The Evangelist
By William R. King

This book is dedicated to my beautiful wife and two girls. I love you so much.

Part 1.

The Evangelist

Chapter 1.   There is Always a Beginning

Looking in the mirror, Phillip weighed the exhaustion in his eyes.

Sitting in the dressing room at the Bridgestone Arena, he rubbed the weariness from his eye. Looking around the dress room he realized he was tired from seeing the same room at every venue for the last four months and then going to the same hotel room with it manufactured sterile coziness., he muttered, "Who am I kidding? Our marriage hasn't been right since I graduated seminary."

Examining his graying hair, he forced a smile, stretched his jaw, rubbed his forehead and tried to get motivated with today's mantra, "One more day; finish well."

Glancing at the freshly laid out suit in his dressing room, he shook his head and thought, "I've not been home for a day, and it's begun," as he splashed cold water in his face.

"Jessica wants more than I can give," found its way back into his consciousness. Not wanting his wife to ruin his last sermon of the rally, he exhaled, closed his eyes, and repeated his mantra, "One more day; finish well."

Removing the crisply ironed shirt and tie from the garment bag, he stretched the tie in front of him and remembered the last time he wore it.

Gripping it he mumbled, "I haven't worn a tie this whole tour, and I can't believe Jessica wants me to wear the tie I wore to Andrew's funeral," as he threw the tie in the trash.

Checking his teeth one last time in the mirror, he started out the door to pray with evangelism team before going on stage. Opening the door, Jessica rushed in the room with uncanny timing saying, "Phillip, there's a packed house! I am so excited all these people came to see you!"

Noticing Phillip's unkempt hair, Jessica snapped, "You are definitely not going out like that. You are the product and you need to be presentable" as she grabbed a hairbrush and gel to improve Phillip's appeal.

Wincing from every vicious pull of the comb, Phillip answered, "Jessica, I pray that they aren't here for me and I'm not the product."

"Do not nitpick and start a fight," Jessica explained as gave him a visual once over.

"I'll be late for the prayer session we share before going on the stage," Phillip said as he turned around as prompted.

Not satisfied, but not able to place what is wrong, Jessica mocked, "You are the boss, they will wait. Tuck your shirt in."

Phillip answered, "I've got to lead by example. We're a team, and I'm one of the leaders. And I don't want to tuck my shirt in!" as he turned for a final inspection.

Wanting the scrutiny to end, he stood up straight and gave a big smile.

As a grimace overtook Jessica's polite smile, she drew in a deep breath and said, "You are not going out there without tucking in your shirt."

Phillip countered, "No, they come to hear me preach, not for me to sell Jesus."

Throwing her hands in the air, Jessica turned her back on Phillip as she whined, "I can't believe you don't value my opinion."

"Jessica. Let's just go," sighed Phillip.

Spinning on her heel, she stared Phillip in the eyes and demanded, "Phillip, if you love me, you will tuck in your shirt. I cannot believe that you would want to go out there looking like a slob. How do you expect people to care about what you say looking like that?"

Lost by her logic, he knew the fight wasn't worth it. So, conceding he tucked in his shirt.

Glancing at his watch, Phillip reiterated, "I really have to leave right now."

Jessica furrowed her eyebrows and began to scan the room, checked under the chair where his shirt had been, and searched the bag. Spotting the tie in the trashcan, she rescued it and began to forcefully tie the tie around his neck.

Exasperated Phillip moans, "Jessica, I don't want to wear the tie. I don't want to tuck in my shirt. I can comb my own hair. It's time to go!"

Jerking Phillip's jaw in her hand, she made sure he focused on her and chastised, "Phillip Ashby! What are we? Four years old now? I cannot believe we are arguing about this. Just wear the tie and make me happy."

Biting his lower lip, he stoically endured what was hopefully Jessica's last inspection.

Satisfied with her creation, she pecked him on his lips and simpered, "I am so glad that I was here to help you. Do well tonight."

Then she exited as quickly as she entered.

Looking at his watch, Phillip donned his jacket, put his grandpa's old pocket Bible from WWII into the breast pocket of the jacket, pulled off the tie, tossed it back in the trashcan, and walked out of the dressing room.

***

Looking over the edge of her balcony seat, a woman with a baggy hoodie looked around the Bridgestone Arena. She felt everyone's tension building as they waited for the rally to begin at.

She sat in her seat as she reminded herself, "I'm a nobody," as she tried to blend in with the crowd.

Glancing at her watch, she murmured, "Already off schedule," as she inspected the empty stage. Looking at the crowd, she muttered, "They're just sheep."

Looking to her left, she felt the bile rising in her throat as she saw a little girl wearing a "Saving a Life" t-shirt. Her nausea didn't come from the girl's parents indoctrinating her into Christianity, but the fact that they were following a creep.

Looking around with her scowl hidden by her hoodie, she thought that the congregation were sheep led to the wolves. She knew there was a verse in the Bible about that.

Her glare softened to compassion as she thought, "Mmmaybe Pastor Phillip is not as 'bad' as I think he is."

Cursing her compassion, she closed her eyes as her head split from excruciating pain. She couldn't win the battle within her. She cursed her hesitation. Her anger burned all other emotions to ash.

The lights dimmed as silence fell on the arena.

Opening her bloodshot eyes, she grumbled, "I can kill 'em all."

***

Standing before the congregation of the thousands who came to his "Saving a Life" rally, Phillip Ashby admired the work that God had done tonight. Hearing his words reverberate around the arena, reminded him that these words were for him as much as them. He preached, "In the beginning, God created the heavens and the earth. Think about this. We believe God created everything. We believe Jesus can help and heal anyone, but we become too caught up in our own struggles and forget that Jesus came to save the lost. He came for the ones who don't know Him.

Jesus sat with the lost. It didn't surprise Him that they were sinners. While His Church complains more than it proclaims, we expect the Lost to act saved! We ostracize Sinners because they cuss, have tattoos, long hair, drink, smoke, have sex outside of marriage, or whatever taboo the Church uses to wall themselves from society. We leave the Lost to be devoured by Satan, while we protect our rituals.

However, Jesus spoke with the woman at the well. He ate with Zacchaeus. He called despised tax collectors to follow Him. He had no wall and got angry with those who prioritize their protocols; so, they would not have to love.

The Lost have enough accusations from Satan and the world. Without needing the church to add to their burden. What they want is to know how things can be different.

What is stopping you from "Saving a Life"? Is it your loyalty to a Bible translation? Is it your devotion to a church denomination? Is it that your church plays drums instead of an organ? These things won't save a life. If you believe that only Jesus can save a life, then be like Jesus and don't fear the Lost just because they act lost. We need to act saved and show them how to be saved."

Murmurs of 'Amen' echoed as applause engulfed the arena.

Phillip began his invitation to the crowd, "If you believe in Jesus Christ, He has one request of you: to bring Him your hurts and shame, your past and failures. Come dirty and broken, so He can wash you clean with blood He freely gave.

Then you can learn more about Him as you follow Him. Each step of faith helps you know His love, so that you can make His love known to others. There is no secret to Jesus a saving a life. It's available to all who believe that Jesus has saved them! Saving you is His plan from the beginning and still His plan now!"

A quiet settled over the crowd as the truth of the message and the pull of the invitation began to break through doubt.

Seeing the first trickle of people come to the altar, Phillip had a swelling pride from giving the message of belief and salvation.

***

Drawing her hoodie tighter, she agreed that Christians shouldn't run away from sinners who are acting lost, but scoff as she remembered how he had run away from her. In the back of her mind, she considered how her actions might have provoked him to run away. Then her headache raged back and doubled her over.

Regaining her senses, she heard a man next to her ask, "Ma'am are you all right?"

Glaring through her pain, she saw him gather his family away to find other seats and heard him say to his wife, "Her eyes were red and swollen. Let's go."

"That's right little lambs, run away," she scoffed as she closed her eyes and strengthened her resolve to blame Phillip.

Phillip back off and let Scott Allen start playing the invitation song, He slowly strummed the intro, then gradually crescendo as he finished the invitation.

As the last note reverberated in the air, Phillip noticed no one was sitting: the young and old, man and woman, black, white, tan, and every nationality came to their feet ready to break into praise.

Jesus, Jesus, Precious Jesus! Oh, for grace to trust Him more!

As the stage lights mirrored the music induced fever, Phillip wondered if livening up those old hymns to make them current with today's music by adding a few verses, repeating a simple verse, or by putting in some power chords to make them relevant for today's generation brought spectacle to the artist, song or God. He quickly dismissed this as he thought that the music didn't make the music Christian, it was the words. Overall, he was grateful the new generation wouldn't lose the truths of these timeless hymns.

Clapping his hands, he joined in worship, "Jesus, Jesus, Precious Jesus! Oh, for grace to trust Him more!" and continued to repeat the phrase, gradually getting louder.

Jesus! Jesus! How I trust Him!

***

Jessica enjoyed the spectacle of seeing wave of people come down to the altar but was brought out of her reverie by the whispering around her. Pursing her lips, she tried to ignore her two daughters beside her in VIP seating.

Closing her eyes, she tried to return to the moment, but couldn't because of Naomi whispering something into Claire's ear and Claire punching out a text on her phone.

She thought about how glad she was that Naomi had traveled from Louisville to be with her on this special night in Nashville and how Claire took time away from the busyness of her job to set with her. She knew she should treat them as the adults they were, but after seeing both girl's grins spread across their faces, she knew she would have to squash their mischief before it got any worse.

Hoping to get their attention, she cleared her throat. Being ignored, she scolded, "Girls! You need to have more respect for me and quit embarrassing me in front of all these people."

"Mom, this crowd doesn't even know you are embarrassed right now. I don't even think anyone cares." chided Claire. "Also, we're in our twenties and not little kids anymore."

Reaching her limit with Claire's rudeness, Jessica interrupted, "Don't give me any sass. There are no ifs, ands, or buts, right now. This isn't open to negotiation. So, stop it right now."

Used to keeping the peace, Naomi consoled, "Mom, she's not giving you any tone. Claire is shouting because of the crowd. Now, let's all settle down, continue to enjoy ourselves, and not let this ruin the night."

Setting her jaw, Jessica huffed heavily and looked back to the stage, but contained her agitation as she heard Claire whisper, "Naomi, she's gotten worse since we've moved out of the house."

Turning on them again, Jessica chided, "Seriously! I can't believe your disrespect! I know I raised you better than this."

Any response and resolution to the argument was lost as the wave of worship increased spontaneously around them, as the whole arena erupted.

Jesus! Jesus! How I trust Him!
***

Stepping out of the spotlight, Phillip looked at the big screen, the lights, massive tower of speakers and thought about how orchestrated these events had become.

He reminisced about when Scott was the headliner with him being the guest preacher in small venues. Now, he was the headliner preaching Jesus with Scott as the special guest.

He prayed Jesus to be the focus through all the attractions and distractions and that he'd still speak truth through all the glitter and glam.

Whispering an Amen, he raised his head and joined the crowd singing.

How I trust Him!
How I trust Him!
Jesus, Jesus, How I need Him!
How I need Him!

Noticing the crowd calming down to a dull roar, Phillip was amazed how music could control the mood of a anyone so easily. Spying Scott's wink, Phillip approached the spotlight as the crowd echoed.

Beneath the cleansing flood!
Beneath the cleansing flood!
Beneath the cleansing flood!

"Tonight, you've heard the gospel: Jesus wants to save your life. Some have responded to His call! If you already believe, pray for others who still need to come. Ask the person beside you if they believe Jesus is able to save them. Then ask if they'd like to have you come to the altar and pray with them," preached Phillip.

As he spoke, people flooded onto the field as if a dam had been broken.

***

Slowly raising her hands, she cursed herself and resolutely planted them in the front pocket of her hoodie. Phillip's words had moved her. She felt she had a reason to believe again. Still, doubt and shame began to creep back in her thoughts, bringing on the debilitating headache. Biting her lip, she couldn't discern truth from lies.

Accepting her raison d'être, she stood to leave but was blocked by a man with his arms open for a hug. Not meeting the person's gaze, she turned and walked in the opposite direction.

***

Claire peered at her notes and then at her watch, and then heard Naomi lean over and whisper, "I know this isn't planned and that it's your job to worry about these things now that you work for dad, but it's OK when the Holy Spirit rewrites what we have planned."

Looking back at her watch, Claire sighed and said, "I should be down there doing my job."

Then both turned and marveled at their mother, who had her hands in the air, eyes closed and dancing to something else other than the music playing.

Incredulous, Naomi studied their mom and asked Claire, "What's she listening too?"

Shaking her head, Claire answered, "I dunno. I bet when she gets to heaven she'll be singing 'Hallelujah' when everyone else is singing 'Hosanna.'"

Naomi added, "Yeah, and she'll be angry because everyone else is worshipping wrong."

Claire continued, "Yep. She'll probably still be wearing the same Victorian style clothes."

Both smirked as they chorused, "With ruffles and flared cuffs!"

"Girls, shhh!", blurted Jessica, "Settle down and quit being a distraction."

Then Claire saw her mother begin bouncing on her toes and waving as she screamed, "Phillip. Hi, Phillip."

Stupefied by her mother's irony, she turned to comment to Naomi and saw that she was also waving. Shaking her head, she mouthed, "Sell out."

Listening to the swelling music in the arena brought Claire into the chorus.

Beneath the cleansing flood!

Beneath the cleansing flood!
Beneath the cleansing flood!

She was brought out of her worship by Naomi shouting in her ear, "Who would we ever get to replace Scott?"

Claire replied, "Take your pick. This is Nashville! Everyone is looking for their big break."

Naomi quipped, "I'm thinking of Dad's ministry. He should have a backup in case Scott quits."

Claire's lip curled with amusement as she responded, "It's my job to worry about this kind of things, not yours. Also, if Scott quits, I'm sure mother will get Dad to make him reconsider."

Naomi commented, "Not funny."

Claire shot back, "Which part? It being my job or Scott quitting?"

Naomi replied, "You know what I mean."

As her smirk grew into a smile, Claire conceded, "Oh, that part. I wasn't trying to be funny."

The music slowly faded as their dad began to give the invitation, "Tonight, you've heard the gospel. Jesus wants to save your life. As you can see, some have come . . ."

***

Amazed, Phillip watched the human flood congregate around the makeshift altar in front of the stage. He marveled as the altar servants who were equipped with a "Life Saver" pamphlet explained the way to salvation. He saw that some came to the altar only for prayer, while others professed their faith in Jesus and to accept Him as their Savior.

Closing his eyes and raising his hands, he listened as the rest of the congregation continued to sing.

Jesus! Jesus! How I trust Him!
How I proved Him o'er and o'er!

Meditating on the words 'o'er and o'er', Phillip thought on how he'd heard this song throughout the tour and how he'd never really rolled the words around in his head.

He contemplated on how they seemed to suggest more than just replacements for the phrase 'over and over.' He puzzled that 'over and over' was like running around in circles, or like watching a clock, or being caught in a time loop.

However, 'o'er and o'er' gave the impression of sailing through rough seas to a new destination. He reckoned the phrase was more about Jesus proving Himself through any struggle. Not sure what the artist meant; the phrase remained stuck in his head.

Letting the words engulf him, he prayed that Jesus would be with him o'er and o'er through any struggle.

Joining the chorus, he couldn't imagine anything ruining this glorious night.

***

Following the crowd to the makeshift altar, the hooded woman snaked her way closer to her mark.

Shuffling by those still in their seats, she became aware that they were applauding, whooping and shouting for her. The closer she came to the altar, some patted her back, some gave thumbs up, some raised their hands into the air praying, while others stood silently with serene smiles on their faces.

Each touch made her withdraw deeper into her hoodie, hugging it closer around herself as she buried her hands deeper in the front pocket caressing the gun that she carried.

Chapter 2.   Lonely Ceremony

"I'd like to introduce a man who helped me with my struggles and helped me to get my head back in the game," said Champ Davis.

Champ, a 6'4" behemoth of a man who was crouched down over a lectern and trying not to eat the microphone, continued, "Without him, I'd still be struggling with my divorce and our hometown team would've had to get another quarterback."

The crowd responded with a quiet boo.

Gesturing toward Ethan, Champ Davis said, "Come over here."

Ethan Pitney stood up next to Champ while fumbling with his coat button. He was fidgeting because being 5'11" and about 215 pounds, he felt dwarfed standing next to Champ. He shook Champs hand as his was swallowed into his mitt. Cameras snapped as Champ gave their photo op.

Finally, after retrieving his hand and standing up to the podium, he watched as Champ left to sit down while shaking everyone's hands enroute.

Ethan nervously started, "Thank you, Champ, for your kind words and letting me leave with my arm still intact." Ethan shook his arm out, mimicking working out the pain before Champ sitting down.

The crowd chortled, and Champ smiled and gave a gun gesture to Ethan.

Ethan knew most of the people in the crowd came to see Champ, but he was the one receiving the award and was going to make this his night.

Ethan continued, "Ladies and Gentlemen, I'd like to thank every one of you for showing up and honoring me with this Pelusa award. When getting into psychiatry I never thought anyone would take notice. I just wanted to help my fellow man. However, as

William James once said, "The greatest discovery of my generation is that human beings can alter their lives by altering their attitudes of mind." I personally think he was an advocate for mind-altering drugs, not just the legal kinds either. Coffee doesn't modify the attitudes of the mind as much as what I can prescribe." Ethan said with a wink and a smile.

Standing in the Opryland Hotel conference room with about two hundred in attendance, Ethan Pitney looked at the crowd as his best and only joke fell flat.

Looking at his note cards he thought to himself about how he'd become one of "those guys" that he typically made fun of while in the audience.

He thought, "Recover. Come on. Recover."

Mouth dry, Ethan adlibbed in his best vaudeville style, "But what medicinal purposes would coffee open up in psychiatry?"

Feeling sweat bead up on his brow, he continued, "We all would have a clinic in every Starbucks."

Giving the required pregnant pause, Ethan heard crickets. Mentally shifting gears, he thought, "Well screw it, they're giving me an award for my work and new book, not my comedy material."

Getting ready to continue speaking, Ethan opened his mouth and accidently hiccupped.

A chuckle made its way through the crowd much to Ethan's chagrin.

Feeling like he had to regain the composure of the crowd, he thought to himself, "This is the last time I have a few drinks before making a speech."

His mind raced and screamed at him, "Recover!"

Champ said out loud, "Maybe coffee could be the cure to hiccups."

Ethan turned sharply at Champ. He wanted to quiet Champ and started to put his index finger up to his lips but changed it to a "Hmmmm" gesture. Once he got his finger to his mouth, he hiccupped again.

The audience started laughing nervously.

Champ pantomimed as if he was drinking and getting tipsy while thumbing over to Ethan.

The crowd guffawed and Ethan thought, "No way is he going to steal my show."

Taking a deep breath, he tried to power through the rest of the speech, "I know they <hiccup> say you're <hiccup> supposed to start a speech with a <hiccup> joke, but you're not <hiccup> supposed to be <hiccup> the joke."

Ethan took a step back watched the audience. Some giving a full belly laugh. Some even had tears come to their eyes.

Feeling someone brush his hand, he saw that someone had brought him a glass of water. Finishing the water, he asked rhetorically, "Ok, where was I?"

Looking at his notes, he saw he was at the beginning: William James' quote.

Champ answered, "<hiccup> Asking for another scotch and bourbon?"

Ethan paused, bit his bottom lip, and thought, "Why can't I catch a break? Recover. Recover."

"All right, now I'm satisfied that the ice has been broken, let's continue. I think we can agree that what William James was getting at is that the change in our lives starts with the change of our attitude in our minds. William James also said, 'The art of being wise is the art of knowing what to overlook.' So, I've taken these two thoughts and not only look at drugs as the answer but how to help other's find the fix within themselves. I want to help others examine that what they've been holding onto could be what was damaging them. That they have several things binding them, anchoring them, and even enslaving them, which can be removed as they find their own healthy life. Lives without the selfishly imposed barriers others have forced upon them, or they had forced on themselves. When I was writing the book "What You Hold on to Is Holding on to You" I wanted to give freedom to the oppressed but had no idea it would make the impact that it has."

Ethan continued his speech with only four more hiccups, two more glasses of water and one loss of control of the audience. Overall, he felt he gotten his point across.

Ending his speech, Ethan said, "And I conclude with Shakespeare's Hamlet musing, "There is nothing either good or bad, but thinking makes it so." I interpret this as meaning 'quit holding onto what society has stated is good or bad' and make the difference in the world by making the change in yourself."

At the end of his notecards, he continued off the cuff, "Not only make a change, but let go of the entangling fingers of family, friends or religion. Find what is holding you back, follow my method, remove it, and find who you are and become it."

Removing himself from the lectern, the audience halfheartedly applauded as Ethan went back to his seat at the table.

Ethan heard Champ say to the man sitting next to him, "That was the best order at the bar I've heard in a long time." Champ imitated a hiccup as an effect.

Ethan thought to himself, "Asshole." However, not wanting to let this man ruin his day he thought, "Great, I'm that guy! Well, at least I'll be remembered."

Champ came back up to the mike and said, "Thank you, Ethan, for your time and congratulations for your award. If you don't mind, we would like to open the floor to some questions."

"Questions?" raced Ethan's mind, "No one said anything about a Q&A session."

Searching the room, he noticed microphones set up for the audience. On the spot, he knew he couldn't say no.

Unprepared he looked at the microphone and hoped no one approached.

Seeing a woman coming up to the microphone, he tried to calm his anxiety by telling himself that this group had given him an award. What hurt could come from a Q&A?

The woman asked, "You said we should let go of what we think is good or bad. But wouldn't that be chaos? I mean, if everyone didn't have a code of good or bad wouldn't everyone be running around doing their own thing?"

Biting his bottom lip, he stood and walked to the microphone. Looking among the crowd, he felt naked without any notecards, yet was glad that the woman was the only one still standing.

Taking a deep breath, he started, "No, you have a duty to your fellow man. I spent a whole chapter on this in my book so I won't continue too far on this. Nevertheless, in living your new free life one should ensure that they are not holding onto something that is holding them back."

The same woman asked, "How does your method provide a different free life?"

Ethan looked at the young lady and stammered, "Well, uh, umm ..."

Taking a drink of water to think about an answer, he finally continued, "Well, I don't base my "method" under fear. You don't have to believe in any superstitious mumbo jumbo for this to work. You only have to find what is holding you back and help yourself find who you are meant to be. Then, be that person to your best ability."

Seeing that the woman hadn't sat down, he continued, "Well, uh, when you become that positive person that you could be. You could remove any obstacles. I figured my method would draw the ire of the religious community, but what doesn't. In my opinion, religion has held society and culture back for far too long."

With this comment, some in the audience looked at each other in agreement. While others murmured and came up to the mike in droves.

"Oh, Shit!" Ethan thought.

Watching the line gather behind the mike, Ethan thought, "Great! The Crazy Conservative Christian Corp is here."

Trying to recover, Ethan continued, "I have no problem with religion per se, it's just not for me. It just holds people back because they are hiding behind it. Thus, crippling themselves."

Not completely satisfied that his answer agreed with his own beliefs, he added, "They hold to their dogma, instead of what is right and wrong for society as a whole. I feel they should release the stranglehold they have on society and culture and let us take care of ourselves."

The young woman left the mike as an older gentleman came up to the microphone and inquired, "So, are you saying religions are good as long as they keep to themselves?"

Ethan knowing that the Q&A had been derailed, he tried to swing the conversation back to his book or his practice, but not religion.

Nervously clearing his throat, Ethan addressed the question in a cautious candor, "Sir, that isn't what I said. However, I do personally feel religions have done severe damage to many people by pigeon-holding them in guilt that today's society and culture doesn't consider viable. Religion will crucify someone for a cuss word but won't help them get through their rough situation. Religions judge people for something that had happened in their past and ensures that they continue to pay penitence for it. Religion will put people in rooms and brainwash them to the point where they think, feel and act the same."

Wanting to change the subject, Ethan called," Next question."

The older gentleman dwelt on the current issue and countered, "Societiesjudge people for things in people's past also. It isn't just religious people. Society also puts people in rooms and brainwash them to the point where they think, feel and act the same. Also, in my long life, I see that society is fickle with determining right and wrong. What was once wrong yesterday, is now right and what was once right now becomes wrong tomorrow. I assume that you're advocating that right and wrong is about people individually only and that no one can judge anyone on their own personal preferences."

Feeling ambushed, the teeth of the trap started to sink into Ethan's leg while his stomach fell to his feet.

He didn't like debating. He liked to be the one in charge while people agree with him because he has the credentials. He desperately wanted to switch the conversation around by not answering the question, but by asking the same answer in return. Thus, missing the trap.

"Sir, since you didn't put forth a question, I'll ask one. Please give me an example where society put people in rooms and brainwashed them to the point where they think, feel and act the same?" questioned Ethan.

The old man stated, "I'd say that the college classroom is an example. It seems colleges are now grading kids on how much they agree with the professor rather than educating them to think for themselves. I was talking to my grandson about what his school was teaching him about liberty and ethics, and he said . . ."

Looking at his award and then at the 'Christian Crusaders' that were lining up to give him his flogging, Ethan persisted, "Well, as I previously stated . . . "

***

"Ethan, you know you brought that all on yourself and that you didn't answer that old man's question also, right?" Liz quipped after the book signing.

She continued, "You just pulled out your official voice and the 'Well, as I previously stated' speech. I also like how you included the 'religion is the company of fools' maxim. Very diplomatic! I told you that you should have done some Toastmasters classes and found a right way to finish your speech instead of hijacking yourself."

Mad that he couldn't see straight, Ethan looked at Liz and shook his head.

She was his book agent and had helped him so much with his book deal that she didn't pull any punches with him.

Liz remarked, "I know you have had a hard year, but leave your demons in the closet or take your own advice and stop them from holding you back."

"I was angry that they got off topic. It wasn't my fault." Ethan responded.

Liz fired back, "No, you got off topic, because you were drunk! There is liquid courage, and then there is making an ass out of yourself. You demonstrated the later."

Defensively, Ethan said, "They got on the topic of religion, and they wouldn't let it go."

"No, Ethan! You got on the subject of religion and then declared 'open season'.. You could have stuck with the 'Father and mothers' being the problem and holding them back, but you didn't. You said the word 'religion' and that was when everything started. It wasn't their fault, it was yours. I'm surprised you got away without inciting a crusade."

Ethan let off, "Well, you didn't tell me to prepare for a Q&A session afterward. I think you're partly to blame."

Liz angrily remarked with sass, "Ethan, I honestly didn't know they were going to do a Q&A, but I figured that you knew your subject well enough and could handle it. You've helped celebrities and athletes to excel as they got their head back in the game. You counsel people for a living. I thought you were a big boy and could handle it. For goodness sake, you wrote a book on the subject, and now you're blaming me because you couldn't deal with a few questions from people who had just given you an award. Thank God, that they weren't your critics."

Weary from the night's events, Ethan repeated, "It wasn't my fault."

Liz eyed Ethan and let it out. "Then whose was it?"

Tired of arguing, he dropped his head in disgust.

Knowing she won, Liz comforted, "Listen, I know your wife going to church and finding religion had you hot and bothered, but if you said the word Islam or Mohammed, it might have been a bloodbath. What were you thinking by bringing religion up?"

"It happened almost a year ago," Ethan replied.

Liz answered, "Oh, Hell Ethan, I don't want to talk about Beth. Especially now. Your screw up is probably going viral so sober up."

Ethan raised his thumbs up.

"Oh, before I forget. You told me to remind you that you took Chap's rotation at the hospital because he is at some rally tonight," Liz said as she left.

Ethan thought to himself, "Now, I can't sleep in."

He called out, "Will you call them and tell them to get someone else to cover?"

Liz said over her shoulder, "No. Nice try. I'll call you in the morning. Go home and sleep everything off," as she turned the corner and was gone.

Ethan looked at his watch and thought, "I need a drink. It's five o'clock somewhere."

Chapter 3.   Following the Devil

Staring at Scott, Jessica pondered, "How can Scott, a single man, get dressed all by himself, when Phillip can't match his socks."

Giving a heavy sigh, she looks up into the rafters and said, "God, You knew Phillip needed me to look after him."

Surveying the arena, she looked for someone else who needed her help.

Hmm! Which one will it be tonight?

Among the crowd she saw a woman in dirty baggy clothes, hiding her hands in her pockets, and shifting her weight from foot to foot. Following her gaze, she noticed that she kept looking up at Phillip and then looking away.

Jessica prayed, "Jesus, if you want me to talk to her and give her the push she needs, then let me know by having her take her hands out of her pockets."

Studying the baggy woman for any confirmation, she became distracted by her daughters pushing each other.

Looking over at the girls, she bellowed, "OK! You two, enough playing around. People are making decisions and now is the time to be reverent. You know better."

Pursing her lip, she stared at them.

Afraid she had lost the distraught woman, she turned back to the crowd. Not seeing her, she wondered if it was a sign from God. Panning the crowd again, she became disturbed as someone shouted "Hallelujah" after someone had received Jesus into their heart.

Sniffling, Jessica looked away from them and thought about how she wanted to help someone in the same way. Looking at the altar, several people were kneeling, and she found her target again with her hands in her pockets.

Seeing her move her shoulder, Jessica almost jumped out of her chair, but the woman only used her sleeve to itch her nose while keeping her hands in her pockets.

Tired of waiting, Jessica thought, "That's close enough."

Jessica told Naomi and Claire "I'm going to speak to that distraught woman down there at the altar."

Naomi answered, "Mom, I think that's an excellent idea. I'll go down with you."

Still anxious, Jessica put out another fleece and prayed, "If she is not talking to anyone when I get to her, it will mean that You want me to talk to her."

Claire replied, "Yeah, I'll go too. I see all the altar call helpers congregating together. I'll go provide some guidance. "

Jessica saw Naomi stop to put her hands on a rocking woman's shoulder as she asked, "Do you need someone to talk to or pray with?"

Looking up with swollen eyes, the woman replied to Naomi and Jessica "I've come up with so many excuses, but tonight . . ."

Leaving the woman with Naomi, Jessica straight-lined to her woman at the altar.

Dodging elbows and people stopping abruptly, she finally made it to her goal.

Stopping and straightening up her clothing, an altar worker swooped in and began talking to her woman and Jessica thought, "Well, Jesus, someone got to her before me."

About to turn away, Jessica saw the baggy clothed woman walk back to her seating area. "Well, that's confirmation enough for me", thought Jessica as she received her sign to talk to her. Keeping the woman in her peripheral, she turned her gaze to what she was staring at. She saw Phillip walk to the other side of the stage and noticed that she was walking parallel to him.

Straightening up her dress, she whispered, "Showtime," as she stepped in front of the vagabond, held out her hand, and boisterously said, "Hello, sweetheart. Hasn't it been such a beautiful night?"

Seeing the unkempt vagabond woman shirk back and looking bewildered, Jessica wondered as to why someone would mix within a crowd during an altar call and then want everyone to leave her alone.

As the woman looked at Phillip, then her feet in displeasure, Jessica smiled as she thought, "This is her lucky day."

Curving her neck, Jessica looked the woman in the face and said, "Sorry if I've frightened you. I saw you down here at the altar all alone and just wanted to know if I can help you? My name is ..."

The woman replied, "You're Jessica Ashby."

Flustered in being recognized, Jessica replied, "Well, yes I am, sweetheart! Yes, I am! Like I said, I saw you down here and just wanted to know if I can help you?"

Seeing the woman squirm, Jessica tried to get away from the crowd around them, so she put her arm around the woman, but stopped when the woman bristled and planted her feet. All the while, shuffling her hands in her pockets.

Taking a step back, Jessica became aware that the woman's hair had an inch of dark roots showing and that her hoodie smelled. She had the look as if she had once taken care of herself but had let herself go.

The woman shrugged her shoulders forward. Cradling a secret in her pockets.

Feeling insecure, Jessica got on her tiptoes and tried to gain the attention of one of the altar helpers to come and help speak to this woman.

Gently touching the woman on the shoulder, Jessica became more distraught as the woman collapsed and began crying.

Jessica thought, "Goodness, what a drama queen."

Regretting that she wanted to speak to this woman, she looked up to heaven and jokingly accused, "Look, what you got me into now," as she wished someone would swoop in and take over.

Not finding a rescuer, she got on one knee and asked, "Would you like to talk to someone else?"

Between sobs, the woman asked, "Does he love you? Or does he tolerate you?"

Cocking her head in confusion, Jessica thought about Phillip not wearing the tie, but regained her composure as she looked to the sky hoping she could find the right words. She stammered, "Well, uh. You see . . . Hmmm! Jesus first loved us, so we love Him in return!"

Jessica thought to herself, "Good job!" and continued saying, "As per the second question, well, I don't quite understand what you mean. Phillip and me, we don't tolerate each other. We love each other. I'd say that's the same with God and us."

Noticing that she stopped crying, Jessica looked around for any helper, but all were busy with others.

"You're the pastor's wife? Right?", whispered the woman as she began eyeing Phillip again.

Looking at Phillip, Jessica mustered her best smile and proudly replied, "Yes, Phillip is my husband. What is your name?"

The woman glanced at Jessica and smiled.

Jessica smiled back and waited patiently for her name.

The woman looked at the crowd and back to Phillip, then leaned in close to Jessica's ear and asked, "Do you think Pastor Ashby'll talk to me?"

Grateful that God had provided a way for her to get out of this puzzle, Jessica helped the woman to her feet and then straightened her own clothes and hair.

Still not having her name, Jessica replied, "I'm sure he'd love to talk to you, darling. If not, I'll make sure he will. What is your name?"

Jessica watched as the woman looked at Phillip again, put her hands back in her pockets, and begin shuffling with something in her pockets.

Tired from the silence treatment, Jessica thought about how fidgety this woman was and how she needed more help than her husband could give.

With the roar of the crowd and the music, Jessica heard the woman cautiously reply, "Ma'am, my name is Tracy."

***

Hearing his name over the crowd, Phillip saw Jessica dragging someone to meet him with all her bracelets clanging together over the music. He smirked at how she could drag someone in a dignified manner with her honey curls tressed over her face and modest NY&Co dress.

Phillip winked at Scott, as noticed that he brought the music to a slower pace. Making his way down to the altar, a person blocked his way as he thanked him profusely.

Looking at the Jessica and back at the man, he said, "Don't thank me. I'm just an ambassador to Jesus' kingdom. He's the one you need to praise."

The man looked quizzically at Phillip for a few moments, looked up to the sky and started singing to the song playing.

Taking another step down off the stage, the crowd surrounded him. Wanting to congratulate him and shake his hand. He looked over to Jessica and shrugged his shoulders as if to say, "I'm sorry."

***

Seeing the swarm around Phillip, Jessica gave him the "Hurry up!" stare.

Tracy commented, "Looks like he's popular. I can wait for him."

Under her breath, Jessica whispered, "You're not the only one who does."

Seeing security thinning the crowd around Phillip, she turned to Tracy with the biggest smile and said, "He always has someone who wants to talk to him. Let's see if we can get you someone else."

Tracy replied, "Ms. Ashby, I'd really like to talk to Mr. Ashby, I think he'd understand me better. We knew each other a long time ago."

Not hearing what Tracy said at the end because of the crowd cheering, Jessica got on her tip-toes and craned her neck around the altar area looking for someone free and replied, "Are you sure you wouldn't like to speak with someone your own age? They'd probably understand better than Phillip."

At that moment, she heard Phillip's voice say, "Jessica, you can stop looking. I got free, and I'm here right now. So, who is this that we have here?"

Jessica snapped at Phillip, "Finally, you're here. This is Tracy, and she wants to speak with you directly."

Feeling foolish, Jessica came down off her tiptoes and regained her patience and composure. Knowing that she was too direct, she moved some hair away from her forehead and kindly introduce Tracy again, "Phillip, this is Tracy. She came here looking for you specifically."

Jessica looked at Tracy and then to Phillip visually introducing them to each other. Thankful for an escape, she put her hand on Tracy's shoulder stating, "Tracy, you're in good hands. Phillip has helped a lot of people in your situation. Especially people like you."

Looking at Phillip, Jessica said, "Love you, honey, I'll talk to you later," as she marched away.

***

Shaking his head in disbelief from Jessica's condescension, Phillip turned his attention to Tracy who had her eyes downcast and hair matted up. He noticed that she kept her body as small as she could and looked at other people from the corner of her eyes while shying away when her space was invaded. He also observed that she was fidgeting with something in her disheveled Baja sweater's huge front pocket.

He held out his hand to Tracy's downhearted stare, trying to gain her interest instead of the ground.

Still keeping her hands in her pockets, Tracy looked up at Phillip with acute eyes.

Phillip thought to himself, "What has happened to you, Tracy?" as he withdrew his hand and asked, "How may I help you?"

Phillip felt like he was transparent and that Tracy looking through him. He wished that Jessica didn't leave so he could use the goodwill that she had built with Tracy

Staring in her vacant eyes, he asked again, "How may I help you? You look troubled. Did the message speak to you tonight?"

Phillip began getting the vibe that he was dealing with an abuse victim and thought that she'd speak with one of his female altar helpers or that one should be onsite with him now.

As he began to slowly back away, Tracy finally replied sheepishly, "No, I'd like to talk to you alone." Gathering her courage, she straightened herself. Yet, still shifting her hands around in her pockets and speaking to the floor, "Do you remember me?"

Relieved, Phillip watched her shoulders drop the weight she'd been carrying. Examining her, he didn't recognize her because her downcast face didn't reveal much. He answered, "I don't know. Please, lift up your head and let me see."

Lifting her gaze, but keeping her face downcast, Phillip acknowledged that he still didn't recognize her.

He did see her furrow her brow, as she added, "I'm sorry for the loss of your brother. It was a shame it was a closed casket funeral."

Surprised, Phillip felt a pang in his heart and gave closer look at Tracy. But due to losing touch with his brother after High School, he was not familiar with many of his brother's friends and didn't remember seeing this woman at the funeral.

"Ma'am, my brother died recently, and I don't know who you are," Phillip replied. Trying to get the conversation back on topic for the altar call he added, "I'd like to talk about this with you later . . ."

"Do you love her, or do you tolerate her?", interrupted Tracy.

"What do you mean?"

Finally, raising her head, she asked, "Do you love her, or do you tolerate her? Your wife?"

"Ma'am, I don't feel comfortable talking to you about my wife and I. Especially, when I don't understand the question, nor the context. I'm afraid that I don't know who you are, nor how you relate with my brother, but if you'd like, I can exchange my work information with you and speak more tomorrow. So, if you don't mind, do you have any questions about the message tonight or Jesus? Or can we extend the conversation later?" replied Phillip.

Phillip saw her drop her head again, so he looked for Claire or any help.

Jessica incredulously blurted out, "Is it true that I only have to believe in Jesus, and He will save me no matter what I do?"

Glad to be on a topic, Phillip responded, "Well, you heard the message tonight and it's the truth that I believe in and what I know to be true. Jesus is all about saving lives."

Tracy prodded, "So, if I only believe in Jesus, and I pray to Him. He forgives me no matter what I do?"

Phillip smiled and returned "Oh Tracy, there's nothing that Jesus can't forgive for those who believe in Him."

Digging further, Tracy asked, "And that is it? I believe, pray for forgiveness and then everything is all right? There is nothing else I have to do?"

Unsettled by Tracy's questions, Phillip noticed her fidgeting with her hands in her pockets but dismissed it because he had seen several people nervous at the altar before doing all types of things. For all he knew she was recording this conversation.

Getting a bit worried, he began backing up towards the stage and gave a careful look towards security. However, they were watching big clumps of people and ensuring this event met fire code standards.

Turning back to Tracy and only seeing her cold, gray eyes, he said a little prayer, "Dear Jesus, please give me the words," and replied, "Yes, believing saves you, then you get baptized just like Jesus did as your first act of obedience. I can get you in touch with an altar call helper so we can get you connected with a local church if you don't have ...",

Seeing her bow her head and mouth the words, "Forgive me," Phillip went to console Tracy as he saw her lift her gaze, pull a .22 revolver out of her pocket, aim at his heart and pull the trigger.

Surprised by the punch of the bullet and that he couldn't hear the gunshot over the music, Phillip fell back and grabbed his chest. In disbelief, he looked at Tracy and tried to catch his breath to scream for security over the music.

Falling to the ground, he thought about how there was a crowd around him with hands raised in the air and with their eye closed as he was going to die with no one was paying attention.

He heard Scott singing, "Just from Jesus simply taking life and rest, and joy and peace."

He thought about Jessica bringing Tracy to him and abandoning him.

He was alone with a woman who had shot him for no reason.

Landing hard on the ground, he heard security behind him shout, "GUN!!!!"

Immediately, the crowd saw security running towards Phillip and at Tracy who still had her arm extended holding a gun as they hit the ground or began scampering away.

He saw a smile cross Tracy's face, then to shock.

Checking his expected wound; there was no blood and he understood her confusion. Looking back up at Tracy he saw her lift the gun again and take aim at his head. Then he saw security grabbing her arm while she was pulling the trigger.

Feeling searing pain in his thigh and hip area, he rolled around writhing in burning agony for the offhandedly shot

Lying motionless, he felt his blood drain out of him and his eyes getting heavy. Feeling someone force his eyes open, he read the rally's banner that was above him: Saving a Life. He smiled to himself at the irony.

Being poked and prodded, he heard Scott still playing the song and went back to his previous puzzle: What does 'o'er and o'er' mean?

Blood pooling towards his face, he watched everyone running away from him, except for the paramedics who surrounded him and began rolling him to his side.

Feeling pressure on his thigh, excruciating pain seared through his body, as he could feel his pulse rush out of him.

Closing his eyes and taking deep shallow breaths, he became startled by snapping fingers in front of his face as one paramedic called for an ambulance.

He heard a soft voice say, "I am with you," as other people cried, and some asked how they could help.

Phillip passed out as Scott obliviously kept singing,

And I know that He is with me,
He'll be with me to the end.

Chapter 4.   Lonely Celebration

Ethan sat at the bar looking into his drink, watching his reflection in the ripples. He picked the glass up, swirled it around, and then looked into it again. He put the glass down and laid his head on the counter.

"Get out of your own head." Ethan jeered as he sat at the bar with Champ.

"What's that bub?" asked Max.

Not lifting his head, Ethan answered, "Nothing Max! Nothing at all!"

"Ya done or do you want another?" asked Max.

Still looking at his reflection in his whiskey glass, Ethan quickly downed it and felt the smooth warmth in his chest, then let out his breath as the fire sought a way to escape.

Looking Max in the eye, he responded, "Sure, Max, give me another."

Max served Champ and Ethan up the drinks and ensured that he was available to them. Considering the slow night, he should give one on one treatment.

Ethan was still distraught on how his evening went and forgot he was interviewed by the news. Ethan asked Max, "What channels do you get that TV on?"

"Watching the news now, gotta see what happened today. Maybe something good," answered Max.

"Yeah, perhaps some good, Max." Ethan let out.

Champ threw his gorilla arms around Ethan and slurred, "Maybe you be. Ahhhh! Maybe you'll be TV."

Ethan scoffed as he thought about how Champ couldn't hold his liquor. He knew he had a TV interview, but he was sure he'd be buried in the newscast; If he was given any airtime at all.

Ethan answered, "Champ, you'd probably get more airtime than me."

Champ vainly laughed, "Chey innaview me ev'vah week." Then he let out a low burp.

Ethan reached for his wallet to pay for his drink. He fumbled to get his debit card out and then dropped it on the floor. He reached down and tried to get his fingernail under the card, but it kept sliding around. He finally got out of his seat retrieving the slippery card.

As Ethan was raising back up into his chair, he heard Champ say, "Hey, Ethan it's ch'you on dah news trailer? Oh my God, dat is ch'you." Champ grabbed Ethan and shook him saying, Gots me a celebrity cheer. Da drinks on me."

Ethan looked around the bar and chuckled because it was only Max, Champ and him there. He asked Max for a double of what he had last.

Max looked at Ethan and the TV replying, "On the house. It's not every day that I get a celebrity. Do you think you could bring me a picture shot of your head? Dang! What are those things called? You know, a picture of your head like some other bars and restaurants have when celebrities eat or drink there."

"Headshots?" Ethan answered questioningly.

Then Ethan thought to himself that he did not have any headshots. Then he remembered the picture in his book's sleeve. He would have to get Liz to get him a few of those pictures.

Ethan looked up at the TV as Max turned the volume up.

The newscaster said, ". . . I am here with Ethan Pitney, the writer of the book, "What You Hold on to Is Holding on to You" and recipient of the Pelusa award. We know the work you do for our beloved football team and the great help you have been with Champ Davis in helping him keep his focus and not let the world get him down."

Ethan whispered to himself, "Finally, a break. Something good that can be salvaged from the day."

Champ slammed him on the shoulder and slurred, "You are on the TV <hiccup>. Hey, man I'm you at the podium. <hiccup> "

Ignoring him, Ethan smiled. Glad the stars were lining up for him.

In the TV interview, Ethan responded, "Thank you, Anne, it has been my pleasure to . . ."

Then the interview was interrupted with a Breaking New splash on the TV as the news anchor said, "We interrupt this interview with Ethan Pitney with some breaking news happening live at the Bridgestone Arena. We have a report that renowned Christian pastor and author Phillip Ashby has been shot during his arena rally tonight."

"Damn it to hell," Ethan cursed through gritted teeth.

Max agreed, "I know. It's another high-profile shooting. I'm really getting tired of these shootings."

Ethan thought to himself that this was the worst day that he had ever had and didn't want to get into a second amendment debate with Max. So, he moved to an empty booth behind him; leaving Champ and Max fix the country's problems.

Situating himself in the booth, he pulled out his phone so he could start texting Liz but was disturbed as Max turned the TV up.

"Damn Max's passive aggressiveness," he cursed as he heard the TV say, "Police have the suspect in custody and Pastor Phillip is in critical condition . . ."

Ethan thought to himself, "That's one way to shut them religious bigots up. They're so convinced they're right, and nothing shuts them up. Let's see if this works."

Catching himself in the mirror across from the bar, he thought to himself about how cynical he was against religion especially while he was drunk and murmured, "Maybe Liz is right. I do need to quit drinking."

Remembering he was going to text Liz, he got sidetracked again as he heard the news reporter ask, "Officer Parks, do you think that this is the beginning of the attack on Christianity?"

Ethan watched as the left-field question dumbfounded the police officer. Watching the officer purse his lips and reply, "Ma'am, we have no knowledge of any other attacks on Christians at this moment, we believe this is just an isolated incident. We are still investigating . . .," caused Ethan's drunken mind to let the words bounce around his head. Killing his buzz.

"The beginning of the attack on Christianity. What a crock of horseshit. Attacking Christianity has been the norm since Jesus died. Anyways, they're in the majority now. What attack is there on them? It's their fault anyways, they're usually the aggressors with all of their boycotting."

Tired of listening to the ignorance that passed as news, Ethan tuned it out and looked at his phone. He just stared at his phone wishing it would remind him why he had it open. He stared at it for a while waiting for the answer to come to him. Then he saw Beth's text: **Can't wait 2 C U at home!**

After reading this, Ethan downed the rest of his whiskey and looked at his ring finger and thought, "I know, I know."

Tired from the day's events, He thought about how he didn't want to handle this right now. He bit his bottom lip, ran his hands through his hair, took a deep breath and let it out as he stared at Beth's text.

Max came to the booth and asked him if he needed anything.

Looking up at Max, he realized that he didn't know how much time had passed. He looked at the TV and saw the news was no longer on.

He replied, "No, I'm good Max."

"You need me to call you a cab?" asked Max.

"Max, you know I live right down the road. You might get Champ one though. Give me a few minutes and let me puzzle some thing's out and then I'll be on my way," said Ethan.

"I was being honest when I asked for the . . . the . . . " Max paused.

Ethan waited to see if he would remember.

Then Max followed with, "the picture."

Immediately, Ethan remembered why he had his phone in his hands. He told Max to hold his thought and texted Liz to get him some headshots and to see if she could get him another interview or have the interrupted one play at another time.

Sending the text, Ethan became mesmerized at Beth's text again.

Seeing Ethan reading his wife' text again, Max gestured to Ethan's cup and asked, "So, you sure you don't want another?"

Putting his hand over his cup, Ethan said, "I finished this off about an hour ago. I should be good."

Looking at the time on his phone, Ethan exclaimed, "Holy shit! It was 12:19 pm!"

Then became distracted again by Beth's text.

Can't wait 2 C U at home!

Taking a deep breath, Ethan put his phone away, got up from his seat and then walked out the door.

Part 2.

The Calm

Chapter 5.   Argument in the Purgatory

After a driving through all the red-lights, Scott and Jessica arrived at the hospital's ER passenger drop-off.

Holding the door handle, Jessica turned in her seat and pleaded, "Scott, thank you for driving me here, but I need another favor. Would go in there with me? I don't think I can do this alone."

Scott replied, "You're not going to be alone though. Naomi and Claire will be there."

"Scott, I would rather not discuss it any further, but I think a man's presence would be helpful, and besides you are essentially family," said Jessica.

Seeing him shake his head in confusion, she released her breath when Scott put the truck in to drive and began to look for a parking space.

Overwhelmed the night's events, Jessica began to sob, "Scott, I didn't know. How could I've known that ..."

Yet, interrupted by him rolling his window down and grabbing the parking garage ticket, he replied, "There was no way anyone could've known."

Looking for a parking spot, he heard Jessica whisper, "Do you think he is going to make it?"

That question had been on Scott's mind also. Seeing the blood pooling at the shooting site and at the shooter's gun, he was amazed such a little gun could cause so much blood.

Knowing he had to be strong for the Ashby family, he said, "God will get him through this. Phillip is a strong one."

Finally finding a parking space on the second level, they got out of the truck headed to the emergency room. The closer they got to the hospital emergency room; Jessica began to break into a run. Seeing that she was still wearing her heels, Scott prayed that she wouldn't twist her ankle or anything else worse.

Arriving at the waiting area, Claire greeted them brusquely saying, "Glad you could make it."

Scott replied, "We got here as fast as we could."

Claire jokingly added, "What? Your adoring fans wouldn't let you go. Goodness, you kept playing as long as you could. What did you think? That the Titanic was sinking, and the band had to keep playing."

Used to working with Claire, he shot back with a smile, "We got caught in the traffic while leaving the arena. We didn't get the privilege of following the ambulance like you."

Claire replied, "Well, Naomi and I followed till we ran the third red light, then we stopped because we didn't want to be another reason y'all got here so late."

Knowing that they have done this song and dance before at the office, Jessica watched Scott and Claire bantering back and forth. Not thinking this was the appropriate time nor place, she cleared her throat and asked, "Where is Phillip?"

Tensing from Claire spinning on her heel and responding matter-of-factly, "He's in surgery and cannot have visitors right now," Jessica looked at Claire crossed and had found her target to unload all her feelings about this night. She thought, "How dare her joke and be sarcastic right now. Doesn't she know what I have gone through tonight? She doesn't know what I did. "

Noticing the tension, Scott stepped back. Because he was fully aware that Jessica's headstrong nature and Claire's sarcasm was going to make this a long night regardless of the occasion. Having worked with Claire for the last few years, he knew her sarcasm and joking manner was a front, especially when she wasn't in control. He also knew Jessica for the better part of his life. He knew she was sensitive, covered her temper with passive aggressiveness, and could blow up during stressful situations.

Knowing he needed an ally, he scanned around the emergency waiting room, Scott asked, "Where's Naomi?" Then he finished the sentence in his mind: ... because I need help diffusing these type A's and she has had years of practice with mediating between Jessica and Claire.

Claire responded, "She's in the restroom, trying to get in touch with Jonathan."

He urgently asked, "Will you please take us to her?"

Claire led them to the uncomfortable chairs they'd claimed in the ER's waiting room.

Scott sat between Jessica and Claire and prayed that nothing would ignite their tempers. Remembering Phillip saying that he felt like a referee between them, Scott questioned what he had signed up for.

Glad that both women were silent, he watched the clock in front of them and prayed a quick prayer in his mind. "Dear Jesus, please make Naomi hurry up."

Watching Jessica tense from seeing Claire taking her phone out and started fiddling around with it, Scott thought, "Nope."

Jessica sneered at Claire, "How can you play a game on your phone at a time like this?"

Peering at her mother above the phone, Claire replied, "I'm not playing a game. I'm reading the Bible."

Jessica coldly said, "You are not. You are playing a game like you always do. I swear you are addicted to that thing."

Shifting her eyes to her mother and then back to the phone, Claire replied, "If I was playing a game, what does it matter to you?"

Losing her patience Jessica said, "It matters because you have no respect and should be praying for your dad right now."

Claire responded, "Mother, I can game, read the Bible and pray at the same time. Regardless of which I do, it will be because I am doing it for God, not you."

Jessica responded, "Claire don't you know what you're doing right now is grieving my spirit."

"Mom, don't you know what you're doing right now is making me angry," Claire retorted, "You're the one who is picking a fight right now."

Jessica flustered, "Well, young lady, your dad should be on the top of your list right now."

Curling her mouth and measuring every word, Claire responded, "Mother, never insinuate that I don't love daddy. This time is as stressful to me right now as it is to you, but because I don't handle things the way you do, doesn't mean that I'm not grieving."

Aware of all the attention they were gathering, Scott gave brief smiles to each spectator and was so glad that he was single.

Jessica said, "Well, I thought you would at least think of others before you do things just to spite them. You're not the only person in this family."

Claire responded, "Mother what does it say about you when all of your arguments seem to apply to you more than they do everyone else. At least I don't act like the whole world revolves around me, where I don't' care about anyone but myself. I'm willing to bet that you are more worried about how everyone thinks about you in this room more than …"

Jessica barked, "OK, what are you reading?"

"I'm reading about how Jesus went off to be by himself," Claire said as she got up and walked away.

Surprised and relieved that Claire had relented, Scott relaxed his shoulder, but his heart sunk when Claire turned before walking past the sliding door and asked them, "I'm going to get something to eat, does anyone need anything while I'm gone?"

Hearing a weak, small voice behind him say, "I'm so glad y'all made it," Scott turned to see Naomi.

Jessica jumped up, wrapped her arms around her, and put all her weight on her as she hugged her. Naomi shifted her stance so she could handle the added weight. Naomi put her arms around her mother for several minutes, and they cried together.

Then Jessica stepped back and asked if there had been any update on Phillips conditions.

Still standing in front of the door, Claire waited to see if there was an update, as the sliding door opened and closed behind her while.

Naomi answered, "Well, I just came from the receptionist, and she said that the doctor will see us when they have more information," as she sat in the chair across from her mother.

Scott watched as Claire come back and sit next to Naomi. Relieved, he exhaled his held breath and put his arm around Jessica to console her.

Jessica leaned into Scott as he moved his arm.

Claire looked at Scott and asked, "Am I going to be the only one to say it? Scott, why are you still here?"

Jessica tensed up at Claire's rudeness and was about to answer Claire's question, but Naomi answered by calmly saying, "Claire, Scott's a good friend of the family, and it is sweet of him to be here right now."

As Naomi was speaking, Scott removed his arm and tried to escape, but was pulled back down by Jessica, who gently pushed at his chest and added, "He is also a pastor, and we are in need of some comfort that a pastor can give."

Famished and exasperated, Claire conceded the battle, but wanted to separate Scott and her mother. She knew they had known each other for years even before her mother had met her dad. Still she wanted this time to be their nuclear family, and not with Scott who was intruding on her mother's affections.

Claire finally blurted out, "Does anyone want anything to eat? Scott let's go get something."

Scott stood and left with Claire leaving Naomi and Jessica alone.

Jessica seethed, "That girl is … is …"

Naomi answered, "It's hard for her also."

Jessica shot back, "Don't you mean she makes it hard for everyone?"

Naomi tried to hide her smile as she replied, "It must be genetics."

For a time, there was quiet in their corner of the Emergency waiting room as Jessica fought back her loneliness and Naomi held back her sorrow.

Jessica, not satisfied with any awkward quietness, asked, "So, did you get in touch with Jonathan."

Naomi held up her smartphone and exclaimed, "No! We have all this technology and it seems we can never get in contact with each other. Especially during an emergency or when you really have something important to talk about."

With tears pooling up in her eyes, Jessica sobbed, "That is what your father would say about me."

Naomi switched to a closer seat to her mom and put her arm around her. Feeling the wetness of the tears soaking through her clothing, made her think about how she'd been in them for too long.

They stayed there that way until Scott and Claire arrived with burgers and fries.

Scott said, "We didn't know what anyone wanted. So, we got several burgers all dressed the same."

"You're so sweet. Thank you," responded Naomi.

As Jessica accepted the burger, she pursed her lips and looked away from Claire.

They all sat there eating in awkward silence.

Naomi and Scott made small talk, about how married life was, how she likes living in Louisville, about how she and Jonathan were doing and what her plans were for work.

After Claire had finished off two hamburgers, she asked, "Does anyone know what happened? All I know is what the news has said."

"I was wondering the same thing, "Naomi added.

Scott leaned forward and said, "I was finishing up the final song and was looking for Phillip to see how the altar call had been doing. I saw a commotion and realized that it was Phillip. I saw him in the crowd falling backward not understanding what was going on. I chuckled to myself thinking he had tripped. Then I saw the woman holding a gun out and taking aim at him again. It was eerie that she was relaxed and smiling. Then I saw the security team tackle her and saw Phillip floundering on the ground in pain."

Naomi added, "I did not even hear the gun fire."

Scott said, "Security wrestled away a .22 revolver. It is a small bullet and with how loud we were playing no one would have heard it."

Claire added, "I was directing the altar call team to people who needed someone to speak with then. I saw the security team rush towards the altar. Following them there, I saw dad ... I saw ..."

Trying to chock back her tears, she finished, "My heart sank when I saw him lying there."

Naomi put her arms around Claire as she regained her composure.

She continued, "He wasn't moving, and blood was pooling all around him. I didn't know if he was alive or dead. Security was handling the shooter, and the crowd was running away once they knew what was going on. Others stared at dad and shook their head in disbelief. Dad was there all alone, and no one was doing anything to help him. I came up to them and told them to find a doctor."

Naomi recounted, "I was praying with a woman named Evelyn. I tell you that poor woman was a wreck. She told me how her husband had passed away about two years ago and that her daughter's boyfriend had thrown her out. She said that taking ..."

Scott asked, "Who threw who out. The daughter or the mother."

Naomi smiled and continued, "She said that taking her daughter back in the house made it hard for her to make ends meet. So, I told her ..."

Claire looked at Scott, wanting to hurry Naomi up. He shook his shoulders implying all they had was time. Claire was not satisfied and snapped her fingers at Naomi.

Flustered, Naomi looked at Claire and raised her eyebrows.

Naomi goaded Claire as she continued, "As I was saying. I told her she ought to see if her daughter could get a job and help. Then I heard a stir behind me but didn't think anything of it. So, Evelyn and I started talking again. Bless her heart; I could not imagine being in the situation she was in."

Claire took a deep breath and let it out.

Naomi was satisfied that she had annoyed her sister enough, continued, "Then the crowd started to press into us a little roughly. I heard someone say 'Gun' and I shielded Evelyn as I helped her up. I walked her out of the arena's main floor, and she told me she would be all right the rest of the way. She was such a lovely lady. Then I turned back to go to our seating area to meet with you and mom. But neither of you were there. "

Scott saw that Claire was looking at her mother as she was mentioned. He also noticed, just like Claire, that Jessica wasn't interested in joining the conversation.

Naomi continued, "I got back to the floor and saw that mom was yelling at the lady who was on the ground by security. I took mom away from there and asked her what she knew. Mom started to cry on my shoulder. I asked her if she knew what was going on and all she said was it was not her fault."

Scott, Naomi, and Claire looked at Jessica as she looked away from the group and studied her fingernails.

Naomi added, "I asked her what her fault was, and she just looked at me wildly and continued on saying it was not her fault. Then she walked away."

Claire looked back and forth from Naomi to her mother while Naomi was telling her story. Claire cleared her throat to ask her mother what was on her mind.

Jessica saw Claire was looking at her and looked away. She put her hands in her lap, fidgeted for a bit and then started to chew on her fingernails.

Scott interjected, "Claire, you are usually in the thick of things. Do you know anything about the shooter?"

Claire looked at her mother and knew that she knew something. She looked at Scott and Naomi and noticed they were both looking at her.

Claire responded, "No, I saw that the crowd running like herd animals and tried to get some people to help maintain some order. I didn't see anything; all I know is what the news report has said. That she was in custody."

Then Claire zeroed onto her mother and asked, "Mother, is there anything you'd like to add?"

Jessica looked at all three of them and said, "Everything was so crazy! I was so far away from it all. I saw that Tracy was wrestled down by security. Then, I headed back to our seats so it could not have been my fault."

Claire asked Jessica, "Who is Tracy? What was not your fault?"

Jessica looked at Claire and asked, "What do you mean?"

Claire answered, "What I mean is who is Tracy. Was Tracy the shooter?"

Jessica sat with a blank face and looked to Scott for help.

Claire returned, "Mother, you said 'it could not have been your fault.'"

Jessica replied, "What I meant to say was I could not see who was at fault."

Naomi confusedly said, "Mom, you clearly said 'It could not have been my fault.' How would you be to blame?"

Claire added, "Why would you even think of the word 'fault'? I believe that you know something about Tracy."

Jessica pursed her lips and squinted her eyes in the 'how dare you manner' with anger rising from her shirt collar. She was tired of Claire trying to make her responsible for everything that goes wrong in life.

Claire asked again, "Mother, what was not your fault?"

Jessica shifted looks between Claire and Naomi and said, "I do not have to take this from my own family. Can't you see I am hurting?"

Naomi replied, "Mom, we are all hurting."

Claire added, "We just want to know what you know."

Jessica looked at Scott and asked him to lead them in prayer.

Claire responded, "Mother, I don't want to pray right now. I want to know what happened. I think we all want to know what Tracy did and why."

Jessica said, "Claire you are grieving my spirit, and I want to pray for God to touch the doctor's hands during your dad's surgery. Now, Scott will you start praying,"

Naomi, Jessica and Scott took each other's hands.

Raising her hands in the air, Claire chided, "Mom, where did you go? You were not there when dad was there on the ground bleeding. From what Naomi said, you were yelling at the woman who shot dad. Now, you are trying to divert all attention from yourself as if you are guilty. What do you know?"

Jessica looked for help from Naomi, but she could tell she was also interested in the answer. She looked at Scott as he nodded toward Naomi and Claire, suggesting that they are family, and they overrule him.

Jessica desperately begged, "Naomi, please stop your sister from rebuking me."

Naomi said, "All right, let's take some time and think about what we're saying before we jump to conclusions and say something we regret."

Claire raised her voice and pointed her finger at her mother as she exclaimed, "Mother, the world does not revolve around you! You have to quit thinking only about yourself."

Jessica tried to control her anger during the last accusation. She wanted to tell Claire all the sacrifices she had made for her entire life, but only muttered, "How dare you."

Claire continued, "Dad is the one in surgery fighting for his life. We are trying to talk about the issue of Tracy, and you are acting as if this is an attack on you. You know something more about Tracy. Is that why you hid from the cops and us?"

At the mention of the name Tracy, Jessica's eyes dilated.

Release her mother and Scott's hands, Naomi looked around and was embarrassed that Claire had made a scene again. Hoping that the situation would not escalate any further, she calmly said, "Claire, please walk away."

Claire answered, "It is not my fault. If she'd just respond to the question, we would not have ..."

Jessica tossed her hands in the air and let them land on the coffee table in front of her.

The whole ER turned their attention to them.

Jessica went into full attack mode, "Enough. Do you understand me? I have had it with your accusations. You are not helping by attacking me. You cannot possibly know what it is like to have someone nitpick you to death on little meaningless issues. You always make this about how I cannot do anything right.

All I wanted was to be happy tonight, but I have to sit here and listen to you accuse me of killing your dad.

Naomi said, "No one said you killed …"

Jessica steamrolled on, "Everything I have done is never enough. You have not thought of my feeling once through this whole ordeal. I give, give, and give, and you take, take, and take. You have no gratitude, mercy or grace. You cannot understand what it is like having someone always leech your joy, to always complain all the time, and to always accuse you and to take advantage of you."

Claire answered her mother, "Yes, I can. I've lived like that my whole life."

She then looked at Naomi and said, "You're right, it is time for me to take a walk."

Claire walked out of the ER with all eyes looking at her with compassion as she went out and removed all the nails put on her cross.

Naomi tried to hide her disgust, and was relieved when her phone rang, and she walked to an opposite corner of the room.

Jessica took a deep breath, was glad to relieve herself of her burden, and walked to the restroom.

Scott looked around the waiting room. Shrugged his shoulders and said, "Women!"

Chapter 6. Ethan's Brand New Day

Ethan startled, as he lifted his head from his pillow.

The alarm blared, like a klaxon warning sailors to abandon ship. It pierced, wailed, and assaulted Ethan's senses. He opened his eyes, but the clock would not come into focus. He tried to reach and tilt his phone so he could see the time, but having slept on his arms wrong, he had problems moving them. His clogged nose from the cold air loosened as his taste buds came to life and he wished they didn't work.

He rolled over and flopped his arm towards the alarm. He was reminded of his night's events as his head throbbed from drinks last night, but he remembered drinking two cups of water and a Tylenol before passing out so it should not have been throbbing this terribly.

Swinging his arm towards his phone, he managed to hit the alarm apps snooze bar, as the feeling started to come back into his hand, like stars piercing as needle pricks through the darkness.

He laid back on the pillow trying to get a few more minutes of sleep, promising himself that he would get to bed at a decent hour tonight.

The alarm sounded again, jolting him from sleep again.

Finding his phone, he snoozed the alarm again.

He cupped his arm, swung his legs off the bed, and sat himself up.

His vision started coming into focus, and he wondered why he was up so early. He smacked his lips together and smelled the stench of mashed corn beef with cabbage and gasoline.

The clock said 4:56 and he wondered why he set the alarm at the time. Then he remembered he was covering for the chaplain this morning until he got back. Then the alarm went off again. He looked at the alarm, and it showed "Relief for the Reverend, love Liz."

"Cute, she never leaves me alone," Ethan grumbled as he stroked his chin stubble and continued muttering, "Time to get clean and professional. "

Ethan cleaned himself up, got a protein shake out of the fridge, and headed to the garage. He started the car, and the radio came to life.

"Right now, I have a witness who was at the arena when Phillip Ashby got shot. Please tell us what happened," said the DJ.

"Great! I can't get away from this," thought Ethan.

The female caller responded with a thick backwoods southern accent," I tell ya what, it was crazy, everything'was just going crazy."

The DJ prodded, "Yes ma'am but what can you tell us about the shooting?"

The interviewee answered, "Well, I didn't see it. I's in the high seats. But I saw people scootin' out, so I headed out too."

"So, you know no more than we do?" asked the DJ.

"Well, I was th . . ." answered the caller before the DJ went to the next caller.

"Why are the most uninformed the most vocal?" thought Ethan.

"All right, let's see if we can get a caller who knows something. Right now, all we know is that a female shot Phillip Ashby and by the account from the last caller, 'Things got crazy.' Hmmm! Let see if the next caller is more informed. You're on the air."

A man who was clearly not good at public speaking answered. One could hear someone whispering encouragement in the caller's ear. The caller said, "Hello, I was at the Bridgestone Arena last night when it happened, the shooter didn't say anything to him. She raised her gun, and she shot him dead. "

"Sir, do you know for a fact that Pastor Ashby is dead, or did he look like he was dead?" prodded the DJ.

There was silence for five seconds and then a click.

"Wow, since when has misinformation become informative? Co'mon everyone, this is the information age people. Next caller." bellowed the DJ

"All right, we have had the uninformed, the guy who called into a radio station and doesn't want to talk. Let's see who'll be next. I am sure it would be 'Mr. Rude who wants to argue' or 'Mr. Let's change the subject'," thought Ethan.

"DJ Joe, thanks for taking my call. I don't know what the big deal is about Pastor Phil getting shot, a whole lot of other people are shot, and we do not make a big whoop-de-do about it. Also, that last guy was full of it. I was there talking to one of the people on the floor. I did not see Pastor Phil get shot, but I saw a lot of blood, and he was still breathing. I think this is the beginning."

DJ Joe responded, "OK, I'll bite. This is the beginning of what?"

The caller answered, "The attacks on Christianity, of course."

Ethan smirked to himself, thinking about how he loved this game. He had gotten both in one person.

Then he yelled at the radio, "Why don't I call in and change the subject. Why aren't we talking about me winning my award last night? Maybe I have to get shot for that to happen."

"Well, thank you for that insight," replied DJ Joe as he hung up on the caller. "We still don't have any information on the condition of Pastor Ashby, nor do we have any information about the shooter. No one can even tell us which hospital he is in. Stay tuned and we will speak with the police chief after these messages."

Ethan turned the radio off and decided to enjoy the quiet. Driving down the road, he let his mind wander to last night. He imagined how his interview with DJ Joe would be.

"Thank you, DJ Joe. It is my pleasure to be here. I got the idea of my book when Quincy "Champ" Stanley came into my office. Yes, that Quincy "Champ" Stanley. Yes, the All-American center who was on the top of his game last year. Anyways, he was telling me how he was having trouble getting his head in the game. He told me about how his divorce had affected him. He told me she had taken almost everything from him and that he was having trouble sleeping. He said that he wanted to get to the root of his mental block."

"So, I asked him what he thought the problem was, and he told me that his ex-wife was his high school sweetheart. That they promised to be together forever. You know how it is. He was troubled because he couldn't let her go.

Then, I asked him, 'Why are you still hanging onto her? She's moved on, living a healthy life. You should you also.' After working with Quincy for a few months, his game came back as did his fortune, fame, and more women.

Working with Champ was the beginning of the idea for this book. We hold onto so many things. We let things bind us to one place. If we could move on and let go, life would be better."

Imaginary DJ Joe replied, "You know that almost sounds like what Christians say, 'Let go and let God.'"

"What, no. Ah! You see that is a platitude for a bumper sticker. There is no God to help you through anything. We are what we make of ourselves," answered Ethan.

"Well, let's stop right there and take a break. Let's take some calls when we get back," smiled imaginary DJ Joe.

Ethan looked in the rearview mirror coming back to reality. "Great, I can't even catch a break in my own head, let alone in the here and now. I spent the past last year and a half working on this book, and now I am overshadowed by a Christian being shot. Why couldn't it be someone I respected have been shot? Now this preacher will be a martyr, and I will be forgotten. Maybe I seriously do need to get shot."

Ethan walked into the back door of the hospital, got to the receptionist and told her he was filling in for the chaplain.

She said that the chaplain usually starts at the emergency room, then to the ICU and then to the nursery floor.

Ethan thanked her and went on his way. He saw that every TV had last night's shooting on. Every conversation he walked by was about the same subject.

Ethan thought to himself that he could not wait until the shooting had blown over and he would not be bothered about it any longer. He crossed the parking lot, took a deep breath, and walked to the emergency room.

Chapter 7.   Phillip's Dream

Phillip startled and took a deep breath.

He felt like he was laying on a cold flat surface but had nothing under him. Only emptiness.

He opened his eyes and saw nothing. He did not see blackness because blackness would depend on only one of your senses. Nevertheless, this was nothingness, a void.

Looking around, he found no color. There was nothing to smell, no wind, wetness nor dryness. There was simply the void. He only existed. Switching his eyes back and forth, he found no points of reference for him to gain any bearings. Smacking his lips together, he discovered the air had no taste.

Seeing a glint of a shadow in the darkness, Phillip watched it twitch as hope started his heart racing.

He felt around, trying to find anything to lift himself up to gain a better handhold, but found nothing to grasp. Not even a place where he could raise himself up by his elbows.

Sweat started furrowing on his brow, as the nothingness swallowed the shadow and any peace he had.

In his peripheral, he saw the glint of the shadow again, but when he turned to view it, "it" stayed in his periphery. Kind of like when one looks into the light, then they go into complete darkness. Finding a shadow outline of what they last saw moving around when they move their eyes.

Trying to find his voice, he attempted to speak to the shadow, but the silence could not be broken. Everything was engulfed in the void. He trembled as each attempt failed. His lips moved. He felt the movement of his vocal cords, but the void swallowed the sound.

Phillip stayed in the silence. He gained solace that his thoughts were something within this void. His despair lifted as he found something that he owned and could control.

The shadow scrambled along in the corner of his vision.

Phillip squinted his eyes trying to make out the peripheral shadow, but whatever it was, knew his thoughts and scurried away. It never went out of sight or tried to flee, it taunted him like a shadow in the darkness. He ignored it and went back to trying to break the void by doing anything. Nothing seemed to exist. The only thing he found he had was his mind, emotion and will.

Gaining more perspective, he found he was only bound by his body. He let his soul start to find comfort in Jesus, as he thought of the song, "Jesus how I trust You. How I proved You o'er and o'er."

The shadow in his periphery flashed. He flailed, as he felt the sensation of falling. Trying to get his arms under him but there was nothing there. He did not feel the pull of anything on him except the sensation of falling.

The void echoed all around him, "Do you love her, or do you tolerate her?"

Then he remembered what had happened. The pain from the bullet and falling. Then those thoughts escaped him as he started to see the beginning of a glow growing brighter like the breaking of the morning.

The void began to give way to the visible. He thought he was laying down, but the world orientated itself around him. The perspective changed from him laying down to where his feet settled under him sturdily on the ground.

He looked around and saw he was in a field with several flocks of sheep. They were not one huge flock but separate as if they had created their own order for themselves. All the flocks were active and jumping up and down.

He noticed the bleating of a lone sheep. He thought it was ironic to have all these sheep, but he only heard one. The sound came directly ahead of him, so he started to walk towards it. His movement was disorienting because as he walked, he felt like he was staying in one place, as the sheep appeared to be coming toward him. He stopped, and all movement stopped. He walked backward, and the same sensation occurred. He thought this must be like playing one of those virtual reality games where you put the helmet on.

After orienting himself, he looked at himself and noticed he had a shepherd's crook in his hand and was walking with a limp, so he leaned upon the staff. He looked at his hands and saw they were calloused and broken as if his had been doing hard work with them. He checked his garments and felt they were torn, and he had a scar on his right hip.

He heard the sheep bleating again in the background. He started walking towards it again. He drew closer to the flock and saw several sheep biting and jumping up and down on something as in defense. He strained his neck around to see if he could get a fix on what they were defending themselves against, but the distance within the nothingness did not allow him to focus. He could not recall when he had ever seen this behavior among sheep before. He limped faster to the flock so he could be some help.

Closing in the gap, he saw that the flock was not defending themselves but had blood on their hooves and on the side of their mouths as they jumped and bit at a black sheep. The black sheep tried to push the other attacking sheep away but was too broken and was bleating out in pain.

Phillip recognized the black sheep as the sheep he heard.

He called out to the white sheep to stop abusing this black sheep and pulled them away with his crook in this hand. Once they turned their attention to him, they cocked their head at him as if they were collectively deciding if they were going to obey his command. They looked at him, to the black sheep and then to the distance, giving a snort through their nostrils as they walked away, leaving the black sheep laying on the ground.

The black sheep tried to get to its feet and away from Phillip, but it did not have the strength to stand. As it saw Phillip coming, it started bleating at him as if cursing him. Phillip approached the beaten sheep with his hands up, and it snapped at him as best as it could. It turned and snarled. But it could not get any distance. Watching its broken body trying to get away made it seem like a slithering snake.

Phillip remembered his staff and used it to hook the black sheep's back legs. It struggled and moaned, but it did not have any more fight in it. Phillip finally got control of the sheep's head and somehow muzzled its mouth. He started to brush and pat the sheep and then noticed the sheep was not black at all but had so many bruises it appeared to be black. The skin was torn from where it had bite marks, but not with typical bite marks from any animal, but the bite marks were from an animal with flat teeth and not fangs.

Phillip thought, "I have never seen sheep turn on one of their own and then keep attacking." Then he grimaced as sorrow filled his heart, as he had to acknowledge he had seen this action take place before many times, but not from an actual sheep.

Phillip then saw the periphery shadow again. He still could not focus on it but knew it was there. The black sheep took the moment of distraction to get its mouth free. It started bleating for something else to help it. Phillip tried stopping the sheep from bleating as he looked around to spy out any more danger.

After several bleats, Phillip wanted to shush the animal, but he still could not make a sound. Then Phillip noticed he began to hear wolves howling in the distance, Spotting them out among the landscape of nothingness.

Some wolves stalked some lone sheep or an entire flock itself, he spotted another wolf chewing on bones while others mixed in with the sheep, and the flock tolerated them in their midst. He noticed some flocks just watched as a wolf just took a sheep from among them, and they did not help or put up a defense; they just watched apathetically and seem relieved they were safe from harm. All the while, the wolves circled and mingled amongst them.

Some flocks abandoned their young. A few flocks bleated to the sky for rescue but seemed oblivious to the environment around them. He saw some of the wolves wore sheepskins. Some flocks were small while others were larger. He spotted one sheep trying to get into a flock. It desperately bleated, but the flock was so tightly knitted that it did not see, nor care about the sheep trying to join.

Phillip absentmindedly stroked the fur of the sheep, as it stopped bleating and laid its head in his lap. Phillip winced in pain as the sheep put its full weight on him.

Noticing the shadow in his periphery, he tried recognizing the silhouette again, but it hid like it wanted its identity to be concealed. It moved further into the outskirts of the void because it was akin to the darkness and it did not want to come to the light to be fully known. He could not see the outline of it, but the blur distinguished its definition.

A light immediately distracted Phillip as it flashed on the other side of the void. Phillip squinted as he began seeing a shadow of a snake rising to strike. The movement of the snake was syncopated like it was taking place with a strobe light. The shadow snake lifted its head and bore down onto another sheep in the distance like the disabled sheep in his care. The distant sheep was caught in a trance, as it looked into the eyes of the shadow snake and then it transformed into a wolf.

"Lord Jesu help me!" convulsed in his head, as sweat beaded on his forehead, his pulse deafened his ears, his breathing became erratic, and his chest was thudding like a drum. He replayed the horrific event in his mind and became more frightened on each loop of the event.

He looked back to find where the shadow snake was but could not find it any longer. He was transfixed on the transformed wolf, watching it licking its wounds and snarling to keep the flocks of sheep away from it. He saw other wolves were trying to join it, but it bared its teeth as it gave a low rumble, as it wanted to be alone.

Unnerved, the other wolves surrounded the new wolf.

Flummoxed, the newly created wolf lowered its head; submitting to its fate. One of the larger wolves approached with its hair bristled. It lifted its paw and placed it firm on the initiate wolf's head. Pushing his head firmly into the ground, the alpha wolf bent down and put its muzzle to the transformed wolf's ear. Then all the wolves suddenly turned and looked at Phillip.

Phillip did not know how much anxiety he could take. Phillip found himself praying, "Jesus, please help me." He tried to retreat but felt the weight of the sheep in his lap.

He decided to move the sheep, but it had him pinned and did not give any assistance. Phillip looked back at the pack and noticed they had not moved. They were staring and licking their lips.

Phillip heard a rustle to his right and found the torturing sheep stalking him. He looked back to the left and saw that the pack of wolves had come closer. However, they were in the same position still licking their lips.

Phillip winced in pain as he pushed the wounded sheep off his lap. He managed to maneuver free and positioned himself between the bruised sheep and the wolf pack and the stalking sheep herd.

Then the shadow of the snake silently rose from behind him. Fear engulfed him as the whole void had a haze of untruth and confusion around it while under its gloom. The bruised sheep and the wolf pack backed away as the serpent's silhouette towered over them all, including the periphery shadow.

Turning around, Phillip saw the snake shadow open its mouth and start to strike. He went to grab the black sheep but felt searing pain as the sheep bit into his offered hand. In disbelief, Phillip looked into the sheep's yellow eyes as the sheep's wool was between transformation between wool and fur. Phillip looked at his pierced hand and noticed the teeth of the sheep, as they became more and more like a wolf.

Phillip turned toward the stalking torturing sheep to seek solace, but they had turned away and deserted him. He noted that the stalking wolf pack was still where he last saw them.

Phillip jerked around towards the snake shadow but could not find any evidence of its existence.

The void surrounded him and engulfed everything until it was only him, the black sheep wolf and the peripheral shadow.

The black sheep wolf pounced on him and called his name as it looked into his eyes. It snarled and placed it paw in his injured thigh. Phillip jerked in pain but could not move. The wolf smiled and said, "You are not ready."

The void suddenly appeared as everything shrunk to nothingness again.

Phillip was alone again with only the periphery shadow. He tried to focus on the shadow, but it would erratically jump when directly looked at.

He was finally able to speak and said, "Who are you? What just happened?"

The shadow fidgeted as it huddled in the left of his periphery and seemed more like a smudge in the darkness than it did a shadow. He tried to approach the shadow, but it moved as he drew closer.

Phillip called out again, "Who are you? What just happened?" He saw the shadow finally paid attention to him as it quickly snuck a peek at him, but turned and went about its business

Phillip watched as best as he could. He saw the thing lift its head from resting on its arms. It still stayed turned away from him but clearly spoke with a hollow and muffled voice, "You have always had a memory of me, but I was put in a corner and forgotten. I am left in this place, with the migration of the sheeples, left to lose my relevancy."

Phillip shouted, "Who are you?"

The shadow turned its head, and Phillip saw its piercing red eyes. The eyes gave a radiance to its facial features, but he could not recognize it. He could tell the smile on its face as it said, "When you know. Know you when? Who are you? You are who. The questions are meaningless. Understand that trying is the truth to you. Then trying to understand that is you. I may be in your now or your later. I may be part of this story, or I could be on the first page of the next book."

"What is your name?" shouted Phillip.

"Your name is what?" taunted the shadow.

"Stop with the riddles. Tell me." Phillip screamed.

A faint glow came across the void, and the shadow began to fade. It laughed as it disappeared saying, "You know me, but you don't know me. You did things with me, but I did not do everything with you. Understand that trying is the truth to you. Then try to understand."

Phillip saw the dullness of light like when the sun is beyond the horizon. His ears became alert, and he heard things like when he was stirring but not fully awake. He felt air rushing into his lungs and hands around his thigh. He felt the presence of others around him. He heard someone say, "He is still with us. He is starting to come too."

Then darkness brought solace to him. He was glad it was not the void and rested in the darkness.

Part 3.

The Beginning

Chapter 8.   Is Seeing Believing?

Once Ethan entered the emergency room, he stopped and looked at the huddles around the waiting room. He saw three huddles. One huddle had three people who absent-mindedly watched TV. Ethan looked at the TV and saw infomercials about some product that could remove stains with no water. The second huddle tried to do their best to rest but could not because of the third huddle. The third huddle seemed to be creating drama worthy of an Emmy. Ethan chuckled to himself, "I know who is getting voted off the island."

He headed toward the receptionist hoping she did not have anyone for him to counsel. His head started to ache, and he did not know how he would respond if someone started any crap with him.

"I know I am filling in for the chaplain, but please tell me I am going to have an easy time consoling these people," Ethan jokingly demanded of the receptionist.

Ethan looked at the receptionist, and all he could see is the gap in her teeth. He mentally said to himself, "Don't look. Don't look. Don't look." However, he found himself looking at the gap in her teeth.

The receptionist jested with a toothy smile, "Son, you are not going to be so lucky. You get to see people at their worst here. And tonight," as she nodded towards the third huddle, "has not been any exception. I should have brought my popcorn for this evening's show."

Ethan tried not to look at the canyon in the woman's mouth and looked away at the people in the ER. Rubbing his brow to remove his headache and not wanting to deal with anyone he stalled as he said, "Did you hear about my special night last night?"

"No. What happened? Did you win the lottery?" joked the smiling receptionist.

"No, I would not be here if I did," Ethan sent back.

"You're not telling me anything I don't know," quipped the receptionist with a healthy laugh.

"I was honored at the Opryland Hotel last night for my book. I am a hometown hero," Ethan said while straightening up and looking her in the face. Seeing her smile, he immediately thought, "Damn it," as he turned to his watch.

The receptionist responded, "You were the one at the hotel last night; I saw the flyers around the hospital about it. That was you. Well, congratulations."

"Thank you. Thank you very much," Ethan said doing his best Elvis imitation.

"What was that?" the receptionist chided, "Was your book on comedy? If it was, what were your sources? Don't quit your day job."

Ethan had always hated that saying. Do not quit your day job. He thought to himself that he wrote a book, and it was not his day job. It was not easy, but he wrote it anyway, regardless of his day job or not. He thought about how many people had been held down because of this simple phrase.

Exasperated, Ethan asked. "Ok, what do I have?"

"Well, before we get to that, how did last night go?" the receptionist asked.

Ethan was glad to have someone interested in his book. He spoke about the night and finished by saying, "It would have been a great night if Christians weren't easily offended by everything. They ruin everything." As the words were leaving his mouth, he noticed the receptionist's cross necklace. He hoped it was for jewelry.

The receptionist gave a crossed look which confirmed her beliefs. She acted professionally again and asked, "So, OK. Are you filling in for Chap?"

Hearing his phone ring and seeing that it was Liz, Ethan told the receptionist, "I've got to take this."

Seeing that she waved him on, he went outside.

"Hello, Liz. What is the news?" Ethan asked.

"Did you get enough sleep last night or are you still showing your ass to everyone?" Liz asked.

Ethan asked, "What is it about you and asses here lately? You were full of it last night."

"I have a fondness of Jack's," said Liz.

Ignoring her quip, he asked, "What did you find out?"

"Did you get up on time?" Liz asked stringing Ethan along.

"What did you find out? Am I going to get the interview shown tonight since it did not show last night?

"Sorry, hon. That is a no can do. This Phillip Ashby situation has all the news in a tizzy trying to gain more information. You are not even on the radar. There is nothing I can do." Liz answered solemnly.

"Seriously?" Ethan asked and then he took the phone away from his mouth and imitated a shout in the air. He looked around, saw no one was around, and jumped up and down frustrated that nothing was going his way.

"There is no way I can catch a break! No radio, newspaper, anything?" Ethan asked.

"Hon, you could put an ad on any of those, but the time has gone. You just have to write another book, and then we will see what happens." Liz said apologetically.

"Write another book? About what? Holding you again the sequel: Choosing what holds you? Or what about Jacks and Asses?" Ethan said.

"Ethan, I know you are upset. Maybe something will come to you. And Jack's and Asses is mine, so don't make me sue you for plagiarism." Liz laughingly comforted.

"OK. It is what it is. Right? Maybe, something will fall into my lap." Ethan agreed.

"You OK? I know you have had a bad year, and I know I did not make things better. Do not go off the rails on me. Maybe you have to get past yourself and actually help someone again," Liz consoled.

"I am OK, I thought more people would be aware of me than they are. But no, everyone is talking about the preacher from last night's shooting. He did not do anything except being shot. What do I have to do? Get shot?" Ethan rambled

"Honey, you getting shot would not get you any further than you are now. Phillip Ashby is not spread all over the news because he was only shot. He has a bigger audience than you do." Liz said.

Ethan cursed, "I can't catch a break."

"Listen, you can feel sorry for yourself on someone else's time. I have one more thing to tell you. Your book seems to be heading to the New York best sellers list. Cross your fingers. We will see on Sunday." Liz encouraged.

Ethan said, "Finally, a ray of hope."

"Yeah, so get to work on the second book," said Liz.

"Now?! Right! Bye Liz," Ethan said as he hung up the phone.

Then he looked at his text from the night before: "Can't wait 2 see U at home." He sighed and walked into the ER waiting room.

The receptionist looked at Ethan with a conniving smile and said, "Glad to have you back." She sat back in her chair with a bowl of popcorn in hand, "I'm ready to enjoy the rest of the show. I'm sure you'd be a great addition."

Chapter 9.   The Mirror Does Not Lie.

Struggling with not embracing her apathy, Jessica gazed into the mirror with tired eyes. Trying to make sense of the jumbled emotions scattering her attention, she leaned into her visage and shared, "It's just you and me again."

Turning the faucet on, she let the water pool and splashed it on her face wishing to rejuvenate herself.

She looked back in the mirror and chided, "If you don't look out. Your insecurities will start showing."

She turned the faucet off and reflected about her last dealings with Phillip before the rally. She regarded how her last meaningful conversation with him was over a silly tie.

"What is wrong with you," she spat. She stared awaiting a response and recognized that her disgust with herself was sufficient.

She clenched the cold porcelain sink, trying to persevere. Hoping that staring with herself would help her ignore her loss of control throughout the day. But her eyes darted to everything around her. The bad paint job between the wall and the ceiling, the smell of the air freshener working overtime to cut the staleness. She heard the drip of a leaky faucet, only to find her tears were the only contributor to the ripples in the sink of water.

Her feelings were hollow. She wanted meaning for her emptiness, but she only stared at her bare vacant eyes staring back at her.

She contemplated about how Phillip being away during the rally and her being alone now was no different. She felt she was a reservoir of anger and tried to be remorseful, but the emotional drought had killed everything.

Captured by her image, she laughed because it did not capture the abundance of fury fighting her emptiness and numbness. She raged inside. Her emotions churned like lava in a volcano. Her feelings stirred like magma. Her self-control was cooling the thin crust of control as bitterness burned her remorse away as an impurity.

"He's going to die, and I'm going to be alone." escaped her lips as tears continued trailing down her cheek.

Agitated, she pursed her lips and scolded her reflection, "Don't give me that look." As echoes of Tracy's words thundered within her: Does he love you? Or does he only tolerate you?

She blew her nose as Tracy's echo endured. She had always had the answer to that question before ever knowing it. She did not wonder why? Their marriage was all expectation and no appreciation. She bore the weight of her wedding ring and admitted, "I'm trapped, alone and tired. I could be free."

The eleutheromania [1]engulfed her as she shuddered from the feeling of euphoria. Then she regretted feeling relief.

"Ok, quick, quick! What can I do to make this all better?" she thought as her mind addled further from the thought of being without Phillip if he died. She weighed the shooting and considered how she did not leave him in the hands of a killer but was helping someone else who needed her. She couldn't be responsible for Tracy shooting Phillip. How could've she known she'd try to kill him?"

Seeking justification, she asked the mirror, "Why is it I have to pay the price every time? Why am I the one who carries the blame? I give and give with no one to lean on for help. Why do I have to be the strong one alone?"

She grimaced as she considered what it was going to be like if Phillip survives. She reflected on how he already comes home and expects to be pampered, and now he will have a valid reason.

Trying to allow herself to feel for the first time through the day, she was unsure of why she was so numb? Shrugging her shoulders, she felt that it was to be expected because nothing had changed for years."

"I want to feel important," flowed from her being to her lips.

---

[1] An intense and irresistible desire for freedom

Closing her eyes, she pondered about the times she felt taken for granted. How her attempts to make herself understood only brought ridicule and shame. How she had to set limits to protect her heart.

Her eyes welled up with tears, her countenance filled with anguish as she scowled at herself, "What is wrong with you? Phillip is a good man, and God has placed you in his life to take care of him. So, buck it up and get over it. This is the life that has been dealt you."

She leaned forward into the mirror and checked her make up. Inhaling deeply, she confirmed to herself, "I am just going to do what I have always done."

Straightening her dress and attempting at fixing her hair the best she could, Jessica tried to repress her sincere feelings. She looked at the mirror trying to emulate feeling fine again. Searching around, she noticed that she did not have her purse with her to cover up. Giving up the search she felt foul and had to look away from the mirror.

"Why would Tracy do such a thing?" she cracked as a wash of emotions overwhelmed her. Several other questions flooded her mind.

"What did Phillip do to her?"

"Was there no other way?"

"Was it Phillip's fault he was shot?"

She felt Phillip could have sorted this all out if Tracy would have given him time. Cycling through the rushing thoughts, she settled on, "Why would she do this to me?"

At this thought, she was startled that she had said it. Nevertheless, it was the truth of how she felt.

She realized that Tracy had spotlighted a giant hole in their marriage, which was her pride and selfishness. She fled the moment Phillip was shot. Her thoughts were not with him but caught up in the facts of how the shooting affected her.

She didn't like the fact that when she was yelling at Tracy, she wasn't defending Phillip's honor, but her own ambitions.

She tried to quell her feelings by thinking about how Phillip was fighting for his life. But her thoughts kept alternating to how it affected her.

"I should've noticed her shiftiness. I should've understood her words and intent. I should've told her that Phillip was the best example of what a husband could be," flowed through her mind.

She tried to rationalize the thought with, "Phillip and I have been married several years, and when he hurts, I hurt." But that view was abandoned with "Why did Tracy do this to her?" or "Why would Tracy want to change my life?"

She thought about how she didn't do anything to Tracy and why she had to pay the penalty.

She began meditating on Phillip getting better. She started to whisper, "Phillip, get better." She kept chanting that phrase, and she felt her tortured soul begin to get relief.

Her mood began to improve. Her mind started quietening, only to have her mind dart to Claire.

"Why can't Claire understand that I'm hurting right now? I am tired that she's got to make it about herself all the time. I thought she'd been taught better. Why does she act like she deserves a reward every time she cuts me down?"

Jessica's blood pressure rose, as Claire's last words engulfed her, "The world does not revolve around you!"

Seething from the abusive judgment, Jessica gripped the sink trying to anchor herself from Claire's overwhelming indignation. "Claire should have known how those words had hurt me so. What have I done to make her think that? She should know that the world does not revolve around her either."

Concentrating on her breathing, Jessica counted each breath. She felt the volcano start to calm. She tried to motivate herself, "OK, Jessica snap out of this. Phillip is going to make it. Everything is going to be all right. The world is going to right itself, and me with it. It was not your fault."

In the mirror, she saw Naomi walk into the bathroom with the phone to her ear.

She heard Naomi say, "Thank you, Jonathan for understanding, and we will be waiting for you. Be safe and I love you!" Then she made a kissy noise and then hung up.

Jessica wiped the tears from her eyes and choked back her feelings. She splashed water on her face and examined the puffiness in her eyes. She did not know how she was going to salvage this.

"Hi, mom. That was Jonathan; he will be driving down here tonight." Naomi stated.

Jessica protested, "It is well past midnight, tell him to wait till morning."

Naomi said, "Mom, I already told him that, but he would not see it any other way. He said he would be here in about 3-4 hours." Imitating her husband, Naomi continued. "He said that family should be together during rough times."

"You got a good one there," Jessica said while blowing her nose.

"Mom, you should not be alone either. Please come out here with the rest of us." Naomi said.

"I am in no condition to be with people," replied Jessica.

Naomi put her arm on her mom's shoulder and said, "Mom, we all are hurting, and we are not just common people. We are family! Come on out here and be with us."

Jessica reminisced, "You know I once was as sweet as you. You are such a blessing."

Naomi reminded, "Both Claire and I are blessings, and we have both you and daddy to thank."

"Agh! That girl. Sometimes I think she does stuff just to make me blow up." Jessica said as she looked in the mirror again and tried to search for her purse again.

Naomi shot back, "Claire has no control over your reactions," as she tried to guide her mother out with the rest of the group.

Jessica cringed as Naomi led her to the bathroom exit.

She replied, "Naomi, I need to get myself ready, can't you see that I am a mess. When people see me, they need to see that I have it all together. Above all, I am a pastor's wife, and they do not want to see me like this with my hair as a disaster and ..."

Naomi looked in the mirror and saw she was unkempt also but knew that now was not a time of pride and vanity. She interrupted, "My hair is a disaster too. We all have not slept tonight. Come here!"

Then Naomi reached out her arms and Jessica received the hug. She started sobbing all over again.

Naomi reached over her mom and began to walk towards the door.

Jessica grabbed a tissue and blew her nose. She straightened herself up, looked at Naomi, and then looked at the door.

Naomi assured, "You're ready. You're not alone. We're all hurting."

Jessica couldn't concentrate on Naomi any longer because all she heard was the echo of herself screaming at Tracy, "Why did you do this to me!"

She felt ashamed because she was more worried about how Phillip being shot affected her more than anyone else. The memory continued taunting her. She looked at her feet, knowing that she had to deal with it, but she did not have the strength nor desire to admit that Phillip being shot was partly her fault.

Not able to cover up behind makeup, she decided that she would let her façade carry her through.

She looked at Naomi, straightened her dress again, and assured herself, "I am ready!"

Then Naomi opened the door, and they both exited the restroom.

The first thing Jessica saw was Claire fiddling on her phone with her feet kicked up in relaxation. She took a deep breath and let it out slowly. She could not imagine hiding behind her phone and a game.

Naomi took her mother's hand, walked to Scott and Claire and said, "Ok, let's pray."

Naomi still held her mother's hand as she took Claire's in her other hand.

Claire took Scott's hand, and he put his arm around Jessica.

She leaned into Scott, hoping to gather strength to make it through the night, as Claire pursed her lips in disgust.

***

Ethan saw the four of them praying. He shook his head and muttered, "Great, Christians."

He turned to leave, but the receptionist smiled as she pointed him in their direction.

He took a seat next to them. Watching them pray, like a spotlight was on them in an auditorium.

Ethan saw the older gentleman with his arm around the older woman. He concluded that they must have been husband and wife with their two girls, who had gotten back from a show at the TPAC.

He figured that one of them must have been touched by a homeless man, and they wanted to be checked to see if they had leprosy or going blind.

Ethan saw their heads go down and waited to hear their chanting.

Ethan was surprised when he heard the man starting to speak. He could hear every word like this man used to projecting his voice.

He thought, "Well, let the show begin."

***

Within the prayer circle, all four bowed their heads as Scott started the prayer:

"Heavenly Father, Creator of our life, the beginning and the end, the Healer who took our shame of sin and death. Lord, we just humbly come before You to just pray You will just hold our dear brother and Your son in the palm of Your hand. Just touch and guide

the hands of the doctor and pray that You
would just envelop our brother with Your
love and peace and understanding.

Holy One, Healer, Comforter, Divine
Judge, You are perfect in every way and have
set man upon Your own heart. Lord, we just
don't understand what's going on right now,
but Holy Spirit we just trust in You and know
Your will, will be done, and Your ways are
greater than our way. Please just breathe
love and peace to this beautiful family. We
just praise You for the work You are going to
do and just place our brother in Your hands,
our Mighty Healer.

We just ask that You would just get us
through this stressful time, and we love You
so much.

We are broken and sinners and just ask
that Your holiness and righteousness would
break through tonight and that You would
just give us peace and rest in You."

***

Ethan snickered to himself because he just could not get the
word "just" out of his mind. He mimicked the older gentleman in
his imagination, "Dear God 'just' help me in my form of wishful
thinking and aid me in bolstering my delusions."

Ethan stifled a laugh, as the older gentleman became more
animated. He nearly guffawed as one of the girls almost got hit by
the man's flailing arms.

Ethan wondered if there were any extra points for
calisthenics during a prayer. Smirking, he thought it would be
horrible if his daughter were knocked out. Then he looked around
and shrugged his shoulders as he thought, "Well, at least they are
in the right place in case he does."

He saw the old woman start. She shot her head straight back
as if she was radiating light through her eyes and mouth. Almost

like a movie he had seen once. He found himself looking up to check what she was seeing.

Shaking his head, he thought that they would be perfect patients in his part of the hospital.

***

Jessica lifted her head up as if speaking to the ceiling as she prayed:

"Father God, we speak in existence
Your power to save my husband. We believe
in faith that what we ask, we will receive.
Father God, we are not looking to
things that are seen, but to the things that
are not seen. We cast Satan out of this place.
He has no place here as we lift up Your name.
Father God, we know You say life and death
are in the tongue, and we give your angels
permission to heal Phillip and to restore him
to full health again. Father God, we rebuke
the evil works of the enemy and give charge
to your angels to fight the battle for Phillip's
life.

Father God, we believe all things are
possible because You said they are. Father
God, please help us to pray for the things we
don't know what to pray for.

Father God, we rebuke the devil for
him sending one of his agents of death to kill
my husband. Father God, we place her in
your hands to judge her for her sins.

God, we believe. God, we believe. God,
we believe.

Answer our prayers."

***

Ethan didn't catch all of the words she was saying, but he thought that she was demanding something to happen. He had never seen someone stamp their foot during a prayer circle but laughed to himself that she was like a horse counting for a trainer.

Ethan mimicked, "Grandpa Joe, we love this steak you made. Grandpa Joe, thank you for killing and cooking this cow so we can live. Grandpa Joe, thanks for the garden you grew so we can have these vegetables. Grandpa Joe thank you so much."

Ethan snickered at himself, as one of the daughters started to pray.

She looked like she had spunk, but he saw that she had humbled herself.

She began to speak, but he barely understood her. It was not like she was mumbling but like she was directly speaking to someone she cherished.

***

Barely audible, Claire prayed:
> "God, please save my daddy and keep
> him well. I have faith in You and know You
> are able to do all things.
> Please save my daddy.
> Amen."

***

Ethan felt that her words were authentic but sighed because he knew that all four of them might as well be writing a Christmas list to Santa. He considered how the daughter's prayer was like the genuineness of a child, who would kiss their daddy good night before going to sleep and knowing that all will be well.

Ethan furled his brow because he was surprised to hear her say "daddy."

So, he ruled out that the older gentleman was the dad, but he became more confused at the closeness of the older gentleman and the older woman.

Ethan scratched his head as he looked at the ER receptionist.

She grabbed a handful of popcorn and chewed. Smiling, she gave a head nod; acknowledging that this is what he was here for while filling in for the chaplain.

He reluctantly stood up and checked his breath to ensure that he didn't smell like last night's spirits. As a precaution, he popped a breath mint in his mouth as he headed toward them.

He stood patiently as the last woman continued praying.

***

Naomi finished the prayer:

"Jesus, we don't know why this happened. We don't know what the outcome is going to be. We do know You that are God and You created us. We are aware that You took the pain of sin and death so we can be saved by Your cleansing blood. We ask that You take this evil the enemy has done and turn it too good in the only way You can. We ask that You orchestrate Your saving grace for the shooter and help us to not think evil of her but ask that You will reveal Yourself to her and bring her to the saving grace that only You can do. We ask that You please give us the mercy and grace to love the shooter as You do.

Jesus, I am selfish, and I still want my dad to be here with the rest of us. I know that You are not done with him and ask that You will please keep him here with us and not with You just yet.

I pray that You will give each one of us strength, courage, peace, faith, hope, and love, that only You can give to get us through this.

Even though one of us is hurt, I ask that You please continue to protect all of us. We thank You that no one else got hurt during this tragic event.

Help us to see You working in all things.

Please open our ears, eyes and hearts to Your will.

Amen. "

***

Ethan thought that she had said her prayer deliberately like she was capturing every thought and feeling of that moment.

He also thought it was a nice touch that she was asking and not demanding as she said please a few times. He thought if he were a god, he would like to be spoken to reverently like this.

He was also amazed that she prayed for a shooter.

His eyes grew wide, and heart skipped, as he realized whom he was about to comfort.

He looked at them and then at the ER receptionist.

She took her hand out of the popcorn and urged him on to talk to them.

Realizing that he was with Phillip Ashby's family, Ethan shook his head no.

The ER receptionist pointed her finger at the family and stomped her foot.

Ethan swore to himself under his breath, "Jesus Christ."

At that, the four of them said, "Amen!" and then turned to look at Ethan.

Ethan's mind was befuddled as he thought about how unlucky he was.

Finally finding his voice, Ethan offered, "Hello, my name is Ethan Pitney. I am here to fill in for the chaplain, Is there anything you need or need help with?"

The four of them introduced themselves to Ethan. Confirming that he was with Phillip Ashby's family.

Ethan became the official sounding board for all of their question. They flung them as darts to a dartboard. They all ask him about Phillip, wanted to know if he was all right, or if he was out of surgery, or if he was going to still be able to walk, or if he was alive at all.

Then almost in synchronous timing, they asked him if he would pray with them.

Finding himself not knowing what to do, he said yes.

Ethan then realized what he agreed to do.

He played the barrage of questions again in his head and then got to the part of them asking him to pray and him saying yes.

He could not believe the place that he was in now. He looked up and thought to himself, that if there were a God, He would be laughing at him right now as He was about to zap him with lightning.

As Ethan looked up, they all took hands and bowed their heads.

Ethan's gut turned because he did not want his first praying outing to be about Phillip Ashby.

Ethan stammered, "I am sorry I led y'all on. I don't really . . ."

Then a doctor called for the Ashby family.

The family looked at Ethan, dropped their hands and then went to the calling doctor.

Relieved, Ethan tried to make his getaway, but Claire took Ethan's hand and said, "Co'mon, we will need all the help we can get."

Ethan continued to stammer, "I should really get going. The surgeon can help you now, and I have others to help."

Claire shook her head in non-acknowledgement, kept her arm around his as they continued walking toward the surgeon.

The surgeon waited till the whole family had gathered.

He smirked when he saw Ethan and the Phillip Ashby's family.

Ethan had met this surgeon on occasion and knew he was a member of a church in the Belmont area. He was aware that he led a small Bible study in the cafeteria with some of the other doctors and the chaplain.

Ethan shrugged his shoulders as if to say, "Get on with it."

The surgeon stated that they had removed the entire bullet, and they had stopped all the bleeding.

He explained that the bullet had hit the femoral vein and that Phillip was lucky to be alive. He also stated that Phillip should be able to keep his leg, and there was no damage to the bone, muscle or nerves.

He said that with a lot of prayer and hard work Phillip should be out of the hospital in about two weeks.

Jessica shouted, "Praise God!"

Then she rebuked, "It was not luck. It is God! It is a miracle."

She dramatically threw her hands in the air and finally settled down, as she laid her head on Scott's shoulder.

Ethan saw Claire cast a glance at Naomi, as they both put a finger up to their lips, shushing each other.

He was surprised that their reaction was similar to his. He concluded they must be used to the drama.

The surgeon looked at Jessica. He let her have her time and stammered, "OK, well he has been moved to ICU for observation." Gesturing to Ethan with a grin he said, "I see you have one of our finest doctors here with you."

The surgeon looked at Ethan and smirked as he said, "I assume, Dr. Pitney, you'll continue supporting this family?"

Ethan looked at the doctor and said, "No. I'm just filling in for the chaplain."

The surgeon grabbed some popcorn from the receptionist's bowl, as he continued, "I'm sure you are doing a great job. Do you mind taking them to the waiting room at the ICU? You do know where it is?"

Ethan paused as he glowered at the receptionist and the surgeon, who only smiled back as they chomped on their popcorn.

He thought, "I hope you both choke on it," as he nodded in acceptance of responsibility for the Ashby family.

The surgeon said, "Thank you for your time and understanding. Just follow Dr. Pitney to the ICU waiting room. Please know that Pastor Phil is in my prayers. If you don't mind, I have others to take care of."

Then the surgeon disappeared into the ER, and the whole family looked at Ethan for leadership.

Startled, Ethan started walking into the interior of the hospital. Pausing at each corner, because he knew how to get to the ICU from his office, but not from the ER.

Ethan did manage to get the family to the ICU waiting room.

Once there, he said, "Well, it has been a privilege to help y'all. A nurse will be here to let you know which room Phillip is in."

Desperately wanting to get away and get back to his office, he said he would go to the nurse's station and get the whereabouts of Phillip.

As Ethan turned to leave, he ran into a nurse who was coming out to meet the Ashby family.

Ethan regained his composure. He stepped aside and gestured for the nurse to enter the waiting room, but she stared at him, so he went in before the nurse as she followed.

Claire sided up next to him as the nurse said Phillip is awake and can have visitors.

"Praise Jesus!" exclaimed Jessica as the rest said, "Amen" in response.

Ethan furrowed his brow, hoping that he did not physically roll his eyes. He was glad that he had a getaway while the family followed the nurse, but Claire caught his arm and said, "Tonight, you're a temporary Ashby. It's been a long night for me, and I need someone else there to help me to keep my sanity."

Ethan chuckled, "Well, that is my field. I am a psychiatrist."

Claire looked at Ethan and stated, "We all thought you were one of the chaplain's minions."

Ethan cocked his head and asked, "Minions?"

"You know what I mean. One of his helpers." Claire clarified.

Ethan offered, "Well, let's say that I know the chaplain, and he owes me a huge favor,"

"OK, well you are doing a great job, but we still need some more help. C'mon," Claire said as she took his arm and caught up with her family.

Ethan still could not believe his rotten luck. He considered the events of the past few days and ventured that if God did exist, then He must be punishing him for all he had done.

Chapter 10.   Alive and Awake

Phillip shifted his eyes around the room, as he struggled with locating the cause of the ringing in his ears. Getting familiar with his surroundings, he was surprised that he was lying in a hospital bed.

He tried sitting up but had to lie back down because the room was tilting back and forth. Looking at the ceiling he started gathering his thoughts, and they immediately shifted to Tracy leveling the gun at him, intermixed with the dream of the bruised sheep.

Examining the wires and tubes connected to him, he attempted to recall the reason he was in a hospital. Lifting his arm to see the IV there, he said, "It has to be these drugs I'm on."

Thinking about getting shot, he remembered the phrase o'er and o'er, then his memory shifted to him lying on the ground bleeding. He was all alone with his blood flowing away from him. He felt the drain as each pump of his heart made him weaker.

He shuttered and felt a chill like someone had walked over his grave.

Feeling exasperated, he found it difficult concentrating on Tracy, because the shadow of years cloaked her. He couldn't keep his concentration on her without seeing the gun leveling at him again.

Struggling to remember her face, he tried singling her out from anyone in his past. But her face was hidden behind the barrel. He tried seeing beyond the weapon, but all his attention and focus was on the gun pointed at him.

Jumping when the shot was fired, he saw the strike of the shadow snake from his dream. The jerk from the jump, caused him to wince in pain, as he quickly found he didn't have the mobility in his leg. He also found himself massaging a bruise on his chest, remembering that he was shot twice. Then he looked at his hand to see if he still had the bite mark from the sheep but found that was where the IV was inserted.

Taking deep breaths, the pain seemed to subside with every exhale.

Looking up to God he said, "I know I've consoled others in this position or worse, but it's me this time. God, how could You allow someone to shoot me?"

Biting his bottom lip, he shook in frustration, trying his best to not be angry. Balling up his fist, he willed them loose as he sat himself up through the pain.

When he saw himself in a mirror, he watched the barrel of the gun aimed at him again.

Flinching out of the way, his leg hurt more.

Anger finally overtook him, and he pleaded with God, "After all I've done in Your name. After all the sacrifices I've made."

Trying to quiet his mind and seeking some solace, he heard the ringing in his ears as he waited for God to answer. Listening in faith, the ringing pierced his patience, so he decided to concentrate on the ringing, discovering that everything else faded away.

He watched the second hand on the clock. Every movement made him feel woozy like he was on a ship with light chop.

Closing his eyes, he felt the weight of abandonment. His restlessness would not allow him to keep his thoughts still.

He cried out to God, "Don't you abandon me! I'm a good man."

Phillip thought of how many times he had heard that argument, and now here he was claiming his own goodness as a reason to be noticed by God.

Finding that keeping his eyes closed helped him to adjust to the pitch and yaw of the room. His equilibrium settled as he stayed in judgment of himself.

He felt justified in being mad. He considered Jonah, who was angry at God and sought justification. Then he remembered God's reply to each of them, "Who are you and who am I?" He let the questions calm him, as he reflected on God speaking to Elijah through the stillness of the storm.

"I know I am the chief of sinners," Phillip humbly acknowledged. "I know my inner thoughts and deeds. I know You know them also. Dear God, I do not have the strength right now. Please, help me to be strong."

Phillip looked out his window and door and watched all the shadows and silhouettes floating by. Everything was zooming in and out in his vision. He held his breath and shifted his eyes to every movement.

Phillip gripped his chest. Wanting to will the world to slow down. Wanting a chance to catch up.

Two nurses walked by having an intense conversation. There was an elderly woman with a cane who looked into his room and continued past his door. He saw a man with a white doctor's lab coat and a tablet. Phillip gasped as he tried to look at his eyes. He was sure he saw a hint of red, just like the man in his dream.

Phillip tried to be still as the man stopped outside of his door and examined his chart. He found himself holding his breath and felt a chill and tried to shake off the dread that was overtaking him.

He forced himself to see the man's eyes better. He tried to reassure himself that the man's eyes had a broken blood vessel.

"This has to be one of Tracy's people, "Phillip thought.

He screamed, but his voice had escaped him. He struggled in finding the nurse call button but couldn't find it while fumbling around. He removed his gaze from the doctor as he quickly glanced down and found it. Then immediately shot his eyes back at the shadowy figure and saw that he had moved out of his view and started to speak to someone.

Phillip thought he heard the man say, "I can finish him up."

Phillip watched the man's silhouette grab something out of his pocket as he turned towards his door. His bed seemed to swallow him, trapping him in place. Phillip wrestled with his bed sheets as he tried finding the nurses button attached to his bed. Finally finding the button, he squeezed it several times.

The man turned to pass into Phillip's view again, but Phillip was startled to hear the words "Honey, I am so glad you are well."

It was Jessica.

Phillip arched his neck around Jessica, trying to see the shadowy man behind her, but he had lost him.

She cried, "I thought you were dead. I'm so glad to see you alive."

She bent down and gave him a big kiss.

Phillip winced because she was oblivious to the pain, she was putting him in by her sudden attack.

"Honey, your pillow is soaked, and you're all clammy. Are they taking care of you?" chided Jessica.

Phillip realized that he had balled his hands into fists. He started to relax as more of his family walked in.

Phillip strained to see around his family filing in the door, trying to find out who the mysterious man was, but his family walking in must had scared him away.

Scott came in next, "Lazarus, it's good to see you alive and well. Welcome back to the land of the living."

Glad to have the security of his familiar group, Phillip relaxed and hoarsely replied, "Did you weep? Jesus wept." The words came out more backward and slurred than he expected.

Scott quipped, "No, you weren't gone for four days."

Phillip gave a small grin and a weak laugh.

He finally saw past Scott and couldn't find the red-eye man. Satisfied that the strange man was not hanging around; Phillip gave his complete attention to everyone coming into his room.

He laid down too quickly, and the room started to spin.

Remembering that he was on a potent cocktail for his pain, he reminded himself, "Move slowly."

Naomi followed Scott, showing the weariness of the night. She came in and gave him a kiss on the forehead whispering, "I love you."

Phillip whispered back, "You, all right?" At least that's what he thought he said.

"I am now," answered Naomi.

Phillip tensed as he saw Claire come into view with a man with a white doctor's coat. Letting out an audible gasp, terror made his heart monitor start beeping excessively.

Claire put her cheek to his as she made a kissy noise and said, "Daddy, I'm so glad you're alive."

While receiving her hug, Phillip examined the doctor. He noticed that he had bloodshot eyes but not to the degree of the person beforehand.

Then Claire lifted his sheet and saw all his bandages. He was glad he was covered, but knowing Claire's personality, he allowed her the moment to see his wound.

"So, doc, do you think he's going to live?" Claire asked the doctor in her tow.

Jessica barked, "Claire, for goodness sakes. What are you thinking?"

The doctor replied, "I am not that kind of doctor, but I think he will live."

Then holding out his hand, he said, "Hello sir, I'm Ethan Pitney. I'm a doctor here and was helping your family out while you were in surgery."

Phillip wanted to be cordial with the doctor, but he couldn't remember a word he said. He looked at the IV in his hand and ventured what cocktail they had him on. He smacked his lip and noticed that the room was swaying again.

Claire said, "Ok Dr. Ethan Pitney, let's go over here," as they walked to a corner furthest away from Jessica.

Phillip searched the doctor's face and could tell that he'd rather be somewhere else.

Phillip then examined everyone else's faces. Sensing that there were hidden tempers under their false countenances of control, he understood the silence that became a heavyweight smothering any joy.

Looking into Scott's eyes, he saw a referee who'd taking a few licks during a game.

On the other hand, the medicine could be giving him false pretenses.

Phillip slurred, "Y'all been right?"

Then a nurse walked in saying, "Do you need anything?"

Phillip remembered that he had pushed the nurse call button.

Phillip managed, "No, I pushed it earlier, but everything is all right now."

The nurse acknowledged him and proceeded to check his IV.

The silence stayed and everyone watched the nurse work.

Scott broke the silence by asking, "What cocktail is he on?"

The nurse replied, "Morphine, he is in a lot of pain."

Jessica looked at Phillip and then the nurse, " Does he need to be on it? He doesn't look like he's in that much pain."

The nurse turned her head to Jessica. In awe of the stupidest question that she had heard that day. She then looked to the other family members for support.

Taking her mom's hand, Naomi said, "Mom, dad's been shot. I know it's hard to see him this way, but he's going to get better. These nurses are doing their very best to help dad heal by giving the best care that they can."

Jessica said, "Let's just pray that Jesus takes the pain away."

Claire blurted, "Mother! He's not in pain because of the morphine. Sheesh!"

Jessica shook her head and gave a heavy sigh, giving Phillip's the confirmation of his suspicions that nerves were raw. Swaying back in forth, he followed the emotion of the conversation, hearing their words but not understanding them.

"Ma'am, Phillip is in control of the drip. See this button here," replied Ethan as he pointed to what looked like a stick grip with a button on top of it. "When he presses this, he will . . ."

"I am not stupid! I just know that morphine is addictive," said Jessica.

Ethan tried to continue, "It is, but Phillip is in control of . . ."

"Listen, Mister . . ." said Jessica as she tried to find Ethan's nametag. After not finding it she continued, "You obviously don't know who this is. My husband is a well-known pastor and if others hear that he's on drugs. . ."

Trying to gain his lucidity, Phillip interrupted, "Jessica, it'll be all right. Please take a deep breath."

The nurse looked at everyone and then at Phillip.

Phillip filled in her thoughts, "Seriously?"

The nurse said, "If you need a nurse again, just page us."

As she walked out Jonathan walked in.

Phillip saw Naomi visibly relax as Jonathan came to her and she put her head on his shoulder.

Jonathan took her into his arms and gave her a huge hug. They both giggled and smiled as they kissed and released each other.

Phillip looked at Jessica, who wasn't at his side but next to Scott's.

Jonathan looked at Naomi and the whole family and said, "I got here as fast as I could. "

Jessica replied, "It's OK, you're here now."

Jonathan came to Phillip, giving him a gentle 'guy hug' and said, "I'm glad to see you're well, sir."

Phillip only nodded his head.

Jonathan asked the group if they've been keeping up with what the news was saying.

The whole group looked at him waiting for an answer.

Jonathan continued, "There is a lot of speculation. There are reports that the shooter had killed herself and didn't make it to the police station; another said that she was in a cult while another says that it is the beginning of the war against Christianity. Then there's the report that the shooting was because of a love triangle that had come to its head. But all of them want you to come back after these messages."

Everyone looked at Jonathan with the weary look that it wasn't a time to joke around.

However, Phillip did manage to get a laugh out and said while coughing, "Come back after these messages so they can hear nothing at all."

Claire answered Jonathan, "So, what you're telling us is that no one knows anything."

"Yeah, pretty much," Jonathan said, "So, what can you tell me?"

Phillip thought about each of the situations Jonathan listed. The third solution was ludicrous. He did get around when he was young, but God got a hold of him, and he'd been faithful to his wife their whole marriage. He felt more at ease with the first solution that the woman attempted to kill him was now dead, but then he had compassion for her.

He tried to dwell on that a bit, but then he saw the man with the red eyes looking at him from the hallway. Upon a clearer look, he noticed the stranger looked familiar.

Phillip gasped and asked Jonathan to close the door to the room.

"Honey, don't you think it'll get too hot in here with all these people and the door closed," argued Jessica.

Agitated Phillip yelled, "I want it closed!"

Phillip saw everyone back away with astonishment. He had to calm himself, but tension gnawed at him. He closed his eyes and concentrated on his breathing. He heard the murmuring in the room.

Opening his eyes, he investigated the shadows from the door and was satisfied that he had quelled his fears.

His family was still aghast.

He panned the room and saw disbelief, except the doctor who seemed to be scrutinizing his behavior.

***

Ethan watched the reaction from the family and deduced that Phillip generally didn't lose his temper. He did a mental checklist of the events that he had seen Phillip exhibit and was sure he was suffering from anxiety.

He watched the machine monitoring Phillip's vitals and kept a mental note.

***

Phillip felt like he needed to apologize. Instead, he collected himself and said, "Jonathan, please continue," as he uncurled his fist.

"Well, that's it. It's only hearsay," said Jonathan.

Claire asked, "Was it the police or the media?"

Jonathan shrugged his shoulders and answered, "Well, I don't know. I think it's only the radio stations."

Phillip saw Claire's public relations mind kick in as she said, "They probably have some talking heads speculating because they don't have anything else to go on."

Phillip mumbled, "Have we put out a statement?"

"No, because I don't know what our stance is. No one seems to know anything other than you being shot," said Claire.

Phillip answered, "Your mom was there."

Claire said, "I knew it," as the whole room's attention turned to Jessica.

Phillip's dream tried to surface, but he quickly dismissed it.

He slurred, "Didn't she say anything? She was the one who introduced me to Tracy and then she left us alone. "

Phillip watched Jessica try to hide into the walls.

Claire glared at her, and then he saw Jessica's countenance change.

He could have sworn she was mimicking the dream sheep's eyes transforming but remembered was from a drug induced dream.

He watched Jessica seeking solace, but the tension was like daggers trying to dig out the truth.

Jessica looked directly at Phillip and pleaded, "It was not my fault."

Crossing her arms, Claire said, "Well dad, that's interesting that mother only says is that it wasn't her fault."

Phillip wanted to stop the escalation before it was too late. But he couldn't concentrate on creating a coherent sentence. He was also afraid that his tone would be misconstrued as anger.

Giving a heavy sigh, he dwelled on how he didn't want to be referee right now.

He somehow managed, "Please stop," but it was too late.

Jessica raised her voice over Claire's and said, "Phillip, why are you accusing me?"

Claire injected, "Dad hasn't accused you. He just stated the truth. Don't turn this around on him. "

"Don't start with me again young lady," bellowed Jessica.

Claire shot back, "Why did you let dad be alone with a killer? Why did you lie about endangering dad?"

Jessica stammered, "Well, I didn't think she'd shoot him."

She turned to Phillip and probed, "Why did she shoot you?"

Before Phillip could stop, he scowled," Probably because I didn't have my tie on."

Jessica stood with her mouth open and fury burning in her eyes, but speechless from his sarcasm.

Naomi tried to calm everyone down.

Being new to the family, Jonathan knew his place and kept quiet.

Scott played the fine line he always played when dealing with the Ashby family.

Ethan watched the dysfunction with amusement.

Claire covered her mouth, masking her snickers.

Jessica pursed her lips and broke the silence, "How dare you. This is why I didn't want to bring it up. I knew you'd side with them and make this all my fault."

Ethan put his hand on Claire's shoulder while Scott stood in front of Jessica.

Claire managed to get the last word in, "Why are there secrets when we're family?"

Silence rushed back into the vacuum.

Phillip watched Jessica nest herself into Scott's arms. Seeing that Scott has assumed the role of surrogate husband, he wanted to say something but reminded himself that he was heavily drugged.

Naomi leaned forward, looked at her mother and said, "Mom, we aren't blaming you for what happened." Looking at her sister, she continued, "There was no way any of us could've known this would've happened."

Phillip smiled, glad that Naomi would settle this mess. He leaned back and settled into his drugged bliss instead of fighting it.

Naomi let out a sigh and continued talking to the room, "This has been a long night. We are still wearing the same clothes as last night, and we didn't get any rest. I for one am ready to get a decent bite to eat, get clean, and sleep."

Jonathan said, "I agree, but could someone tell me what just happened."

***

Ethan listened to Phillip try to tell his story as lucidly as possible. He noticed that he didn't say anything about being shot.

He only mentioned Tracy raising the gun and then him blacking out.

Making mental notes, he listened to Claire, Scott and Naomi tiredly give their account.

He watched Phillip lie down and close his eyes.

After their version, he saw Phillip wake up as Jessica started hers.

***

Jessica started, "Well, you heard that I introduced Tracy to Phillip and then I left them alone."

Phillip shuddered when he heard her say the word 'alone.'

Then was surprised that he remembered that she was shouting at Tracy, instead of supporting him in his time of need.

He figured she was defending him as the only way she knew how. He felt bile rising in the back of his throat because he was aware that was 'wishful thinking.'

Phillip regarded his family, knowing the events of the night had taken their toll on them too.

"Y'all are still in your dressy clothes, and I am sure you need your rest. I'm alive and awake. I'm still here and don't intend on going anywhere," Phillip said as he gestured to all of the medical devices connected to him.

He continued, "Get your rest and I'll get mine."

They all looked at each other in agreement, turned and wearily left.

Phillip considered on how Claire held onto Dr. Pitney's arm as she led him to leave. It struck Phillip odd to see her so clingy.

She had always been a daddy's girl but had always been sure of herself also. Phillip thought about how the night's events showed that even she was vulnerable and just using Ethan as a crutch.

He furled his eyebrows as Ethan walked Claire to the door and then told her she should go. He finally convinced her by saying that he had to speak to Phillip alone.

Claire blew a kiss to Phillip and said, "I love you, daddy, "as she walked out the door.

Phillip thought that it was odd that Claire was the only one to say goodbye. He justified Naomi because she now had Jonathan. But Jessica ...

He rejected that line of thinking and saw Ethan approaching.

Ethan quipped, "Well, you've got a lively bunch."

Phillip slurred, "You're right. I sure do!"

Ethan placed his card on the nightstand and continued, "Phillip, we weren't properly introduced. I'm Ethan Pitney, a psychiatrist for this hospital. I'm available when you need to talk to someone."

Phillip looked at the card and garbled, "Thank you, Ethan, I don't know how you got caught up in this mess, but thanks for being here. I don't need your services, but thanks anyways."

Ethan retorted, "Sir if you don't mind, I've noticed that you're showing signs of,"

But Phillip cut him off, "I'll pray about this," Phillip somehow continued with an edge in his incoherent ramblings, "Please don't take this the wrong way, but I don't think you can help me."

Ethan insisted, "Sir, you've been through a traumatic situation. I recommend that you get some professional assistance."

Phillip closed his eyes from exhaustion, and dismissed Ethan, "So, again thank you for the offer. If I need to talk, I've got Christian counselors where I work."

Ethan looked to the door but knew that he'd never get a chance to speak to Phillip again. He knew that he was drugged and having a hard time staying lucid, but he had to know the answer to the question that was gnawing at his mind.

He turned back to Phillip as asked in a cordial manner, "Sir, do you mind answering a question for my curiosity. Is your family the typical Christian family?"

Phillip opened his eyes, ready to be done with this questioning.

He wanted this man to know that he was spent, but somehow graciousness prevailed as he managed, "Goodness sakes, No! But, what do you mean?"

Ethan clarified, "I mean it seems that they all ignore the fact that you're lucky to be alive. They act oblivious to the fact that you could have died but act naïve in believing that God could be in control during this horrible event."

Phillip noticed that Ethan had blatantly shown his hand about his beliefs about Christians. Trying to clear his head, he blinked a few times and responded, "Ethan this is not a good time. Please come back later."

Ethan knew that he was taking advantage of this man, but he didn't really care. He waited patiently regardless if Phillip was lucid or not.

Phillip pushed the nurse's button, wanting someone to save him. Waiting for the nurse, he prayed for a clear mind so he could reason, because he sensed this man wouldn't stop.

He answered, "Crisis times are the best time to believe in God. As per my family, they're dealing with God themselves. I've tried to teach them to pursue God always, especially when the world is fraying at the edges. You've seen us at our worst moment. I pray that we haven't shamed God with our actions. "

Ethan realized that Phillip had had a rough few hours, but also didn't know when he would have another chance to have a one on one with a traveling preacher whose job is to explain God.

He decided to forgo formality and asked, "Sir, you believe God is good and in control of all things. But if He is good and in control, why did you get shot? I mean, what happened to you was evil and 'God' allowed it."

Phillip prayed that his response wouldn't be tainted by his circumstances.

Ethan was correct that Phillip had dealt with this question several times, and he answered on autopilot, "This is not a new question. 'How could God who claims to be good allow so much evil, pain, and suffering? How could God just not care? Or better yet, 'Why did God allow this to happen to me? Which I think is the nobler question."

Phillip managed a smile because these issues were the ones, he had been asking himself. He thought that expressing his thoughts would help him.

Ethan blurted out, "So, you're not ignorant that God failed, and didn't protect you?"

Phillip paused and thought of saying, "The truth is I do believe God did protect me, which is why I am able to talk to you right now. Just because bad things happen, doesn't mean that God is not in control. We live in a world of sin by our own choosing. The Bible says the rain falls on the just and the unjust. I'm not removed from the consequences of living in this fallen world because I'm a Christian."

However, all he managed was, "I'm still here."

"Ok, what about when God fails, and they die then?" asked Ethan.

Phillip watched Ethan instinctively go for his phone when he asked the last question. Noticing that he was fixated on it, he figured that this question wasn't just to satisfy his curiosity, nor about him getting shot and answering the question of where God was, but something more intimate.

Knowing that he had morphine in his system and that this conversation was personal for Ethan, he offered, "Sir, would you do me a favor. You're asking excellent questions, and I'd love to talk to you about this, but I'm not fully in my right mind now. So, can we talk about this later."

Defeated, Ethan pursed his lips and left the room.

Phillip saw that Claire was waiting on him, and they walked away.

He was glad that Ethan had left and that he was alone with his measuring thoughts. But he was disturbed that his thoughts continued in their loop "Am I a good man? I cannot believe I am sitting here in this bed. Why did it have to happen to me? Who was Tracy? Why did she single me out and shoot me? Who is the strange red-eyed man that was outside?"

Alone with himself again, he heard the ringing in his ears. He felt his leg throbbing.

He closed his eyes to pray and saw the gun being leveled at him again.

He decided to pray past the cacophony of distractions.

"Dear Jesus,
Help me to trust in You during this time
and not let me be defined by what happened
to me. I know You are willing and able to
handle all the stuff that is going on right now,
so I give it to You.

Help me to think of others before I
think of myself.

I pray You will somehow use this to
Your glory.

I pray for Tracy. I don't know how to
pray for her, so I ask that You would for me. I
pray for her salvation and ..."

At that time, Phillip's mind got distracted as he thought of Tracy's words to him: Do you love your wife? Does Jesus save you no matter what? Forgive me?

Phillip rolled those words through again, "Forgive me?"

The sarcasm of her using the phrase made him desperately try to puzzle out who she was.

Closing his eyes, he paraded all the women he'd known his whole life. Narrowing it down to women he knew with his brother. He shuffled through his childhood, college, seminary, family events, holidays and he could not remember any person named Tracy.

Closing his eyes tighter, he stared into the barrel of her gun. He tried to focus on her face, but then a shiver went up his spine, and his mind went blank.

Lost, he concentrated in the distance outside his room's window. His thoughts stumbling in locating the memory of whom Tracy was. Circling around the memory, he heard the gun go off again.

Phillip shrieked in panic, causing him to scream in pain because of his leg moving during the jolt. Doubling over in pain, he reached for the morphine drip and pushed the button.

He pushed it again.

Again.

Then held the button down.

As the pain started subsiding, he looked around his room and found nothing to comfort him.

Remembering that he was praying, he couldn't remember what he was praying about.

Discouragement engulfed him, as he thought about how his prayers hadn't comforted him either.

The room started to move like the waves with each breath he took.

Absentmindedly, he sang "'Tis so sweet to trust in Jesus,' not because the words comforted him but because it was the first thing that came to his mind.

He labored in singing, as each breath began to rise and fall with his vision. He closed his eyes so he wouldn't fall out of his bed. He kept singing the chorus:

Jesus, Jesus, how I trust Him!
How I've proved Him o'er and o'er;
Jesus, Jesus, precious Jesus!
Oh, for grace to trust Him more!

"Dear God, please help me!" cried Phillip as tears rolled down his face. "Please, help me!"

The room started to settle like a top beginning to waver and then fall.

Phillip sank in his bed and felt the pain wash away as he continued praying, "God, have I proved You o'er and o'er? Right now, I'm hurting, scared, and feeling lost. Please don't be silent. What did I do wrong? What did I say wrong? Help me to know that

You're with me, regardless of what other say and what I feel right now. Help me in my unbelief."

As Phillip slipped into sleep's darkness, he thought, "O'er and O'er, O'er and O'er. O'er and Oar, Oar and oar, Oar and ore, Ore and or, Or and or . . ."

Part 4.

The Fall

Chapter 11. Hurricane Jessica

Claire enjoyed watching her mother hold onto the 'oh crap handle' in the car. She really loved when her mother stiffened like a board trying to find the brake.

"I wish you'd slow down Claire; I don't think my nerves can take any more of this. Are we in a race to get to your father?" pleaded Jessica.

Jessica looked back to see if Claire was causing any disasters behind them.

Claire continued weaving between the traffic on I-40.

"Mom, we're OK. Will you just relax? This is how I drive. I've been in control the whole time. I'm going the speed limit anyways," comforted Claire with a curl in her smile.

Claire swerved over, hitting the braille bumps in the road on purpose, and jumped back in her lane.

"Will you just watch the road?" screeched Jessica.

"Listen, I'm a safe driver, and you need to calm down," said Claire as she gripped the steering wheel tighter.

"I wish we took my car," mumbled Jessica.

"Your car is a boat and drinks gas. Don't you care about the environment?" asked Claire.

"Speeding wastes just as much gas. So, don't give me any lip about the environment," argued Jessica.

Claire turned the radio on but had the speakers on too loud from before.

Before Claire could reach for the dial to turn the stereo down, Jessica screamed, "Will you turn that down? Goodness, do you have anything that doesn't have guitars and someone screaming at you."

"No, I always have someone screaming at me; most of the time without the guitars," remarked Claire. Then she turned the volume down.

"What was that?" asked Jessica.

Claire covered, "I said: Look, they are letting a little water out from the dam,"

"Why? There hasn't been any rain for weeks," stated Jessica.

"Mom, they let the water out at different times during the day, not because it has rained or not," answered Claire.

"No, they don't. I've lived here my whole life, and that's the first time I've heard that," said Jessica.

Claire responded by turning up the stereo.

The rest of the trip was uneventful except Jessica trying to help Claire with the bumpy I- 440 during rush hour.

Arriving at the hospital, Claire immediately saw the news reporters with their cameras and microphones. The newshounds have enjoyed eating the scraps that were offered to them. They had been gnawing on it, satiated until now.

The press hadn't been around in the past two weeks ago after she had given them a statement that specified that Phillip was well and that he had no recollection of who Tracy was, nor why she had shot him in the first place.

Within the past two weeks, the press reported that Tracy wasn't dead but was in jail. No new information had been available, so Claire was confused about the media's arrival now. She did not schedule a press conference, which meant they had some information that she didn't.

Jessica didn't notice the press at all as she stepped out of the car and then started trotting to the front door.

Claire noticed the press starting towards her mother, and she double-timed it to her and got there before they did.

She coached her saying, "Mother, the answer to any question they ask you is 'No comment.' Let me do all the talking. Do you understand me?"

Still unaware of the reporters, Jessica looked at Claire and asked, "What are you talking about?"

Claire couldn't repeat herself as the first reporter shoved their microphone in front of Jessica as the cameras zeroed in, "Mrs. Ashby do you have a statement about Tracy confessing that she and your husband allegedly had sexual relations together?"

Claire tried to intervene and gain control of the ambush, but she saw her mother's bewildered eye's as she stared at the reporter and stammered, "What? When? Where?"

The reporter continued, "Mrs. Ashby, you didn't know? Tracy's lawyer released this information this morning. "

Jessica responded, "What are you talking about? Phillip and Tracy had ... had ..."

At a loss for words, she looked at the camera and was trapped in the void of the single lens piercing stare. She switched her attention to the reporter, trying not to hyperventilate as the weight of the betrayal overcame her, she stammered, "When did they have time to... I mean ..." as she stopped again dumbfounded.

Taking advantage of the confusion, Claire asserted herself in front of the cameras saying, "Hello, I'm Claire Ashby, the daughter of Phillip and Jessica Ashby and PR for my family. In answer to your question, we have no statement about any relations between my dad and Tracy, who tried and failed to take his life. Thank you very much."

Claire put her arms around her mother's shoulder, hurrying her into the hospital.

She heard the reporter finish, "You get it here, Mrs. Ashby had no knowledge of the secret love affair between Phillip Ashby and Tracy."

Through the press corps gauntlet, they made their way to the hospital door, other reporters screamed their questions: Was this a crime of passion? How long did it go on? Is this the first time? Are there others? What does this mean for the ministry?

Once inside the hospital, Claire and pushed the button for the ICU floor and noticed that her mother was getting visually angry. She was fuming also, because of the sensationalism of the accusation instead of fact, but she did not know how to handle her mother when she was outraged. She thought to herself, "What would Naomi do?" and remembered that Naomi would always put her arm around people and speak to them in a light tone.

Claire walked up to her mother and began lifting her arms.

But Jessica seethed, "Listen, I don't need any flap from you, especially now. Just do whatever you do with your phone and leave me alone."

Claire said, "Mom, I was trying to . . ."

"Well, quit trying. Just leave me alone," hissed Jessica.

Claire backed off and thought to herself, "Thank God she didn't bite me."

However, Claire pulled out her phone and started to write in her journal, putting her hurt and pain where she always had.

The elevator door opened and Jessica straight-lined it to Phillip's room.

The nurses tried to say hello, but Jessica waved them off, saving all her words and emotions for Phillip.

Opening his door, Phillip stood smiling and steadying himself on a cane with a head of a hand-carved dove. He greeted, "Hi, hon. Love you. Thank you for this beautiful cane. "

He gestured towards his packed bags and finished, "I'm ready to go."

Jessica answered, "Don't 'hi hon' me," as she spread herself out as large as she could in the doorframe.

Claire stuck her head around her mother's tiny frame, attempting to update her dad about Tracy's statement.

Jessica tried to slam the door, but she struggled with the automatic door closer. So, she continued pushing the door with her foot, allowing no one entry nor escape.

Phillip looked at Jessica and said, "I can tell that you are angry, but I honestly don't know what this is about."

Jessica's scowl filled her face, as she waited for him to come clean.

Betrayed, Phillip looked at Jessica desperately wanting to know what had set her off and requested, "Please tell me what has you so upset."

Jessica shot back, "I'm not the one upset. You're the one who is upset. How could you betray me like this?"

Phillip didn't understand her last statement. He knew this was about Tracy, but he was no closer to making sense of what happen to him. He finally could think of her without seeing the gun every time.

Changing tactics, Phillip said, "'Hon'"

Jessica acerbically chided, "Don't call me 'hon.'"

Phillip started again, "Jess, you know how one has a dream that seems so vivid, but, it was just a dream. You can't explain it fully to the other person because they weren't there. I think that's what's going on here, it's all in your head, and you expect me to just know what's going on."

Setting her eyes on Phillip, Jessica punctuated every word saying, "Don't tell me it's all in my head."

Phillip tried to correct, "That isn't what I was saying. I'm saying I don't understand because you've got me playing this guessing game."

Jessica crossed her arms and probed, "So, you think this is a game?"

Phillip answered, "No, I'm trying to say that I don't understand, and I want you to tell what is bothering you."

Jessica responded, "So, which is it? A dream I can't get someone to understand or something that is only bothering me but not you. You see that's the problem, you don't hold me in honor."

Phillip leaned on his cane, aware that he'd played this game before with Jessica and knew that anything else he said wouldn't help the situation and said, "I'm just saying that..."

Jessica venomously attacked, "I know what you're trying to say. You're trying to say that you're better than I am. That you deserve sympathy because you were the one who was shot, But what about me? No one even cares about how I feel."

Phillip went from the joy of going home to being stuffed in a box with no defense. He calmly answered, "Can we just go?"

Claiming victory, Jessica snapped, "Can you just go? Are you ready to go? Where are you going to go? The arms of Tracy? The one you're having... you're having.... having, well you know."

Defeated, Phillip ignored Jessica and saw Claire watching the ordeal through the door window.

He thought about how he had gained strength the last few days because he assumed, he was going home to those who loved him, but now he didn't care.

Sitting on the bed, all the pain that he'd ignored because he thought he'd be hindered by them, overwhelmed him as he resolved that he was crushed.

Behind Jessica, his eyes met Claire's as he bowed his head in shame.

Jessica was in full stride and kept the rant going, "How dare you! After all, I have been through these last two weeks, and this is how you repay me. What is it? Are you so much like the animals that you have to leave your scent everywhere? Have I not met your needs? Are you not satisfied with all I have done?"

Phillip rubbed his leg, realizing that he had no more hope. He thought that Tracy might as well have shot him again and finish the job this time.

Claire shook the doorknob, trying to get in the room to let her dad know that he was not abandoned.

But Jessica continued ignoring Phillip and Claire, as she raged, "There has been an elephant in our marriage for years and now I want to talk about it. I know that you try to come off squeaky clean to the public, but I know who you really are. I know all about your past, but now I know there are other things you have been hiding."

Crossing her arms, she started tapping her foot, taunting, "Well, it's all caught up with you now. Are you listening to me?"

Staring through her, he quelled his anger and remained silent.

Jessica accused, "How'd you expect me to not find out? Everyone else knows about her except me. When were you going to tell me?"

He considered how his last week has been, laying in the hospital bed banging his head against the mental block of Tracy. His torment of not remembering meeting her before. About how he did not know who she was.

Running his hands through his hair he looked at the door, Claire held a sheet of paper up, "Tracy says she and you had sex."

Now he wondered if the gap in his mind was because Jessica may be right and that he did do something inappropriately.

Shaking his head at the absurdity of the notion, he vowed that he'd never give into the lie that he had sex with Tracy.

He prayed, "God, where are you?"

Listening, he heard nothing. He felt nothing.

With more fervency, he prayed, "God, I need you now."

Coming to grips that everything was collapsing, and that God was silent, he tuned back into Jessica hoping that he could rescue his marriage.

Jessica still had her foot at the base of the door, in control of any exit or entry. Gaining strength from his silence, she spewed, "Did I not love you enough? Did you need someone who was prettier? Don't you know how hard I have worked to make everything work thus far? I can't live like this anymore. It ends right now."

Hoping he could salvage the discussion and some hope, he answered, "Can we sit down and discuss this. Let's think this through. This has been hard on all of us. I'll do anything. I have no problem if we get a counselor."

Jessica fumed, "Counseling is for those who have had infidelity. Notice that you brought it up first, not me. My mind is settled."

Phillip thought about Jessica's irrationality, about how he couldn't handle going home to her continuous accusation, about how he needed someone to help him think things out before he broke down any further.

Jessica raged, "We couldn't go to your counselors at work because they'd be biased. What would we talk about? Let's see, we could talk about me being in limbo while I made sure that I am pretty enough, loving enough, and raising our kids. I kept the house; I cooked your meals, and always put the pretty smile on. I always thought the long nights in the office and traveling the country was because of your work for God," then she venomously spat, "but I see what you worship now."

Phillip sat dejected as Jessica dripped with sarcasm as her wrath was unconstrained. Rubbing his leg because his hip started to hurt, he reflected on how Jessica had only visited him five times since being shot. How he was ready to reconnect with Jessica after a long rally across the states. Now he was sitting on his bed feeling more alone with Jessica here.

Jessica walked away from the door and went over to him and towered over him.

Phillip saw that Claire tried to come in, and he waved her away.

"Have you been listening to me? Do you even care about the way I feel?" attacked Jessica.

Phillip looked Jessica in the eye, calmly answering, "Jessica, I'd love to work through these concerns, but right now I have no answers for you. I have more questions than you do. I don't know who Tracy is. The lie of Tracy and I having sex is just that, a lie. I did do bad things before I became a Christian, but God got a hold onto me, and we have discussed these things. Please don't let this lie bring you to the point to where you want to leave me. Please understand that I'm trying to figure this all out, and I need you more than ever right now."

Phillip couldn't continue because Jessica blurted out, "I know that you did things when you were younger, but I didn't think they would come and show their face now. Why have you lied to me? You've only thought about yourself during these last two weeks, and I have supported you. What else have you done? Are there any drugs, children, and other women I need to know about other than Tracy? I am tired of your excuses."

Wringing his hands, Phillip remained calm and pleaded, "I am not offering excuses, I think it's important that you'd let me finish."

With tears starting to trail down her cheek, Jessica said, "No, Phillip we're finished, and I'm done listening."

Phillip wanted to comfort her, but Jessica turned and walked away. She opened the door, saw Claire, and ordered, "I'm ready to go! This was a waste of my time."

Phillip heard her stomping down through the hall. Hearing her steps growing fainter, Phillip put his head in his hands and wept.

***

Standing there, Claire looked at her battered dad and thought about how much her family's world had changed. How her mother was reacting to Tracy, instead of loving her dad. Speechless she kissed him on the top of this head.

Claire somehow got out, "I love you, daddy."

A nurse walked into the room with the discharge papers and her hat in her hand. Lost for words, she finally stated, "Mr. Ashby, we heard the whole thing, but I am afraid you are well enough now and . . . Well, uh." She looked over at the nurse's station for courage.

Claire understood that she had drawn the shortest straw and knew that what she was trying to say was that this room was for people in Intensive Care. She wanted to tell the nurse that this wasn't the time, but she decided to respond instead of reacting.

"Thank you, we'll find another place to stay. We won't be in your hair much longer," Claire replied.

The nurse bowed out and left Claire and her dad alone.

Looking at her dad, she could tell that he was just a shell of who he'd once had been. She could tell that he was crying, reduced to rubble from Hurricane Jessica.

She mentally listed all the places he could go, "Naomi was in Louisville. Her apartment was a studio apartment."

She looked up and prayed, "Help," and spotted Dr. Pitney's business card on the drawer next to the room phone.

Dialing Ethan's office number, she got the receptionist and asked to speak to Ethan.

She watched her dad still shaking and trying to hide his crying from her. She stood up and walked out of the room.

After waiting a few minutes, Ethan got on the line, and she explained the whole situation to Ethan.

Claire whispered into her phone not wanting her dad to hear, "I think he needs someone to help him through everything. He really needs someone to talk to, and I know that he's not going to talk to me."

Ethan asked, "Has he talked about the trauma with anyone?"

Claire replied, "Not that I know of."

Ethan continued, "Is he having a hard time sleeping?"

Claire answered, "The nurses have told me that he is. I don't think he is going to get any better alone."

Ethan asked, "So, what did your mother do?"

Claire thought of being on the other side of the door listening to her mother's outburst. She was used to being on the receiving end of her tirades but had never been tore into the way that she had done her dad and said, "She took all of her problems and dumped them on him,"

Ethan sympathetically said, "We have a room ready; you can bring him over and sign him in."

Claire's phone let her know that she had another call on the other line. She quickly glanced and saw that it was her mother.

She quickly responded, "I'm my mom's ride. Can you do me a favor and send someone here and pick him up from the ICU and I'll handle the paperwork later today."

The phone quit the second call notification but started again when Ethan started, "OK, that is not right procedures, but I got your number now, and I'll give you a call when he's here."

Claire quickly said, "Ok thanks, got to go!" as she switched the call to her mother.

Jessica chided, "Aren't you done yet? I'm ready to go."

Disgusted Claire answered, "I'm on my way. There's some cleanup I had to do after the mess you made."

She hung the phone up and sat next to her dad. She put her head on his shoulder and said, "Someone's coming to pick you up, and I'll see you later."

With swollen cheeks, Phillip looked up and acknowledged, "Please take care of your mom."

Claire replied in disbelief, "OK, I will."

She stood, kissed her dad on the cheek and left the disaster area.

Seeing her mother at the hospital's lobby entrance, she kept walking through the doors, past her mother and straight to the car.

The press was gone. Apparently, the sharks had had their fill for the day.

They both got into the car, and they headed back to Mt Juliet.

Thirteen miles down the road, Jessica said, "I should've listened to my friends who told me to make sure that I'm taken care of. It's my fault. I should've set boundaries just like they said, but I was afraid I would've been overbearing."

Claire bit her lip and looked over at the dam; watching the water rush out. She looked at her mother and decided silence was best as she drove over the braille bumps in the road.

Chapter 12. Surviving the Storm

Not believing how his life had come crashing down, Phillip looked at the mirror in his room and saw his red face. Closing his eyes, he let his mind wander.

He thought about his dream where the sheep became the wolf and it turns on him. He wanted to let his mind try to figure out that puzzle, wanting to ignore how Jessica fit this description.

He scolded himself. "How could you want to think about a dream when you have real problems? You have to remember who Tracy is. She said that she was sorry for the loss of my brother. Did she have anything to do with his death? Is she taking revenge on me because of something that he did? She said she knew him and me. Co'mon, think. Think. Think."

Opening his eyes, he saw a glimpse of a person walking away from him in the mirror. A scream escaped his lips as he turned to see that no one was behind him. He checked the hall and did not see anyone there. He splashed water on his face and thought that now was not a good time for paranoia. However, fear won.

As terror filled him about Tracy and this nameless man, dread started its game by filling hopelessness about his failure with Jessica.

He prayed that Jesus would stop being silent and come to his rescue.

A nurse came running to the room and saw that Phillip was flush and sweating. The nurse asked. "Mr. Ashby, are you OK?"

With fear still overtaking him, he took her by the shoulder, and pleaded, "Who was that? Did you see him? I have seen him here before."

Releasing his grasp, he noticed the nurse backing out of the room as she said, "Mr. Ashby, no one has been here after your wife and daughter left."

"He was just here, you couldn't have missed him," Phillip continued with wildness in his eyes, "Y'all are not paying attention. He has been here several times, and I'm still in danger and you nurses could care less."

"Mr. Ashby, you've had a hard day. Please settle down," she said as a man came from behind her.

This man was in a white orderly's uniform. He stood about 6' 4" and was as thick as a wall. He had an assuredness about himself like a lion, yet his stare was calming and gentle.

Phillip screamed, "I want to know who was just in my room!"

The orderly put his huge hand on Phillip's shoulder as he looked at the nurse and asked, "Is this, Mr. Phillip Ashby?"

The nurse quickly nodded her head as she stepped behind the orderly, putting the orderly between her and Phillip.

Phillip realized that his agitation had him crossing all social barriers he'd normally never cross as the nurse hurried away.

He muttered to himself, "I've lost control, and I need to gain control of myself."

Looking up at the orderly, he realized that this man who so easily restrained him was the person that Ethan had sent for him.

Embarrassed that his first impression had not been a good one, and never not being in control, he did not know what to do to regain confidence from this man.

He met the large man's gaze and then glanced at his nametag. Straightening himself, he thrust his hand and as calmly as he could manage, he said, "Mr. Abiel, I'm Phillip Ashby. Are you the person Dr. Pitney sent to get me?"

The large man looked at Phillip's outstretched hand and said, "Follow me."

"Yes sir," Phillip said as he hobbled over to get his suitcase and bag.

Passing the nurse's station with all his luggage on rollers, Phillip turned toward the nurse, apologized for his behavior, and thanked her and the rest of the nurses' staff for their help.

The cautious nurse said, "Mr. Ashby, I don't know how I'd handle things if I were in your situation. Thank you for talking with me yesterday about my son. We're all praying for you to get well."

Phillip turned, noticing that he needed to catch up with Mr. Abiel. He followed this man, ashamed and wanting to apologize for losing control of himself.

Insignificance was now the badge that he wore. Plunging into the depths of himself, he felt he was at the edge of his faith. Hope against hope, he knew that he needed some time away to regain his serenity. An accusation crossed his mind, "Oh, how the mighty have fallen," as he followed the orderly outside the hospital and then across the street to the psych ward.

Struggling with his cane, suitcase and his injured leg, he hobbled up the steps of the psych ward. Stopping at the front door, he caught his breath and silently prayed, "God, please help me! I don't know what's going on. I'm tired of trying to figure out who Tracy is and why she did what she did. Please reveal yourself to Jessica and change her mind. Please help me to depend on You and not let this doubt and uncertainty consume me. Please lead me."

Phillip walked through the door that Mr. Abiel had opened for him.

Mr. Abiel said, "I'll take you to your room."

While en route to his new room, Phillip remembered counseling people in his current state and telling them, "When you don't know what is going on it is a great chance to take a step of faith."

He thought of the times in his life when every step he took was a step into the unknown and unfamiliar. Or the Psalms that said God would lead you through the valley of the shadow of death, but not to fear because God was with you. Or how God is with us and that we should not be afraid.

"God, I'll follow You. Not only in the good times but also in the …" Phillip paused as he contemplated if he still had the faith to follow God even during his current bad times.

Mr. Abiel stopped and gestured to an open door.

Phillip looked around the room and saw that it was a 20x20 room with a small bed, nightstand, three-drawer chest and a small desk with a lamp on it. He was relieved to see that the room had a private small full bathroom.

As he entered his room, Mr. Abiel walked away.

Phillip watched him and thought, "Not much for goodbyes I guess."

While he was putting away his luggage, a dog flew into the room before Phillip was settled.

The dog hid under the bed as a man came around the corner chasing the dog. The man abruptly stopped at the threshold of the room when he noticed Phillip.

He was in sweats and a sweater that did not match. Standing to his full height, he scowled at the dog and then Phillip.

Understanding that the dog was under his bed for sanctuary, Phillip turned to the man and queried, "May I help you?"

He looked at Phillip and gruffly said, "Nothing that I can't take care of later" as he turned and walked away.

Phillip sat on the bed as the dog came out. The dog was a beagle with a coat mostly white, but with brown ears and brown and black markings. Reaching down at the collar, Phillip found the dog's name was Lilly.

Lilly looked at Phillip with downcast eyes, seemingly asking for permission to join him on the bed. Tired of waiting she jumped on the bed and leaned on him.

Startled by Lilly's impetuousness, Phillip said, "Well, OK! Come on up."

She jumped into his lap, looked into his eyes, and started smelling his breath.

Phillip sat there not knowing what to do as Lilly burped into his face.

Turning Lilly's head away, he had to admit that he still liked her. Smiling, he thought as how this was the first time he had smiled today. He also thought about how much God must love us despite our rudeness, vanity, and righteousness getting in the way.

Rubbing her ears, she started to lay down.

"Well, I see you met the welcoming committee," Ethan said as he walked into the room.

Phillip realized that he had lost track of time rubbing Lilly's ears.

Ethan continued, "I'm sorry that I couldn't meet you upon your arrival, but this was short notice."

Ethan sat on the bed and started itching Lilly's back.

Lilly rolled over and sighed as both men rubbed her belly.

Ethan resumed, "Lilly is also a guest here. She seems to be good therapy for the patients, but really, she is only a pet. I figured that some patients have their "imaginary cats" and adding a real dog to the mix should shake things up."

Lilly wagged her tail and licked her lips in joy.

"It looks like she has adopted you. You two will be good for each other," said Ethan.

"Yeah, I guess I'll take her in. By the way, thanks for taking me in on short notice," said Phillip.

"About that, this is not a hotel. I know that you've been struggling with your memories about your shooter, and Claire had said something had happened today that you would need help with. Think of me as your guide to help you see what is holding you back. We will be meeting once a day for now. So, I'll see you tomorrow morning in my office at 8 sharp," said Ethan.

Phillip said, "OK, I guess I do need someone to talk to."

Ethan suggested, "You do know that I may have to take the kid gloves off and put rhetoric under the microscope."

Phillip asked, "What do you mean?"

"Let's talk about this tomorrow," Ethan said as got up and started to leave.

"I do have a few questions. What's the dress code and how do I take care of Lilly?" asked Phillip.

Ethan answered, "The dress code is 'get comfortable' and whatever that means to you, but clothes are necessary. As per Lilly, let some of the help know if she has to do her duty and they will assist you in taking her out. We have a bag of food for her in the office, and she usually handles her own sleeping conditions. Anything else?"

"Can I contact the outside world?" asked Phillip.

"You can write letters, and you can receive phone calls. Which reminds me. Do you have a cell phone on you?"

Phillip answered, "No, I don't carry it with me when I preach, and it got lost in the shuffle during that …"

Ethan noticed that Phillip had trailed off. He also made a mental check that he also didn't recognize the fact the he was shot.

Getting Phillip's attention and said, "OK, that's good. I do not mean it is good you lost your phone. I mean they're not allowed. We find they're more of a distraction instead of being a help. Anything else?"

Ethan wished he could easily forget about his cell phone. He was sure it was more of a distraction instead of being a help in his life, but he felt chained to it like concrete around his ankles. He reminded himself: What You Hold on to Is Holding on to You. He scolded himself to get back on task.

"No, I'm good," Phillip replied.

"Oh, before I forget again. What did you say to Tennessee Jack when he was in your room?" inquired Ethan.

Phillip answered, "Who?"

"The gentleman who tried to follow Lilly in here," helped Ethan.

Phillip answered, "Oh, him. I asked if I could help him and he said that …"

Phillip furrowed his eyebrows and tried hard to remember Tennessee Jack's reply but couldn't.

"You know I don't remember what he said," Phillip answered.

"Have you been forgetting any other information?" asked Ethan.

"Yes, I forgot completely about having a cell phone until you brought it up. Is that a problem?" asked Phillip.

Ethan answered "It's probably nothing, but it could be that you have been suppressing the shooting incident, or you are trying to remember repressed memories, and you did not store what TJ said. A helpful hint leave TJ and Frank alone. OK?

Phillip cautiously replied, "OK? Who is Frank?"

Ethan kept lecturing, "Also, remember that you are in a psych ward, things are different here."

Phillip nodded in agreement.

Ethan continued, "Good, for the rest of the day I want you to relax and then see me at 4 pm. Do you have anything else?"

Phillip answered, "No, I'm still good."

Ethan left, and Lilly snuggled closer to Phillip.

He looked down at Lilly and said, "You're pitiful. Your world is OK, long as you get your 'lovin'."

Lilly yawned, licked her chops, and adjusted herself to get rubbed on her side.

Phillip tried to get up as Lilly laid in his lap like a sack of potatoes. Phillip gently nudged her, and she just laid there with no motivation to move. Phillip got his arms under her 25lb frame and slowly moved her as she leaned even more onto him. He finally moved her onto the floor. She moved two feet away and stared at him.

Getting his cane, Phillip lifted himself up and finished unpacking.

Seeing dog hair all over his hoodie, he took it off and looked at Lilly.

She looked back at him as she seemed to be asking, "Why did you get up?"

Phillip chuckled to himself. He thought about how when God moves, we watch Him do His thing, and we think only about ourselves. Wondering when God is going to settle down again so we can get comfortable again.

Lilly sat there with her orange-brown eyes and yawned. Waiting for him to finish.

As Phillip was unpacking, he got to the bag that the hospital put his belongings into while he was in the ER. He moved things around in the bag trying to find his Bible but became frustrated and dumped the contents onto his bed.

Motion activated and possibly looking for food, Lilly jumped up and started to sniff everything. He pushed her away and rummaged through the contents.

Then he found it.

It was "The Heart Shield Soldier's Bible" that his grandfather had given him when he started his ministry. His grandfather said that it was the Bible that had gotten him through the World War II, and he wanted to pass it onto him. It was a plated steel with the Shield of Faith, and he had always carried it with him while he was preaching.

He read the worn inscription "May the Lord be With You" and then rubbed his hand over the cover as a chill rushed over him. He felt the dent of where it stopped the first bullet when Tracy shot him.

Phillip collapsed onto the bed. He wept and prayed, "Thank you, Jesus, for being with me. Thank you for protecting me. Thank you for this shield of faith. This explains the impossible look on Tracy's eyes that day. Thank You! Thank You, Jesus! Thank You for saving me and continuing to save me."

Lilly nosed her snout under his arms and tried licking every one of Phillip's tears as she comforts him.

Phillip cradled Lilly in his arms, trying to think more about Tracy other than her leveling a gun at him. Trying to reason out why she had shot him, the memory played out as it always had, but instead of ending, the memory continued with her confused face after the first shot.

He was elated because this was the first time the memory didn't end with gunfire, but the joy diminished as he saw her level the gun at him again.

Exhausted from the exercise, he put his Bible back in the bag and laid down on the bed crying and praying to Jesus.

"Thank you for a bit of hope but help me to get through this pain. Keep protecting me from the enemy. Please keep the enemy away from Jessica. I still love her and please let her know my love for her during this time."

Weeping and praying, Phillip finally fell to sleep with Lilly curled next to him snoring.

Chapter 13. Weathered by Pride

Straightening his desk, Ethan moved files around, ensured all pens and pencils were assorted and made sure he had business cards by his name placard. He checked that his newest award was prominent among his other credentials and accreditations.

This was the third time that he had performed this ritual. He couldn't believe his luck. Phillip Ashby had taken him up on his offer. Smirking, Ethan replayed Phillip's words in his mind from his last conversation with him, "I don't think you can help me." Ethan thought that in the psych ward, he would be the only help Phillip had. Overall, good or bad he couldn't wait to see Phillip Ashby.

Checking his desk one more time, he spotted his phone placed face down. He reached for it, then paused. Running his hands through his hair, he wanted to scream but settled with a sigh.

Deciding to call Liz, he reached out and picked up his phone.

He smiled that its weight had lessened. He turned the screen on, and then stared at the home screen, forgetting the reason he had picked his phone up. He bit the inside of his cheek and switched to look at the text from his wife, "Can't wait 2 see U at home."

Staring at the text, he shook his head remembering why he'd picked it up.

Dialing Liz's number, he smirked because he had to share this and couldn't keep this to himself.

Hearing the phone ring twice, Ethan thought he'd get voice mail. Rehearsing his message in his head, he heard Liz say, "Ethan you've got me out of a meeting, make it quick!"

Surprised that she'd answered the phone, Ethan teased, "Guess who I'll have in my office today?"

"Damn it, Ethan! I don't have time for these games! Don't you have anyone else to bother?" Then there was a heavy sigh and Liz guessed, "Let's see, someone who has convinced you that you are Sigmund Freud?"

Relishing that he had something that Liz didn't know, Ethan said, "Nope, let me give you a hint. His book ensured that mine wasn't on the New York Times best seller's list a few weeks ago."

Liz exclaimed, "Jesus Christ, really?"

"No, not Jesus, but close," Ethan joked, enjoying pulling Liz's strings.

"Seriously, I know it isn't Jesus Christ, but Phillip Ashby? I thought he told you it would be a cold day in hell if he needed your services. What changed?"

Ethan explained the events that had led up to this and ended with saying, "Anyways he doesn't have anywhere else to go."

Liz replied, "Go ahead if you think you can handle this, just don't screw this one up and . . ."

Ethan felt hurt by Liz's distrust and bluntness. He knew he was qualified and thought that should get him some credit.

He batted back by saying, "Don't screw this up? I'm a professional, and I've helped several others. How's Phillip Ashby any different?"

Liz followed, "First, you didn't let me finish. I've known you for a while now, Ethan, and take it from me. You're professional most of the time, except when it comes to Christians. Considering your batting average and experience with them right now, I personally think your wounds are too fresh, and this is too early. You're still wrestling with being at fault, who was right, and who was wrong. But the opportunity did fall into your lap, so what does any of that matter?"

Falling for the bait, Ethan exclaimed, "It wasn't my fault. I don't like how they think they are the only ones who are right!"

Overjoyed that she succeeded in pushing Ethan's buttons, Liz exclaimed, "Wow! Really? See what I mean? Isn't that how everyone thinks, Christian or not?"

Liz noticing that Ethan was silent on the other end of the line continued, "Never mind. Second, you might have your next best seller about the person who knocked you off the list only because he was shot. I'm just saying that caution is warranted for both of your sakes. I wouldn't be surprised if you've cussed him out by the end of your first session."

Ethan replied half listening, "Yep, OK. Whatever. That's all I called about!"

Seeing Phillip walk out of his room, Ethan said, "Well, I've got to go, he's coming right now. Bye."

Hanging his phone up, Ethan started straightening his desk again. He then decided to grab a pencil and paper to look busy. Then he chose to not put any pretenses on and waited for Phillip by sitting in his chair like a throne.

A firm knock disturbed the silence of the office as Ethan confidently sat in his throne and answered, "Come in."

The door rattled.

Then it shook.

Then the knock came again.

Then Ethan remembered he locked the door for his conversation with Liz.

Ethan whispered to himself, "Damn it!" as he jumped from the chair, destroying the whole persona.

Ethan opened the door, feeling like a servant as Phillip hobbled in with his cane.

Phillip looked around and furrowed his eyebrows, as he said, "Nice office, where is the couch?"

Missing the joke and feeling off kilter because the locked door had disturbed the presence he was trying to portray, Ethan replied, "Huh?!" He knew this wasn't the most professional response, but it came out anyways.

"Oh, well never mind," Phillip said as he hobbled to the chair in front of Ethan's desk. Resting his cane in his lap.

Closing the door, Ethan knew he had lost. He knew Phillip was a counselor in his own right and that he was familiar with publicity, authority, and control.

Thinking of his mantra, "<u>What You Hold on to Is Holding on to You."</u> He remembered step seven, "Name what you lost and let it go." He took a deep breath and decided to ignore step 7 and focused on winning back control.

Thankful that Phillip didn't take his chair, Ethan sat down asking, "Mr. Ashby, are you getting settled?"

Phillip replied, "Yes sir, I'm unpacked and had a great nap."

Ethan stated, "Well, I'm glad you're settled. First off, I'm sorry for all the events that have taken place in your life recently. I want you to know that I really want to help you."

Phillip simply answered, "OK."

Expecting more, Ethan paused to allow Phillip time to respond.

Ethan watched Phillip sit calmly with his hands in his lap and looking at all his rewards with no reaction.

Finally, satisfied that there wouldn't be any more reply, Ethan continued, "OK. Well, based on what your daughter and nurses have shared with me, do you think you're simply OK? How are you dealing with the events of the past few weeks?"

Phillip answered, "Well, I don't know what you mean. If you want me to start telling you all about my problems, I already have someone for that."

"Who?" asked Ethan?

"Well, Jesus, of course," answered Phillip.

Ethan forced his whole body to relax, knowing the reply shouldn't have surprised him because he knew that he would have to handle talk about Jesus and religion with Phillip, but he didn't expect it at the forefront of the conversation.

He also knew that people who suffered from Post-Traumatic Stress Disorder (PTSD) usually try to cope with it the best they can with the tools they are familiar with, and of course, Phillip would use religion to hide.

Still feeling that Phillip was in control, Ethan decided to change tactics. He remembered helping other patients by using journals. He also remembered how they had let him use their journals to write his last book.

"Mr. Ashby, do you keep a journal?" asked Ethan as he handed Phillip the pen and pad of paper.

Phillip answered, "Only when I have something to say, but otherwise, no, I never saw the need," as he left the bundle in Ethan's hands.

"I'd like for you to start keeping one now. It'll help you to gather your thoughts of recent events and document them. This will help you release your mental activity on things that you've written down already and give you a sense of accomplishment. Then you can go back and be accountable to your own emotions and thoughts," Ethan answered as he tried to hand the pen and paper to Phillip.

"What use would I have for that?" asked Phillip still ignoring the bundle.

Ethan pursed his lips, knowing that Phillip was deflecting by giving curt responses and playing a game. He needed to get Phillip talking and was surprised that Phillip being a counselor himself didn't want to get to the root of his problems. He wanted him to name the things that had happened to him so he could start the healing process.

Ethan replied, "Well, I find that a lot of people rationalize their behaviors and tend to excuse themselves. They see the world as something happening to them or around them. Victimized, they think themselves blameless and forget that their own past or present actions may have made them participants in the event, so when they examine the event, they can see misconceptions . . ."

Phillip noticed Ethan was using a lot of psychological jargon and seemed to be purposefully ambiguous. Nevertheless, he also saw how it could line up with his beliefs. As a step of trust, Phillip received the notebook and with curiosity asked, "Which thoughts? All of them? Do all my thoughts matter? Which actions? Do all of my thoughts of the event's that happened to me justify them?"

Taking in a slow breath, Ethan tried to not react to Phillip, knowing that he was purposefully being hard to get along with. Still he was becoming frustrated with his rapid-fire questioning, but was glad he took the pen and paper, so he gestured to the journal bundle and answered, "Try it for tonight and see how everything goes. It couldn't hurt. Write about anything. People usually find out what their addictions are by doing this," replied Ethan.

His last statement on addictions caught Ethan odd, as he tried to think out the conversation and find why he brought it up. He thought of previous patients working through addictions, but he couldn't think of a correlation with Phillip and addictions. Glad that he had Phillip talking, he hoped that this wouldn't shut him down again."

Phillip responded, "Well if everyone were to give up their true addiction, I think we all would be better."

Ethan asked, "Which addiction are you referencing?" as he thought about how glad he was that he hadn't ruined this interview. He was going to have to rub Liz's nose in it later.

Phillip beheld all of Ethan's recognitions on his wall and answered, "It's what I hate to see in someone else but tolerate in my own life. I'd say it's the one thing that everyone struggles with daily. Today's culture doesn't see it as a vice but as a virtue."

Wanting to keep Phillip engaged, Ethan replied, "You've piqued my interest. What is it?"

Phillip leaned forward, looked Ethan in the eye and replied, "Pride. It's what keeps me from other people. It defines how and what I criticize without including myself in that criticism. I fall into this pit with a shovel still in my hand. It's my vanity, self-pity, willfulness, and self-love. It stops me from looking out for others before myself or hearing what others have to say before thinking of my reply or enjoy watching what others do instead of thinking about how I'd do it better. The deception in myself makes me always look for more glorification. Pride gives me a table of one and tells me to be satisfied with only wanting more of myself."

Ethan wasn't sure if Phillip was trying to give him a lecture or was opening up.

He replayed the whole conversation in his head and wasn't sure where to go with it. Looking around the room at all his self-promotion, he thought about how he was trying to gain Phillip's trust yet didn't know if he could trust Phillip himself.

Ethan cautiously asked, "Do you think pride is more destructive than being 'holier than thou' which does more harm in the world than helping it?"

Phillip replied, "I think everyone is in competition with one another. Also, some Christians and non-Christians alike have pride in thinking they are doing 'better at being good' than others or as you say, 'Holier than thou.' I do agree with you wholeheartedly that this is not helping the world."

Glad that he had found common ground, Ethan replied, "I'm amazed to hear you say this about Christians. Because, it seems, a lot of them don't see pride and arrogance in their own lives and actions. But are all too willing to put themselves or others down by telling them what is wrong and what is right based on rules that don't apply to today's world. I think Christians set themselves up for failure when they expect others to follow rules, they fail to keep themselves. I didn't expect to get to this right now. I'm glad that we agree."

Phillip replied, "I was speaking about everyone in general: not just Christians.,"

Then Phillip set back and contorted his face, as he cautiously asked, "And what do we agree on?"

Knowing his response would determine how the rest of the sessions with Phillip would go, Ethan felt the noose gently placed around his neck. He didn't want to tell Phillip what he felt about his beliefs, but he wanted to be true to his own.

Then hearing Liz's voice in his head, "Don't mess this up." He thought to himself, "Too late!"

Ethan thought about how he could get things back on track, but he shelved that idea because they were playing in his yard and with his ball.

Ethan smugly replied, "Again, Christian arrogance and pride is destructive and being 'holier than thou' does more harm in the world than helping it. Christians believe that God exists and that everyone should follow blindly with no thought."

Not understanding this session, Phillip sat quietly with the pen and pad of paper in his hands. He had always thought that the psychiatrist held the pen and pad of paper with a clipboard and only shook his head and said "Uh, huh" while asking about people's relationship with their parents. Now, he had the pen and pad and felt like he was on the defensive. Analyzing Ethan statement's, he figured that he'd been wounded by Christians before.

Looking around the room at Ethan's degrees, Phillip considered if this was normal behavior for a secular psychiatrist and if he'd be the best person to help him.

Phillip didn't feel any indication that Ethan was worried about his health nor well-being.

Wanting to see what had caused Ethan's wounds, Phillip questioned, "You don't like Christians that much, do you?" You're probably one of those that think I blindly believe in a fairy tale with no thought or reason. You possibly think that I deserve to be in here because of those beliefs."

Feeling the noose tightened tightly around his neck, Ethan assessed how he could salvage this session without the bottom dropping from underneath him.

Amazed at how Phillip seemed to have read his mind about how he thought that Christians were mass delusional. He dismissed the thought because they were pretty much harmless and that they had the freedom of religion as much as he had the freedom of not having one.

He just didn't understand their superstition about a person raising from the dead who'd make a home for them after they died that has lollipops and rainbows when their current life is rotten. Why not try to make their current life better, instead of thinking so much about an imaginary life after this one?

Remembering that Phillip had asked him a question, he found his voice and stammered, "Well. No."

Phillip asked, "No, to which? You not liking Christians or that we Christians are crazy by your standards?"

Ethan replied, "I think we're getting off topic and need to get back to it. What can you tell me about Tracy?"

Phillip leaned forward and pressed, "No, I don't want to talk about Tracy, my wife, nor anything else right now. So, which is it? Do you like Christians or do you think we are deserving of long sleeve jackets that are tied up in the back?"

Ethan questioned, "Why does it matter? I'm a professional, and my views won't affect your treatment."

Phillip answered, "It matters to me! I've got to feel secure that you can help me."

Ethan gestured to all of his credentials and then said, "These aren't just trophies. I've earned these and have helped others."

Phillip continued, "I have a hard time putting my trust with someone who thinks it's all right to have pride in being an atheist or agnostic. Saying that there is no God just because they believe there isn't would be worse than the pride of Satan. He, at least, acknowledges God's existence."

Ethan choked back is rage from being called a fool, and sternly answered, "I'm not here to have a debate about the existence or the idea of God or Satan. I'm here to help you get to an understanding on Tracy, your wife, and the shooting. That's the reality. That's your 'now' that I'm trying to assist you with. You need to stay on the task at hand."

Ethan's voice had risen to a yell, and Phillip sat back and waited for Ethan to continue.

Heedless of the noose, Ethan's impudence seized his mind as the ground dropped and his rage left him dangling unprofessionally.

Steadfast, Phillip asked, "So, what do you believe? Are you saying that everyone should have their own set of rules they follow as long as they don't affect anyone else?

Ethan emphatically answered "Yes. I'd say everyone is able to believe what he or she wants to believe. I've found that people who don't believe in God are more compassionate and generous to others because we're worried about the world during the here and now, and not consumed about heaven or the afterlife."

Amazed at the speed that Ethan replied, Phillip continued asking, "So, are you of the opinion that Christian's beliefs are worthless?"

Ethan replied, "Well, I'd say that their beliefs are not worthless, but their ... well their ..."

Phillip interrupted, "Please know understand that I am part of the 'their' you're talking about."

Ethan cursed his penchant for political correctness. He wanted to just say 'yes' but couldn't spin it in a nice way.

Ignoring Ethan's stammering, Phillip continued, "Do you also believe that you're smarter, better and more enlightened than Christians because you think you're right and that we're wrong."

Ethan replied, "Come on. Is there an end to this?"

Phillip answered, "Sure, that was the last question. So, what is your answer?"

Growing tired of this questioning and wanting it to be done, Ethan replied, "Yes, but Christians are the same way."

Phillip finished, "That brings us full circle."

Trying to understand the statement, Ethan stammered "What? My beliefs? Huh? What do you mean?"

Phillip looked down at the floor and gathered his thoughts.

Finally, satisfied that he could articulate his thoughts properly, he looked into Ethan's eyes, he said, "Granted. Your beliefs and my beliefs don't agree, nevertheless, my original statement about people needing to deal with our pride, Christians and non-Christians alike, still stands. We are too busy colliding into each other and exploding. Leaving a devastating mess. Both sides come off with 'holier than thou' attitudes. Both sides think the other side's arguments are worthless. Both sides are trying to convince the other they're right and the other that they're wrong. However, what would the conversation be like if we set aside our pride and reasoned together? I don't want to convince you Christianity is correct, that isn't my job. My job is to tell others about Jesus so they can make their choice themselves."

Ethan countered, "But Jesus was prideful enough to say that He was God."

Nodding his head, Phillip clarified, "You're correct. However, it isn't prideful for Him to state the truth, no more prideful than a child to say whom his Father is if it's true. Now, we're dealing with belief and faith, and you take that statement of Jesus and base your belief or non-belief in it. "

Ethan shot back, "Wouldn't you say that God is prideful by wanting all the praise, honor, and glory?"

Phillip templed his fingers and answered, "Would it be prideful for a soldier who's deserved acknowledgement for putting themselves in harm's way to keep us safe from harm. Or a doctor to receive honor for saving someone's life. I believe that God is worthy of the praise, honor and glory that is given to Him."

Feeling his blood pressure rising and not wanting to talk about things that was not his expertise, Ethan decided to bring the conversation back to the physical world as he countered, "How's it not prideful of you building a ministry based on the brand of your own name?

Laughing, Phillip replied, "Dear Lord, I hope people don't only come for me."

Ethan keyed in saying, "You said they did not only come for you. See you are prideful!"

Phillip responded, "How's it prideful when I lift up Jesus' name above my own? That I work for God's glory and not my own."

Feeling like he was in a wrestling match, Ethan thought he'd have Phillip pinned and could get a foothold to gain the upper hand by now. But he felt that Phillip was slipping through his arguments too easily. He was use to Christian's capitulating by now. But he wanted to prove that he was in control.

Exhausted from his own ideas, he tried Gandhi's by saying, "Yeah, well I would probably feel better about Jesus if it weren't for his followers."

Phillip smiled and said, "Well, if Christians were only following the idea of Jesus, but not the person of Jesus, I'd agree with you. But I think too many Christians are too busy trying to get people to like them while they table Christ on the idolatry of acceptance.

On the other hand, quite simply a lot of Christians just don't know who Jesus is because they have not read the Bible themselves.

You alluded earlier that the secular is only worried about the world, but Christians are to care for the world also. The Bible tells Christian's that true religion is to look after the orphans and the widows, but in the same breath, we're also told to keep ourselves from being polluted by the world. Overall, Jesus has always meant to create a response in someone's life. He wants to separate light from dark, life from death, the spirit from the flesh, the truth from a lie."

Ethan shot back, "As long as it's the Christians' thoughts on truth, life, light, and dark, etc."

Phillip shook his head and countered, "You continue slanting this conversation towards Christians failings. Your thoughts about Jesus shouldn't solely be based on his followers. That's a copout. Deal with Jesus first and then his followers next."

Sitting with his jaw dropped, Ethan had to admit to himself that he wasn't prepared for this and was dumbfounded that a Christian was standing up to him. Liz's last words nagged at him about not doing well around Christians.

He assumed he'd be in control of this conversation, being in his own office and practice. Knowing that a lecture was coming or to be preached by Phillip, he decided to pull the "this is my office" card just like he pulled the "I'm on the mike, and my opinion only matters card" during his award ceremony.

Wanting to turn the conversation away from himself and Christianity and back onto Phillip's problems, Ethan said, "Mr. Ashby, let's talk about why you're here. As I said before, you've had several traumatic events take place in your life recently and from what I observed, I'd say that you're dealing with Post Traumatic Stress Disorder.

Phillip asked, "Isn't PTSD something that soldiers have?"

Ethan added, "Yes, but it isn't isolated to them only. It also encompasses for those who've been in a traumatic event and may have any of these symptoms: emotional numbing to the disturbing event, trouble concentrating, difficulty remembering things, or being irritable. Sufferers also have a hard time sleeping and dealing with triggers that cause them to remember the incident. Recent events with your wife have made matters worse. So, let's focus on this and how I can help."

Ethan saw Phillip look up and to the left as he mulled over the diagnosis. Ethan grinned, feeling that he had finally gained control.

Ethan continued, "Another thing that a PTSD sufferer does is avoidance. They may position themselves to where they avoid places, people, and experiences that remind them of the event. Or they become numb."

Tensing his whole body, Phillip said, "Listen, I know that you believe this is what you think I'm dealing with. But, honestly, the main obstacle is that you're not a Christian, and you don't have a high opinion of me. I don't know if I can trust you digging around in my head."

Ethan managed his disgust and said, "You may rationalize your feelings any way you want, but overall we're not here to discuss religion, and this is what I'd like for us to start dealing with."

Looking at the clock, Ethan said, "Well, unfortunately, our session is over. We'll get together tomorrow morning. I want you to spend the rest of the day resting and working in your journal. Also, get out and become acquainted with the natives. I'll see you in my office tomorrow in the morning"

Phillip replied, "Ok, I'll see you then," as he rose from his seat and left the room, letting the door close and lock.

Thinking of Liz's comments, Ethan mused, "Well, at least I didn't cuss him out."

He grabbed his phone and stared at the text from his wife.

Putting the phone down, he felt the indentation of where his wedding band used to be. He rubbed the grooves in his ring finger and recalled why he had taken it off.

Tearing up, he didn't want to have a breakdown here.

"So much for removing what is holding onto me," Ethan whispered to himself.

He wiped his eyes, put away his phone, packed his backpack, and left for a lunch cocktail at Max's.

***

Phillip left Ethan's office and wanted to go straight to his room. Turning into the common room, everyone examined him.

A man with a butterfly bathrobe approached him.

Not wanting to deal with anyone, Phillip tried to walk faster, but his limp and cane didn't allow him his fast getaway.

The butterfly guy intercepted Phillip before he got to his room. He was heavy set and breathing hard. He stood in between Phillip and his room and finally asked, "Do you like butterflies?"

Trying his best not to be annoyed, he was surprised the man sounded intelligent, but started the conversation with such a banal question. It was obvious this man did like butterflies, so he turned the question back to him, "I never really thought about it. Do you like butterflies?"

Glad to have someone's attention, he replied in a hurry, "Yes I do. Let me tell you why. You see they start as caterpillars and then they seem like they die but they build themselves a cocoon, which is also known as a chrysalis, and then they metamorphasize and then they break through the cocoon and become a beautiful butterfly."

Phillip thought of the Looney Tunes Rocky and Mugsy. He knew it wasn't a good comparison because the man was coherent, except the using the word metamorphasize instead of metamorphosis.

The Butterfly guy asked, "Are you the pastor guy who got shot? I saw it all on the TV, and Frank over there said it wasn't you because you only were shot and that your head is all right, but I told him it was. So, are you?"

Phillip held out his hand and said, "I am he."

The man shook his hand, and Phillip was able to get around him.

Still exaggeratedly shaking hands, the man said, "I like butterflies."

Phillip trying to rescue his balance and his arm replied, "Listen, I'll be here tomorrow. Can we continue this conversation then?"

Butterfly guy said, "Yeah, OK. I'll see you tomorrow."

Then he ran off towards a man stroking a couch pillow. He smirked as he imagined how that conversation went.

Snapping out of his reverie, Mr. Abiel was in front of him.

"So, how did it go?" asked Mr. Abiel.

Phillip answered, "It went worse than I expected. I'm used to my own surroundings and like-minded people. Overall, I'm having a hard time now."

"I want you to know that it's my job to make sure you're taken care of during this hard time," answered Mr. Abiel.

"Thanks, so I get your one on one service?" quipped Phillip knowing that Mr. Abiel meant "you" as a collective instead of singular.

"No, I'm here for everyone when they need me. It's one of the things I do, but you have my one on one attention now," answered Mr. Abiel.

Glad to have a character reference for Ethan, Phillip asked, "So, how long have you worked for Mr. Pitney?"

"Well, I like to think that I work for someone higher," Mr. Abiel said with a wink.

Phillip asked, "So, are you a Christian?"

Mr. Abiel replied with a smile, "Well, not in the sense that you mean. Let's say we have a common boss," and without skipping a beat asked, "Again, back to my original question. How did it go?"

Excited that he found a like-minded person, Phillip let his defenses down and said, "Well, I don't think it went well at all. I don't think he likes me."

Mr. Abiel answered, "You'll find that it's more of who you represent than it being who you are,"

Phillip replied, "You're probably right, I can see that he has awards and education, but it seems that he's taking me and my case personally."

"Let's just say that he's working through things just like you are. Believe it or not, you two are good for each other," answered Mr. Abiel.

Phillip answered, "Really, I was thinking about getting one of my own counselors to help me."

Nodding his head in acknowledgment, Mr. Abiel took a breath and said, "If we follow and trust in God, He has a way of helping others through our own pain."

Phillip turned towards his room, then looked back at Mr. Abiel and bit his lip.

Aware of the awkwardness, Mr. Abiel stood and awaited Phillip's response.

Phillip finally said, "Well, I'm going to try to get some sleep. Thanks for what you do." "Have a good night," Mr. Abiel said as Phillip walked into his room.

Phillip got ready for bed and ritualistically said his nightly prayer.

He thought about Mr. Abiel's last words about him and Ethan being good for each other.

He smirked, as it seemed to be a confirmation. It let him know that he was to endure being a patient here.

Taking the pen and pad of paper that Ethan had given him, Phillip started a prayer list. He added his marriage, wife and Ethan to it.

He prayed for each item on his list and then closed his eyes and tried to sleep.

Part 5.

The Test

Chapter 14. Sharing Your Bed

Phillip didn't stir but opened one eye, as he sought to find where the horrible noise was coming from. Being as still as possible, he looked around and examined all the different gray in his new room.

He had to admit Ethan was right that he'd been having a hard time sleeping because he was fighting the pity party that was dwelling deep within him.

Letting out a deep breath, he had a hard time getting back to sleep because his new roommate was a snorer, hogged the whole bed and got dog fur everywhere, especially in his nose.

His mind switched on and then he role played arguments with Ethan. Riling from his imagined accusations, "How is it you can have hope in your Big Fairy in the sky when He has let your wife leave you and let you get shot? Was he asleep? It's time to quit clinging onto fantasy and get back to reality."

After each word, Phillip noticed that the room grew stiller, and the darkness started to engulf the light from his room. He checked Lilly and saw her chest was rising, but she wasn't snoring.

The rustling happened again, sounding like something the size of a raccoon scampering around his room.

He looked for his cane, but it was out of reach at the foot of his bed.

Breathing in short quick breaths, he noticed the room was so cold that he could see it. Then, feeling sweat trailing down his brow as he watched the shadow in his room was becoming larger.

Trying to lift his arms and to move his head, he found himself paralyzed. Only being able to roll his eyes to the scampering around the foot of his bed. Hearing it stop, his eyes bulged as a wolf jumped up onto his bed.

Peering into his eyes, it snarled, then turned then smell at Lilly who was oblivious to the whole situation.

Frustrated at his immobilization, Phillip's heart ached that he couldn't help.

Tired of smelling Lilly, the wolf nudged her with no response. Then it glowered at Phillip as it started to make its way up to the bed.

Phillip felt every footfall as it stepped on his chest and stared into his eyes again with its fangs bared.

The wolf reared back and then cocked its head. It sniffed the air and appeared to be listening to something in the distance. Then brought its attention back to Phillip, as it drew close to Phillip, eye to eye.

Phillip felt the full weight of the wolf and the moisture from its breath as it said, "You're not ready!".

Phillip started screaming and shaking in terror as it jumped out of his window.

Finally, able to move, Phillip felt Lilly licking on his face as he shot up still screaming.

Looking toward the window that the wolf jumped, he saw a man outside with a hint of red eyes.

Phillip renewed his alarm until Mr. Abiel came into the room.

Wild that someone else was in his room, Phillip fell out of his bed. Wincing from the pain in his hip from the fall, he crawled in to one of the bathroom's corners, still shrieking in terror and pain from his wound.

Mr. Abiel carefully approached Phillip and softly said, "Shalom, my brother. Peace."

Coming out of his fog of the dream and realizing that Mr. Abiel was with him, Phillip tried to look around him to see if the person as still at his window.

Mr. Abiel helped him to his feet and back into his bed, as he stared out the window.

Not seeing any man or wolf, but only his reflection, his mind raced as he tried to create some correlation between the wolf and the man with red eyes.

Finding his voice, he wildly stared into Mr. Abiel's tranquil eyes and said, "A man! A wolf! Here! But gone."

Mr. Abiel went to the bathroom, got a towel, and started to wipe off Phillip's sweat.

Phillip blurted out, "Why is this happening to me?"

Mr. Abiel answered, "Who else should it happen too?"

Not getting the sympathy that he wanted, Phillip quelled his frustration and answered, "That isn't what I meant. I mean, why was I shot? Why did Jessica leave me? Why am I here?"

Mr. Abiel smiled and answered, "Why not? Maybe you are right where God wants you."

Albeit, he had to admit that Mr. Abiel's solution was the same he had when he rolled them around in his head. He knew the rest of the world had problems also. His insulating bubble had burst, and the world's problems showed up at his feet and affected him.

Phillip started to cry.

Mr. Abiel sat on the bed with his arm around him. Comforting him with the words, "Peace is with you. Do not fear."

Phillip angrily answered, "How can you say that peace is with me. Peace hasn't been with me since being shot."

Phillip thought about that night and expected to see the gun, but new memories surfaced as he continued saying, "All I remember from that night is that I was laying on the concrete. Concentrating on my breathing and not wanting to die. I looked to my side and saw Tracy subdued on the ground by security. Chaos had consumed the people at the altar. Security was shouting for a paramedic and for someone to call the cops.

The crowd was separating from the sound of gunfire, manically tripping over each other and destroying the front row of folded chairs.

Tracy stole a glance at me in between everyone's legs as I laid there with blood pulling all around me. I cannot forget that she was smiling. Seemingly relieved she had done what she had come to do.

All I could think about was her last questions, "And that is it? I believe, pray for forgiveness and then everything is all right? There's nothing else I have to do?" "

Then his mind went to the Bible verse about how the demons believe that there is one God[2]. Phillip started to shiver as he started to blur Tracy's eyes with the wolf from his dream. His mind started to cloud with not knowing who Tracy was, even though she seemed familiar with him. Then there was the nagging question of why she would have shot him.

Phillip swallowed hard and continued, "I felt the paramedics rolling me to my side as they were poking and prodding me. I recall yelling in pain and trying to push them away because of the excruciating pain. I felt like vomiting as the world was spinning like a top which was about to fall.

One paramedic rested me onto my back and wrestled my arms away from my hip as another paramedic checked my arms and chest. I remember fighting them because I didn't want anyone else touching me, yet I was drained and too weak to fight

Disoriented, I saw another person coming closer and then further away from my vision. I know that other people gathered around me, but I only saw their mouths moving with gibberish. I made out, "We're losing him. . . "

Staring at the wall, Phillip stopped at those words. Oblivious to anything else, he felt released from trying to remember that dreadful night.

Lilly pushed her head under Phillip's hand, rested, and let out a heavy sigh.

Phillip looked at Mr. Abiel and resumed, "I tried to look at the people around me. I felt so cold and alone because none of them were my family.

I'd close my eyes and listened to the craziness around me.

---

[2] James 2:19

I thought I heard Jessica screaming at Tracy, "How could you have done this to me? Why? Tell me why? What did we do to you?"

Someone started snapping their fingers at me. One person asked where the ambulance was. Then amid the chaos, I heard …. I heard ….someone say 'Peace, I'm with you."

Mr. Abiel spoke softly, "Phillip, I'm so sorry those things happened to you."

Phillip choked his tears back and asked, "Why did Tracy do what she did to me?"

Mr. Abiel responded, "Phillip, bad things happen. The rain falls on the just and the unjust. However, we can't give up on others or ourselves. There's a wealth of information in the rest of someone else's story, but only when you decide that the story isn't only about you. We can't get to page three of someone's story and then give up on them because we're more worried about our own, or because we don't like their outside appearance, or because we're too busy with our frivolous endeavors."

Phillip missed Mr. Abiel's words as sleep started to cover his senses and he replayed echoes of the phrase, "Peace, I'm with you."

Mr. Abiel tucked Phillip back into his bed. He put his hand on Phillip's head and calmly soothed him as a mother would a crying child. Phillip laid back down, and Mr. Abiel continued saying, "I'm here. You're safe now. The demons are gone now. Peace. Peace."

Sleep welcomed Phillip back for the rest of the night in dreamless peace.

Chapter 15. Round Two

Stumbling into his office, Ethan was glad that the ward was at a dull roar and that nothing needed his attention.

Looking at his watch, he found that it was 7:05 a.m.

He closed the blinds in his office apart from those looking at Phillip's room. Then he turned off his overhead lights, leaving his desk lamp to be the only source of light.

Sitting in his chair, he tried his best to stop his head from throbbing, so he took two aspirins from his desk and swallowing them down, laughing at the coincidence of being a doctor taking two aspirins in the morning.

He wished he didn't go out last night, but he was too frustrated about letting Phillip get under his skin. Then he laughed at himself because he was giving Phillip too much credit to blame his hangover on him.

Waiting for the medicine to take effect, he closed his eyes and repeated his mantra, "What You Hold on to Is Holding on to You." Then he repeated step two: "Don't blame others for what is your own fault."

Wanting to be ready for Phillip this time, he ensured his door was unlocked.

Leaning back in his chair, he watched Phillip let Lilly outside.

Then he thought to himself, "Why am I waiting on him? I have other duties here."

Looking at the paperwork on his desk, he decided he didn't want to tackle it.

Thumbing his phone on, he saw that he had missed a text from Liz. He decided to ignore it because he knew she only wanted to gloat.

With the text app open, he saw Beth's text, which he could not bring himself to deal with. He wished he were able to remove it but knew it was the last thing he had from her.

He turned his phone off and then looked at his watch.

It read 7:10 a.m.

He looked back at his paperwork and scowled. He knew that he'd have to deal with it sometime throughout the day, so he shuffled through it for low hanging fruit.

Ethan noticed that a note fell to the ground. He wanted to ignore it until he saw Phillip's name on it.

Bending over to pick up the note, his hangover almost helped him to double over completely onto the ground. Finally reaching the note, he rose too quickly which made his head feel like it was swimming.

The note stated Phillip had a rough night sleeping.

Ethan thought, "Serves him right. Glad that I wasn't the only one suffering from yesterday."

Then he thought about step two again: Don't blame others for what is your own fault.

He thought, "I'm a damn hypocrite. "How am I going to expect others to follow my methods when I can't? Phillip was right about pride and that it wasn't only Christians who were guilty of hypocrisy."

Ethan tried to not beat himself up, but he kept thinking about how Phillip had pushed his buttons.

He cursed, "Jesus, what is wrong with me?"

Then he remembered his books step 5: "Expect the change in yourself, not others."

He thought again, "I'm a damn hypocrite."

Tired of the boomerang his thoughts became, he started to chant in his head, "OK, OK, OK. Change your perspective: I'm responsible for my own actions, not anyone else's. Change your perspective: Fix what you can; me not you. Change your perspective: . . ."

Massaging his temples, he slumped further in his chair as his thoughts boomeranged to another well-worn subject.

Looking at his phone, he examined the grooves in his ring finger and brooded, "Why am I tortured by her? Why can't I let this go? Why does this text have such a great hold on me?"

His peripheral caught Phillip hobbling back in with Lilly.

With the note in hand, he was glad to have a reason to get out of his office and headed towards Phillip's room.

Ethan was interrupted as soon as he opened his door.

Looking at Frank, Ethan asked, "Frank, how can I help you?"

TJ responded, "How can you confuse me with that sniveling idiot?"

Ethan answered, "Sorry, I have a hard time telling you two apart. What do you want?"

Feeling his headache throb, Ethan sucked at his teeth, trying to figure out how to quicken the conversation so he could get out of his office.

TJ growled, "Why does the new guy get the dog in his room?"

Ethan looked into TJ's eyes and could tell this wasn't a good time to be alone with him.

He didn't like having to deal with TJ by himself when he was like this. Especially when he had to say something TJ wasn't going to like.

Looking for a staff member, but none was around.

Ethan positioned himself where he was able to get away and answered, "Jack, you know we spoke about this before. Lilly can go anywhere she chooses. We can't make her do what we want her to do, just like we can't make the..."

TJ quickly responded, "Yes we can, she's a dog."

Ethan continued, "... just like we can't make the world or people do exactly what we want them to do."

Smirking, TJ said, "Yes we can."

Ethan said, "We brought Lilly into help everyone. If you'd be nicer to her, she'd probably come to you."

"Get real, Nice is a place in France. I am from Hell, Michigan," TJ said while cracking his knuckles.

Relieved, Ethan was glad to see TJ joking, as he chided, "No you aren't. You're from Tennessee, Jack."

TJ replied, "Yes I am! Doc, I can't believe that you won't help me. Lilly can't play favorites."

Ethan replied, "Well, I gotta go," as he turned and continued to Phillip's room.

Glad to have that over, he walked into Phillip's room.

He squinted because Phillip had his windows wide open to let the sun in.

As his headache throbbed, he thought that he'd made a mistake, but he shielded his eyes and cursed his hangover, he decided to carry on.

He saw Phillip laughing at Lilly.

Ethan opened, "So, what's so funny?"

Surprised that Ethan was in his room, Phillip turned and said, "Ah, nothing. Just learning more about myself through this dog and I just have to laugh."

Wanting to share the joke, Ethan asked, "So, what happened?"

"Well, I was feeding Lilly this morning, and she had this big bowl of food available," said Phillip, "But she chased this morsel across the floor. I started thinking about how we chase after things that are fleeting, instead of the big bowl set before us."

Ethan thought about it in respect to his own life and had to chuckle. He thought about how his message from his wife was a morsel, relative to the big bowl of life that was before him, and how he had to be released and start enjoying the here and now.

He replied, "Yeah, I guess it's kind of funny when you look at it that way."

Wanting to set the tone and to have control, Ethan decided to get to the point and said in a professional manner, "You do know Lilly is the hospital dog and should be allowed to come and go as she pleases."

Asking for permission to get into his lap, Lilly put her paw onto Phillip's leg.

Phillip raised his hands to pat his legs, but Lilly had already jumped in his lap. Rubbing her belly, hair flew everywhere.

He replied, "I figured I left the door open so she can come and go as she pleases."

Tired of having the dog hair stirred up, Phillip pushed her onto the ground.

She went in front of the window and sunned herself.

Still trying to shy away from the sunlight, Ethan continued in his professional manner and said, "I heard that you had a hard time sleeping last night. Do you need me to prescribe something for you so you can rest better tonight?"

Looking out at the great oak in the lawn, Phillip answered, "No, your staff helped enough last night."

Not wanting Phillip to divert his attention, Ethan moved over into Phillip's gaze and was glad to have the sun at his back.

He asked, "OK, tell me what happened?"

Phillip looked at Ethan and replied, "No, really I'm good. Nothing has happened that God and I can't handle."

Trying to hold back his disgust on Phillip's arrogance, Ethan knew that he couldn't be successful, so he sneered, "So, you and God are good?"

"I hope things won't get any worse, so I hope so," answered Phillip.

Tired of all the brightness in the room, Ethan closed the blinds. Then he thought about how he could knock Phillip off his spiritual high horse.

He disparaged, "You hope so. All right then let us get down to it. Do you think you need help?"

Phillip looked at Ethan and said, "Yes I need help, which is why I'm staying here."

Ethan continued staring at Phillip wanting him to continue.

Phillip understood that the pregnant pause was his cue to continue, so he resumed, "I'm at a loss on Tracy. I don't remember her or know if I should know her. I feel that I'm coming close to a memory of her, but it seems something is cloaking that memory."

Ethan was pleased that Phillip was talking. He offered, "So, tell me what you do remember about her."

Phillip looked into Ethan's eyes and noticed that they were bloodshot. Wanting to comment on it, he stopped as he recalled Mr. Abiel saying that Ethan was working through things and that they were good for each other.

Phillip knew how he could be good for Ethan, but struggled on the 'how' someone who was drunk could help him.

Phillip finally replied, "Well, I had more memories of the night that I was shot last night, other than looking down the barrel of a gun.

Ethan nodded his head and said, "Uh-huh?"

Phillip continued, "That's it. I don't know who she is still. I don't know why she did what she did. During the first week in the hospital, I struggled with trying to remember anything about her, but then all I saw was her leveling the gun at me and shooting me. I saw glimpses of her face but only like looking through a foggy mirror."

Ethan was pleased that Phillip was dumping the puzzle pieces of the shooting out and that he was finding other pieces. He needed to show Phillip that he was trying to help him by sorting the pieces out by the edges and then matching the like colors.

He asked, "Do you remember anything else about her?"

Phillip burrowed through the memories and remembered, "She said that she was sorry for the loss of my brother."

Ethan replied, "Ok, so tell me about your brother."

At that, Phillip and Ethan both noticed that Lilly started snoring with her eyes open. She kept her head laid down but switched her eyes back and forth between both men and snored again.

Ethan shook his head and said, "I didn't know that she did that."

Phillip answered, "I didn't either."

Wanting to get back on track in between the snores, Ethan asked again, "What about your brother?"

Phillip answered, "He and I lost touch after he moved away. I don't know exactly what it was that he did, but it was something for the government. He died recently and somewhat suddenly. The government said that it had something to do with a training exercise, but it just didn't sit well. Overall, I knew that he knew Jesus and that Jesus knew Andrew, so I know he's better now."

Ethan unconsciously coughed, as he listened intently because he wasn't aware that Phillip had a brother who died recently. He wondered if the Tracy puzzle had to do more with Phillip's brother than with Phillip himself.

Phillip noticed that Ethan was engaged, but also noticed that Ethan didn't like the conversation when Jesus entered. Not wanting to compromise his beliefs, he kept Jesus as part of the conversation because He was part of his brother and his life.

Phillip replied, "I've got faith that Jesus will reveal everything in His due time. He's never let me down yet."

Ethan replied, "You may believe that Jesus knows everything, but we don't down here, so don't quit. Keep trying."

Phillip clammed up after noticing Ethan had shirked off his comment about Jesus.

Ethan noticed this and couldn't think of anything that he said that was offensive. He asked, "Don't you think that you're being defensive?"

Phillip just sat staring at Ethan.

Ethan shrugged his shoulders and asked, "What?"

Phillip crossed his arms.

Stopping himself from swearing "Jesus Christ," Ethan instead continued with, "You're hiding behind platitudes which are preventing you from getting to the crux of your problem. This is just like you Christians; you deflect everything onto God. Which I'm OK with you believing in because it normally doesn't affect me, but you're here in my hospital and wanting to receive my help so it does."

Phillip said, "You need to deal with Jesus if you're going to deal with me."

Ethan's frustration grew because he thought he was about to get resolution on Tracy, on Phillip's PTSD, information about him and his wife or his anxiety.

Nevertheless, Phillip kept turning the subject to Jesus again and again.

Not wanting to pander to Phillip's coyness, and because his head was swimming from his hangover, Ethan finally threw his hands up and said, "Ok, so answer me these questions. How's your hope in a higher being going to help you with your PTSD and your anxiety? How's this hope you are talking about going to help you and your wife's marriage? How's your hope going to help you figure out more about Tracy and why she shot you?"

Knowing that he should stop, but not finished with his deluge of infuriation with Christians, Ethan continued, "Why do Christians think they can judge everyone, but have no judgment when dealing with themselves?"

In disbelief, Phillip watched but knew that Ethan was venting. He calmly stared at Ethan waiting for him to be finished.

Ethan was about to start again but figured he should try his best to keep his calm and use language that wouldn't offend Phillip.

Through gritted teeth, he continued, "I'm right here, right now, and I want to help you." Almost pleading, he continued, "I just need to have some cooperation on your part, but it's frustrating when you live in this Pollyanna delusional world where you don't have to deal with anything personal."

Knowing that he was going to have this lecture sometime or another, Phillip licked his lips and kept looking at Ethan. Then he smiled, as he thought about how he liked the movie Pollyanna, especially the part about the minister not taking the recommendations of what to preach.

Ethan continued, "You Christians act superior. Expecting everyone to follow rules that you say your God has set, but you conveniently don't follow them yourselves. Then you put on a façade of perfection, but, your actions betray you because you're as biased to the rest of the world as you try to make it something that it'll never be. You're quick to call people sinners but from what I see, Christians are no different than the rest of us sinners."

Rolling all his reactions through his head, Phillip remained speechless as he wrestled with not getting angry with Ethan because the hypocrisy that Ethan was trying to get at were not only specific to Christians but non-Christians alike. Non-Christians also set rules that they expect other to follow that they don't obey themselves. He wanted to disagree that Christians should be different, because holiness means that we are set apart from the world to be use of God, but that was an argument more for believers than it was for non-believers.

Looking at the mirror in his room, Phillip decided that he should give Ethan a reflection of himself.

Phillip finally replied, "I've got a problem when you lump all Christians into the same pot. Not recognizing the double standard, which is that the problems you are mentioning are not Christian specific but problems that everyone has."

Ethan replied, "All you Christians justify your behavior by hiding behind God. This God that no one can see, touch, or fully explain."

Phillip replied, "Ok. So, are you speaking as an expert on Christian behavior? If so, where did you study to get your specialized knowledge?"

Not expecting Phillip's impertinence, Ethan drew back because through his previous experiences dealing with Christians, that they were usually passive doormats and kowtow any questioning on explaining God. Knowing that he was dumbfounded, he ensured that his mouth was not open.

He also wanted to ensure that Phillip wouldn't usurp his authority again and answered not based on the question but on his feelings, Ethan said, "You hypocrite. What do you mean to come here and challenge my education and me personally as you parrot some ancient dogma? You come here and want this to be a hotel. I already told you this is not going to be a holiday. I told you that the kid gloves would have to come off so I can deal with the religion of fools."

Ethan knew that he'd done it now. Either he would be rid of Phillip or Phillip would start to work with him, make some progress, and he'd be able to gain back control.

He also imagined Liz's response, "Really, out of all the things that you could've said. You could've mentioned the validity of the Bible or that it is just a myth. Or better yet, you could've mentioned homosexuality or dinosaurs, but you had to go with hypocrisy?"

Phillip paused. Surprised that Ethan had come into his room and attacked his beliefs. Wondering about what had set him off, he remembered his conversation the previous day about Ethan not liking Christians.

Sitting back and letting Ethan have his tirade, Phillip thought about how he'd had heard it all before, never being surprised on how it always sounds the same.

He quietly prayed the Bible verse, "A calm answer turns away wrath."

Straightening himself up, he calmly replied, "You're correct that some Christians falsely use the Bible to justify their own actions, and some have the 'religion of fools' when their faith selfishly deals with themselves and not the world around them. But that doesn't mean that all Christians do.

You also stated that you think that I'm a hypocrite. I wonder what you're basing that on. Is it because I stand for my beliefs as I believe I am called to do, or because I don't line up with your worldview? You should afford me the same respect that you afford yourself when you stand for your beliefs. Or are you only 'parroting some dogma' that is as ancient as mine. Do you truly practice these beliefs or are you deflecting, because you only believe in yourself and don't really believe and follow them 100% either?"

Feeling convicted, Ethan justified himself, "I'm a good man."

Phillip answered, "By whose standard? Humanism's dogma, which says everyone, is capable of being moral without God or religion, yet leaves morals wide open. So, who or what defines the standard of what is good or what is bad? And when someone does stand and says that something is the standard of good, what does that make them relative to the rest?"

Feeling the room starting to close in on him, Ethan didn't like having someone talk to him in this fashion. Especially talking to him like this a second time.

He tried to think of what the right words to say, but every thought seemed hollow. He tried to fall back on his training, but his training had escaped him now.

He stood there with nothing but the emptiness inside himself. But not just emptiness, but anger welled within him. Not because of Phillip's words, but because he did not have a response.

Feeling petty, he wanted to respond "Well, oh yeah, what about …," but now he got angry with himself because he had failed in preparation. Calling a Christian a hypocrite was the end of his argument. So, he said it all over again with different words, "Well what about the Christians who don't do what they are told to do based on the Bible?"

Not waiting for a heartbeat, Phillip responded, "All right, since you hold all Christians to such a high standard, do you do the same for others who follow philosophies and other religions like Plato, Confucius, and Mohammed? Do you expect perfection in them? Forget about other religions, do you even follow your own beliefs 100 percent of the time? Or do you latch onto beliefs just so you can use them to argue with and get a sense of superiority. One of the arguments that prevails is that all religions are equal, but every religion has different views of how we're are equal. In Christianity we do define what makes us all equal: we live, we die, we sin, and we are all in need of a Savior because we are powerless to save ourselves."

Ethan's head started to swim from last night's outing. Wanting to have the conversation over, he asked, "Ok, so what does this have to do with what we're talking about?"

Phillip answered, "Don't you see that you have defined your moral path above mine? You've deemed yourself an authority with bias and superiority? Wouldn't that be hypocritical too?"

Phillip waited a few moments and let his words sink in.

Rubbing his forehead, Ethan wished he could go back to his office and have this conversation where it was much darker.

Powering though his headache, Ethan thought, "Why won't he shut up? I used to tell a Christian that they are hypocritical, or that the whole church is hypocritical, and the conversation would be over. It would usually shut them down or shut them up."

Pinching the bridge of his nose, Ethan was quietly examining himself about how he didn't like to be shown that he qualified for the title of hypocrite also. Then he cursed, as he thought about how Phillip had turned the tables on him again.

Or was it the hangover?

Satisfied with the brief respite, Phillip continued, "Further hypocrisy is evident when there's a culture that rules and judges people by their own sensitivity. Judging people to the point where one can't say anything that disagrees with someone else because it might offend that other person and their personal liberties while disavowing any others person's right and liberties of free thought and expression.

Personally, I think that some people need to be offended. Just to see that we're all the same.

Further proof of your hypocrisy is that you are talking about something that you do not know anything about as fact.

Have you studied the Bible?

Have you tried the Christian life?

Have you tried to understand God's love for you?

Your comparison of all Christians being hypocrites is like looking at a hospital and expecting everyone to be a doctor. While you forget that some are the patients, the nurses, the janitor, etc.

You look at Christians as a whole, but we Christians look at each as a family knowing that each of us are at different stages of our Christian lives.

You see a young Christian not following what you believe the Bible to say and condemn them as a hypocrite. But we see them as family and try to help them to understand God's love more.

You see an older Christian and see they have stumbled, and you hold that up as proof that their faith is false and that they are a hypocrite. But we see them as brothers and sisters, who just like us, deserves compassion and grace, and to be reminded of what they believe."

Waiting for Ethan to interject, Phillip gave pause.

Ethan stood and walked to the door with his eyes downcast like a scolded child.

Phillip continued, "That's why we pray to God. It's why we read the Bible together. We do these things not because we forget, but because this life is so complicated with the evil and the lies of the enemy, we need reminding that God is in control. We're still sinners in need of a Savior and Jesus fulfilled that need."

Ethan turned and asked, "What need is that?"

Phillip started, "Protection, hope, justification, purpose, love, endurance, salvation, provision, ..."

Knowing that Phillip could continue spouting virtues, Ethan interrupted, "Ok, I get it, but Jesus fulfilled these needs?"

Feeling that this was the first question that Ethan had asked that was genuine, Phillip smiled and relax his posture. Looking into Ethan's eyes, Phillip was content with Ethan's intent on asking the question, so he calmly answered, "Ethan, you distinguish things as Christians versus the world, but Christians see the difference as being between believers or non-believers."

Ethan cut in, "We've already covered that."

Phillip nodded his head in agreement, and continued, "Ok. Christians believe that Jesus is who He says He is, which is God's Son and the Christ. We believe that He did what He said He would do, which was to live the perfect life without sin, to substitute His sacrifice for the death that we all deserve, and to rise from the dead proving He is the Son of God. Finally, we Christians believe that Jesus is where we go to get our needs fulfilled. Jesus is God's help for us to become Sons of God. I know in my own life I had tried to fill my needs by ..."

Trying his best to listen and keep his head in the conversation, Ethan had a hard time with the simple description of believers that Phillip was giving.

He hadn't been listening to Phillip past his "believers and non-believers" comment and wanting clarification he asked, "Ok. So, who do I follow? The Baptist? The Methodist? The Mormons?"

Phillip replied, "Are you not listening? The answer is Jesus Christ. Truthfully, it isn't any denomination that saves anyone.

One simply has to believe that Jesus Christ is the Son of God. That Jesus led a sinless life. That He is willing and able to forgive anyone of their sins. That Jesus died on a cross in their place as payment for those sins. That Jesus rose again proving He is who He says He is and that he is able to do what He said He can do."

Ethan felt his eyes starting to roll to the back of his head and responded, "As I said earlier, I'm a good person, so do me a favor and keep all this to yourself. Try practicing your Bible and judge not lest you be judged[3]."

Phillip knew that this verse was a favorite for those who had never read the whole Bible and replied, "You're correct that is in the Bible, but do you know where? Do you know what the text and context of this verse is? Do you know how it really applies to the Christian life?"

Ethan disinterestedly shrugged his shoulders.

Phillip continued, "Since you brought it up, let me tell you. Do you remember when I talked about brothers and sisters who deserve compassion and help to discern truth? About those who need to be corrected and to be reminded of what they believe?"

Ethan drew a deep breath in and let it out loudly.

---

[3] http://www.Biblegateway.com/resources/commentaries/IVP-

NT/Matt/Do-Not-Judge-Others

http://www.studylight.org/com/mhm/view.cgi?book=mt&chapter=007

Phillip continued, "That verse is the beginning of Matthew 7, but it's more about taking care of the log in one's eye before taking care of the speck in someone else's eye.

To understand this more, let's take a doctor as an example again. Would anyone want a blind doctor helping a blind patient see?"

Ethan scoffed, "Of course not."

Phillip continued, "You're right. So, the meaning of the verse is that a Christian should examine themselves before going to help someone else with their problem because they may be doing so in the wrong spirit."

Feeling remorse because he had come to work with a hangover, Ethan began to see some of the truth in his own life.

But not wanting to get Phillip an inch of leverage, Ethan smiled and replied, "Kind of like a Christian, who should be dealing with himself about being shot and losing his wife, before trying to help the doctor who is trying to help him."

Phillip stared through Ethan, as he worked through the pain of conviction.

He had to force himself to blink.

Ashamed that he'd crossed a boundary, he resolved that he wasn't on the rally's stage and that this wasn't his forum.

Understanding his denial, he thought that he was trying to sum up himself for Ethan so Ethan could help him.

Phillip shivered as he realized that Ethan was enduring everything he dished out because he really did want to help him.

He still didn't know if he could trust him, but could he trust Jesus to use this man to speak into his life?

Ethan identified Phillip's silence as agreement that his point was made

He stepped towards Phillip and said," I want to help you with your PTSD, but you're deflecting. As much as I haven't enjoyed our last two talks, I can tell that you're not going to open up and deal with the events of your life. You seem to be wanting to help me more than you want to help yourself. So, instead of meeting with me in my office as we planned earlier, I want you to be at the next group meeting that will have in a few hours. I'm sure you will be such a big help for everyone."

With his voice breaking, Phillip replied, "If I'm to trust you, there are some things I want to work out with you before I can continue."

Ethan replied, "We'll see."

Phillip responded, "As much as you've reacted to me, I'm guilty of reacting to you. I'm having a hard time trusting you, but I do want your help. I'll try to change my reaction. Will you forgive me?"

Ethan sighed and tiredly responded, "Whatever you've got to say to make yourself feel better."

Then he walked out with a smug smile leading his way.

Lilly jumped up onto Phillip's lap and looked into his eyes, licked his hands and decided to lay down at his feet.

Phillip opened his Bible and reread Matthew 7 and then prayed

Dear Jesus,
You're so awesome and thank you
for keeping me from death.

Nothing has been the same since I've
been shot.

I don't have any normalcy anymore,
and I need help in not being Pharisaical. I
know that I haven't done right by Ethan,
but Ethan sees everything I say about You
as a reason to attack Christians.

Please help me to take the plank out
of my own eye and not to be blind or
rationalize my own guilt. Help me to know
my place here and to learn something more
of myself and of You. Help me to do what
You have called me to do.

Thank you for reminding me that You
are God and that I'm not.

Help me to temper everything I say and do with Your love. Please, speak to him and give him someone to counsel him about You. Please don't let me be in the way of him finding You.

God, I'm so tired, because the more I try to get the answers to one thing, more things keep popping up. I guess I'm part of the world that keeps spinning. Please resolve all this mess so I can be a help for You.

All of this is becoming more than I can bear. There's Tracy, Jessica and now Ethan is in my face. Help me to get through this PTSD and let me bring my anxiety to You. I guess this is all part of the o'er and o'er.

Please help me through these trials. Please reveal yourself, I so desperately need to know You are here."

Concentrating on the words, he didn't feel adequate and worthy of them. Especially after the beating Ethan gave him.

He always thought to pray for others but not himself. So, this was the first time that he had spent time praying and struggling with the weight of being shot, Jessica leaving him and being in a psychiatric ward.

Thinking about going to the group meeting, He prayed that the rest of the day would get better.

Defeated and not having any more words to say, he whispered, "Amen."

***

Ethan entered his office and checked his voicemail from Champ Davis.

"Hey, doc. I'm having some problems sleeping. It's nothing big, I just need something to take the edge off so I can sleep at night. You know my pharmacy to send the prescription."

Putting in the prescription, Ethan left a note on his desk to call Champ next and left for lunch ecstatic that he'd finally shut Pastor Phillip Ashby up.

Chapter 16.   Population +1

"Tracy … Jessica … gun … red eyes ……… Tracy … gun … Ethan … hypocrite …. wolf … Jessica …."

Sitting at his desk, Phillip closed his eyes as the torturous loop ran its course through his brain. Breathing in and out, he tried relieving himself from all the stress. Concentrating on the oak tree outside his window, he tried to calm his mind.

"Oak tree …. Oak tree …. Oak tree, slow my breathing, oak tree, rustling leaves, knock, knock, knock … gun … Tracy …"

Perking his eyebrows up, he recognized the knocking behind him. He turned to see Mr. Abiel knocking on the door again.

"How're you doing? Is there something I can help you with?" asked Phillip.

Mr. Abiel answered, "I need to take Lilly out so she can do her business."

Nodding, Phillip said, "Thank you, but she's the hospital's dog, so you always have permission."

Mr. Abiel replied, "I know, but I like to be respectful anyways."

Then he called to Lilly, and she bounded to the door.

Looking back out at the oak tree, he tried to change the rut his mind was in, but all he could think about was how he wasn't ready for the rest of the day's craziness. He looked at his desk and stared at his journal and Bible.

He closed his eyes and prayed that the rest of the day he could keep his head low and get better so he could get out of here.

"God I hope You give me clear direction
on how to get this log out of my eye. Please help
me to remember who Tracy is and bring about
healing and restoration between my wife and
me.

Amen!"

He then opened his Bible and read.

"So do not be afraid of them, for there is
nothing concealed that will not be disclosed or
hidden that will not be made known. What I tell you
in the dark, speak in the daylight; what is whispered
in your ear, proclaim from the roofs. Do not be
afraid of those who kill the body but cannot kill the
soul. Rather, be afraid of the One who can destroy
both soul and body in hell. Are not two sparrows
sold for a penny? Yet not one of them will fall to the
ground outside your Father's care. And even the
very hairs of your head are all numbered. So don't
be afraid; you are worth more than many sparrows.
    "Whoever acknowledges me before others,
I will also acknowledge before my Father in heaven.
But whoever disowns me before others, I will
disown before my Father in heaven.[4]

Phillip looked up from reading. He felt caught in the contrast
of this verse and his conversation with Ethan earlier about being a
hypocrite.
    He said to God, "How can I balance the strength that You
expect of me and the vulnerability it is going to take for me to
heal?
    I feel useless while I'm paralyzed by the same thought loops
of Tracy shooting me, Jessica leaving me, and Ethan accusing me
keeps revolving in my thoughts."
    Phillip recognized that he was praying and being irreverent,
and wanted to get on his knees as best as he could with his injured
leg to continue praying to God, but the verse in Ecclesiastes about

----

[4] Matthew 10:26-33

there being a time for everything quickened into his mind and figured he was to take the time to heal.

Sitting at his desk, seeking God to stop the torturous loops addling his mind, he continued to think, "God … Jesus … healing …. Faith …. Jesus … hypocrite."

Frustrated, he sighed, opened his eyes and continued reading.

> "Do not suppose that I have come to bring
> peace to the earth. I did not come to bring peace,
> but a sword. For I have come to turn
> "'a man against his father,
>   a daughter against her mother,
> a daughter-in-law against her mother-in-law—
> a man's enemies will be the members of his own
> household.'
> Anyone who loves their father or mother
> more than me is not worthy of me; anyone who
> loves their son or daughter more than me is not
> worthy of me. Whoever does not take up their cross
> and follow me is not worthy of me. Whoever finds
> their life will lose it, and whoever loses their life for
> my sake will find it.[5]

Phillip closed his eyes and tried to rewrite to loop.

"Jesus   … love my life   …. lose it … worthy   … peace   … hypocrite   … gun …. Tracy."

Not getting the comfort that he wanted from his study, Phillip shook his head muttering, "It's going to be one of those days."

Closing his Bible, he started writing in his journal.

> "God, I feel like I'm getting pulled in so many
> directions. Everyone has their expectation on how I'm
> to get better.

[5] Matthew 10:34-39

Ethan feels like I should abandon everything that I've known my whole life for what he believes to be true, with no proof other than his belief that he is right.

Jessica's behaving like she's the one who has been wounded and wants me to acquiesce, despite my injury and confusion.

God, I know that You want me to keep acknowledging my faith in You and to tell others. I just read that You tell me You didn't come to bring peace, but a sword ..."

Weary, he lifted the pen from the paper. Normally, he wouldn't deliberate about being God's instrument, but now abandonment overwhelmed him.

Struggling with being honest with himself and God, he continued writing:

"You're going to have to fight because I'm tired. I feel like I'm a black hole attracting everyone's pain.

I don't want to be the whoever mentioned in Matthew.

I don't want to be the lone sheep to be devoured.

Help me to submit to You and take up my cross and follow You."

Closing his journal, he decided to get lunch. Seeing his cane at his door, he walked past it because he was tired of feeling like an old man hobbling around with it.

While eating lunch, Ethan's words and the harshness of his manner made Phillip want to reconsider staying here. He felt that if his day continued like this, he'd get Claire to find him a Christian counselor to get him away and to some proper care.

He saw Mr. Abiel walking around the cafeteria, and remembered his words, "You two are good for each other."

He scoffed at the thought and brought what looked like mashed potatoes to his mouth, and immediately drank his entire glass of water.

Putting his glass down, he was surprised by the "Butterfly guy' sitting across from him. He was wearing another bathrobe that looked like a gleaming boxers robe with a huge butterfly on the left breast.

Noticing that he had Phillip's attention, the 'Butterfly guy' instructed, "Did you know that butterflies' taste with their feet?"

Feigning interest, Phillip nodded.

"It's true, when they're walking on you, they are also licking you," continued the 'Butterfly guy.'

Phillip sustained his uninterested nod and mashed his potatoes more, wondering what they really were.

The 'Butterfly guy' reached out his hand and said, "How rude of me. I haven't introduced myself. My name is Kevin."

Phillip dropped his fork and shook his hand and gave his own name.

Kevin gripped Phillip's hand firmly and said, "MMMMM! You taste good."

Jerking his hand out of Kevin's hand, Phillip started wiping it off with his napkin.

Ignoring his own weirdness, Kevin continued pointing out others around the room.

He pointed to a table and said, "That's Frank and Tennessee Jack. TJ is mean and dangerous which is why he is here. I don't think he and Frank are getting better. TJ, he don't like nobody. He and Frank..."

Phillip interrupted, "Yeah, I met him briefly."

Kevin continued, "Well, he doesn't like you at all. He mads at you because of Lilly. A little secret about TJ. We don't talk about him being out a touch of reality. If you know what I mean."

Phillip looked over at Frank and TJ and slowly nodded in understanding.

Kevin then pointed to a squirrelly woman and said, "That's Mary, she ..."

Phillip interrupted, "Kevin, thanks for trying to get me acquainted with everyone, but I usually like to get to know people myself."

Kevin tilted his head, smiled and asked, "Really?"

Phillip saw that others were starting to leave, grabbed his tray and said, "Yes and thank you for your time."

He followed the crowd to a room with easels and several paints, and tables that had pen and paper.

Taking a seat along the wall, he studied how everyone simply went to their art projects like little children.

He watched Kevin painting several butterflies and grinned when he noticed that Kevin's boxers robe had a huge butterfly on the back of it. He wondered why Kevin loved butterflies so much.

Feeling someone take his hand, he thought it was someone who was going to lead him to an art station but was startled when the person intertwined their fingers with his.

He turned to see a somewhat attractive woman, who then leaned on his shoulder and stared up at him longingly.

He stood up and let go of the woman's hand.

She said, "Please, don't go."

He created some distance from her, but in doing so, it landed him by Frank and TJ.

They screamed in horror, "Get off the cat's tail."

Not knowing that there was a cat in the ward, Phillip jumped away only to find TJ laughing hysterically.

TJ said between laughter, "Frank, the imaginary cat gets them every time."

Frank answered, "It's not imaginary."

TJ kept laughing, "Right, just like you don't have other imaginary friends."

Frank had had enough and started yelling and screaming about nothing which made TJ laugh all the more.

Unnerved from the conversation, Phillip tried to calm Frank down and noticed that there were bruises on his arms.

"Where did these come from?" asked Phillip.

TJ gravelly replied, "Shock treatment."

Phillip asked, "What is shock treatment?"

TJ answered, "It's what happens when I don't get what I want. Get it?"

Phillip looked at Frank and asked, "Is he hurting you?"

Frank looked deep within himself, found no courage against TJ, and shook his head. "No," silently escaped Frank's lips as he looked around nervously.

Phillip gestured to Frank's arms and asked, "Who did this? How did this happen?"

Frank eye's dilated as he whispered, "I did it."

Phillip kept looking at Frank and TJ responded, "See, I didn't do it."

Then Frank gained control of himself and started screaming, "I did it. I did it," as he drenched his paintbrush with red and acted like it was a knife

As Frank danced around his canvas, scoring it with red like blood so thick that it started to drip, Phillip noticed Frank's scar on his wrists and backed away.

TJ laughed and bellowed, "Boy, you aren't in the real world anymore. We're all crazy in here. This is your shock treatment."

Phillip slowly left the paint area as the words echoed with him.

"Not real world …. I did it … Don't go …. Jesus … Jesus … Jesus …."

He sat alone at the writing station, trying to get his anxiety under control. He blinked his eyes as he tried to stop staring at all the people around him.

"I'm sure you will be such a big help for everyone ….. Whatever you've got to say to make yourself feel better …… We'll see."

Wanting to work out the events from the day, he decided to write whatever came to his mind. His focus concentrated on the awkwardness he felt. How he felt like he was dense and compact. How his life was spinning out of control. How his wife, his helper had left him, and no one was able to really see or understand what he was going through. How he felt like he was only consuming space. How all the events and misunderstanding since the shooting had put him into a tailspin and that the only thing, he had was God.

Looking at the scribbles on the page, he read:

Black Hole

I am a black hole
Keeping everything to myself;
Nothing escapes me.

The Light is consumed within me,
But do not get too close
Or I will have you too.

I am here affecting those around me
But you cannot see me.
I know the Light but cannot make it known right now.

Only a miracle …
Only a miracle can save me …
Only a miracle can save me from collapse.

Dunamis; the Light's power within me
Stronger than my pull.
The Light is sanctifying me.

Supernovae; Light making itself known.
Radiating beyond my borders.
Giving Light for another Black Hole.

Amazed that his free writing had summed up how he felt about being here, he was sure that the day couldn't get any worse.

He tucked the paper into his pocket and felt drained. He played through the day, trying to realize what had caused his exhaustion. He thought about the disparity of the patients, or that

Jessica had left him here, or that he hadn't had a good night sleep, or that he saw red eyes around each corner he passed.

He heard a slight tone of the overhead paging system and watched how the group filed out of the room.

Glad that art time was done, he followed them all to the common room. Being the last in line, everyone else had gone to their designated place.

The room was spacious with a huge bay window showing the lawn with the same oak tree that he could see from his room. There was a sectional couch facing a TV, a table with people putting together a puzzle and some playing cards. Then there was a high back chair facing the outside window.

Walking in, he felt like everyone was looking at him. Like he was intruding into their sanctuary.

With a dozen people scattered about the room, he observed how everyone stayed out of TJ's way, but noticed that TJ didn't do the same as he belligerently walked around daring someone to intrude in his bubble when he forced it into their space.

Phillip knew that he'd have to deal with him sometime as he finally took a seat in the high back chair looking out the window.

Looking to the other side of the room by the TV, he noticed Kevin looking out the window expectantly.

Feeling that Kevin would be the friendliest to be with, Phillip decided to sit on the first couch closest to him. However, Kevin was excitedly distracted with something outside.

Phillip couldn't see from where he was, so he stretched his neck and still couldn't manage to see out the window, so he lifted himself with his arms and caught site of Lilly sniffing around.

He was glad to see that Lilly brought joy to others without even knowing it. He wondered if others projected some of their experiences onto the dog like he did.

Without a warning, a woman jumped into his lap facing him.

Looking directly into his face, he saw that it was the same woman who held his hand. Her auburn hair tickled his nose, and her brown eyes were searching for something within his. She was attractive, but Phillip had decided that Jessica would be his definition of beauty a long time ago.

Tired of looking into his eyes, she leaned back and gave a big smile.

He tried to maneuver himself away from her, but she had pinned his arms under him. Feeling the soreness in his leg, he was thankful that his leg had healed at bit, but he didn't know how much it could take.

Recognizing that there was no one able to help him, Phillip wished that Mr. Abiel wasn't letting Lilly out, or that Ethan wasn't stuck in his office. He knew that everyone else was paying attention to them but wasn't offering any assistance.

He tried to wiggle free, but the more he moved, the more she mimicked that she was riding a bronco, and it didn't help his manhood, so he stopped moving.

Panic washed over him, as he slowly came to the realization that he was at this woman's mercy and discretion.

Now, he wished that he hadn't left his cane in his room.

He thought about how far he'd fallen since his current events and prayed that God would get him out of this.

She took his face into her hands, and he leaned back as far as he could, but instead he inadvertently was thrusting his body upward as the woman shrilled with glee.

She leaned forward and forcefully grabbed a hold of his face and stared into his eyes, and said, "OK, let's see why you're in here?"

She put her hand to her lip as if she was thinking hard about the question, as she also swayed side to side.

Phillip prayed that she'd just set still, but she kept squirming in his lap. He tried to roll over so he could get her off his lap, but his hip started to hurt under this pressure.

Giving a pouty look, she pulled back his hair and checked his forehead and said, "I got it. You're crazy just like the rest of us."

He replied, "I'm not crazy. I just have to take a break to figure things out."

Still pinning him down, she maneuvered her leg around him and leaned back and said, "Ok, so what do you think about my figure?"

Having enough of this, Phillip desperately wanted to get her off his lap because he was about to have another problem when he became aroused.

Taking a deep breath so he could yell for some help, she leaned forward and covered his mouth and whispered in a deeper breathy voice, almost like she was imitating a man's voice, "There's no need to scream, just set back and enjoy this."

Sweat rolled down his brow, as fear overtook Phillip. Beforehand he thought this woman was naïve about what she was doing, but now he knew that she was purposely doing it.

Remembering Ethan saying that he wasn't in a hotel, his current reality had finally cemented that he was in a mental ward.

His muffled screams enthused her even more, so he let out a desperate prayer that it couldn't get any worse.

As if on cue, someone cleared their throat.

The young woman sultrily looked up and replied to the people behind Phillip, "Oh, he's already taken. Move on!"

Turning his neck as far as he could, Phillip saw Jessica with crossed arms and Claire holding a box behind Jessica.

Claire tried to come to her dad's aid, but Jessica put her arm in front of Claire and said with disgust, "Phillip, I see that you're making 'good' friends."

Phillip's heart unexpectedly dropped as he renewed his attempt to get up again.

Delighted that she had an audience, the woman in his lap squealed with each exertion.

Exhausted and still pinned, Phillip managed to muffle through the woman's covering hand, "It's not what you think it is."

The woman removed her hand from Phillip's face and held it out to Jessica and said, "Hi, I'm Mary. I'm pleased to meet you."

Not taking Mary's hand, Jessica replied, "Missy, I don't give a hoot about who you are, and Phillip is my husband."

Mary asked, "Who's Phillip?"

Jessica pointed at Phillip and then started inspecting her fingernails.

Mary looked at Phillip and said, "Oh, just my luck another one taken."

Slowly raising her eyes from inspecting her fingernails, Jessica said to Phillip, "I was going to give you the benefit of the doubt. I thought we could put everything behind us and try to start again. But after seeing this, I don't think I can believe you anymore. You just don't care about anyone else but yourself."

Phillip struggled in guarding himself against Jessica's anger, but he couldn't stop from being exposed.

Jessica tempestuously continued, "I've been replaced by your work, this Tracy and now a tramp who you've just met. You've never cared about anything that I care for. It has always been about you."

He strained to get his arms free again, and Mary moaned in exhilaration.

Jessica stormed away in self-righteousness. Each stride made in disgust.

Exasperated, he brooded, "This day got worse."

Phillip somehow wrenched one of his arms free, enabling him to thrust Mary off his lap. Wincing from the blood rushing back into his leg, he tried to ignore the pain, but it became more intense than anything he had felt before.

Mary grasped his arms pleading, "Please don't go. Everyone always leaves me. I can do better. I promise. Please don't go."

Freeing himself from Mary's grasp, Phillip stood up to pursue Jessica, only to fall onto the side of the couch and roll to the floor exposing his arousal. Embarrassed at his lack of control he tried to hide but knew that everyone had judged him the same as Jessica had.

Mary squeaked, "Uh Oh!" and scampered away.

He stroked his leg, tried to work out the numbness, and cursed himself that he didn't bring his cane.

The rest of the common room stopped what they were doing, giggled, and murmured to themselves as they enjoyed Mary's affair.

Claire put down the box she was carrying and struggled to help her daddy up.

Kevin gently moved past Claire and lifted Phillip quickly. Putting Phillip's arm around himself, he looked at Claire for instructions.

Claire pointed to the couch, and Kevin obliviously dropped Phillip down.

Wincing in pain, Phillip examined his leg and didn't see any blood, he rested on the couch as he tried to slow his breathing again.

Phillip noticed that Claire's phone rang and that she quickly silenced it.

In between the pain, he said to Claire, "I know that's your mom. You have to tell her that what she thinks she saw wasn't real."

Waving her Dad's comment away, Claire said, "Dad, she's just mad at the world right now. You just happen to be the target. You know what she's like, she acts as if her desire gives her the right to control."

Plopping next to her dad, she continued, "It took me an hour to get her to come and visit you. I asked her what it would look like if she didn't visit her husband at the hospital. That's when she agreed to come. I don't understand how y'all love each other."

Phillip divulged, "I know that it seems that everything is rotten between your mom and I right now, but I do still love her."

Kevin squeezed in between Phillip and Claire and interjected, "I'm so glad you've come, my name is Kevin. Do you like butterflies?"

Claire looked around Kevin as Phillip pleaded his case, "Just tell her that what she saw wasn't what she thought it was. I've been in my room since I've been here. This is the first time that I've come out here."

Kevin leaned forward, tried to help and said, "It's true. Today's the first time he's come out of his room. So, do you like butterflies?"

Claire gave a 'get lost' look to Kevin, but he just smiled back at her waiting for her answer.

Losing patience, she leaned back and continued her story, "You owe me big time. Driving here, all I heard was how bad my driving is, about how awful you've been to her and about how hard she has it. "

Kevin leaned back and put his feet up on the ottoman. Giving up on his questioning, he blurted out, "Dont'cha worry about Mary. She'd been passed around so much like the Queen of Hearts. That why she's confused on what proper behavior is for people to like her."

Still rubbing his leg, Phillip collected his thoughts and saw that Kevin and Claire were chatting. Since they were distracted with each other, he looked around.

He saw Mary stealing glances his way as she rocked back and forth in a corner with her knees to her chin.

He looked into Ethan's office and saw him staring intently at his phone. He cocked his head and wondered what he was doing on it.

Then he looked at the high back chair facing the window and saw a hand stroking a pillow.

* * *

Claire relented and decided to pump Kevin for information. She asked, "Thank you for the help, Kevin. Is there anything else we need to know?"

Kevin shifted his weight and answered. "Well, there is Frank and Tennessee Jack. ..."

Listening to Kevin talk about TJ, Claire realized the possible danger she'd put her father in.

She leaned across Kevin and tried to get her dad's attention. She looked at where he was looking and saw Ethan sitting in his office.

She made a mental note to talk with him before she left.

* * *

Phillip felt someone touch his knee. He went flush and turned to ensure that Mary was still in her corner. Still seeing her there, he felt someone tap him on the shoulder.

He turned and saw Claire and Kevin staring at him.

Kevin said, "Don't you wish you were a butterfly? Did you know that Monarch butterflies travel long distances to lay their eggs and die?"

Phillip answered, "OK?"

Claire stood up and intervened, "Dad, I'll try to get you out of here as fast as I can. Let's get away from Mr. Butterfly so we can talk."

Phillip's heart sank when Claire said that she wanted to get him out of here. He recalled Mr. Abiel saying that he and Ethan were good for each other.

He looked at Claire and answered, "I don't think so. Right now, I believe that this is where God wants me. I've got to stand for Him and try to be his ambassador here. Ethan's challenged me to do some good here, and I shouldn't run from those who stand against Him."

Kevin clapped his hands and said, "All right! Let's do some good."

Irritated, Claire glared at Kevin, who was oblivious that he was in a private conversation.

Noticing that Claire had acknowledged his presence, Kevin continued to give the rundown of the place.

He pointed at the high back chair where someone sat stroking a couch pillow as a cat and said, "That's Frank. I talked about him earlier. He's OCD. I think it's fun to tell him he missed a button to his shirt and then walk away. He usually wants to be alone, but he's never alone."

While Kevin was cackling at his own joke, Claire picked up the box and gave her dad the stare that it was time to leave.

Phillip shook Kevin's hand and said, "Kevin, I'm so glad to know your name now and thank you for all of your help, but I have to go."

Kevin kept a hold of Phillip's hand and looked around to ensure that no one was listening. Then in his usual voice, he said, "Wait, I gotta tell you about the big man."

Phillip looked at Claire. Claire shrugged her shoulders and mocked, "*He has to tell you about the big man.*"

Ready to hear what Kevin would say, Phillip waited.

Phillip looked at Claire. She shrugged her shoulders with contempt.

Waiting longer than he thought he should, Phillip whispered, "OK, what about the big man."

Kevin said, "He's lost something, and he's mad at who took it from him."

Puzzled over his statement, Phillip wondered if he was talking about God, TJ or his own make-believe person.

Liking a good riddle, Claire asked, "What did he lose?"

Kevin looked at her and said, "Not what, but who."

They both waited for the answer, until Phillip finally asked, "OK, Who?"

Kevin shh'd them both and then answered, "We don't know much. He did talk to Mary briefly about it. But he isn't the same."

Phillip asked, "Who are we talking about? Who's the big man?"

Kevin laughed and answered, "You know. The big man. I saw you talking to him earlier, so I figured you'd know."

Phillip quizzically answered, "Ethan?"

Kevin shushed Phillip and said, "Be quiet."

Looking over his shoulder, Kevin whispered in Phillip's ear, "His phone, he just stares at it all the time."

Claire rolled her eyes, shuffled the box to one hand and took her dad's hand to lead him to his room.

Letting go of Claire's hand, Phillip exclaimed, "I knew it!" and asked, "What happened?"

Kevin replied, "The only people here that know is Mary and the big man."

Phillip looked over at Mary and knew that he wasn't going to try to get any information from her.

Claire took his hand again saying, "Co'mon dad, we got to go."

Phillip remembered that during his session with Ethan, he'd thought he'd seen Ethan reach for his phone a few times. He was glad that he had confirmation that he was troubled by what was on it.

Then he reminded himself that he was here to get himself well, not Ethan.

Over her shoulder, Claire shouted to Kevin, "It was nice meeting you Kevin and thank you for all your help." As she quickly escorted her dad to his room.

Chapter 17. Taking Care of Business

Claire carried the box in one hand, helped her dad with the other and wished that she could turn her phone off by sheer will.

Agitation slowly ate at her while her phone vibrated in her pocket.

It was the sixth time that it had demanded her attention after her mother had stomped away from the common room.

She supposed that her mother's persistence should be something to admire, but she wondered how her dad handled all her mother's hassling and burdens.

Her dad's pace quickened, as he smiled and said, "I've got a surprise for you when we get to my room. "

Upon reaching his room, Phillip exclaimed, "Wow, that was nice of them."

"What was nice of them?" asked Claire as she put the box down on the nearest table.

Phillip answered, "Oh nothing much, they just made my bed."

Claire teased, "Is this the surprise?"

Phillip said, "No," as he sat on the bed and let out a weary sigh.

Claire joked, "What a beautiful hotel. Did they leave chocolate on the pillow?"

Phillip scoffed, "No, Dr. Pitney was very adamant about me not treating this place like a hotel. He informed me that I wasn't on vacation and that I'd have to deal with some hard things."

Claire said, "OK. Not considering what I just witnessed, how are you doing otherwise?"

Giving a heavy sigh and looking at the floor, Phillip said, "Well, I've only been here for two days, so you'd think there wouldn't be much to report, but what you've seen has been situation normal. Dr. Pitney and I don't seem to be getting along. I thought that he'd be the one person in this place who'd be dedicated to helping me, but he's a religious bigot, and I only make him angry. When he says that I've got to deal with 'hard things,' he means that I have to accept his views on religion."

Claire said, "I thought that he was a Christian. He seemed like one when we were in the ER."

Massaging his leg, Phillip continued, "Well, I don't think he is. But Mr. Abiel says that Ethan and I are a good help for each other."

Claire cocked her head and asked, "Who is ...," but her phone vibrated again.

Tired of the interruption, she retrieved it, turned it off and set it next to the box.

Phillip advised, "You really should answer that. We don't need to make things worse."

Unperturbed, Claire responded, "No dad, I'm not dividing my attention now. This is our time. Anyways, Who's Mr. Abiel?"

"A bigger help than Ethan is," Phillip ridiculed as he hobbled over to his cane, then made his way to the window and stared at the oak.

Claire stood next to him and matched his silence.

Looking at the oak, she considered how she never had taken any time to just stop and behold a tree. Solitude crossed her mind, spirit, and soul. Relaxing her as she slowly respected it standing against the wind and establishing itself amongst the cityscape

Her attention was broken, as her dad dropped his head and sobbed.

She contemplated on what she should do. She decided to give her daddy a hug as his vigor eroded.

Regaining composure, Phillip dried his eyes.

Claire looked into them, drowning in their weariness.

He finally said, "Besides Dr. Pitney, I've got a young woman who thinks I'm her plaything. Another woman, who seems to know me, shot me even though I don't have the earthliest idea who she is. My marriage is falling apart because your mom can't get past herself. I've had horrible nightmares and some guy with red eyes following me around. I'm afraid to ask what is next, because every time I do, something else happens."

Claire moved over to the bed and sat down.

Phillip whispered, "You're the first person I can talk to unguarded. I'm losing it, and I'm beginning to believe that I really do belong here. I don't know how much more I can handle."

Claire struggled with reconciling her daddy's earlier positivity about being God's ambassador and being where God wanted him, compared to him now. She replayed the list of his strife and wondered how she'd do.

Never seeing him this vulnerable before, she thought about how he only worked things out between him and God. Recognizing that him opening like this was a sign of his breaking point, she quietly prayed for strength for all the things that had been forced upon her.

Curiosity gripped her as a smile came across her daddy's face. She had never seen his manner change so quickly before.

He started searching his floor, as she joined him and asked, "What are we looking for?"

He looked in his bathroom and said, "It's the surprise I was telling you about. I've got a dog."

Still searching and not seeing any evidence of a dog, she asked, "You've got a dog. What type?"

Looking out into the hallway, Phillip replied, "She's a beagle with beautiful markings."

Claire struggled to find one dog hair. Knowing that beagles were a social animal, and wouldn't be hiding, she furrowed her brow. She feared that her dad was correct that he was beginning to lose it.

She answered, "Are you sure?"

She watched her dad's agitation grow as he breathed deeply and said, "Of course I'm sure, she was in the bed with me last night and snored the whole time."

She started to check the bed but remembered her dad saying that they had cleaned his room, including making his bed.

She checked for dog hair on her dad's clothes and came up empty. She began to think that her dad may have cracked and that she was looking for an imaginary dog.

Hoping against her fears, she asked, "Is she in here now?"

Phillip matter-of-factly replied, "I remember now. She's outside. Also, will you do me a favor? I'd like to get her a bed so she could sleep on her own, instead of mine. "

Flummoxed about the dog and not finding any evidence, she decided to go along with it and said, "So, you've got a dog, and it snores."

Phillip answered, "Yes. She snores when she's awake also."

Claire corrected herself, "And she snores when she's awake."

Phillip added, "It's the weirdest thing. I think she just wants attention when she does that."

Claire asked, "Has anyone else seen this dog?"

Not understanding the reasoning for the question, Phillip answered, "Yes, of course, others have seen Lilly."

Claire ruminated about the man stroking his imaginary cat and grabbed her dad by his shoulders and asked, "Dad, I'm worried about you. Are you sure that you're going to be all right?"

Phillip abandoned his search and gazed down at the floor.

She could see that he was mulling things around in his mind, and decided to help by saying, "Dad, I'm here for you."

He finally answered, "I see a gun every time I close my eyes. I don't remember a Tracy that I'd know. The only thing I know about her is that she knew your uncle and that she felt justified enough to shoot me. I have prayed to God, but I don't get an answer."

Claire encouraged, "Daddy, don't give up."

Phillip continued, "It's frustrating. I know God wants me to help others but being here I don't think that I can. I know that I should be concentrating on getting well, but I feel so guilty only thinking about myself."

Claire replied, "Daddy, it's all right to take care of yourself right now. You need to get well so you can be a better help to others."

Phillip replied, "Yes, but Jesus was taking care of others while he was on the cross."

Claire snapped, "Daddy, you aren't Jesus. You've got to take care of yourself before you can be a help to anyone else. You've told me about the verse that said we should deal with the plank in your own eye before dealing with the speck in someone else's."

Phillip interjected, "But, I'm a minister of ..."

Claire interrupted, "Dad, you're not above needing help. Do you remember telling me that dealing with the plank would make me humbler and able to empathize with the person after I had examined myself."

Claire felt she should stop, but saw her dad sit quietly so she continued, "You told me fools were everywhere and that I was to not become one of them, but to always pursue God even when it doesn't make sense."

She knew that her words hurt for a moment, but he knew that it was for his good ultimately.

She resumed, "Dad, I agree that you're a victim, but don't just sit by the pool waiting for the angel to stir the water but listen to Jesus' voice. Do what he says and seek His comfort and not the comfort of the world. He will be your defense.""

Then she heard him whisper, "Do you want to be well?"

She cocked her head.

He continued, "The man at Bethesda. Jesus asked him if he wanted to be well."

Claire watched her dad physically shake and asked, "Are you OK?"

Phillip answered, "I'm all right, it is just from the confirmation I just had. You talked about the man at Bethesda at the same time I thought of the same thing."

Claire cautiously answered, "OK?"

Her dad's whole demeanor changed; his downcast face became uplifted.

Taking her hands, he said, "Please don't take this the wrong way, but I'm surprised that I'm hearing this from you because you're usually the headstrong one and quiet about your faith. I would've expected it from Naomi, but not you. I'm so glad that God has made your faith deep.

Unruffled, Claire gripped her dad's hands for emphasis as she said, "Daddy, I understand that you're letting God be your defense. Trust me! I understand. But I always remember you telling me to learn something about Him while he does. To make an altar of remembrance like they did in Abraham and Moses' time."

Trying to search for the words, she grabbed her phone to ensure that she said the quote exactly.

Turning her phone on, it chirped and buzzed notifying her that she had several voicemails and text. She perused one text and then looked at her dad as she joshed, "You don't want to know."

Ignoring the rest of the notifications, she found what she was looking for and said, "All right, I want to read it exactly as you said it. You ready?"

Phillip joked back, "Well, If I said it and you wrote it down, it must have been profound."

Claire read, "'Everything I endure is to shape me in the image of Christ.'"

She gave time for his words to permeate. She supposed he was struggling with that truth again. However, the atmosphere was interrupted by her phone giving another notification.

Her dad gave a knowing nod, as she powered it off and put it in her pocket

He said, "You know, she can be ignored only for so long. Trust me! I know."

Then she saw her dad's countenance change again. His face contorted, but she didn't understand what was going on in his mind.

She felt she was done but felt urged to continue. So, she said, "Dad, you're broken, and you're trying to be strong, but let your weakness show God's strength. Let Jesus mold you to be more like Him. Let Him make you holy, as He is holy. You can't do it any other way."

Phillip angrily protested, "I am!"

Surprised at his outburst, she paid attention to him covering his mouth. She smiled and nodded as she waited for him to work out his shame.

She observed him bowing his head, as he said, "O'er and O'er."

He then lifted his head, and with calm control said, "I'm listening, please continue."

She asked, "What is o'er and o'er?"

Smiling, he answered, "It was the song that was playing when I was shot. For some reason, I just chose it to calm myself down. It also reminds me that everything you've said hasn't been something I haven't known, but it was some things that I needed reminded of again. Hence, o'er and o'er."

Claire not missing a beat said, "All right, let's continue. You need to deal with surviving. We both know that God didn't keep you here on Earth without a reason. Please take this new lease on life and use it, but also take some time and be still and quit hiding behind the God of your understanding. You need to come to grips with God again, seeking not only God from yesterday but today and forever. God is always the same, but our understanding of him changes. Also, don't be like some who get angry with God, asking why He let things happen or selfishly asking why He allowed it to happen to them. Please, deal with the events in your life and ask for His new word."

Frustrated, Phillip blurted, "But, He's been silent."

Claire pursed her lips, waiting to see if there was more. After allowing an awkward pause, she assumed she had consent to continue.

She admonished, "Dad, I've heard you tell others that they may have run ahead of Jesus and not learned what he is teaching them. So, they had to go back to the last thing that God's told them and to understand it deeper. God doesn't get us over things, but through them."

Phillip pleaded, "Claire, it's been hard, I can't do this anymore."

She wanted to quote some Bible verses at him, but decided to say, "Dad, let Jesus make your burden easy. He's on the yoke with you; carrying the load with you. You must let Him guide you. Let Him do the work. Let Him take this time to teach you again."

Claire felt a peace wash over her.

Then she was amazed to see her dad have a tear fall to down his cheek as he said, "I'm so thankful that you didn't tell me to be stronger. You don't know what it has been like to hear that freedom comes from resting in Jesus, instead of from the world or from within.

Calmness and peace comforted Claire, as sat down by her dad and started to pray.

"God, I thank You for saving my daddy. Please help him to get well. I have faith in You and know that You can do all things. Please show Your love to him, more than You've done before. You tell us to cast our cares, worries and anxiety onto You, and I pray that you will reveal Yourself and help us to see You working. Thank you for not letting my daddy die.

Amen."

She saw her dad look up to heaven as he prayed,

Jesus, I receive this prayer. I'm in awe of the work that You are doing with my daughter. Please keep her willing to be Your child. I'll treasure this time with her always. Thank you.

Amen"

She helped her dad up and onto his bed, as she wiped her eyes and then stood up, straightened her clothing just as her mother would and began giving a status report like she'd give at work.

She saw her dad smirk, as he said, "I'm amazed on how you could switch tact so easily."

She informed, "OK, quick update for work. Our website has been updated, and we've released press statements letting everyone know that you're alive and well. We've answered many letters from well-wishers, handled trolls who said they wished you had died and have dealt with several whose faith was shaken because they had put their confidence in you instead of Jesus.

What the press doesn't know about is you and mom being separated, and you being in this hospital.

I believe we need to get a statement out about your mental health before someone else finds out and reports about it.

About you and mom, I believe y'all will get things worked out. I don't need another press fiasco who had a field day with mom's comments about your suggested sexual relations with Tracy.

About Tracy, I've been dealing with a lot of speculation about you two. I've stated that you have no recollection of her and don't understand why you have been singled out. I feel a statement about you trying to understand the truth about who Tracy is. Then I'll pad it with something like 'We will let the world know when more information becomes available.'"

After shotgunning the report, she took a deep breath and gave a pregnant pause so Phillip could speak.

He answered, "Well, I figure that Tracy's lawyer is placating to the press and that my silence gives their voices more strength. I don't want my good to be spoken evil of because of my silence, but honestly, I have no answers nor defense.

How can I prove that I'm the victim of one person's actions; when I feel that the world is ready to swallow me completely. Not because of my conviction, but because of their speculations.

So, tell the press that I'd appreciate some time to work things out. That I'll give answers when I'm satisfied with the truth."

Trying to keep her calm, she wasn't satisfied with her dad just repeating her with different words. So, she pressed on saying, "Dad, some believe that this is the beginning of attacks on Christianity. From hearing people talk, you'd think that some believe that non-Christians have pet lions at home hungry for us. Others think that you're just like the rest of the 'hypocrites' and that it is a sex scandal. A statement needs to go out before someone says they have had your love child."

Her dad raised his hands and voice, "I don't know. Why is that so hard for anyone to understand? I don't know."

Putting her hands up in defeat, she said, "OK, we will just tell them that you are trying to work it out. It'll just have to be good enough."

Blushing from his sudden outburst, he flustered, "I'm sorry. I didn't mean to take anything out on you. It's just that I'm angry with myself because of this exact reason. I'm scared because there is too much I don't know. I don't know anything about Tracy. It feels like she's in control and has all the answers. I don't know what is going on between your mom and me. I don't know if Ethan is a help or hindrance. All these things have challenged me to the core. I don't doubt God, but not knowing all these things makes me wonder about what I do know about Him. I feel like the enemy has won."

Claire said, "Maybe Mr. Pitney can help?"

Phillip shrugged his shoulders, "Maybe, but I don't trust him. We don't have the same foundation."

Claire said, "Dad, he's helped others. At least let him try."

Phillip replied, "Yeah maybe."

Claire got up and gave her dad a hug, "Well, I've got to go. I love you, daddy."

Phillip asked, "So, you were going to leave without me opening the box?"

Claire released Phillip from the hug and said, "Oh yeah, I completely forgot about it."

Bringing the box to the bed, Claire said, "It's the things that you had on your desk."

Phillip opened it, finding his Study Bible, concordance, a hoodie, and slippers.

Then he jumped up as best as he could and grabbed a stack of letters for Jessica. He gave them to Claire and said, "Please give these to your mom."

Surprised at the thickness of the stack, she raised her eyebrow and asked, "All of these are for her?"

Phillip replied, "Yes, and please remind her that what she saw wasn't what she thought it was. If your help to her is the same that you've provided for me, I know that your mom is in good hands. Thank you for what you are doing. I know I haven't given you an easy task."

Taking her phone out of her pocket, she asked, "How many messages do you think I have now?"

Phillip silently shook his head and shrugged his shoulders.

Claire hugged her dad again and said, "You're welcome, and you're understating the task you've given me. Please pray for mother and me."

She turned to leave, and her dad closed the door behind her.

***

Silence filled the vacuum after Claire left.

Phillip enjoyed it, but the moment faded as the slight ringing in his ears reminded him of the shooting. The weight of being alone, made him think about being the only Christian.

He sat on his bed and sighed, trying his best to not lose his mind.

A knock on the door broke the calm as Mr. Abiel peaked his head in.

Lilly nosed her the door the rest of the way but stopped short because of the leash.

Phillip stood, glad to see them.

Mr. Abiel let the leash off Lilly and said, "She came straight here from being outside. You've been adopted."

Phillip opened his arms to receive Lilly, but after she was released from the leash, she bolted and ran straight past Phillip and to the last place her food bowl was.

Phillip looked at Mr. Abiel, and said, "Well, I see where I rank."

He went to his bathroom and retrieved the dog bowl and put some food in it.

Mr. Abiel said, "Yeah, my children do the same thing. They look for what I can give them instead of just loving me for who I am."

Phillip said, "Speaking of children, you just missed my youngest. Claire was here."

Mr. Abiel replied, "I bet she is just like you."

Phillip smirked, "Yeah, but she is her own person too. She surely surprised me today by revealing that she listens to what I say as she repeated it back to me."

Mr. Abiel replied, "Yeah mine surprise me a lot also. I like when they take the love, I have for them and share it with others."

Phillip and Mr. Abiel sat looking at Lilly while nodding in agreement.

Mr. Abiel continued, "There are times when they do take the words I have said and throw them back at me. They intend to hurt me, but I know they just don't understand what I meant. They usually remember my love for them, return, and we work things out."

Phillip chuckled, "Yeah, I remember one time when Naomi thought I said that she was ugly. I meant that she was being ugly to her sister, but it was a hard time trying to get her to understand. It's hard being a Dad and letting them know what they did was wrong. But I do it because I love them."

Mr. Abiel agreed, "Yeah, things can get lost in translation sometimes. I pray they know that I continually love them. And that I am always there for them especially when they are hurting. I just want them to know that I am accessible for them."

Phillip asked, "So, how many kids do you have?"

Mr. Abiel thought hard and said, "More than I can …."

Distracted by Lilly moving her bowl around, they both observed her checking to see if she had overlooked any more food.

Satisfied that she hadn't missed anything, she perked her ears up and studied them. She came over and sniffed to see if they had more for her.

Phillip replied, "Silly dog, you're only looking for more than you already have had."

Mr. Abiel produced a rawhide treat.

Lilly sat down with her tail swishing the floor.

Mr. Abiel gave a hand command and Lilly rolled over.

Phillip was impressed that she knew how to do this and said, "What else does she know?"

Mr. Abiel gave other hand gestures that had her dance, chase her tail, shake and roll over.

Pleased, he gave her the rawhide as she went to a corner and loudly gnawed on it.

Mr. Abiel turned and asked Phillip, "So, what else did you and Claire talk about?"

Phillip responded, "Well, she's also my PR person, so we spoke about how I should respond to the public. I've always disliked how evil prevails through gossip and speculation. It seems that society desires celebrities to mess up, so they can gossip about them and not feel that bad about their own lives. They don't seem to want to witness anyone doing well."

Mr. Abiel asked, "So, what I hear you saying is that you've got a PR person so your good won't be spoken evil of?"

Phillip nodded in agreement and said, "Yeah that is it. It's like you personally have to broadcast what good that's being done. I had a friend of mine that said, 'Live your life in such a way that people have to make up stuff to discredit you."

Mr. Abiel asked, "So, is that what is happening with you right now?"

Phillip answered, "That's what's bothering Jessica and Claire right now. They both are worried about what other people think. One because it's their job and the other because that is the way she's always been."

Mr. Abiel asked, "OK, so what is happening with you right now?"

Phillip sighed and answered, "I don't know, I think I'm struggling with figuring out what was going on in Tracy's and Jessica's minds."

Mr. Abiel asked, "About what?"

Frustrated, Phillip continued, "Well, that's what Claire and I were talking about. I don't recall anything about Tracy. I don't understand what's going on with Jessica and me. I can't identify why Ethan is so antagonistic against me. I can't determine why I am here?"

Mr. Abiel jested, "Maybe, you're here so you, and I can have these talks."

Shrugging the comment off, Phillip construed, "Yeah, maybe. I just don't feel any closer to any answers. I feel farther away from God and more worthless."

Shaking his head, Mr. Abiel said, "Maybe 'I don't know' is an opportunity for faith."

Turning the word around in his head, he had to admit that he currently regarded faith as unobtainable. However, the simplicity and the depth of Mr. Abiel's statement made him consider how yielding to faith would look like in all his circumstances?

A liberation inundated him when he meditated on how trusting and believing in God was an opportunity.

Claire's rebuke about being mad at God because things had happened to you personally washed over him. He thought about Bible characters who did awesome things because they chose faith when they had the opportunity.

Chastened, he bowed his head.

Mr. Abiel resumed, "When God is the only one you can depend on, isn't that a good place to be?"

Phillip tried to form a reply, but the truth of the statement resonated in his soul and chipped away at his being.

Knowing that he heard the truth, questions flooded within. Had he put this whole situation in faith? Into God's hands?

Being crushed by all the recent events, he admitted that depending on God was his only option.

Defeated, he understood, "Oh, how I've failed."

Lifting his head, Phillip asked, "What am I called to do?"

Mr. Abiel answered, "That's a better question than all the anxieties you've had about the shooter, your wife, and Ethan."

Phillip agreed, "You're a wise person. Thanks."

Mr. Abiel humbly bowed and took his leave.

***

Claire knocked on Ethan's office door, stuck her head in and saw him quickly putting his phone down.

Ethan greeted, "Claire, how may I help you?"

Claire said, "Thank you for your help on such short notice. I trust my daddy is in good hands."

Ethan answered, "Absolutely."

Claire asked, "Do you mind if I ask you a question?"

Ethan answered, "Sure, I think you already have."

Claire asked, "Who is Lilly?"

Ethan asked, "Why do you want to know?"

Claire asked, "Just tell me that she is real?"

Ethan answered, "Some patients have imaginary friends, some cradle dead babies, some like butterflies. Some have a dog."

Furrowing her brow, Claire waited for more of an answer, but nothing came, so she left his office and prayed that Jesus would protect her dad.

***

Knowing that he didn't answer her question 100%, Ethan justified his prevarication, because he did say 'Some have a dog.' Even though he didn't specify real or not.

Chuckling to himself, he went back to meditating on the text on his phone and his smile turned to sorrow.

Chapter 18. You Don't Care About Anyone
Else, But Yourself

Claire exclaimed, "Mother, will you watch the road," as she watched her mother with her hands in the air and singing along with her Bill Gaither/Imperials CD mix.

Wishing that she had driven, Claire tried to find the 'oh crap handle', but her mother driving was one of the stipulations for her to visit Phillip.

Flabbergasted that she had to bribe her mother to visit her own husband, Claire considered how she didn't know how to apply logic to emotions. She was tired of her mother crying and making things about herself.

She wanted to talk about their visit to her dad, but she was relieved that they weren't arguing about her turning her phone off anymore.

Jessica stopped singing enough to say, "I've driven longer than you have, so just settle down. Anyways, I'm not going that fast."

Then raising her hands back into the air, singing at the top of her range and driving with her knees, Jessica tested the limits of her inattention.

Claire gazed at the speedometer and saw that they were going 55 MPH on the interstate and said, "You being below the speed limit isn't what I'm worried about, not staying in our lane is what's driving me crazy."

Annoyed that she couldn't enjoy her praise music peacefully, Jessica looked at Claire and said, "I've been in the right lane the whole time."

Claire had to admit that she was right, even when she didn't get over into the other lane when someone was trying to merge on the interstate.

Claire replied, "Staying in the same lane does not constitute safe driving."

Having no reply, Claire knew that her mother had started to ignore her, so she began to fill in the blanks, "Why can't you be like your sister and just enjoy the ride while singing along with me."

She looked out the passenger's side window and snickered at a frustrated driver who was trying to merge onto the interstate. He summed up her feelings about her mother, but she knew that she wouldn't use that type of language.

She decided to pull her out her phone so she could do her devotional, but the proverbial elephant in the car wouldn't let her.

Putting her phone down and turning down the music Claire said, "Mother, let's talk about dad."

Jessica answered, "There is nothing to say. He is in the hospital getting the care he needs."

Claire shot back, "OK, let's talk about you then."

Jessica curtly said, "I'm all right."

Rolling her eyes, Claire said, "Mother, you're the furthest thing from fine."

Jessica cautioned, "I don't want to talk."

Tired of the evasiveness, Claire retorted, "OK, I'll talk."

She thought hard on several subjects but decided on a topic that she'd approach her mother about for years.

Breathing in deeply, Claire started, "If you don't want to talk about daddy, let's talk about Scott. About how you've talked to him more than you've talked to dad."

She started counting inside her head as she watched her mother's color change shades multiple time.

She got to nine.

Jessica brusquely replied, "He's just a good friend of the family," as she brought her hands back onto the wheel and turning the music back up louder.

Knowing that she had struck a nerve and that her mother was being evasive, Claire smiled as she reached over and turned the radio back down.

She started again, "Mother, let's talk about Sc ..."

Flying into an outrage, Jessica objected, "He's helping me through this trying time. He's being my rock and lighthouse."

Claire said, "So, what you're saying is that he's being a substitute for daddy?"

Infuriated, Jessica said, "Listen, young lady, when you're married then you can lecture me about this."

Claire shot back, "So, let's get Naomi on the phone."

Gripping the steering wheel, Jessica said, "He understands what I'm going through. He's been there for me many times before, and I thank God that he's here now."

Claire countered, "So, daddy hasn't been there for you, and he doesn't understand what you're going through?

Jessica burst out, "That isn't what I said."

Claire corrected, "So, daddy hasn't been there for you, and he doesn't understand what you're going through as much as Scott does?"

Indignantly Jessica responded, "You make it sound like I'm having an adulterous relationship with Scott! We haven't done anything wrong. We're just friends, and that's it."

Shocked at the strength of her mother's response, Claire answered, "Mother, I'm worried about your relationship with daddy. You're abandoning him, and I'm doing what you should be doing."

Jessica pulled the car over onto the side of the road. With tears streaking through her makeup, she glared at Claire and asked, "Why are you doing this?"

Astounded, Claire repeated, "Why am I doing this?"

Rolling the words in her mind, Claire only found blame within the question. Amazed at her mother's mentality, she tried to figure out why she was to blame.

Claire noticed that they'd parked in front of the dam as she absentmindedly observed traces of water streaming from the dam.

She then followed the stream and then studied that the vegetation around the river the dam fed was dying. She wondered how much was ruined because of the flood that was being held back.

Knowing that she was stating the truth, Claire contained her frustration because she was unarmed against the tears. She speculated on if her mother used her tears as a weapon instead of defense.

Setting her eyes on her mother, Claire determined to get past her mother's excuses and attempts to sidestep all issues.

Claire beamed as she recognized that it was just her and her mother. There was no referee to interfere and no one to shelter her.

Gathering her courage, she began, "Mother, you're too busy being hurt to not see the hurt that you're causing others. From my standpoint, you don't care about anyone else but yourself. You …"

As Claire faced her mother, she looked into her eyes and stopped her rant because she knew she'd lost her attention as she gazed into their void.

***

"YOU DON'T CARE! You don't care about anyone else but yourself. Don't you know you aren't the only person in this family?" Jessica heard her dad fume with narrowed eyes.

Stomping her foot, Jessica snapped, "But Jeannie got to go to the prom and get a new dress. Why can't I?"

Through clenched teeth, her dad responded, "Yes, but things were different then. I had a job, your mom was still alive, and we weren't scraping by trying to make ends meet. We can get your sisters dress refitted for you."

Outraged at the suggestion, Claire answered, "Jeannie's dress is two years old. I want my own dress."

Her dad looked at the mantle at the last family picture taken with his wife and then looked at Jessica, "I wish things were different, but they aren't. One day you'll understand that having a house over your head and food on the table is more important than a silly dress."

Jessica snapped, "It's not a silly dress."

Her dad snapped back, "Jess, you knew that this prom was coming for a while now. Where did all the money go from your babysitting jobs?"

Jessica's pupils narrowed and eyes bulged as she tried to get her mind wrapped around the change of events. She exclaimed, "What!?! You want me to spend my own money. Jeannie didn't have too, why should I?"

Her dad replied, "I'm doing the best I can, and a brand-new dress isn't happening."

Jessica looked away from her dad and with tears streaming down her face said, "Your best is not good enough."

Her father took a deep breath, looked away and unclenched his jaw. Spending time settling down and gathering his thoughts, he said, "I've had enough of this. Young lady, you're coming dangerously close to not going to the prom at all."

Jessica furrowed her brow, crossed her arms and retorted, "Well, it'll be all your fault."

Waving his finger under his daughter's nose, Jessica's dad said, "Listen, I've given you many ways we can work this out. If none of them are good enough, then you come up with a better solution."

Jessica's tears began to flow as she started to bury a part of her childhood. Not wanting to acknowledge there was any other solution she screamed, "IT'S NOT FAIR! Why are you doing this?"

Her dad responded, "Who said the world is fair? Someday, you're going to look back and see how much you have."

Without thinking, Jessica said, "One day, I'll have so much that I won't have to look back."

***

James sat in the driver's seat of his car. He was pouting because she had rejected him again. He looked out of the foggy windows and muttered, "You don't care about anyone else but yourself."

Jessica lifted the handle to erect the passenger's seat and looked out her window, "That is not true, and you know it. You just want too much."

She was exhausted from having this conversation with James, she could almost recite it back to him because it was the same way every time: "A man has his needs.," "Everyone else is doing it," and her all-time favorite, "You know you want it too."

Drawing in her breath, she looked over James' direction and waited for him to start.

She watched James sulk as he sought to find another angle. Wondering how long he would be, she got tired of waiting and decided to cut the tension and said his name.

Upon hearing his name, James said, "Jeez Jes, Annie would do it. She told me you'd be a prude and that you'd drive me crazy."

She knew Annie liked James, but James had asked her out to prom and not Annie. So, her and Annie's friendship dissolved because going to the prom as a sophomore meant more to her than Annie did.

Not knowing how to respond, Jessica's eyes welled up with tears as she said, "Why are you doing this?"

James answered, "Are you serious? It's because you only care about yourself. I need someone who'd care for my needs. I wish I had picked Annie."

With her dad isolating himself by a drunken stupor every night, he had left her to fend for herself.

Tired of cleaning up after their drunk father, Jeannie escaped from them both to an out of state college. Too busy, she didn't come home for the holidays.

Alone, Jessica desperately wanted to feel the love that she supposed that she was missing. After all, society said that everyone had the right to happiness.

Looking into his eyes, she evaluated if she could trust him.

Kissing her on the lips, neck and then her shirt line, he peeked up at her and smiled.

Despondent, she smiled back as she permitted his hands to track downwards.

She gave up, gave in and gave herself away.

Two weeks later James started to go out with Annie.

***

"All right! Places," the director said as he clapped his hands and sat in the pew.

Jessica and her father decided to give church a chance. Her dad had been rehired at his previous job and took it as a sign that things were looking up again, so he decided that they'd go to the church where her dad's AA meetings were.

She was elated he had been sober for 5 months.

She had met new friends, but she kept them at a distance because they could find out what she'd done with James that night in the car.

She thought of the irony of wanting to talk about what happened, but not wanting to talk about her thoughts.

She heard about Jesus in Sunday School, but her new friends taught her more about how to play church or how to be excited about the latest Christian fads. She was amused at how the "church" world wasn't that different from the rest of civilization. There was henpecking, gossiping and slandering just like the real world

She had to admit that everyone wasn't that way and that some did take God seriously; except for when they didn't get their way.

She didn't notice it that much personally until she got the lead and solo in the next church play: "Playing Christian."

The director had heard her singing in the church hallway and asked her to try out for the lead part. She was surprised that she got the role as much as her friends were. However, that was when the whispering started. Grumbling about her dad's sobriety and how she got the part out of pity. Murmuring about how she was stuck up and wouldn't talk to anyone.

The irony was that she was living the lead part in real life.

Her character was the new person at a church, the youth group was separated into cliques, and she was alone among God's 'children'.

It dealt heavily with the subject that we should love others as we love ourselves.

Her solo gave her a chance to speak her mind. It was a sassy song called, "You Don't Care About Anyone Else, But Yourself. "

She still remembered the chorus.

> You say that you care. But you don't take a chance to be fair.
> You say that you love. But you just push and shove.
> Trying to get to the top. When will it stop?
> You Don't Care About Anyone Else, But Yourself

Jessica knew that the play wasn't Broadway material but within its hour showing the play's youth group discovered that Jesus loves all and that they all have failed in showing His love to others.

The youth group leader did a study about cliques, and it opened the hearts of the group. They accepted Jessica in the group, and the group became more open to new people

The rest of her high school career, the youth group became her family that she needed. They taught her how to worship in the Spirit, how to pray when no one was looking and how to pray so you can keep up your appearances.

She unknowingly was still playing the part in the play: She learned all the words, she looked the part, and she was the center of attention. She got too good at playing Christian.

***

Sitting in class and thinking about how much she loved her sophomore year in college, Jessica felt like she had a new lease on life.

She tried not to become so jaded, as she thought about her dad looking for answers in the bottom of a bottle again and having lost his job.

Recently, her dad had asked for her help, but being exhausted from being his surrogate wife, she told him that he'd gotten what he deserved and that it was time for him to start taking care of himself.

She completely understood why her sister didn't often visit while she was in college and decided that she didn't want to have to take care of anyone else again and that it was her time to be taken care of.

Barely paying attention to class, she heard Ms. Johnson ask, "So, what can someone tell me about the Nacirema people?"

Jessica loved her Folklore class, more than any other she had taken thus far. She especially enjoyed Ms. Johnson because she carried herself like a someone you wouldn't want to trifle with.

Mostly, she loved Ms. Johnson's sense of fashion.

Her clothes were a lesson in irony itself, there were soft and sharp, comfortable and elegant, close and supercilious. She mostly wore Victorian shirts with flaired cuffs and a vest. Her jewelry was simple and never overpowered the rest of her wardrobe. She always ensured her clothing was tidy and had no wrinkles.

Jessica emulated her teacher's style more than what other college girls were wearing.

But it wasn't just her fashion sense that she sought to imitate, she also revered how Ms. Johnson carried herself. She was thoughtful, but firm. She didn't carry her passions on her sleeve and always forced people to back up their beliefs.

Jessica's biggest hindrance in imitating Ms. Johnson was trying to keep the facade up when her emotions erupted to the surface.

Ms. Johnson asked, "Why do we concentrate on diversity over similarities?"

The other reason that Jessica loved this class raised his hand.

Ms. Johnson acknowledged Scott.

He answered, "I personally think that we justify our decisions and behaviors because we think we're all the same. When we all come from different cultures and see the world differently.

But to your point, we also concentrate on our diversities over any similarities that we may have, because we all want to feel unique. Unfortunately, that leads to conflict.

This is demonstrated when we're at war with different cultures. We demonize them and give them different names, so we don't have to acknowledge that they're just like us, a child of God that is in need of a Savior. That our main similarity is that we're all sinners that ..."

Cutting Scott off, Ms. Johnson rolled her eyes and corrected, "Thank you, Scott. You're correct to a point. Please remember that everyone doesn't ..."

Not listening to Ms. Johnson any further, Jessica gazed at Scott and decided he was the type of man she liked.

From the first time she had met him, she was captivated by his devil may care attitude and his assuredness in his beliefs. However, she didn't appreciate that he wanted to be a rock 'n' roll star and that he spent most of his time as the worship leader for the college's Bible study group. She wished that he didn't have such strong beliefs and that she didn't have to share him with his groupies.

Not having been to church since she had left home, she decided to go to the Bible study group to spend more time with Scott.

Spending almost every waking hour together, she was weary of him saying that he enjoyed her company and their talks, but never getting a clue.

Tired of waiting, she confronted him, "Why don't you like me?"

He smiled and said, "I do like you."

She listened as he reasoned around the subject. His explanation was that he had dedicated himself to God and music and that he wasn't looking for a heavy relationship with anyone but Jesus. He gave other excuses to alleviate himself from a relationship, like him enjoying her company but them not having common ground, and her not accepting Jesus as her Savior.

All she heard from him was that she wasn't good enough and the faint echo, "You don't care about anyone else, but yourself."

Still going to the Bible studies, she chased after him into her junior year, hoping that he would change.

Coming late to the Bible study one night, she had missed Scott's set and was surprised to see a new person teaching. Being late, she also had missed the introduction of the new speaker but learned that he was a student who had transferred in from out of state to finish his studies.

He shared about a mission trip in Mexico that had changed his life forever. He didn't talk about the Bible, and its stories like Scott had but talked about having a personal relationship with Jesus. He instructed that being a Christian means that you don't just acknowledge that Jesus exists, but that you have to live your life like you believe that Jesus is alive in you.

He also talked about God convicting him about not caring about anyone else but himself.

After hearing him say that phrase, she sat up in her chair captivated.

She shuddered as he gave testimony about how his mother had died and how his father turned inward.

She empathized when he revealed that he had pursued the wrong things in life and had only gotten hurt in return.

She identified with him as he explained about being a counterfeit Christian for so long, that he never really examined his self-centered beliefs.

Conviction overcame her when he testified that he worried more about how he appeared to others, instead of how he was playing make believe with God.

Putting her arms around herself, she felt that he was talking about her life.

Rage began to burn within her because she thought that he was unfair to others who didn't believe in God as he did. Then she realized that she wasn't angry with this new person, but with God.

She wanted to run away. She didn't want to look God in the face and Him see that she was mad at Him.

But her wrath of all the unanswered questions that she had had welled up to the surface and wouldn't be buried any longer.

She accused God, "How could You have taken my mother away? How could You have left me with a drunken father? "

The new person said, "Jesus offers to take all of our hurt, shame and pain," as she languished on if she could give it up.

She realized that she liked her hurt because it defined who she was. Without it, she'd have to come up with another reason to be angry.

She recognized that she had let shame define her, as she shielded her real self. That part of herself that she protected, but she knew that it was really exposed.

She embraced her pain because it was proof that she was still able to feel.

The new person pleaded, "Jesus wants us to be free. He said that His yoke is easy and that His burden is light. He wants to come beside us, take our burden, and carry it for us.

With all the technology that we have today, we don't see or understand yokes that often. Nevertheless, many years ago in order to plow a field, a farmer had to put two animals together to get more work done. The thing that would connect them together was called a yoke.

The yoke shows that Jesus is a servant with us.

You see, Jesus doesn't tell anyone to do anything by themselves because He isn't the farmer in this instance. He is the other animal working with us that is connected by the yoke. He is there carrying the brunt of the load with us. He is there to guide us and help us to keep our path straight."

She trembled as he said, "I'm sure that the Holy Spirit has already gone before us and has prepared some hearts for this message. Please know that You aren't alone, and that Jesus will really help you. He has really done all the work. All we have to do is accept Him as your Lord and Savior."

Battling within herself, Jessica had one part wanting to bolt and the other wanting to stay. She'd never had heard of Jesus being a servant, especially a servant that still serves today.

With tears welling up, she scolded herself for letting her emotions show. However, she couldn't help it because after hearing that she had to accept Jesus as her Savior, she realized she had never accepted his help or strength.

Epiphanies overwhelmed her as understanding flooded into her being.

Her thirsty heart had finally had a drop of water that quenched her deepest longing, and her soul wanted more.

A veil was removed, and she was surprised at the weight of it.

She wanted this more than a relationship with Scott or her father.

She felt Jesus next to her, and that He wanted to reveal more of himself than what she had accepted ever before.

Excited, she wanted to talk to someone.

She noticed that Scott was playing and that the new guy was giving an invitation.

She didn't go up to the front because the group already thought she was a Christian. Nevertheless, she went up after the study and met this new teacher and asked if she could talk to him more.

Seeing Scott up there, she was surprised that she didn't think about flirting with him.

Scott put his arm around the new guy and said, "Jessica, have you met my newest best friend!"

The new guy teased back, "Scott, we just met."

The new guy turned to her and said, "Nice to meet you. I'm Phillip."

Phillip and Scott explained to Jessica about salvation and the price that Jesus had paid.

Jessica was stunned to see Scott wiping tears from his eyes as she followed Phillip through the sinner's prayer and her accepting Jesus as her Lord and Savior.

All done, Jessica stood up and straightened her clothes and her hair. She was sure she looked like shit.

Catching herself, she thought that she couldn't talk or think that way anymore.

Looking past Scott at Phillip, she noted that he was shabbily dressed and thought, "He's not that bad, I'm sure that I can fix him."

***

Hearing the car door shut, Jessica poised to pounce.

Waiting, she looked around her and Phillip's one-bedroom apartment.

There was Phillip's desk, which was completely full of all of his books. The floor had baby toys strewn across it. The kitchen had sitting dishes, with a hamper full of dirty clothes in the corner.

Glimpsing out the window, she saw that he wasn't in the car any longer.

She took a deep breath, as she thought about not signing up to be a slave when she got married.

She heard Phillip fumbling with the lock and saw the lock twist.

Bedraggled, he finally came in with one of his gloves in his mouth, his hair unkempt and his shirt was untucked. Seeing Jessica, he managed, "Helwo wove" through the glove.

She stared needles at him as she imagined slapping his silly grin off him.

Phillip spit the glove out, continued smiling at Jessica and asked, "What, you don't have any love back for me?"

Jessica retorted, "Yeah, love you too," and then quickly started to whine, "There's nothing to do."

She left Phillip standing in the doorway, knowing that he was trying to figure out why she was angry.

He finally said, "Honey, we've talked about how this semester was going to be hard and that you should get together with some of the women in our Sunday school class. I promise you that things will change in two months when I'm done with seminary."

Defiantly, Jessica said in a slow terse tone, "I don't want their help. I didn't even want to move here. You dragged me out here away from all of my friends. Why should I make friends now when we are going to up and leave again in two months."

Phillip gave a heavy sigh, put his stuff on the desk, and started to clean the toys off the floor. Yearning to do anything else but argue with Jessica again.

Jessica keyed in on the sigh and said, "Yeah, that's right. We're going to have this 'discussion' again. I'm not here just to take care of you and Naomi. "

Jessica contained her outrage as she watched Phillip rub his eyes. She knew that he had been reading and writing papers and listening to lectures all day, but she did not care.

Plopping down on the couch, he said, "Honey, you knew that I was called to preach before you married me. This is part of it. This is just a season. We will be done soon, and then things will be better."

Jessica sat down, crossed her arms, and said, "I want you to help me more around the apartment. A little more help could not hurt."

Glimpsing that Phillip was settling in, she threw her arms up and said, "All I do is take care of you and Naomi."

Phillip reached over, put his arms around her and said, "Honey, that's not fair, this is what Jesus has called us to do."

Shrugging Phillip's advance off, she said, "You always hide behind Jesus."

Jessica watched the confusion on Phillip's face spread.

He mumbled, "Where else should I hide? What other defense do I have?"

As the argument progressed, Jessica began enjoying knocking down every defense Phillip had.

After an hour of being dumped on, Phillip hollered, "Listen, all I've heard from you is 'I,' 'me' and how your needs aren't being met. I could bring up how I'm the one who wakes up with Naomi so you could get more sleep because I'm already up doing homework. Or how I'm trying to finish seminary, work an eight-hour job, an intern at our church and try to devote time to you and Naomi before hitting the books. I just wish you …"

Then he stammered and settled on, "I think that you don't care about anyone else but yourself. I understand that it's hard right now. It's hard for me also, but we'll get through this."

He stood up, picked up the dirty laundry and moved it to the door. Putting his jacket and gloves back on, he turned to her and said, "If you don't mind, I'm going to do something productive."

Surprised that he had lost his temper, she wanted to let him leave. But she went to the catalyst of what had started her whole meltdown. Holding the note from Scott in her hand, she was angry that he had called for Phillip over her.

She stood in front of the door, holding a note out to him. She notified, "Well, Scott called about a gig that he had and wanted to know if you'd want to preach at it."

Taking the note in one hand and the dirty laundry in the other, he waited for her to move.

She stared into his dead eyes, as he moved forward and nudged her out of the way with the basket and walked out the door.

Nonplussed, she stared at the closed door as the headlights danced across the room.

She wondered if he'd ever come back.

As the darkness settled in, she cursed herself, "Why was I so … so …"

The words trailed off as she let the tears begin to fall.

Isolation settled in as she thought about her obstinacy.

She knew that he was guaranteed a job at the church that he was currently serving at and that they'd be able to spend more time together.

She looked at the door, wishing that he'd walk back in. She played the conversation in her head, realizing that she'd never heard Phillip raise his voice before. She was surprised that they hadn't woken Naomi up

Startling her out of her reverie, she heard the phone ring.

She picked up the phone and answered, "Hello?"

Scott kidded, "Well, Hello yourself. Have you been crying?"

Wiping the tears from her eyes, she lied, "No, I'm cutting an onion."

Confused by her feelings, she drove her argument from Phillip out of her mind, and said, "It's so good to hear your voice."

He asked, "So, did you pass the invitation to Phillip? We need an answer quickly. Also, this could be a long-term gig. This could be the thing he does till the day he dies."

She sniffled and said, "He said that he's got to pray about it first and then he would call you."

Scott cheerfully said, "All right! Are you sure that you are all right?"

She contemplated about telling him about her and Phillip's fight or about her slight feelings for him, but she settled on saying, "I'm just confused right now."

Scott quipped, "Aren't we all. Well, I've got to go. Whether the answer is yes or no, make sure that he calls me. Then I'll have a chance to make sure that he says yes."

Hanging up the phone, she fell to her knees as she let the tears freely fall.

Tired of sobbing, she decided that since she was on her knees, she might as well pray.

She whispered, "Father God, I don't want to ..."

Thoughts of humility, patience, and suffering in her own life engulfed her mind and caused her to stop.

Feeling her heart beating, she started again.

> Father God, everyone is right. I'm a disaster.
> I don't care about anyone else, but myself.
> Please help me to remember that Phillip is
> going through this with me also. Help me to change
> and learn to be a better wife and mom. Help me to
> be the help Phillip needs right now. Help him in the
> decisions that he makes for our family."

Trying to think of more to say, she felt spent and quietly said, "Amen!"

***

She beheld the maître d' as he sat them in a cozy corner booth. She was overjoyed that she and Phillip could be secluded together with candlelight and no kids.

She recollected how Phillip told her to get dressed up to go out, but she still felt under dressed at this place. She should have known something was up when Phillip put on a suit jacket without her asking him.

She looked into his eyes and wondered where the 20 years have gone.

Noticing that she had caught his eyes and that he was smiling back, she asked, "So, what made you pick this place?"

Phillip answered, "You're surprised?"

She replied, "Oh yes, very surprised."

Phillip answered, "Well, I'm afraid to admit this, but Naomi's boyfriend brought her here on their 6-month anniversary, and they told me that I needed to bring you here sometime. I thought that this would be a great 'sometime' to surprise you."

The waiter arrived, took their order and brought their food. She wanted to relish the moment and make it memorable, but time seemed to be rushing past.

She pleasured in sharing stories of their past years while they ate, but she really wanted to get past his buffers and know what he was feeling, although she knew that he'd never discuss things like that with her.

As if on cue, he began sharing his feelings, telling stories on himself and dreaming with her.

She was thrilled to have a conversation with him, not talking at or about things, but with each other. They laughed so hard that she thought they were going to get kicked out.

Phillip imparted, "Well, I was thinking about how the girls now having boyfriends. About how they better not ever lay a finger on them, because I've never done such a thing and ..."

Jessica's mind keyed on that statement, and she said, "Well, there was that one time."

He answered, "One time? What do you mean?"

She looked up from her dessert and saw that his whole demeanor had changed. Her stomach dropped as she met his somber stare, as she wished that she hadn't commented at all.

She whispered, "Well, I mean there was that one time that you pushed me out of your way when we were in that little apartment while you were in Seminary."

She noticed that he recollected the moment. Putting her fork down and her hands in her lap, she waited for his reaction. While waiting, she recollected on how they'd been enjoying themselves, and how they could recapture that moment. Maybe, there was something that she could say, but she knew that she'd said enough.

Searching for comfort in his eyes, she knew there would be no refuge there while he was exposed.

She cursed herself, then she reflected on why she was dismayed.

Comforted by her self-assurance that she didn't do anything wrong but speak the truth, she picked up her fork and continued enjoying their dessert.

Done with her half of the dessert, Phillip began with a measured cadence of calmness, "I didn't push you. I … I … I …" Phillip paused and took a deep breath and continued, "I remember that you were standing in front of the door frame, in my way and …"

"Phillip Ashby?" asked a middle-aged woman who disrupted them both.

They both turned to stare at her, Phillip with his stage smile and Jessica suppressing her disgust.

She watched Phillip hobnob with her, as she turned her attention to the rest of the dessert that she was relishing more with every bite.

She saw Phillip kindly decline the woman's request for an autograph, as she then asked for prayer for something. He took her hands and prayed with her. Then she just stood there after saying "Amen."

Phillip said, "Well, I hope everything gets better. If you'll excuse us, my wife and I are on our 20th-anniversary dinner and …"

Finally acknowledging her, the woman congratulated them both. She said to Jessica, "You've got a good man of God there."

Then she gave Phillip a quick hug and said, "Thanks for all you do. I'm so glad to have met you."

As she left, Phillip turned his attention back to her and said, "OK, where were we?

Jessica finished the last bite of dessert, wiped her mouth with the napkin, corrected her posture, straightened out any wrinkles, dusted off any crumbs and stated," You know what? I'm tired of me **and** Your Ministry **and** Your next book **and** your fans **and** the kids **and** whatever else."

Phillip looked quizzically and asked, "What?"

She continued, "Get rid of all the 'ands' and be with me. The only thing I want you to have before me is Jesus."

"What do you want from me?" asked Phillip.

Calming her hysteria, she said, "You never talk to me about what matters most to you. You'll talk about the kids, work, Jesus, but you won't let me in. You won't let me get past your defenses."

Then she watched him sit in his chair, brooding just like he does every time she brings up something serious.

Phillip finally broke the silence, "Every time I do, I feel condescended. I don't talk about personal things because I feel that I'll be cut by it later. I can't 'feel' around you because you've got that area covered and tell me that your feelings surpass mine. Honestly, I just don't trust you."

Jessica said through pursed lips, "Well, you just ignore me. You never take my side with the kids. You just come home from one of your trips and don't want to do anything. You say that you've traveled too much and that you just want to stay home. You say that you've eaten out so much, that you just want a home-cooked meal. Those are the last things that I want to do. You come home and don't care about anything else but yourself."

Phillip countered, "Well, OK, I guess I don't have anything more to say another than that I don't see things the way you do. "

Taking the bill, Phillip walked up to the front and paid it.

Following him out of the door and into the car, they both endured the silent drive home that communicated more than they did at dinner.

***

Aggravated, Claire kicked her feet up on the dash of the car. She had never seen her mother space out like this before.

Deciding to busy herself on the journal on her phone, she typed, "My whole family is losing it. God, you've got to help me to stay sane."

She tried to write more but figured that little bit sufficed.

In the corner of her eye, she saw her mother came out of her reverie.

Jessica looked at Claire and felt her heart fall.

She thought, "I wish I were dealing with Naomi instead of Claire."

Not wanting to start another argument, Jessica softly declared, "I don't know if I can handle all that is going on, you're going to have to be patient with me."

Claire turned towards her mother and calmly said, "Mother, this is hard on all of us. What helps me is redefining normal."

Not understanding her, Jessica tilted her head and asked, "Redefining normal?"

Claire continued, "Everyone has a normal state that they try to get back to. However, there are some life-changing events: like marriage, having a baby, moving out of the house. But redefining normal is where you cannot go back to that everyday state. We cannot act as if nothing has changed and that it did not affect us. We have to learn to make a new normal."

Jessica started the car and responded, "Claire that sounds like crazy talk."

Understanding that the conversation was over, Claire looked at the dam one last time before they left.

Looking back at the dam, she noticed that the stream of water was no longer running, but she detected the black streaks from where the water normally flowed.

Jessica turned her music back on, and Claire fooled around on her phone.

After having an uneventful drive back home, they both got out of the car, ready to have some separation between each other.

Gathering her stuff from the backseat, Claire came across the letters her dad wanted her to give to her mother.

Getting to the entrance, Claire handed the bundle to her mother and said, "Daddy wants you to have these."

Taking the letters, Jessica dropped her keys.

Jessica's anger at Claire rekindled because she couldn't believe that she didn't wait to get into the house to hand her the letters.

Standing next to the door, Claire waited for her mother to make this her fault somehow.

Claire gathered the keys and handed them to Jessica.

She was surprised that her mother unlocked the door, walked into the house and went straight upstairs without a word.

Jessica walked to her bedroom and closed the door with her foot.

Disturbing the dust next to her dusty Bible, she dropped the letter bundle down on her dresser.

She took out her phone and called Scott to get some sympathy.

Chapter 19. Shipwrecked/Group Therapy

Phillip awoke from his nap, wishing that this day was over.

Lying in bed, he wished that he had progressed towards getting better, but wave after wave of attacks had him retreating into weariness.

Lilly snuggled up against him, demanding him to not move.

Ignoring her, he sat up in his bed.

Drained from seeing those red piercing eyes looking at him as if he was mutton during sleep, he gently kicked his legs over and shivered as his feet touched the cold linoleum. Yawning, he wiped the sleepies away from his eyes.

Lilly put her paw on his leg, urging him to not move any further.

He petted her on her head and willed himself out of the bed.

Lilly stretched and licked her chops.

Tasting the dryness from the nap in his mouth, he cleared his throat a little and said to Lilly, "Yeah, I know. Me too."

Lilly rolled over on her back and wagged her tail as she waited for him to rub her belly.

Phillip hobbled to the bathroom, finished his morning duties, and then stared at the mirror. Thinking about the metaphorical log in his eye that he and Ethan spoke about, he became more depressed as he thought about how that had happened this morning.

He muttered, "This day has to end."

Phillip heard Lilly sneeze, jump off the bed, and then the clip clap of her nails on the floor.

He turned to see her stopped at the threshold of the bathroom door. Patting his legs, he tried to get her to cross the threshold, but no urging ever worked. He figured that she had a bad memory from when she had crossed it before, and had it etched into her behavior for life.

He put the leash on her as she started to dance around. Phillip grabbed his cane and took her out in the little garden area in the square the smokers used. He let the leash off Lilly and let her have a smelling party and time to do her duty.

He sat on the bench and was glad to have some solace to himself.

He tried to force himself to remember something new about Tracy. However, Ethan's odd behavior of reaching for his phone every time he spoke about Jesus and Christianity was at the forefront of his mind.

Phillip attempted to divert his attention to his and Jessica's problems, as he recalled bits and pieces of the dream he had during his nap.

He remembered weathering several waves and storms on a ship that he'd sailed familiarly on for years.

Then the ship's sails were caught out during a sudden storm, the mast was broken, and he was cast off the boat.

Desperately holding onto debris, he watched the storm set his boat adrift further away from him. Abandoned to the elements, his ship betrayed him as the storm surged and it floated away.

With hunger and thirst overtaking him, hope was hidden as the world moved around and below him ready to devour him.

He yelled at the world, "I'm still here!" while holding onto debris.

The only thing that hadn't failed him yet.

Coming out of his reverie, he decided this is how he wanted to be: facing the world while holding onto Jesus.

Nevertheless, his dream pressed on.

Screaming at the world had parched his throat, but he couldn't drink because all the water around him wasn't life sustaining.

He remembered praying for life-giving water as he was grieved that another storm was gathering.

However, he later rejoiced because the storm brought salt-free water as it also drove the predators deeper and away from him.

Then, his strength gave way from him as he lost his grip from the debris.

Sinking, despair wasn't dragging him down. It enveloped him to the point where he could not do anything except sink in it.

He recalled praying for something to lift him up, but only finding that he was opening his eyes to the same shipwrecked day.

Phillip came out of his reflection with Kevin and Frank arguing about the checkers game they were playing. Kevin had crowned his black checker with one of Frank's red checkers.

Frank cursed, "You're cheating."

Kevin argued back, "How's I'm cheating. I's only put a checker on top of mine and moved the checker in a legally crowned checker move."

Frank said, "You're cheating because you used my checker."

Kevin examined the checkered King and said as he switched the checkers around, "You's right, I did it wrong. I'm winning so my checker should be on top,"

Putting the crowned checker back on the board, he grinned at Frank and said, "OK, it's your turn."

Frank said, "I'm not playing until you start to play correctly."

Kevin replied, "What's it matter what color I use to King."

Frank began to shake as he bellowed, "It's wrong."

Kevin said, "Come on Frank. You know how it's with two sides of the coin. Let's ask TJ to get a second opinion."

Frank bellowed, "Let's keep TJ out of this."

Kevin looked at Phillip and motioned him over and said, "How 'bout Pastor Phillip?."

Phillip called for Lilly and put the leash back on her as he answered, "I'm not getting into this."

Walking back to his room and releasing Lilly from her leash, Lilly ran to her bowl and then back to him. She continued dancing around till he understood that it was food time.

Phillip filled her bowl and then saw Mr. Abiel at his door.

He gave a half wave to Mr. Abiel, as he heard him respond, "Peace to you friend."

Phillip replied, "Peace back at ya!"

A smile began to break, as he thought that there was perhaps some joy in this place.

Mr. Abiel said, "It's time for group therapy."

Phillip's anxiety convulsed within him as he thought about who was going to be at the therapy session. His mouth went dry as he considered if Ethan would be professional or make him a target.

Mr. Abiel said, "Don't worry, I'll be there if things get out of hand."

He asked, "How often do things get out of hand."

Mr. Abiel smirked and replied, "It depends on who shows up and what mood they're in."

Phillip still wasn't used to walking with a cane but managed to follow along.

They made it to the therapy room, and Phillip already wanted to get this over with so he could get back to his room and rest. He hoped that he could lie low and not make anyone angry.

Entering the room, Phillip was immediately overpowered by a citrus and pine disinfectant smell. Looking around, he saw nothing but a circle of metal folding chairs.

There were no windows and only one exit, which was the door that they had entered.

Mr. Abiel moved to a corner in the room and nodded to him, confirming that he wasn't leaving.

Phillip moved to a chair across the room, where he could see everyone entering, with Mr. Abiel over his right shoulder.

The next person to arrive was Mary, who came and sat right next to him.

She looked around the room, not acknowledging Mr. Abiel's presence and hiked her legs up under her chin.

After a few awkward moments, she asked, "So, are you doing better?"

Phillip noticed that he had missed the clock on the wall over the door and saw that he had 5 minutes to make small talk.

Out of all the people in the building, she was the one who unsettled him the most. Not wanting to be rude, he cared more for his self-interest than hers at this time and kept quiet with his eyes forward.

Still not getting the message that Phillip wasn't interested in talking, Mary continued, "I always get uncomfortable during these sessions. It seems to me that everyone is trying to outdo each other in their problems."

Thinking the same beforehand, Phillip agreed, "I know."

Not able to get his complete thought out, he was shocked by Mary resting her head on his shoulder as Kevin walked in with Frank at his heels.

Kevin took the other seat next to him with Frank taking the seat next to Kevin.

Frank still complained about how Kevin had cheated at their last checker game.

Phillip chuckled to himself a bit because he knew that Kevin was enjoying himself as he kept pushing Frank's OCD buttons.

Kevin jibbed Phillip in the gut in a "Hey, watch this" manner and called to Frank, "That special crowned king should have been able to do double moves."

Frank's blood rose up to his ears as he said, "There is no such rule."

Kevin leaned onto Phillip's shoulder and guffawed.

TJ emerged after Frank had settled himself back down from his frenzy. He turned to Phillip and said, "Oh how sweet! Mary's found someone to keep her company."

He stood and sat at a seat opposite of them in the circle.

Not wanting to give the wrong impression, Phillip shrugged his shoulder, giving an indication to Mary that he was going to stand.

He moved to another seat as TJ said, "Don't stop on my account. Or are you two having a lover's quarrel. Young love is so short."

Phillip saw Mr. Abiel carefully observing the whole situation.

Mary placed her heel on the floor and screamed at TJ. "Stop it!"

TJ jibbed, "Pastor P.A., don't worry. She'll get over you. From my understanding, she has already been over you."

Mary yelled, "Just stop it!"

Feeling awkward and wanting to remove himself from the hen-pecking, Phillip wanted to go get a drink of water. He knew that he should have come to Mary's aid but knew it would only encourage TJ even more and be misconstrued by Mary.

Catching Mr. Abiel's eyes, he saw that he was disappointed in his nonresponse.

Phillip averted his eyes from everyone and turned to the clock as he waited.

Ethan came in and took the seat right next to Phillip with TJ on his other side.

He asked Phillip with a sly grin, "Have you been any help to anyone?"

Phillip decided the question was rhetorical and didn't deserve an answer because he knew it was Ethan exerting his authority, so he kept his eyes on the clock.

Everyone quieted as Ethan cleared his throat to start the session.

Ethan opened, "Today's topic is about accepting the blame for what harm we have caused. Granted, others have harmed us, or we can shift the blame onto others, but I want everyone to be introspective and accept their responsibility. Each of you have different ways of coping with problems but remember we are here to get better and getting better means we do not have to have a narrowed view of life but should be open to all points of view. So, let's take this time and help each other by reasoning together."

Phillip was always amazed when his belief in God was considered a narrowed view of life and how he should be open to all beliefs when God is rejected as one of the beliefs. Having no right to his own faith, he felt like a bound and gagged prisoner who was executed or mocked for their convictions. He felt dazed from Ethan's seemingly open dialogue that had channeled the conversation to where he was sovereign and could dictate what truth was.

TJ interrupted, "Doc, what's all this shit about us all getting along with each other and remembering our differences. We all know that Pastor P.A. is new here because some broad shot him because he did what every other "real man" has done. Let's cut all the bullshit that you're sugarcoating. Personally, I'm glad that he's here because I have some questions for him."

Visibly irritated by the interruption, Ethan continued, "Well TJ, thank you for your thoughts, but if you don't mind, the topic we're going to concentrate on is not blaming others for what is your own fault."

Phillip deeply exhaled as he watched TJ dramatically wringing his hands together.

Ethan started to ask, "Ok, let's start with …"

But TJ blurted out, "Let's start with Pastor P.A. Let's have him tell us why a loving God would let such a bad thing happen to him? After all, this is a God who loves him. Right?"

Ethan attempted to impede TJ, but Kevin interjected, "TJ, you're a bully."

Glaring at Kevin, TJ answered, "Really? That's it. Doc, tell him how we're supposed to talk about what we've done and how we're not to blame anyone else."

Phillip believed that TJ had perfectly displayed what was wrong with hurt people trying to help each other. Simply that hurt people, hurt others.

They have no qualms about breaking the rules to show someone else's failing but request favor or political correctness when someone calls them out on their offense.

He thanked God for His grace that he still believed to be true.

TJ kept prodding, "So, Pastor P.A. what's the answer to the question? Does God love you?"

Phillip looked around the room, seeing that every eye was on him. Even Ethan leaned back waiting for his response.

He nervously chuckled to himself, knowing that TJ wasn't offended by what he'd done or said because he hadn't said anything to the group yet. But perceived that he was angry only because he's a Christian.

Phillip was familiar with TJ's type and was sure that he didn't believe that Jesus was real. He could only speculate as to why TJ was so offended if he thought that Jesus did not exist in the first place. Phillip didn't understand why one would spend so much energy being offended about what they considered a fairy-tale.

He also thought about Ethan's introduction and how he was confined by it. He did want to reason with everyone, but he didn't think that reasoning meant that you sacrifice your beliefs for being tolerant of all points of views.

Then his mind flipped to Ethan calling him a hypocrite and him not dealing with the plank in his own eye.

Paralyzed in thought, Phillip just sat there.

He came out of his fog once he saw TJ standup.

He stood over Phillip and snapped his fingers as he sarcastically said, "Hello, are you listening?"

Still standing in front of Phillip with the 'What are you going to do about it?' attitude, he addressed the rest of the room, "You see, he has no defense because he knows I'm right."

Phillip's blood pressure rose, but he was still speechless. He wondered where his incisiveness had gone. He was sure that it was stuck in the mire of 'Judge not', or the web of 'the plank in his own eye' or the quagmire of 'casting your pearls before the swine'. He desperately craved that his intellect to be freed from the stifling circles his mind raced on about.

Wanting to hyperventilate, he bowed and prayed, "Jesus, You are my defense, You are the judge, You are my helper, You are God. Please, help me."

Phillip watched as TJ's shadow shrunk back.

Looking up, he saw Mr. Abiel was in between him and TJ.

Phillip was glad that Mr. Abiel was so quick to do his job despite Ethan not doing his. He was also amazed at how Mr. Abiel could get TJ to easily back down.

With TJ glaring at him as he sat back down, Phillip didn't know what he had done to cause such a reaction.

Phillip observed TJ looking around at the group, seemingly proud that he had "put someone in their place."

TJ sucked his teeth and tilted his head. Then leaning forward on his knees, he squared up on Phillip again saying, "You aren't any different than any other Christians. You talk a big game until someone smacks you with the truth."

Phillip saw that TJ was about to stand up for an encore, but perceived that Mr. Abiel was ready to intervene once again.

But TJ only kicked his feet out and leaned back with his hands clasped behind his head, as he gruffed in a typical thug fashion and relented.

Several moments passed as no one said anything.

Phillip wasn't impressed with Ethan's facilitating skills. He thought that if he were leading, he'd be prepared for the incident that just took place between him and TJ, and ready to mitigate the silence. He couldn't fault Ethan entirely, at least had the presence of mind to have Mr. Abiel there.

Kevin cleared his throat as he broke the silence by saying, "I try my best to not blame anyone for what happened to my …"

Phillip tried to listen but was still not prepared to be a participant in this menagerie of indifference. Looking around the circle, he saw that everyone's mask was removed and that their faces carried all weight of their hopelessness.

He speculated on what his face was like. He was certain that it didn't convey the joy of Jesus.

Remembering that to get out of here he had to come down to some answers. He thought, "Tracy, Tracy, Tracy."

He paused.

Then he got irritated that he couldn't conjure up anything. He supposed that she blamed him for some sexual encounter that he knew he hadn't been responsible for.

Phillip thought about all the women he had been with before God had gotten a hold of him.

He reflected on heavy petting with several girls throughout high school. He loved the temporary good feelings that were there when he enjoyed their company but remembered how fleeting the pleasure was compared to the vastness of the guilt that followed.

Shame began creeping in, because he even called himself a Christian during this time but dismissed it because he knew that he was forgiven from them and God.

He remembered their names: JoAnn, Sonya, Destiny. He wondered if Tracy was a middle name for any of them. He thought of more: Yolanda, Jenny, Alice …

He heavy-heartedly sighed, "Alice."

Alice was the only one that he had sex with before marrying Jessica. He also remembered how much both wanted it. It was during a church mission trip to Mexico where they had found a way to get isolated and had sex. It only lasted 10 minutes, but he agonized longer.

He thought about how he felt when they finished. Alice had covered herself as quickly as she could, and she dodged him every time they came in contact.

That was the beginning of his confusion between his way and God's way. He knew that God's way was celibacy until marriage, but he couldn't get his sexual addiction under control.

He remembered that after being with Alice, he heard God's voice as clear as day. God said to him, "What are you doing? Don't you know that I love you more than this?"

Every sexual encounter he had done, lusted about doing, watched and read about had culminated to this moment. He had called it everything else but sin. However, when he heard God ask, "What are you doing? Don't you know that I love you more than this," he knew he was caught and judged for his sin.

He remembered trying to excuse himself because his introduction to sex was at an early age with his female cousins. They were put to bed together at night with the family thinking that nothing would happen.

That was the beginning of his shame and the battle that he had every time as he tried to not think about a woman in a sexual manner.

Now he had God asking him, "What are you doing? Don't you know that I love you more than this?"

He finally admitted to himself that he didn't know what love was or who God was either.

He called this the "Time when God got a hold of him," because he came to the realization that God had protected him this far even though he had jumped off His path into his own destruction. God's love had convicted him, but not with condemnation but with loving grace to restore him.

He knew that the Bible said that God is love. The more he examined himself, he realized he didn't know what love looked like. Consequently, he decided he was going to get to know God, not just his idea of Him.

He buried himself in the Bible and commentaries. He changed his ways and started to teach others how to love God and how to have a real relationship with Him. He went to each cousin and girl he had wronged and repented and apologized to them about his fault in their relationship. Some of them he was able to lead to a relationship with Jesus, some just accepted his apology, and some said they didn't think they did anything wrong.

Phillip breathed a sigh of relief as freedom from his sin had brought him joy again.

Then he tried again to think about Tracy.

He waited.

He fought between trying to prod his mind into action and clearing it to see if any memory of Tracy would surface. All he felt was suffocation by the void created by Tracy's actions.

Phillip silently prayed, "God, I need help."

He grabbed his cane and leaned his chin upon it as he tried to force himself to concentrate on Tracy. However, he was only able to focus on his leg aching. He was sure his was being psychosomatic, but he rubbed his leg trying to dull the pain.

Coming out of his stupor, all he heard was TJ ranting about God not being real and how everyone should come to this belief that God was for fools.

Phillip glanced at Ethan, not understanding why he hadn't stopped TJ from preaching his message, yet he knew that he'd stop him if he said the name of Jesus.

Phillip ruminated on how he was here to get well, and that Jesus could defend himself.

During his sideways glance, he was sure that he noticed that TJ had flashed a look at Ethan and that Ethan had given a slight nod of permission.

Suddenly, TJ stood and grabbed his shirt in his best imitation of an orator. He stared at him as he finished by saying, "Pastor P.A., If God existed and is all-powerful, he could make each of us well, but everyone here is still stuck in our misery."

TJ began pacing and gestured to the circle as he continued lectured, "Just look at us. Every person in this circle is suffering. Now, we could all be narrow-minded like you and follow the teaching of a homeless man just so we can set our mind at ease and say to ourselves that everything is going to be better."

Then he broke his lawyer characterization and began snickering. He said, "Who am I kidding? His followers just torment themselves with all of their impossible rules, which only serves to make them all the same brainwashed clones."

Bound up in his own troubles, Phillip just sat there aloof. He prayed that he could get his troubles taken care of so he could be a better witness. Looking up to heaven, he prayed that the Holy Spirit would intervene on his behalf.

TJ scoffed, "Hello Pastor P.A.? Do you have an answer?"

Wanting to inspect the room so he could gauge TJ's influence, Phillip glimpsed Mary's eyes and saw that she was looking intently at him. Phillip quickly looked away, and prayed, "God, please protect me from her." He stole another look at her and saw that she was downtrodden.

He pondered on how she was different from her first impression that she conveyed. He wanted to help her, but he was afraid he was in no position to help anyone. He couldn't add her to the list of problems he was dealing with.

Triumphantly, TJ claimed, "That's what I thought. He can't answer any real questions."

Phillip became so discouraged from all the distractions of his life.

He saw Mr. Abiel attempting to prod him into action, and he so desperately wanted to respond, but the Gordian Knot that passed as his brain was trying to unravel itself.

TJ continued, "Where was God when Frank's wife left him? Why did he let that happen, huh?"

Then TJ pointed at Kevin and asked, "Where was He when Kevin's son died, and his wife left Him? Why didn't he stop it?"

Kevin replied, "My son is a butterfly, and I see him every day."

Then pointed at Mary, he asked, "What about when she was raped and molested? Where was God then?"

TJ got in front of Phillip's face and said with spittle coming out of his mouth, "Where was He when you were shot and left for dead? Where's He now that your wife has left you here to rot with the rest of us?"

Mr. Abiel came over again and stood between the two men again.

Phillip's tears welled up from the weight of TJ's final questions. The knot tightened, as answers eluded him. He only thought, "Hurt people, only hurt people."

He glared at Ethan, livid from his inattention.

TJ walked away and sat back down. Pointing at Phillip, he said, "There's your man of God. Quiet and small."

Nevertheless, Mr. Abiel was standing in front of Phillip taking all the accusations and finger pointing.

* * *

Ethan dismissed the group and was cognizant of how TJ said the words and thoughts that he believed but was disconcerted after he had heard them said.

He stood at the door and then glanced back at Phillip. He wondered where the obstinate Phillip was at this moment. He was delighted to see Phillip humbled, but knew that the odds were in TJ's favor because of Phillip's brokenness rather than any other reason.

***

With cane in hand, Phillip ambled to his room with Mr. Abiel next to him.

Phillip quipped, "I felt like there should've been a prayer afterward, but everyone just got up and went their own way."

Looking straight ahead, Mr. Abiel asked, "Are you done feeling sorry for yourself?"

Phillip furled his eyebrows and asked, "What do you mean?"

Mr. Abiel continued, "God saved you from death, and you're just sitting around and not doing His work. You're still called."

Phillip stopped, wounded from the sting of the word "called."

Mr. Abiel stopped also and pronounced, "Are you going to stop right here at the threshold of healing? Are you still drifting around in your dreams? Are you smelling everything around you like Lilly, or is the smelling party in the square done? Are you going to complain about checker pieces or still live your life? Stop watching the clock, waiting for your time on this earth to be done. Stop being distracted and quit looking for the problem. You let God take care of all that. Engage and be what He has called you to be. You do what He says."

Phillip answered, "That's the thing. What's God saying? Why is God so far away?"

Mr. Abiel stopped and grabbed Phillip's shoulder. He looked into Phillip's eyes and said, "Do you know what your biggest problem is? It's that you're trying to be Jesus and that you want to be worshiped. Your wife is tired of placating to you. You don't think that people are doing God's work unless they do it your way. You think that everyone should care about what you have to say. You've been God's mouthpiece for so long that you aren't absorbing any of it."

Phillip's nostril's flared as he tried not becoming bitter to the one person who'd been his sanctuary here. After his mind had calmed down, he asked, "OK. What's God saying to me?"

Mr. Abiel countered, "You tell me. What did He last say to you?"

Instantly, a new memory from his last rally "Saving a Life" came to light as he answered, "That everyone needs salvation."

"And?" Mr. Abiel punctuated.

"That we are called to love all people, not just the ones like us," added Phillip.

"And?" Mr. Abiel continued to press.

Then Phillip remembered the rest of his sermon from that rally and said it aloud, "Jesus' request is that we come to Him with our hurts and shame, our past and failures, dirty and broken so He can wash us with His blood that He gave so freely. Then He reveals more of Himself to us as we follow Him. We just have to learn His ways and make Him known to others. All who believe that Jesus can save them will have everlasting life! Saving you was His plan from the beginning and is still His plan now."

Mr. Abiel then asked, "For how long?"

Phillip then thought about his last thoughts that dreadful night and awkwardly said, "O'er and o'er."

Mr. Abiel smiled and peered into His eyes as he remarked, "Get it."

Phillip cadenced "Got it."

Mr. Abiel turned around and said over his shoulder, "Sounds like He's still talking to you to me. Are you listening and doing?"

Watching Mr. Abiel walk away, Phillip didn't think about the plank in his eye anymore. He only felt rightly rebuked in Jesus' name

Part 6.

The Love

Chapter 20.   Turning the Corner

Exhausted from the therapy session, Ethan sat in his office. He knew that he'd enjoy TJ blasting Phillip's 'holier than thou' attitude, but he'd believed that Phillip would try to be a 'better help' for others than he did.

He was pained when assessing Phillip's performance. He wondered if he should appear with Phillip to see how well he was licking his wounds and to see if he'd like to have individual meetings again.

Relishing his victory, he packed up his stuff so he could go home. Then he saw his voicemail light blinking from his work phone.

Knowing that if he chose to not check his messages before leaving would keep him up all night, he listened, "Hey ... uh, Ethan. This is Champ ... I really need some help. Please call me soon."

He finished packing and left a message for himself to call Champ in the morning.

Escaping from his office, his conscience wore at him till he dialed Champ's number. He hung up before his 'Leave a message' spiel began.

Satisfied that he had made an attempt, his conscience was subdued.

Walking to the exit, he was amazed to see a gathering of reporters around his building's entrance door.

He knew it was bound to happen but was surprised at the amount of them. What also surprised him was that it took them so long to catch up with him. Considering that his book had been out about a month now.

He confessed to himself, "About time," as he checked his breath.

As a precaution, he went to the restroom, retrieved his fresh breath spray and tidied up.

Satisfied, he grabbed his briefcase and walked out into the midst of them.

Once outside, the reporters surrounded him while he tried to keep a calm demeanor.

As they all shouted their questions, he counted seven cameras from all the major networks and news services. The noise swelled over him, but the cacophony didn't allow him to make out what they were saying.

Trying to quiet them, he held up his free hand and the roar slowly dulled.

Clearing his throat, he began, "I'll try to answer all of your questions, but personally I'm surprised that it took you so long to find out where I've been. Y'all are some slow investigative reporters."

Letting out a nervous chuckle, he hoped that he wouldn't get the hiccups again.

Glad to finally have the spotlight he believed he deserved, he rambled, "To answer the first question that I heard. I've been here for several years helping many patients improve their lives by facing their inner selves by finding out that what they're holding onto isn't as severe as they think and that they need to release whatever it is that's binding them and work to become the better person they really are."

He justified his babbling because he was shooting from the hip. He thought that if they wanted a prepared statement, they should've been here a few weeks ago when he'd won his award.

Noticing that the reporters were quizzically looking at each other while holding their microphones and tape recorders out towards him, Ethan stood there awaiting the next question.

The reporter who asked the question that Ethan thought he had answered, gave his credentials and then asked, "Mr. Pitney, tell us how Preacher Ashby is handling your unique style of treatment."

The reporters' presence finally dawned onto Ethan that they weren't here because of his book.

Another reporter elbowed their microphone to the front and asked, "Do you have a comment about Preacher Phillip Ashby's condition?"

Angry and embarrassed, Ethan's temper began to color his face as sweat trickle down his neck. He was irritated that Phillip had overshadowed him again in the news.

Many words did circulate in his head about Phillip Ashby, but none of them were appropriate for an interview.

Liz's words rattled in his head also, "Don't screw this up."

He tried to form a response about Phillip's status, but he had to admit that other than diagnosing him, he hadn't provided any real assistance.

Ethan muttered to himself, "How can I help him?"

The reporter stated, "Sorry, Mr. Pitney, we didn't get that."

Turning his attention back to the reporters, they instinctively quieted down as Ethan reported into the closest camera, "I have no comment about the treatment of any of my patients nor can I confirm that Phillip Ashby is a patient of mine. To do so would be a violation of the doctor-patient confidentiality."

Ethan left them, as each reporter spun his statement into their story.

Walking to his car, he confessed to himself, "The more I try to help Phillip the more I feel like that I'm the one who needs help."

Sitting in his car, he couldn't anathematize Phillip from his head. He now recognized that he needed support in dealing with Phillip and began to consider who could help him.

Then he remembered that him subbing for the chaplain was what brought him into this whole predicament in the first place.

Ethan got out of his car and marched towards the hospital chapel.

Becoming more vexed with each step, he mumbled under his breath, "I can't believe that I've been degraded to being a comment for someone else. ...... I should deserve acknowledgment for my own achievement. ..... I'm tired of being a puppet to Phillip. ..... He reminds me of Beth."

He stopped walking, leaned on the closest wall, rubbed the indentation left from his wedding ring and said his last thought aloud, "I feel like crap because he reminds me of my lost wife."

He gave himself the usual pep talk. "Snap out of it. It wasn't your fault. It was her choice. You need to let go of what is holding onto you."

Taking a deep breath, he said aloud, "I can't help Phillip because ..."

"No. No. No. I need to take responsibility for what I did. And I didn't do anything wrong," resolved Ethan.

Grabbing his phone, he brought up the text: **Can't wait 2 C U at home!**

He grimaced and thought, "Time to end this!" as he held his finger over the delete button.

Not being able to do it, as he chided himself again, "Snap out of it. Come on, snap out of it."

He inspected the groove from where his wedding ring used to be.

Biting his bottom lip, he forced memories and emotions away, as he put his phone back into his pocket.

He continued walking towards the chapel.

Once at its front door he looked for the bowl of water that he'd seen in every movie.

Stuck at the threshold, he peered in and saw red carpet, stained-glass windows, and the long benches that made noise every time you moved, but no bowl of holy water.

Conflicted, he believed that it didn't really matter, still he didn't want to upset anyone. Then anger swelled within him, because if the rituals were necessary, they should be easy and standardized. Then he had a mental 'Aha' moment as he discerned that things must be different for this tiny drive-thru church.

He noticed Chap walking in from the front of the room, as he began cleaning and dusting the huge table in the front. He tried to recall Chap's real name but gave up because he never actually tried to learn it. Besides, Chap always responded, so he figured that Chap didn't seem to mind.

Ethan cleared his throat, as Chap turned and saw that he was having a hard time trying to enter in. Ethan still honoring the threshold, and not wanting to yell across the sanctuary, he questionly gestured as to where the bowl of water was.

Chap stretched his neck, as he tried to figure out what he was looking for. He waved Ethan inward and said, "Co'mon in Ethan. I hope everything is going all right. I was meaning to get together with you, to thank you for covering for me that night."

Ethan awkwardly stepped forward one step and then waited. Satisfied that he hadn't been struck down, his mind raged against his paranoia. Why was he so superstitious, when he didn't believe anything that he was trying to honor for Chap's sake?

Chap walked towards him, at home in this sanctuary and said, "Also, my apologies about your wife, I'm sure that it has been hard on you since ..."

Ethan quickly interjected, "Chap, I'm doing as best as you'd expect. I really don't want to talk about that anyways," as he choked down all the feelings that he had just dealt with in the hallway.

Chap held his hands up in a cautious posture.

Ethan knew that ESP didn't exist, still he tried to force his thoughts onto Chap, "Please, don't ask anymore!" as if he had 'The Force' or something.

Chap questioned, "OK. OK. So, what brings you to these parts?" as he placed his hands on Ethan's shoulders.

Ethan thought long and hard, and he couldn't remember as to why he'd come to visit Chap. He ran through his thoughts, "Reporters. Book. Wife. Text. Liz. TJ. Phil ..."

Finally remembering that he came to talk about Phillip, Ethan answered, "I'm having a hard time working with one of my new patients. He's not acting like a normal person."

Chap quipped, "So, psychology has finally standardized on what a normal person is? I don't know what you mean by acting like a normal person?"

Ethan felt disgusted that he had fallen into the same trap that he did every time that he spoke with Chap. He really didn't want to have a discussion on how religion was superior to psychology.

Getting past his regret, Ethan answered, "Well, I mean that my patient isn't grieving or dealing with the pain of what's happened to him."

"So, let's skip to the chase. Are we talking about Phillip Ashby?" asked Chap.

Ethan asked, "How did you know?" as he replayed the conversation in his head, trying to find where he'd telegraphed the information to him. Then the notion came that he'd received the information from God began to mock him.

Removing his hand from Ethan's shoulder, Chap replied, "The reason that you were covering for me was because I was at the conference the night that he was shot. I checked in the next day and saw that he was admitted to our hospital and went to visit him."

Ethan sarcastically drolled, "You're welcome by the way, but that is still a huge leap to get to where he's my patient."

Chap scoffed, "Also, it's been broadcasted all over the national news that you're the one that's caring for him."

Ethan mentally added, "Duh!" to Chap's statement.

Chap continued, "Getting back on subject, are you having problems caring for Pastor Ashby because he's a Christian?"

Taken aback, Ethan barked, "What makes you say that? He's the one that's deflecting."

Chap gave him that look that Ethan interpreted as 'seriously?' as he finally said, "Considering some of the conversations that we've had, I figured that you're having a ... a ... ah..." Chap tried to capture the appropriate word and finally settled on, "... an 'awkward' time with him. "

Ethan answered, "No, the difficulty that I'm having is that every time I attempt to help him, he defends with Jesus."

Chap smirked as he said, "Again, did you ever think it's because he's a Christian? That's what Christians are to do because Christ is our defense."

Ethan snapped, "I meant evades. He evades by Jesus."

Chap gave Ethan the look again, then asked, "Are we really going to get caught up in semantics? Because, you're now defending yourself by evading my question. "

Ethan snapped, "He offends me."

Chap replied, "Well, maybe you need to be offended. Also, did you ever think he's offended by you?"

Ethan defended himself, "Why would he be offended by me. I haven't done anything to him."

Chap probed, "So, you don't think that your outright unbelief and attacks on God wouldn't be an offense to Phillip Ashby or to any Christian?"

Ethan blew a raspberry. He didn't even know why he had come here because this is how every conversation has been between him and Chap. He figured that he'd get some sympathy or some insight, but regretted being wrong.

Chap retorted, "Goodness Ethan, there are times you even offend me."

Ethan replied, "Yeah, but you Christians are supposed to be loving and forgiving first. You know the whole turn the other cheek thing.

Chap took a deep breath and calmly replied, "We are, but we're also called to contend for our faith and to stand for the sake of Jesus' truth and love."

Ethan wondered what was up with the boldness of all the Christians here lately.

Chap paused and then asked, "So, is this how the conversations go between you and him?"

Ethan sulked, "I don't have to take this."

Chap shot back, "You're the one who came to me. Leave if you don't like what I have to say."

Ethan wanted to leave and claim that Chap had no reason to condemn him, but then he took a moment and recognized the

Chap was right. That he had come to him for help and hadn't answered one question. He was guilty.

He meditated on Chap's words, compelled himself to calm down, and recollected all the times that he spoke with Phillip.

Ethan was chastened that Chap was right; Phillip was just standing for what he believed in, and he had eviscerated him psychologically. He let others in his ward have the freedom to stand up for what they believed in. Conviction stopped his critical thoughts, so he decided to change the subject back to why he came.

Ethan pleaded, "His catharsis is being hindered by his altruistic behavior, but he is bottling up the shooting, and all I get is his reflexive responses. "

Chap furrowed his brow and said, "OK, Dr. Ethan Pitney try this diagnoses, is he still reading his Bible and praying?"

Ethan replied, "Yes."

Chap asked, "Does he seem to be at peace?"

Ethan replied, "Uncannily yes."

Chap answered, "Good, you see when Christians face a trial we believe that we should look to God before we look to man. We look for God to bring us provision, security, and understanding that only He can give. The Bible says that God gives Christians a peace that passes all understanding and I think that may be what you're running into ."

Ethan asked, "Yes but doesn't he need to deal with being shot and his wife ..." Ethan stopped himself because he recognized that he had given information that would betray patient confidentiality.

Chap replied, "Yes, but he's working things out between him and God. God is probably revealing Himself to Phillip, and we may never know it."

Relieved that Chap didn't catch the bit about Phillip and his wife having problems, Ethan continued, "Are all Christians like this?"

Chap replied, "I wish all of us were. If we were, there wouldn't be any gossip, slander, backbiting, malice, envy ... You get the idea. You just happen to have Phillip Ashby, who preaches and lives out his faith. He isn't Jesus, but he has my respect."

Trying to understand, Ethan considered that he was conditioned to help guide people through their stressful times and when dealing with their particular battle or addiction. He struggled with Chap telling him to do what was contrary to his training.

He then became fixated on Chap's words: leave Phillip to God and let Him take care of him.

Trying to balance that belief through his own viewpoints, he became absorbed in it as he recalled that Beth told him the same thing after they had an argument.

Beth's memory was a hole that he couldn't fill. Bitterness choked any joy that he used to have from her memory.

Fidgeting with the groove from where his wedding ring used to be, he became aware that Chap had noticed his aloofness also.

Ethan became lost in Chap's compassion, as Chap reiterated, "Are you sure that you're OK? I'm here anytime you want to talk about you and Beth."

Breaking eye contact, Ethan externalized what he was thinking, "The more I reflect on what you're saying, I believe that we're saying the same thing, except you're suggesting that I abandoning him with God whereas I'd leave them alone with their thoughts. Right?"

Chap threw up his arms and exclaimed, "I'm in no way suggesting that you abandon him. Just ensure that God is still speaking to him. Then, I'm sure that he'd open up and then you assist him better."

Shaking his head, Ethan asked, "Why at my ward? Why doesn't he go somewhere else that he trusts and would be better equipped to help him? He is the one who came to me, not the other way around."

Chap queried, "So, are you saying that you can't help him?"

Ethan pouted, "No. It's just … "At a loss for other words, he let out a heavy sigh.

They both sat in the pew as it creaked under the stress.

Ethan's eyes got big as Chap calmed him by saying, "It's normal."

Ethan answered, "Really?"

Chap ignored the question and continued, "I don't claim to know the mind of God, but Jesus probably led him to you. On the question of 'letting you help him', you've probably had and not have known it. Pastor Phillip strikes me as the type of Christian, who'd only trust and seek counsel from their core group that shares the same beliefs they do."

Exasperated, Ethan took his turn at throwing up his hands and said, "Well, then I'm never going to be any help for him."

Chap said, "Remember that he's used to being the person who helps others and is probably trying help others before you can help him."

Ethan replied, "Hence the reason for his altruistic behavior towards me."

Chap countered, "Co'mon. I can tell that you are hurting. I'm sure Pastor Phillip can also."

Ethan chuckled and said, "Well anyways, that's kind of what I suggested for him to do, but for others and not me. I admit I was angry because he wasn't dealing with things."

Chap lifted his finger to inject, but Ethan acknowledged him before he could say anything. "OK, OK, he's dealing with it, but not in the way that I think that progress is made. Currently, he has internalized everything. "

Chap asked, "So, is he just staring off into space or navel gazing?"

Ethan answered, "Neither, I've seen him interact with the patients, but he's only existing and taking up space. He deflects to 'God' when asked a question. Do you know what I mean? I just don't understand why he doesn't allow me to help him get better."

Chap asked, "So, what was the last conversation that you had with him?"

Ethan leaned back in the pew and said, "It was something about specks and logs in people's eyes. I told him to judge not lest you be judged. Then I challenged him that he wasn't dealing with his log and that he was a hypocrite."

Chap replied, "Oh, real subtle. And you thought that would make him want to open up to you?"

Ethan said, "I said I was angry. I need help to salvage this, or I'm not going to be a help to him at all."

Chap started, "Ok, I see what happened, but you have to hear me out."

Ethan said, "I knew you would be able to help me."

Chap reached for one of the Bible's in the pew as Ethan rolled his eyes. Chap gave an "Are you sure you want me to help you" look and Ethan nodded his head in agreement.

Chap found Matthew 7 in the Bible and started, "Well, you know the 'Judge not lest you be judged' verse and I'm sure that Pastor Phillip told you about the rest of the story, but you didn't get the whole verse in context."

Ethan still nodded his head for Chap to continue. He also recalled Phillip saying something similar about taking the Bible in text and context.

Chap cleared his throat and read:

> "You hypocrite, first take the plank out
> of your own eye, and then you will see clearly
> to remove the speck from your brother's eye.
>
> Do not give dogs what is sacred; do not
> throw your pearls to pigs. If you do, they may
> trample them under their feet, and turn and
> tear you to pieces."[6]

Ethan adjusted in his pew and cursed silently as it creaked. He brought his index finger up to his face and looked away. He whispered, "What does that mean?"

Chap put the Bible away and said, "Based on your body language, I'd say that you know what it means. It is just a straight forward as 'judge not', but Jesus did not mean 'judge not" as a defense to shut someone down, but for Christians to examine themselves before trying to be a help to anyone else. Jesus tells us

[6] Matthew 7:5-6

to not to help others or not to call out sin, but he wants us to make sure we are humble in doing so and not more destructive. Still He gave us the warning to beware who to trust."

Still looking away, Ethan despondently said, "I'm a good man." Then he turned to Chap and said, "He can trust me."

Chap answered, "Do you really think that you're able to help him when you can't help yourself? Let's talk about why you're really angry with Phillip. Do you think you are punishing Phillip because of ... "

Through gritted teeth, Ethan tried his best to keep his calm and responded, "Chap, this is not about Beth. So, drop it already."

Chap replied, "You're mad at Phillip because he doesn't want to deal with his own issues. Sounds like you're having the same problem. Should I call you a hypocrite also?"

Stunned at Chap's boldness, Ethan leaped up from the pew and headed for the door. He stopped at the last row of pews and was about to go to his go to phrase 'judge not', but it didn't have the same weight as before.

Infuriated, he turned to lash out but saw Chap's compassion and that he was trying to help. He realized that Chap was his friend and someone who he could trust, but he felt shutdown and ineffective. Then he recalled that he'd shut down Phillip the same way. Then it all clicked, and he stood there working everything out in his head.

Chap stood up, walked to Ethan and said, "I think you understand, but I'll say it anyways. We're all hypocrites and yet we're still called to help each other. The Bible says 'that we are to speak the truth in love.[7]' Sometimes that truth may hurt, but we do so in love.

Today's culture assumes that love is tolerance, but you've got to recognize that isn't true. One cannot tolerate someone hurting themselves or others, love requires one to do something. If they do not, then they show that they don't love them. When we do come to those who are hurt, we're called to come with our piety and self-righteousness but with humility, grace, mercy and

[7] Ephesian 4:15

love. The Bible says, 'God's love always protects, always trusts, always hopes, always perseveres. That His love never fails.[8]'

Ethan replied, "I've heard that before. Is that in the Bible?"

Chap answered, "Yep, 1 Corinthians 13. The Bible also says that we're to repent. Not that we're to only expect the other person to change, but a call for us to examine ourselves and see if we're acting in love and be a change that will last."

While listening to Chap, he remembered seeing the change in his wife's life. That change caused a separation between them, not because she outright judged him, but because he was convicted from her genuineness and happiness. Still she stayed with him as she went to church against his wishes. Going to church was the only thing that Beth had stood up to him about. He remembered her saying that he could sleep in on Sunday while she'd go to church and be home before he woke up.

Setting his jaw and feeling his blood pressure rising, he stopped his reminiscence because he didn't want to go trail down that well-worn path again. He said to Chap, "Well that is nice for you, but I'm not buying."

Chap replied, "That's OK. It isn't for sale. It's already been paid for..."

Ethan bluntly said, "I'm done. OK. Done. I don't want to talk about any of this because my problems are not relevant to Phillip's problems."

Chap shook his head in acknowledgment and raised his hands in surrender. Then he said, "Alright, let's talk about Phillip."

Ethan asked, "Well, how am I going to help him if I don't understand this Christian stuff?

Chap answered, "You're kind of lucky in respect to Phillip."

Ethan furrowed his brow and asked, "How?"

Chap continued, "In Phillip's case you have a wealth of knowledge. He's written books and has done seminars about what he believes in Christ and how to help others, including himself. So, you don't really have any questions about Phillip that he hasn't

---

[8] 1 Corinthians 13:7-8

already provided, you've just got to go and find the answers. That is if you really want to help him."

Deflated, Ethan asked, "You're telling me I need to buy his books and online videos to help him?"

Chap nodded his head yes and added, "Yeah, I'm sure he's got online videos also that will help."

Grabbing one of the Bibles from the pew, Chap handed it to Ethan and said, "It would probably help you to read the Bible for yourself, so you could get in his frame of mind and be able to help him."

Ethan's phone started to buzz, but he decided to ignore it. He looked at Chap and joked, "Sounds like to me you're trying to convert me."

Chap answered back, "Always, it's what I'm told to do by God."

Ethan smiled and shot back, "You Christians are so hard to get along with."

Chap returned, "You non-Christians aren't so easy to get along with either."

With his phone starting to buzz again, Ethan quickly thanked Chap for his help and took out his phone, and pointed at it saying, "I've got to take this."

Chap waved goodbye and walked back to the front of the chapel.

Ethan looked at the phone, saw it was Liz, and answered, "What?"

Liz replied, "Sorry, did I interrupt something important? Working late at night? I'm impressed."

Ethan replied, "No, just getting a list of required reading."

Liz answered, "Huh?! Never mind, anyways what did you do today?"

Ethan answered, "Nothing, why?"

Liz paused, and Ethan could hear her punching the keys on her keyboard and then she finally said, "You sure you didn't do anything recently?"

Ethan thought and then remembered the media. He said, "The press figured out that Pastor Phillip Ashby is one of my patients."

Liz cursed, "Holy shit, that may be what's happening."

Ethan was getting tired of the game and said, "What has been happening."

Liz said, "All right, are you sitting down."

Ethan was about to curse Jesus' name then remembered his proximity to the chapel and said, "Liz, out with it."

Liz said, "You've sold more books today than you have the whole time your book has been out."

Ethan cursed, "Damn it, more books because of Phillip Ashby. Can I just catch a fucking break?"

Liz said, "I thought you'd be happy."

Ethan said, "I would be if it were on my own merit."

Liz said, "Well the cash is green either way you get it. Remember, I'll take a percentage of it. Do you think that you can talk to the President of the United States next?"

Ethan snidely grinned and said, "Maybe later Liz, I've got to go book shopping for now."

Chapter 21.   Forsake All Others

Claire walked in the door and called up the stairway, "Mother, I'm home."

Walking into the kitchen, she saw all the mail on the counter. It looked like someone hadn't checked them for a month while on vacation. She saw there were bills and personal 'Get Well Cards' for her dad.

Claire took a mental note to help her mother with the canned letters at work in responses to all the "Get wells and flowers".

She walked towards the refrigerator and saw that it was open. She shook her head as she thought about how she would have been chewed out if she would have left it open. She closed the door and searched her mind, trying to remember if her mother said that she was going to a friend's house or going out somewhere else.

She rushed to the garage and confirmed that her mother's car was still there.

Frantic, she checked the den and then the dinner room still with no sign of her.

Her mind immediately went to the worst, and she fretted that she hadn't lived up to her bargain with her dad.

She called out again, "Mother, where are you?"

She felt a pang of despair, as the silence began to shadow over her hope.

Running up the stairs, Claire called out to her mother again with a quick prayer in between each call. Still not hearing a response, she quickened her pace.

Reaching the top of the stairs, her heart was racing as her imagination flashed to crime scene police photos.

Hysterical, she called out "Mother. MOM. MOOOM!"

A room loomed ahead with a crack in the door with light bleeding through.

She cautiously approached the room, praying that her week wouldn't get any worse. Shadows move across the light, and she caught her breath.

She peeked in and saw her mother sitting in the middle of the wrecked room with picture albums and loose pictures littered around the floor. She monitored her feverishly shuffling them around.

Noticing adrenaline was following through her, Claire took a deep breath and then thought about how she wasn't prepared for any more of her mother's craziness. Opening the door, she was surprised that her mother didn't even turn to acknowledge her.

She watched her mother turn each photo, moving them into an ocean of memories that were falling and cresting across the years. There were baby pictures, aged Polaroids, love letters, class pictures, video tapes and vacation photos being shuffled by her mother who seemed to be in a catatonic state as she made chaos of all the year's memorials.

Claire put her mother's face in her hands and searched in her eyes as she said, "Mom, are you OK?"

Jessica shot her gaze at Claire as the frantic look softened and the color came back into her eyes as she said, "You called me mom. I so like it when you call me that. I just want things to be like they used to be."

Searching for words, Claire knew that she was ill prepared to help her mother in this state. She thought about how Naomi was the one who handled the feelings department, as she stood there with her mouth shut because she knew any words would be babble.

Jessica moved her face away from Claire's hands as she kept turning every picture and said, "I tried to put my makeup on this morning, but had a hard time because I felt like I was trying to cover up something that cannot be hidden anymore. I'm starting to see what everyone knew all along. I've lost something, and I don't know what it is that I've lost. I feel like I have been in a cave and can't see."

Claire thought about commenting on how it was night, but she knew that her mother had been in a fragile state since their ride home from visiting dad. So, she just sat quietly next to her.

Dropping the pictures that she was holding, Jessica then stared at Claire as she said, "No that isn't what it is. It's like I'm sunblind from staring into the sun too long and I'm not able to notice anything else. I never thought to look for something because I thought everyone else had the problem, not me."

Claire watched her mother start rummaging all the photos again as she muttered, "What is it that I'm looking for? What has gone beyond my grasp?"

Jessica picked up a photo of Phillip, Naomi and herself in their apartment, and held it up to Claire to see as she whispered, "This is when he quit trusting me with his heart. I expected so much of him when he was already overwhelmed."

Claire watched a tear leave a trail on her mom's face as she continued, "... and I was lonely."

Pushing all the pictures away, Jessica dejectedly said, "What is it that everyone else sees that I'm missing? Where did I go wrong? How did I let it get this bad? Why is it that no one loves me anymore?"

Claire held her breath and counted to five, then decided that her comments wouldn't help at this time. Not knowing how to handle her mother, she wished that things between them were better, but her mother's self-centeredness irritated her and led her into apathy.

Jessica grabbed a tissue and said, "No, that isn't it. The right question is 'Why is it that I don't love anyone anymore?'"

Claire decided to go for it and asked, "Mom, what is this about? You aren't making any sense."

Jessica's lip quivered as she took Claire's hands into hers. She opened her mouth and said nothing. Her eyes seemed to be searching for words that were denied her. She finally mustered, "I was thinking about what you said earlier."

Claire fought her defensive reflex because she knew that conversations with her mother never started or ended well. Biting her lip, she waited, ready to endure the coming onslaught.

Jessica confessed, "You're right. I've forsaken your father, and I haven't made him above all others. You called me out on my relationship with Scott, and I was guilty. I was so wrong to get angry with you. Will you please forgive me?"

It was Claire's turn to drop her jaw. She tried to respond, but she couldn't answer her because she was overwhelmed with all the things that she had held against her mother for all the years. Pushing down her anger and disgust that had fueled her relationship with her mother for so long, she thought about how she was totally prepared to go through her whole life not being understood by her mother, as she remembered that she'd forgiven her years ago.

Jessica didn't let the silence linger as she continued, "I've let things get too bad between your dad and I. Scott has become a surrogate husband and my temporary savior. I now realize that I have been having an emotional affair with him. It wasn't that your dad was emotionally distant, but I found myself praying, worrying and caring more about Scott. I prayed more for him to have a wife than I prayed for your dad to continue being the steadfast, loving husband that he has always been. I've taken advantage of your dad's trust and misused it. I didn't know how destructive it was to think that your father 'was strong enough without me.' I figured it was harmless. I've forsaken your father." Jessica choked up and continued, ". . . and forsaken God also. I've turned away from them and did my own thing. All the while, I justified it because I never physically left them. However, I did forsake them. And they never left nor forsook me."

Claire tried to comfort her mother, but all she barely got out was "Mother ...," before Jessica held up her hand to stop her.

Holding an assortment of pictures in her hand, she said, "I've exhausted myself from praying that God would tell me that He loved me while I left my Bible collecting dust on the stand in my bedroom. I put your dad's letters on the stand next to my Bible, as I desperately wanted him to give me a reminder of his love.

Claire received one of the pictures, but before she could glance at it, her mother cried, "Look at all these pictures, I see that he has continually given me a treasure of his love. I see his smile, his laughter, his love for me and you two girls . . ."

Then she reached down and grabbed a photo of her holding her hand out in front of the lens of the camera and said, "… .and this is what I give."

Jessica eyed the photo and started to laugh and cry. Pointing to the drapes in the room, she said, "I've worried more about the color of those curtains than I did loving your father, Naomi, you and others. I'm tired of being worried about the curtains and the color of the wallpaper. I am no different than the world. I've worried about being liked more than following Christ. "

In disgust, Jessica looked at all the pictures and sat there and quietly.

Claire started to talk, as Jessica continued, "Is this the best that I have to offer?"

Ecstatic to hear her mother's confession and contrition, Claire wanted to console her with what God had taught her. Appreciating her mother's candor, she felt like she could take this opportunity to make herself understood.

Saying a quick prayer, she ignored the gnawing impression that she should just listen instead of talk, as she began, "Mom, you don't have to stay this way. You're a child of God, and there's still hope. And we're all guilty at times of being caught up in how shiny our halos and crowns are instead of . . ."

Jessica interrupted, "Claire, you don't understand. . ."

Claire decided to continue saying her piece while her mother was able to listen. Raising her voice over hers, she said, "Mother, I've always struggled on how to trust you because you have been so volatile. It chased me away from God because I looked at you and saw how you thought that you were more perfect and holier than everyone else. I knew that God demanded perfection of His children, but if you were an example of a Christian, I didn't want anything of it."

Claire saw her mother starting to give her the stare she got when they were about to lock horns.

Claire continued, "Mom, please bear with me. I'm going somewhere with this."

Seeing her mother's countenance change, she knew that she had about 5 minutes worth of patience.

Claire continued, "I examined myself and found that I didn't compare to Naomi nor Daddy either. I began searching for other answers while I was in college. I remember being on the precipice of deciding if I was going to make the Christian faith my own or abandon it.

I looked at what the world was selling as success, beauty, fame, and fortune. And it all seemed so hollow to me.

I researched other faiths: atheism, Buddhism, Hinduism, Islam and Mormonism. I saw that they were faiths where one had to save themselves.

I couldn't find freedom, nor salvation, nor perfection until I looked at Christianity again. Not the cover up faith that I saw that you had, but a personal relationship with Jesus. I challenged Him, telling him that He had His chance to prove Himself to me, or I was done with Christianity."

Jessica let out an audible gasp.

Claire ignored her mother's reaction and continued, "God brought a great friend into my life that helped me with all my hard questions. The first thing we dealt with was that I had an identity crisis.

I thought beauty defined perfection, but I learned that grace, mercy and love did. That I had to choose Jesus as my own personal Lord and Savior and not to live in the shadow of daddy's or your salvation.

God then delved into the source of what was separating me from Him, which was that my belief in Him wasn't dependent on how I compared myself to you or anyone else, but on how he compared me to Himself. Humbled, I submitted to Him as He helped me with becoming more like Himself."

Claire paused and waited for her mother to understand. She hoped that her mother could connect her experience with her own.

Jessica looked askance.

Wanting to quit bearing her soul to her deepest skeptic, Claire gave a frustrated sigh as she wondered if she was laying it on too thick.

Closing her eyes to pray, she felt a prodding to continue on. She tried to remember what had sent her down this path. She paused, searched her mind, gestured to all of the pictures and started, "Mother, I think you aren't comparing yourself to what you think Jesus wants you to be, you're comparing yourself to your past.

You said that you are no different than the world, which means that you're comparing yourself to it and your past. You're more worried about what you've got to offer, instead of seeing what Jesus still continues to offer."

Claire saw Jessica wipe a tear from her eyes and asked, "What is it that Jesus still offers?"

Claire answered, "Himself."

Stillness hung in the air, as Claire watched her mom let that truth permeate into her soul.

Claire counted slowly, trying her best to be patient and to not ruin the moment, but she wished her mother would engage. After a seemingly lifetime of counting, she reached fifteen and released her contained explosion, "Mother you've blamed everyone else for your burdens and got angry when none of us could deliver. We can never provide for you what Jesus was expected to carry."

Jessica opened her mouth to speak as Claire winced, waiting for the kickback, but relieved to say what had gnawed at her every time she was around her mother.

She watched her mother close her mouth and start assorting the pictures on the floor as she whispered, "That is what I've been learning her."

She monitored her mother pathetically looking at the pictures and wondered if she was helping.

Struggling to not shake her out of her misery, she hid her frustration as she calmly consoled, "Mother, you can keep going on with your 'You don't understand' or 'woe is me' or 'It's not my fault' drivel, but the truth is that we all have to come to the end of those thoughts and come to Jesus.

We have to come to Jesus with the understanding that there is no temptation that we've come through or will go through that Jesus hasn't crossed. He doesn't get us over things, but through them or provides a way out. Jesus being God who became a man means He is able to identify and have compassion with our weakness. He's not up in Heaven keeping track of our wrongs and waiting to strike us down, but He is struggling with us to become the perfection that He desires.[9] Jesus said, "Take my yoke …"

At those words, Claire was startled at the immediacy that her mother threw open her arms open and hugged her.

Relaxing from not being struck, she heard her mother sobbing, "Your dad's told me about the yoke. It was the night that I was saved and first met him. "

Claire felt the wetness from her mother's blubbering and knew that she would have to change her shirt afterward. Lost at what to do with her mother draped over her, she began to pat her on the back as she sobbed even louder, which made her stop because she didn't know if she was making things worse. She stiffly put her arms around her mother and gave a gentle embrace as she choked a snicker, because she was use to selecting and directing people to handle these type of things against their own comfort, and now she understood why they did it reluctantly.

She balanced on the edge of wondering if there was something wrong with herself, because sympathy for her mother was so foreign to her, and the other edge of biding her time until

[9] Hybrid of Hebrews 2:18 and Hebrews 4:15

the mother that she was familiar with rose up to betray her trust again.

Finally cried out, her mother lifted her head, as Claire tried not to shirk back from her mother's face that was flush and eyes that were puffy. She doubted that she should say more or ensure that she was understood. It seemed to make sense when she was saying it.

Her mother wiped the tears from her eyes, and then took her hands and said, "Would you please pray with me."

Claire grimaced in repulsion, but took a deep breath and stammered, "Well, I don't know mom. I .,,, I ...."

She saw her mom's eyes sparkle as she called her mom.

Still in conflict with her trust issues, Claire took another deep breath and bowed her head. She decided to believe in God more than her mother, as she prayed,

"Dear God,
Help us through the destruction
that we've caused in ours and others
lives. Forgive us where we've failed You
and bring us back to Your will and love.

Amen

Surprised, Claire felt her mother wipe the tears from her face. She jerked away from the grossness of their mixing tears as she realized that she had also been crying.

Inundated by her emotions, Claire was not able to speak. Use to having anger as the overwhelming emotion that she had had tied to her mother for so long, she was not sure as to what to do. Wiping her tears, she tucked her emotions away until she could analyze them later.

Her mother said, "You're straight to the point, and brief prayers have always surprised me. I love that about you."

Claire cocked her head as she tried to swallow the lump in her throat because that was the first time she'd heard such a thing from her mother. She knew that everything wasn't still at a 100% with her mom, but she decided that the spirit of confession was still here so she chanced continuing on.

But she had to get back to work considering the press had found out her dad was in a mental institution. She also did not know how much goodwill was still available between her mother and her,

Claire asked, "Mother is there anything else that you'd like to talk about?"

Jessica said, "You must think that I'm awful. I haven't shown you or your dad how much I really do love you. You've visited your dad more than I have, and when I did go I made a … a … well … I showed my . . . I showed my …"

Claire allowed her mother to struggle as she tried to find a better word. Then she offered, "Mom, I know what you mean. Please continue."

Casting her glance aside, Jessica continued, "I don't know why I covered up knowing who Tracy was when we were at the hospital. I was so befuddled at that time, and I didn't want anyone to be angry with me. I know I shouldn't have left him with her, but I really thought that everything would have been OK. Y'all have every reason to blame me, and I accept the responsibility. It's entirely my fault for leaving him alone with her. Phillip could've died, and it would've been because of what I did and didn't do. That's the reason why I struggle when I visit him. I see my fault every time I see your dad. I don't give him a chance to talk to me because I'm afraid of his reaction."

Claire bit her lip as she tried to not ruin the moment and prayed that God would use this somehow. The more her mother talked, she felt a sense of peace and understanding that was once dammed up, but now was beginning to flow again.

Claire grabbed a tissue and handed it to her mom, as she wiped her eyes and nose. She continued, "Phillip has every reason to be angry with me. That's why I cannot open his letters. I'm afraid of what he's going to say. I sometimes wonder why he's stayed married to me because I've made his life unbearable."

Taking Claire's hand, she confessed, "I think that I struggle so hard because I'm the outsider in this family. I know that you've chosen your father before me. Please understand that I've tried to be fun and caring, but I wanted to spare you and your sister the same struggles that I had in my youth. I wanted you to have the mother I needed when I was your age. However, I don't know what went wrong. The more I tried it seemed the more distant or argumentative you and your sister became.

I don't know how to come back. I love your dad, but I don't think that he'd accept me."

Shaking her head 'no' in response to her mother's last statement, Claire answered, "Mom, he asks about you every time I visit him. He gives me a stack of letters every time I get ready to leave. He always promises me to tell you that he loves you so very much and that he's waiting. Mom, if this is how you feel about Daddy, he loves you even more."

The irony of how her mother instinctively put her dad's letters by her Bible that she hadn't read, caused Claire to regard the parallels between how some people say that they love God but won't read His love story back to them.

Claire added, "Mother, if this is how you feel, you need to ask for forgiveness, I can tell you that daddy has already forgiven you and wants to reconcile, but know that asking for forgiveness is more for you than it is for Daddy. "

Jessica gently voiced, "But how do you know?"

Claire couldn't catch herself before saying, "Mother, duh?! Because, I talk to him, and all he talks about is how much he loves you and how he wants things to be right."

Claire waited and knew that she had just ruined the moment, but was astounded when her mom didn't react to her sarcasm but answered like a child, "Really?"

Glad that she hadn't pushed any buttons, Claire resumed, "Yes, and you don't have to make the first move either. Dad has already reached out to you several times, and he's waiting for you to quit being angry and respond. He doesn't understand why you're so angry with him. He needs you to release him so he can figure other things out.

Jessica tried to contest, "But what about ..."

Claire interrupted, "Mother, quit tying yourself in shoe knots, receive him and let him know that it isn't his fault and that you aren't angry with him anymore. You might find that you're the one who is tightening the strings that bind you as you try to unravel them while daddy has the scissors to cut them to free you."

Claire couldn't believe the words and attitude that was coming through her mouth and that her mom hadn't reacted negatively. She knew it had to be God speaking through her. She prayed she could remember them later and write them down in her journal.

Jessica said, "But you were right when you said I don't care about anyone else but myself. It is a problem that I've had my whole life. There are so many things that I've got to fix before I see your dad."

Claire grew frustrated from the doubt that was encircling her mother like a fly, she decided to swat it down with truth. She went and got her mother's Bible and daddy's letters from her room. Laying them at her mother's feet, she opened the Bible and read:

> What shall we say about such
> wonderful things as these? If God is
> for us, who can ever be against us?
> Since he did not spare even his own
> Son but gave him up for us all, won't
> he also give us everything else? Who
> dares accuse us whom God has
> chosen for his own? No one—for God
> himself has given us right standing
> with himself. Who then will condemn
> us? No one—for Christ Jesus died for
> us and was raised to life for us, and he
> is sitting in the place of honor at God's
> right hand, pleading for us.
>
> Can anything ever separate us
> from Christ's love? Does it mean he no

longer loves us if we have trouble or calamity, or are persecuted, or hungry, or destitute, or in danger, or threatened with death? (As the Scriptures say, "For your sake we are killed every day; we are being slaughtered like sheep.") No, despite all these things, overwhelming victory is ours through Christ, who loved us.

And I am convinced that nothing can ever separate us from God's love. Neither death nor life, neither angels nor demons, neither our fears for today nor our worries about tomorrow—not even the powers of hell can separate us from God's love. No power in the sky above or in the earth below—indeed, nothing in all creation will ever be able to separate us from the love of God that is revealed in Christ Jesus our Lord.[10]

Putting the Bible down, Claire took her mother's hands, and said, "Mother, this verse comforts me when I feel like I'm being accused and condemned. It gives me hope to know Jesus is pleading for us even when I'm the one who has caused my own problems. I know this is how God loves us and how daddy loves you."

She took a letter opener and put her dad's letters in her mother's hand.

She sat there and watched her mother cycle through the letters. During each page turn, she quietly prayed that God's love and her daddy's love would speak and reach her. She knew this was the time her mother would start her dependence upon God.

---

[10] Romans 8:31-39 NLT

She quietly got up, leaving her alone with God as she thought, "What a great place to be."

Grabbing her car keys, she headed back to work, so she could handle the press finding out that her dad was in a mental institution.

Chapter 22. The Passing Storm

Storm clouds billowed and the winds picked up speed as the weather channeled into the valley. The energy in the coming storm was fighting against itself. Light streaked through the clouds and the rapid expansion of the air surrounding the bolt shook and rumbled as the storm announced its presence.

The drought was about to be over.

***

Sitting in his high back chair in his living room, Ethan listened to the howling wind. He closed his eyes and let it calm him.

Giving a heavy sigh, he was glad that this day was about to be over.

Settling in, he cracked open Phillip Ashby's book "Healing through the Valley."

Holding the paperback, he felt a weight from it as he read the back cover.

> "There are times when we all go through the valley of shadows and death, and we call out to God. It's important for us to know that He is with us even then. I began writing this book because of the questions I received during my altar calls, but writing it became cathartic for me when my twin brother passed away."

Ethan had to admit Chap was correct. He had learned more about Phillip reading this one paragraph than he did the whole time he had counseled him.

He grabbed his pen and started taking notes.

He scribbled – Phillip had a twin brother who died.

Looking at the copyright of the book – he added, "Recently."

***

Phillip laid in his bed with his Bible and notepad, still licking his wounds from the day.

He closed his eyes, and his anguishes overwhelmed him: "TJ …. Hypocrite ….. Mary ….. red eyes … Trying to be Jesus .. Ethan …. Wolves…. Tracy …. gun ….. Jessica … worshiped."

Opening his eyes, he realized that he was holding his breath. Releasing it, he looked out of his window and saw the storm clouds chasing away the loose things in the world. He chuckled as he thought about how the flying debris always appeared, even when the world seemed so neat and kept up.

He yawned and rubbed his eyes, never being so glad for a day to come to an end. Still, he dreaded the night. He just wanted to sleep so he could get the torment of it done. He knew the necessity of him getting rest, but he hadn't felt rested since his stay here.

He had rejected all the offered medications to help him rest and to relax, not because he was against taking medication but because he wanted to settle his mind from its knots without being addled.

Looking at his window again, he saw the ominous coming clouds rotating around as they searched for their prey.

Phillip jumped as the first boom of the storm stirred the whole ward. It brought everyone to the edge of their nerves. He knew Mr. Abiel would be busy tonight, and he said a quick prayer for him that he'd keep everyone calm.

***

Jessica sat still in the pile of pictures and papers, unnerved from the wind moving a tree branch across the window.

She was incredulous because she had reminded Phillip about that branch several times for the past last year, and he still hadn't taken care of it.

She scolded herself for thinking these thoughts again. Gritting her teeth, she fought the urge to not get into the same pattern again. She admitted that the rut she was in was more like a valley, and she would have to retrain herself again to take her thoughts captive and rise above them.

The idea did cross her mind as to why she didn't take care of it herself.

But she quickly dismissed it. Then was mad at herself for quickly dismissing it and then failed at giving herself the silent treatment.

Emotions drained, she was done with this day. She was no longer blind to her failure.

A lightning bolt cracked the sky as the tree branch silhouetted a knobby hand onto the wall. It seemed like it was going to reach out and snatch her up.

She laughed at herself because she normally was over dramatic and would blame Phillip about what he hadn't done. Wiping the tears from her eyes, she resolved that she wasn't going to go there again.

She went to shake her fist to the storm in triumph but felt her Bible beside her. Remembering that Claire left it next to her before she left, she took the Bible and raised it to the window; overjoyed in her small victory.

***

Lightning surrounded Ethan while he turned to the dedication page. It read "to those who know Him and for those seeking."

Ethan gave a heavy sigh because he wasn't either of these.

Shaking his head, he conjectured as to why Phillip didn't dedicate the book to his wife or to his deceased brother.

He looked out the window watching the light show as he rubbed the bridge of his nose and yawned. Feeling his eyes weariness, he sighed because he knew that he had to drudge through this book if he was going to learn how to get onto Phillip's level.

He scoffed facetiously because he deliberated on what his wife would think if she saw him reading a book from Pastor Ashby. Sorrow flooded his heart immediately at the thought of Beth. Putting the book down, he went to get Beth's Bible and some wine.

He thought he should get some candles also just in case.

***

In the distance, Phillip saw the lightning cross the sky as the thunder unsettled more than the building.

Phillip heard some of the patients in the building starting to howl, moan and laugh. Phillip hadn't observed this behavior the whole time he had been there and was sure that the storm must be affecting this on some level.

Another lightning bolt streaked across the sky as the thunder instigated the conundrum again.

Phillip tried to open his Bible, but Lilly sprang up onto his bed and onto his chest. She stared into his eyes, demanding to be in bed with him tonight. Not able to take her full weight on his chest, he moved her to his side, and she licked her lips as approval of his decision. She yawned and laid down, leaning her full weight against his side.

Finally opening his Bible, he decided to read its dedication page. He smiled as he read what Jessica had written years ago: To the man who does what God says and leads and guides people to Jesus. Acts 8:35

He knew that the verse was in the story about Phillip leading the Ethiopian eunuch to Christ. Specifically, where Phillip opened his mouth and told about Jesus.

Shame rested on his chest with more weight than Lilly had because he didn't feel like that man right now.

Then he remembered Mr. Abiel's rebukes: "You're trying to be Jesus and that you want to be worshiped. You don't think that people are doing God's work unless they do it your way. You think that everyone should care about what you have to say. You've been God's mouthpiece for so long that you aren't absorbing any of it.," "Are you listening and doing?"

He was sure that Mr. Abiel was right, but his concentration was sidetracked by the familiar Tracy and Jessica rollercoaster that he'd been on, with Mary, TJ, and Ethan being added. Catching himself in the loops, he felt like the devil had put him on it like a merry-go-round with no destination other than going around and around again with all the twists and drops.

A bolt of lightning lit his room, shaking him out of his indecision.

Lilly buried her nose under his arms, and he began to pet her head, he wondered how long he'd been experiencing analysis paralysis.

Phillip closed his Bible and prayed:

> *"Dear Jesus, Help me. Free me from
> these unchained memories on Tracy. Help my
> marriage. Help me too. Help me to be
> continuously drawn to You."*

Phillip thought about the inscription in his Bible from Jesus as he prayed:

> "Help me to bring others to You. Help
> me to be about your business first. Amen."

Freed from any distractions, his mind diverted to the loop again.

Lilly, however, redirected all of his attention to her, as she stretched and rolled over for a belly rub. She let out a heavy sigh from all of his pats and rub downs.

Conviction crushed him on how quickly he allowed Lilly to distract him, but his reaction from any distraction from Jessica was so different.

He babbled, "I'm too busy and ... and ... everything else comes before her."

Understanding his fault, the proverbial train ran off the track and came to an abrupt stop.

The storm inside him released, leaving him to be comforted by Lilly.

***

Lightning danced across the sky, as thunder shook the house.

Jessica scrutinized Phillip and her wedding picture. It was the one where they were shoving wedding cake in each other's face.

Remembering the joy that they brought to each other, she contrasted what her reaction would be today if he had done that now when she was in a beautiful dress.

She sat still trying to think about what had changed but didn't get far because the thunder shook the house and the wind moved the branch across the window again.

Containing her seething agitation of the branches neglect, she stayed on task with her self-condemnation.

She thought back to her wedding and recalled that they had tailored their vows from "The Love Chapter" in the Bible.

The wind chased itself around the house, and the tree branch tapped bad Morse code on the window, but she ignored it all and turned her Bible to I Corinthians 13 and started reading.

> If I had the gift of being able to speak in other languages without learning them and could speak in every language there is in all of heaven and earth, but didn't love others, I would only be making noise. If I had the gift of prophecy and knew all about what is going to happen in the future, knew everything about everything, but didn't love others, what good would it do? Even if I had the gift of faith so that I could speak to a mountain and make it move, I would still be worth nothing at all without love. If I gave everything I have to poor people, and if I were burned alive for preaching the Gospel but didn't love others, it would be of no value whatever.
>
> Love is very patient and kind, never jealous or envious, never boastful or proud, never haughty or selfish or rude. Love does not demand its own way. It is not irritable or touchy. It does not hold grudges and will hardly even notice when others do it wrong. It is never glad about injustice, but rejoices

whenever truth wins out. If you love someone, you will be loyal to him no matter what the cost. You will always believe in him, always expect the best of him, and always stand your ground in defending him.

All the special gifts and powers from God will someday come to an end, but love goes on forever. Someday prophecy and speaking in unknown languages and special knowledge—these gifts will disappear. Now we know so little, even with our special gifts, and the preaching of those most gifted is still so poor. But when we have been made perfect and complete, then the need for these inadequate special gifts will come to an end, and they will disappear.

It's like this: when I was a child I spoke and thought and reasoned as a child does. But when I became a man my thoughts grew far beyond those of my childhood, and now I have put away the childish things. In the same way, we can see and understand only a little about God now, as if we were peering at his reflection in a poor mirror; but someday we are going to see him in his completeness, face-to-face. Now all that I know is hazy and blurred, but then I will see everything clearly, just as clearly as God sees into my heart right now.

There are three things that remain— faith, hope, and love—and the greatest of these is love.[11]

---

[11] I Corinthians 13 (TLB)

Each word brought her to humility because she thought of how much God, her husband, and her family loved her and how she had loved them so poorly.

She tormented herself further, "How could I be deserving of anything from them?"

Tears fell on the Bible's delicate pages like rain falling, liberating her from her self-imposed anathema.

***

The POP of the wine bottle cork coincided with the thunder crackling outside.

With tired eyes, Ethan knew that it was going to be a long night.

Retrieving his stemless wine glasses, his heart became dark as memories of his wife crept up again.

He smirked at the stemless wine glass, remembering that his wife had bought them because he "always" broke the stems off of every one of their previous wine glasses that they received as a wedding gift. He thought about how practical and simple she was.

Massaging the groove in his ring finger, his heart panged at the memory of his wife as he bit his bottom lip and cursed, "I have got too many memories."

The lightning flashed and crackled across the sky.

Several profiles of picture frames that used to be on the wall stood out, reminding him of what they once meant and of when they had put them up. He muttered to himself . . ."The memories are the first thing to go."

He stopped rubbing the depression in his finger and stole a look at his phone sitting on the kitchen counter recharging. Resisting the urge to get it, he breathed, "I couldn't get rid of them all," as he downed his first glass of wine and poured himself another.

He sat the drink down, banged both fists to his forehead in vain and ineffectively comforted himself, "Get a hold of yourself, Ethan. Be a rock. It wasn't your fault she left that night."

Ethan was so done with the torment. He didn't even have to look at his phone because he knew the text by heart. **Can't wait 2 C U at home**."

He downed the drink and poured another as the thunder rolled the storm closer.

With the media aware of him being Phillip's doctor, he was pressured to quickly find a way to reach him just like he had helped Champ Davis.

A thought skimmed his mind, "Are you helping Phillip or yourself?" but he dismissed it with another swig of his drink.

The lightning cracked again, and the storm was right over him.

The emptiness in the house embraced his melancholy, as he grabbed the glass and the bottle and headed toward the living room.

Stopping at the threshold of the kitchen door, he turned around and retrieved another bottle of wine and the corkscrew, thinking to himself that it was going to be a long night.

***

Sheets of rain like waves crashing over and over again began to rush the window as the wind projected it so fast that the window was almost useless.

Phillip puzzled over the words o'er and o'er and how it gave the impression of being on the ocean. Those words had been impressed upon him since Scott was playing when he was shot

He became angry with himself as the rest of the lyrics teased him just out of reach. He couldn't remember the whole song, just the chorus that he started to sing softly to himself.

Jesus, Jesus, how I trust Him!
How I've proved Him o'er and o'er;
Jesus, Jesus, precious Jesus!
Oh, for grace to trust Him more!

He thought the storm was on top of the building and was about to relocate everything. The wind howled through the nooks and crannies of his room, making his room sound like it was breathing. The windows continued taking their beating and he noticed that the rest of the building was oddly quiet.

He watched the outside lights dance through the rain-glazed window as the storm surge onward.

Scratching Lilly behind her ear made her stretch out her legs and roll onto her belly. She sighed in peace, content to lean against him in trust and rest.

That helped him to remember the rest of the lyrics.

> *'Tis so sweet to trust in Jesus,*
> *Just to take Him at His Word;*
> *Just to rest upon His promise,*

Then he heard the crowd chanting, "Beneath the cleansing waves."

The storm continued to rage, as Phillip chuckled to himself that he was beneath the cleansing waves.

Re-experiencing the gun sight fixed on him, he remembered Jessica screaming at Tracy before he passed out, "How could you have done this? What did we do to you?"

He wondered why he had never thought about the same things.

Then he recalled all the paramedics surrounding him as then a soft voice he heard before passing out. He had not thought of that night at all afterward. He just wanted to get back on with life and try to get things back to a sense of normalcy. Nevertheless, the voice was comforting, and he thought to himself that it was the reason why he didn't have to worry.

Amongst the chaos of the night, Phillip mouthed the words he heard "I am with you."

A lightning bolt lit his whole room. His memory flashed to the end of his wolf and sheep dream.

Phillip thought about how his traveling created a void between Jessica and him, how he didn't protect her from the wolves of the world, and how the shadow serpent blocked out the sky.

Considering how the distance between Jessica and him had never been greater, "I'm to blame," escaped his lips.

With his distraught heart collapsing upon itself, he added, "I thought I was doing everything and carrying her, but I failed at the one thing I was supposed to do. Be her covering."

He recalled how the other sheep had left the black one in his lap bruised and bloodied. The dream compacted upon itself, leaving him alone in his inadequacy. His failures assaulted him; each a lash across his soul, "I was to be the shepherd for my family, and I failed. I sacrificed my marriage to my career. I didn't protect my bride from my family. I forsook her. My heart wasn't towards her."

Hearing the rush of rain, he suffered every drop that was wearing down his defenses.

He cried, "I'm no different from Adam, who didn't protect Eve from the serpent. I'm so ashamed. I've blamed her for not being strong enough when I traveled. I've ignored her attempts to help me. I've chosen others above her, and expected her to happy about it."

Ashamed of his shortcomings, he closed his eyes, got out of bed, wept prostrate and confessed to God:

> *"Dear God, I admit that I've been blind to the balance of my faults in my marriage. I wasn't the perfect husband, and Jessica isn't entirely responsible for all the problems in our marriage.*
>
> *Please forgive me and give me another chance to reconcile with her.*
>
> *AMEN!*

He sat up, took a deep breath and stared around the room, feeling like a dated burden had been lifted from him and cast onto Jesus.

The wind settled as the rainfall in tranquility, mirroring the calmness he now felt. Peace settled in his soul, and his mind calmed, safe from his tormenting thoughts.

He prayed to God again, "It's in your hands now," then he smirked as he added, "What a great place for it to be. Thank you for being with me o'er and o'er."

Content, Phillip leaned upon his bed and watched the rain.

Lilly came down, lifted his hand and put her head under it.

He felt an urgent need to continue praying. But not for his behalf, but because someone was fighting a battle that also needed winning.

He dropped his head, sought the Lord, and prayed.

***

The waves of rain wash the window as the tree branch scratched an eerie rhythm.

Jessica decided that it was time to make a drastic change and to cut the branch down. She knew that doing so during a storm wasn't the smartest time, however debating with herself, she argued that she had had plenty time beforehand and didn't do it then.

She rationalized carrying out this endeavor to herself with three points. The first being that the branch is a problem now and that she had forgotten about it every time when there was not a storm. The second being it was time to stop being dependent on everyone else to take care of her. The third was the ladder was wooden, so she figured that she'd be safe.

Getting herself up, she put on her work clothes, went to the garage and picked up the ladder.

As the garage door opened, a lightning bolt lit the whole garage as if to influence her to abandon her effort.

Jessica motivated herself, "It starts now or never."

She marched in the rain, and each raindrop stung her when it pelted her face.

She tightened her resolve and continued like a soldier who was going to take the hill and defeat the army all by herself.

Stretching the ladder out, she chuckled when she thought of commercials that warned, "Don't try this at home."

She measuredly moved up each rung with the saw in tow, sure that she was a sight to be seen.

Misplacing her step on the fifth rung, she waivered.

Gripping the rung, she found her footing. Doubt invaded her mind, as common sense pleaded for her to listen.

The ladder swayed with each renewed step, and the wind tried to keep her from her goal.

She struggled cautiously up the remaining rungs, achieving her final goal.

She closed her eyes and breathed deeply.

Maneuvering the saw into place on the branch, she made only two motions as the ladder exaggerated each effort.

A mighty wind shifted the branch away and back at her.

Wide-eyed, she dropped the saw to shield her face. Knowing that she was going to be walloped by it, she braced herself for the worse as she prayed, "Help!"

She heard the branch break and watched it fall as the wind pushed it away from her ladder, landing three feet away from the house and the fence.

Triumphant that she had finally taken care of the annoying branch, she beamed that she hadn't slipped nor hurt herself.

Examining her situation, she recognized that someone had to be praying for her.

***

The wind carried the rain in sheets over Ethan's window.

Finally, comfortable in his chair, he began Phillip's book again, but the pages had shifted while he was away.

He took a sip of his cup and decided to start where it laid.

> There may be a time where you feel
> that you are responsible for someone's
> death, and it has taken you away from God. It
> could be because you blame God more than
> you do yourself. Or maybe you don't think it
> is your fault, and you shift the blame to God.
>
> But God will not be insulted with our
> sin and wrongdoing, and He will let you know
> that He is God, and He will do everything in
> His power to let you know this truth.
>
> What will God use to get your
> attention? What storm will you have to go
> through until you get the message that He

wants you to believe in Him as your Lord and Savior?

There are many times in the Bible that God had used the loss of someone to bring about his love into someone else's life.

Let's do a comparison study.

David, the man that the Bible said was a man after God's own heart, was caught in adultery and murder. He lost his child because of his disobedience, and he had to choose if he was going to blame God or blame himself.

Pharaoh, a man who thought he was a god, who was responsible for the mistreatment, enslavement, and death of God's chosen people. He lost his child because of his disobedience, and he had to choose if he was going to blame God or blame himself.

Both Pharaoh and David had son's that died because of their disobedience.

Some criticize God in these scenarios and give both Pharaoh and David a 'Get out of jail for free' card. However, the truth is that we should concentrate on Pharaoh and David's response.

Let's do a little mental gymnastics and separate God from these stories and examine their results.

Based on the story of Pharaoh, Moses interceded on behalf of the Israelites, and he was not sorry nor repentant, but full of hate and avarice. Pharoah thought himself to be a god who was above everything, thus giving him the right to do his atrocities.

Then we look at the story of David. When confronted with what he had done, he unknowingly condemned himself. Then when he admitted his sin, he quit covering it up, repented and accepted the consequence for his wrong.

Just like Pharaoh and David, intervention showed them their sin.

We are no different, we still have interventions and consequences today. We look at their sin and deem it less than ours because we read about theirs in a few pages and we know the volumes we've committed.

Then we enter God back into the picture and make him the scapegoat. He gets blamed, and we seek solace in his blasphemy, all because we don't want to believe that He is just. Or some just keep continue with the mental gymnastics and eliminate Him altogether, suffering the hopelessness that reasoning inevitably brings.

So, name your vice and do the same mental exercise of separating God from your sin and examine the results.

Be honest with yourself and confess your sin, not someone else's, but yours. Do not quit, for no one is beyond going through the valley.

The valley of shadow of death is dark and painful. Its labyrinth of twists and snares, which paralyzes us, brings us to despair, tortures us with our own fears.

Now, enter God into this exercise and identify if He is trying to get your attention? Is He your comfort? Is He guiding you? Is He your refuge? Is He your everything so you lack nothing?

Think about what God endures because of us? He suffers our disobedience, rejection, manipulation and pride, sending His Son as His great plan of our salvation; a ransom paying the full price of our disobedience if we receive Him.

God gives us the choice that Pharaoh and David also had. His voice calls, "What else do I have to do to get your attention?" and "Will you choose Me?"

Outside the lightning electrified the sky, the thunder rumbled, the wind stirred, and the rain saturated everything, but the synchronicity of the book and the storm raging outside and within perplexed him.

Each word had pierced him, and some of the phrases echoed within his mind. They drudged up his deficiencies in his marriage, but he still refused to acknowledge and accept that he was mostly to blame.

He recognized that he had ignored, prodded and made fun of her faith. Making things as hard as he could, because he considered himself abandoned and held onto his right to be right.

As the tempest blew through his memory, it reminded him of the similar fateful night that his wife had left him alone, as his mind fixated on the haunting text that he made as her memorial: **Can't wait 2 C U at home!**

"Dear God, help me!" escaped his lips.

Astonished, he covered his mouth and evaluated what had made him compromise his beliefs with that exclamation. The only thing that was atypical was Beth's Bible and Phillip's books in the room with him.

He downed another glass of wine, hoping to invalidate the power within the books. He unsuccessfully collected his composure and chuckled as his vision blurred, "I'm drunk. That's what is impairing me." Then his demeanor soured at this revelation as he cursed himself for his vulnerability.

However, the comparison between Pharaoh and David played tug-of-war inside his mind, as it mentally weaved through his conscience: Which is he? Pharaoh or David. Which is the truth? Is it what Phillip devotes himself to or what I conceal beneath my drinking?

He scoffed, "Let's see what answers Pastor Phillip has," as he continued reading, "Sometimes the Holy Spirit will cry out to God for us. During these times whatever we endure is to make us more in God's image . . ."

Ethan thought of his previous exclamation to God helping him and dropped the book as if it burned him.

Sitting in his chair, he just stared at it.

The storm briefly calmed, allowing him time to collect his thoughts.

He didn't have the confidence nor comfort that the God he'd denied his entire lifetime was trying to reach out to him.

Still, his mind felt like two dogs squaring off for its territory. His heart was beating in his ears.

Keeping his eye on the book, he rose to his feet and encircled it.

He tried to convince himself that everything had been a coincidence and then glared at the Bible.

Emotions surrounded him as the storm allayed.

Eerily, he didn't feel alone and felt the desire to speak to God. But fear overtook him because he was afraid God would answer.

Rallying up his skepticism, he quietly prayed, "Show yourself."

Nothing happened.

With the wine bottle in hand, he toasted the air and scoffed, "That's what I thought." Attempting to sit back in his seat, he tripped into his side table, collapsing with the Bible hitting him in the head and then landing on his chest.

Gathering his senses, he sat up as the Bible slid off his chest. He became aware that the bottle was no longer in his hand. Frantic that the wine would stain the carpet he searched for the bottle. Alleviated, he found it lying down with none of it spilled.

Examining the amount in it, he thought, "I couldn't have drunk that much," as he rubbed his temples.

The thunder shook his house, as he noticed that he had a headache. He continued rubbing his temples, as he turned his attention to the Bible that had hit him in the head.

He sat there, seeing that it was open. He had heard of people finding the answers they needed by this coincidence, and he didn't want to fall into its power, so he closed it.

He took a deep breath, flipped through several pages and read, "Behold, I stand at the door [12]..."

He heard some debris slam into his house, and he tossed the Bible over to where he had thrown Phillip's book earlier.

Exhaustion overwhelmed him, but not from the wine that he'd drunk tonight, but from his continuous struggle that he wanted to become numb to. He recognized that the cost of his selfishness and the consequences that he'd endured was mainly from him having to prove himself right against his wife.

Rubbing the groove in his ring finger, he thought of how no matter how badly he treated her, she was still gracious.

Who was at fault, rushed like trains destined for collision in his thoughts. Wanting to change his line of reasoning, he considered how he wanted her back, and he came full circle on his hatred of God.

Being on speaking terms with God, he scoffed as he prayed again, "Show yourself."

He noticed a small note next to him. He knew that he hadn't seen it earlier and figured that it fell from the Bible when he'd thrown it.

He read the note, and anguish flooded over him as he wept.

Wiping his tears, he dropped the note.

---

[12] Revelations 3:20

He grabbed the wine bottle and struggled up, leaving the books where they laid.

Lightning lit the room, and he swallowed hard.

He grabbed the note, and read it again: I wanted to give this to you. I hope it becomes the treasure to you that it has become to me.

Ethan placed it back into the Bible, finished the second bottle of wine and then drifted off to sleep in his armchair.

***

Phillip opened his eyes from praying and let out a gasp. He didn't know if he was praying for Tracy, Frank or Mary, but knew that he was participating in spiritual warfare and that the Holy Spirit was working.

Looking out the window, he examined the calm after the storm.

Yawning, he didn't feel like he was going to have to fight any more battles tonight. The storm had cleansed him of his apathy.

He hobbled to his bed and saw that Lilly had taken over again while snoring horribly.

He picked her up and placed her on her floor. He felt the strain on his leg, but it was worth the little pain to get a good night's rest.

Closing his eyes, he went to sleep with a smile on his face.

***

Coming down the ladder, Jessica dreaded the mud that she had to trudge through to get out of the rain. Familiar anger swelled up within her, as she thought about getting dirtier.

She closed her eyes, so she could take her thoughts captive. She knew that she heard God whisper through the storm, "It's OK to get dirty, you're cleanable."

Letting out a healthy laugh at herself, she splashed in the mud puddles like a little girl.

She finally made it to the garage: muddy, sop and wet.

Raising her hands in triumph over such an easy task, she laughed because it was not easy at all. Then she remembered that it could have been if she would have done it when conditions were better.

She then wondered on what tasks she now faced would have been easier if she'd handled them when conditions were better.

She prayed, "God, help me with the mess that I've made, and I don't mean all of this mud. Please give me the strength to continue to do what You want of me."

Exhausted, she left her mess where it was and went to bed.

***

The storm carried its fury to its next location, making its presence known and affecting everything in its path.

Effectively, bringing heaven to earth and loosening the weak and testing the strong.

Part 7.

The Revelation

Chapter 23. Getting Affairs in Order

After being purged and cleansed by last night's storm, Jessica thought about the freedom that she now felt. Motivated to not only be satisfied with cutting down a tree limb, she knew that she needed to continue to take action and correct the other relationships in her life.

Several thoughts swirled in her head, as she was inundated by them all vying for her attention. Not being able to grasp them all, she grabbed a pen and paper and wrote down:

1.   Call Scott and tell him my feelings.
2.   Call Naomi and ask for forgiveness.
3.   Call Claire and ask for forgiveness.
4.   Visit Phillip and ask for forgiveness.

Looking at the list, each line was a burden, paralyzing her into inaction. All the other things that she could be doing wrestled for her attention.

She thought about the fallen branch, the ladder, and all the mud that she had left from last night's event. Thinking of that, caused her to think about how she didn't get a chance to clean herself up afterward. Then she thought about how the neighbors wouldn't appreciate her leaving the unsightly mess. Next, she knew that she needed to clean up all the pictures from yesterday also. Later she knew that she'd have to wash the dishes.

Looking back at her list, she said aloud, "God, help me! I know what I must do, and I can't stop myself from going back to my old patterns."

Then convicted that she'd forgotten God, she added above Scott's line:

½.   Spend time with God.

Studying that line, she wondered what that meant for her. She had been a Christian since her 20's and married to a pastor, and she still couldn't define what spending time with God meant.

Looking around her room, she saw the light streaming across her bed. Then she thought about how she should wash the bed. Then she remembered that she had to go shopping and buy laundry detergent. She grabbed her list and began to write down the grocery list and then she caught herself again.

Putting her face into her hands, she started to shake uncontrollably.

The silence in the room was broken, as she tilted her head back and guffawed.

In between trying to catch her breath, she said aloud, "Aren't I the perfect pastor's wife. I can't keep my mind focused on You more than 5 seconds."

Bound and determined that she was going to complete her list, she recalled an old trick she used in college. She went to the kitchen and grabbed a timer and then went back to her bed and twisted it to 20 minutes and said to herself, "OK, I can do this."

Her train of thought before she was distracted doubled back, as she meditated on what spending time with God meant to her.

She began to become distracted again, but this time, she had kept the mantra, "Time with God" in her head to keep her focused.

Spotting her Bible across the room, she went to get it.

She began to sneeze from all the dust that was stirred when she picked it up, and then she saw Phillip's letters that had gathered up.

She ran her finger across the dust, then turned to leave to get some cleaner. Then she focused herself reciting, "Time with God."

Discouraged with herself, she gave a heavy sigh.

Then her heart sank, as she looked at Phillip's letters. Knowing that he would encourage and tell her how much he loved her made her want to so desperately open them.

She heard the timer ticking down the seconds, and regained her focus as the mantra, "Time with God," relapsed in her memory.

She jumped on the bed, opened the Bible, and then closed it quickly because she hadn't prayed. She bowed her head and prayed, "God, please lead me!"

She reopened the Bible and saw that she was in Phillippians 3. She took a deep breath, deciding to read with no interruptions.

No Confidence in the Flesh. [13]

Stopping right there, she looked at the timer and heard it ticking by. She gave a harrumph, thinking, "Isn't this the perfect subject for me, I can't even keep myself on task, of course I have no confidence in the flesh."

Discouraged that she was hampering herself, she put her finger on the page and forced herself to follow.

> Further, my brothers and sisters, rejoice in the Lord! It is no trouble for me to write the same things to you again, and it is a safeguard for you. Watch out for those dogs, those evildoers, those mutilators of the flesh. For it is we who are the circumcision, we who serve God by his Spirit, who boast in Christ Jesus, and who put no confidence in the flesh—though myself I have reasons for such confidence.

Biting her lip and scratching the back of her head, she reread the passage and could only concentrate on the words: dogs, mutilators and circumcision.

Compelling herself to not be distracted, she continued reading.

> If someone else thinks they have reasons to put confidence in the

[13] NIV Bible, Philippians 3 – All references.

flesh, I have more: circumcised on the
eighth day, of the people of Israel, of
the tribe of Benjamin, a Hebrew of
Hebrews; in regard to the law, a
Pharisee; as for zeal, persecuting the
church; as for righteousness based on
the law, faultless.

She pondered about this passage and wondered why
the writer was giving a resume, why he was bragging about
it and why hadn't Jesus been brought up. Feeling her eyes
cross she looked at the timer and saw that she had only
been reading for less than a minute.

Drawing a deep breath, she dove back into the Bible.

But whatever were gains to me
I now consider loss for the sake of
Christ. What is more, I consider
everything a loss because of the
surpassing worth of knowing Christ
Jesus my Lord, for whose sake I have
lost all things. I consider them
garbage, that I may gain Christ and be
found in him, not having a
righteousness of my own that comes
from the law, but that which is
through faith in Christ—the
righteousness that comes from God
on the basis of faith. "I want to know
Christ—yes, to know the power of his
resurrection and participation in his
sufferings, becoming like him in his
death, and so, somehow, attaining to
the resurrection from the dead.

She thought, "Well, now I understand the resume, he
considers it garbage for Christ sake."

Stopping on that thought, she mused, "What is my
garbage?"

She closed her eyes, overwhelmed from judging her own self.

Several words came to her mind about her garbage, each pelting her. She looked back at the same verse and then meditated on the phrase, "... not having a righteousness of my own."

She wondered what that meant and saw a reference to Luke 18:9. She jotted that down to be checked out later as she wrote that phrase on her hand to be meditated upon throughout the day.

She continued studying the same passage and began playing with the phrase, "... knowing the power of his resurrection and participation in his sufferings, becoming like him in his death..."

She jotted down, "How have I participated in Jesus' suffering?"

She dwelled on it a bit and then wrote down, "Failed." Circling it several times.

The timer broke her concentration and she quickly reset it, not wanting to stop her studying.

> Not that I have already
> obtained all this, or have already
> arrived at my goal, but I press on to
> take hold of that for which Christ
> Jesus took hold of me. Brothers and
> sisters, I do not consider myself yet to
> have taken hold of it. But one thing I
> do: Forgetting what is behind and
> straining toward what is ahead, I press
> on toward the goal to win the prize
> for which God has called me
> heavenward in Christ Jesus.

She caught herself smiling because the writer thought the same way she did, or she thought the same way the writer did. Either way, hope started to take root in her soul.

She reread the resume passage again and thought about her own resume. She understood that the writer was talking about him following his own path and thinking that he was perfect from it. The she thought about how she thought she was perfect, and how the writer stated that his perfection was garbage.

She looked at what she wrote on her hand, "... not having a righteousness of my own," and began to understand her fault.

She wrote under it, "It's garbage."

She then scanned the passage that she just read, "Forgetting what is behind and straining toward what is ahead, I press on toward the goal to win the prize for which God has called me heavenward in Christ Jesus."

She fell in love with the prose but felt like she was dealing with a riddle. She wrote, "Forget behind - Press onto goal," on her hand, so she could noodle it through out the day.

She wondered who the writer was and then read the next heading, "**Following Paul's Example.**"

She wrote on the notepad, "Read more Paul, he speaks to me," as the timer went off and she closed the Bible.

Looking at the rest of her list, she checked off "½ Spend time with God."

Then she looked at the next one on the list: Call Scott.

Curling her upper lip in disgust, she forced herself to continue because she knew that this step was more for herself and her marriage.

She went to the guest room where she had laid out all the pictures and grabbed her phone and dialed Scott's number.

It rang once, and Scott answered, "Well, hello Jess. So, why am I blessed to have this time with you?"

Taking a deep breath, Jessica blurted it all out before she could be interrupted, "Scott, you and I have been really good friends for years. Moreover, you know that I value our relationship, but I don't think that I've ever gotten over you, and I suppose that

I've substituted Phillip for you. Most of the time, I pray for you to get a wife more than I think and pray for Phillip's needs. I have spoken to you more this last week than I have with him. It's not that I want to leave Phillip it is that I need to concentrate on him more than being diverted by my feelings and concern for you.

God did some major work on me last night, and this is something that I've needed to do for a long time, but I have not been obedient."

Scott interrupted, "Can I say something?" but she gathered her resolve all the more as she continued, "Scott, please understand that Phillip is going to be my top priority. I thought love was going to be easy and that everything was going to be perfect, but it's been very hard.

The biggest thing that I've recently relearned is that love is a choice and that I have to continue to choose my husband every day, which means that I've got to change my feelings for you."

Scott managed to say, "Jessica, I don't understand ..."

Not wanting to lose her momentum, Jessica steamrolled over him, "I'm sorry that you don't understand, and it's my fault for putting you in the middle. It was a place you were never meant to be. I know that now. The blame lies completely with me. I'm changing things between our relationship and I'd like for you to not call me anymore and not to come over unless Phillip's here."

Jessica paused, relieved that she had progressed this far.

Scott tried to interject during the break, "Jessica, will you please ...," but not wanting to have any influence in her decision, she ignored his pleas and informed, "I choose Phillip and I want to be the wife he deserves. I want to live a life where he's the most important person in my life."

Considering what she had learned in her Bible study this morning, she backpedaled, "Well, God would be first, but Phillip is next, then Naomi and Claire. What I'm trying to say is that I'm going to try my best to live this way. This is my focus. I'm not going to compromise this. OK?"

After saying her piece, she was so pleased with herself for not wavering and waited on the phone for Scott's response.

Scott finally answered, "OK!? I understand that you're upset about something, but I do not know what about. I'm getting bits and pieces of what you're saying because I'm driving in an area with bad cell phone coverage. I heard that 'you are a wife that preserves,' 'Cuban defense for dog years' and 'its debt reads into penetrate autumn.' I'll call you back with I'm in better cell coverage. Bye now."

Rage started to surge within her when she heard the click of the phone hanging up.

She stared at the phone incredulously, because she wanted to get this part behind her before she continued on her list. Especially before she called Claire.

She put the phone down, silently praying to God that He would calm her and give her better perspective.

She decided that the conversation with Scott would be better when Phillip could be there with her.

She went to cross Scott of the list, but put a wavy line and wrote, "To be continued ...."

Not let this stop her, she looked at her scribbles on her hand and decided to press on.

She paused before continuing and acknowledged to herself that she was still being overly melodramatic.

Taking a quick breath, she held down the speed dial for Naomi.

She waited through the rings and heard Naomi's voice, "Hello, this is Naomi."

Jessica launched into her spiel, "Hi, Naomi, this is your mother. I ..."

Naomi answered, "Hello? Hello?"

Jessica restarted, "Hi, Naomi, this is your mother. I ..."

Naomi continued, "... I am not available right now. Please leave a message after the beep."

Jessica closed her eyes and released her grip from the phone as she tried to quell her anger.

She absolutely hated Naomi's voice mail and became frustrated every time she called her.

She relaxed her jaw as she assessed, "I'm trying to change and do well, but I'm being thwarted at every step."

Giving a quick shrug, she thought, "I'm not a victim anymore. Starting right now, I choose to give to them, regardless of what I receive back. I am not just going to be a taker."

Regarding the memento of her Bible study on her hand, she prayed, " Jesus, please help me to be your servant."

Then she remembered that the voicemail was still waiting.

Feeling foolish for all the dead air that she'd left, she stammered but finally hit her stride, "Naomi, I just called to let you know that God has worked on me recently and has helped me to find out that everything's not about me. That I should look at other's struggles and be a help. That what Jesus cares about, I should care also. That what He holds dear I should hold dear likewise.

I thank God for the woman that you are now. I pray that you and Jonathan have a great life together and do the best that you can do with the poor example that I have been."

Pausing, she began to choke up and feel tears well up in her eyes.

Clearing her throat, she continued, "Wow, this is really hard to do on a voicemail. I pray that you, please understand my intent and know that I'm trying to be a better person.

Know that I love you always. Sometimes, I know I don't act like that I do, but y'all don't make it entirely easy for me."

Catching her self-centeredness, she rephrased, "I'm sorry, I know that I'm to blame for not making anything easy for anyone. I can't get past what has happened to our family right now. I thought everything was perfect and that I was invulnerable. Then your dad got shot, and I realized how calloused I've been all along, how demanding that I am and how I apathetically see everything.

I know that I'm rambling, but I want you to know that I'm trying to make amends with your father, you and your sister. I don't hold anything against any of you and thank you for bearing with my overbearing nature. I know that I have a lot to be forgiven for, and I pray that all of y'all can see it in your hearts to forgive me."

The tears began to trail down her cheek as she started to feel the weight of the word 'forgive.'

Looking at her hand, she read, "Forget behind," and deliberated, "How?"

Then she thought about her resume being garbage.

She knew that she was asking for too much, but prayed that she could get some relief.

She bit her lip and thought of how easy everything seemed in her mind when she wrote the list and thought about calling everyone, but now she was tired of the one-sided conversations and wished that she'd get some comfort

She mumbled, "I sure wish that you were here and that I didn't have to do all this alone. My love for you is always and give my love to Jonathan.."

She hung up the phone and let it hang by her side.

Looking at all the smiling faces of her family in all the pictures on the floor, she pushed them away from her because she didn't feel like any of her smiles in the pictures were genuine, but forced. She was amazed that her family somehow found happiness in spite of her.

Trying to shrug away the despair, she shook her head and chanted, "Press on. Press on."

She crossed out Naomi's line on the list and then cringed at handling the next challenge, but she knew that it had to be done.

She prayed, "Dear Jesus, I pray for compassion."

She shook her hands and began to take deep breaths, and then dialed Claire's phone number.

She heard the phone ring on her phone and then heard a ring at the door of the room. During the next ring, the echo repeated.

She felt like cursing her rotten luck. She mollified herself, thinking that just because she was ready to reconcile did not mean they were ready to do it on her time frame.

The phone rang again, and she patiently waited for the voice mail.

She heard the echo for the third time and then heard Claire answer, "Mom, I love you."

She registered that she had just heard Claire in stereo, live and then on the phone.

She turned to the door and saw Claire, answering into the phone, "I love you, too!"

Hanging up the phone, she raced to give Claire a long hug.

Jessica finally managed through her tears, "How long have you been there?"

Claire answered, "Well, I walked into the house from the open garage and followed the muddy trail up to your room. Seeing that the light was on, I almost called out to see if you had left this room or ask about the muddy mess. Getting to the door, I saw that you were on the phone.

In answer to your question, I caught the end of your call to Scott. Around the time, you were saying how you had put Scott in the middle."

Jessica thought about all the conversations that Claire may have overheard but decided that she didn't have anything to cover up anymore.

However, a mild anger welled up within her about her privacy being invaded upon, but she tempered it by remembering that she'd turned a new leaf.

Claire broke her internal criticism by asking, "So, mom what is it that you've got to say?"

Jessica looked at her phone and then back to Claire and explained, "Well, you've heard a majority of it. Let's see. I've recognized that my feelings for Scott were out of line. I'm failing as a wife with your father. I understand that I've been acting like a spoiled princess who demanded my own way and that I've made y'all responsible for my happiness, but now know that I'm responsible for my reactions, and lastly that I've tried to make y'all live up to my expectations, which I didn't even live up to and that God doesn't even expect

I'm sorry for my selfishness, and I'm trying to change. I make no excuses, and I really mean that I'm sorry. Please forgive me; I didn't know how broken I was."

Jessica saw Claire allow her walls to fall as she cried, "Mom, I do love you, and I do forgive you. Let's get through this together."

Through her snot and tears, Jessica blurted out, "I'm sorry for all the criticism ... No, I mean the extreme criticism that I gave because I thought you were trying to make me look bad. You're old enough that I should be more your sister in Christ who is helping you to get on with your life, before being your mother who is pushing her fears onto you. I know that I've been childish and hope that you'd forgive me for everything that I've done and for what I have made you responsible for.

My passions have been so out of control that I didn't notice what I had already. Like a spoiled brat, I looked at what everyone else had and made all of you do the heavy lifting, as I just enjoyed the ride and complained when things got a little bumpy for me."

Jessica stepped away and looked outside for the first time. She almost gasped at the damage that had taken place.

Hearing that Claire had followed, she gazed at the note on her hand and resumed, "Claire, it's just like you said. I thought that I had the perfect Christian resume, but I've found out that I'm no different than the world. I worried more about what others thought of me, about having the right colors, smiling at the right time, or to appear to be all right. Now I know that it's all right for me not to be perfect, but to let God do His work in me."

Seeing her reflection in the window, Jessica continued ranting, "I know that I must look such a mess. I tried to put on make-up this morning and had such a hard time because I felt like I was trying to cover up something that couldn't be hidden anymore. That the cover-up was only for my benefit because my failings were so obvious to everyone else even though I was oblivious to it. Now that I think about it, it's weird; I've cared so much about what others think about me that I've covered everything up which only exposed my problems all the more."

Jessica looked at the branch that she fell last night and felt pride well up within her, then deflated as she continued divulging, "I've also come to find out that I've put too much on your father. He's always been the one that made everything … No, I've made him the one to make everything all right. Then this whole situation happened. You've got to understand that my world has been turned upside down and exposed to the point where I could see all of my illusions. I now understand that your dad is vulnerable and that I have nothing without him. I blamed him, not because I thought he had had an affair. I figured he had let me down, and to no fault of his own. I've held him responsible for things that shouldn't have been his responsibility. I wanted him to be my Savior."

Catching a glimpse of her notes on her hands, she snickered and said, "I didn't even read the Bible for myself. I was entirely dependent on Phillip to be God's mouthpiece, even though God had written everything down in a book about how much He loves me."

Tears began to flow down Jessica's cheek as she whimpered, "Phillip's wrote several letters telling me how much he loves me and I've taken it for granted. I've left them sitting in the dust next to my Bible. The things that I so desperately wanted was for God and your father to tell me how much they loved me and I … and I …."

***

Claire watched her mom's blubbering and wanted to say something, but thought better of it. She didn't want to ruin the moment.

Exhausted, she felt that she had found the edge of her emotions; two days was the limit.

She had wanted to have this moment with her mother as long as she could remember and now that she had it, she fought the urge to look at her watch.

She thought, "Life is so ironic!" as she reached down, took off her watch and placed it in her pocket.

With renewed interest, she put her arms around her mother.

***

Jessica sat at the mess of picture on the floor, grabbed a tissue and blew her nose and continued, "There were times that I felt I was in competition with your dad for you and your sister's love. I thought he was winning and that I had to assert myself. What I didn't recognize was that I was sabotaging myself by trying to win."

Claire answered, "Mom, it was never a game and we lost more than you won."

Jessica grabbed more tissues and buried her face in them, crying hysterically.

Sorrow filled Claire's heart, knowing that she had destroyed the moment. She silently reprimanded herself, "You fool, you don't always have to have something to say," as she waited for her mom to speak.

Jessica tried to calm herself, sobbing less, but still with syncopation between each word, "I don't know how to make things right. How do I come back to Phillip and make everything normal? I don't feel like I'm worth his while. Besides, I know that I deserve it because I'm the one who pushed him away. I'm the one who has forgotten my first love. I've put everything in front of him, thinking that everyone else was more important than he was. It's all my fault that Phillip is alone right now and that he's not in this house. "

Claire shifted her weight from foot to foot, trying her best to allow her mom to express herself, but decided to interrupt her mother's pity party saying, "Mom, let Jesus and dad make their own decisions, instead of you making up their minds for them. Trust them and let them love you.

Please just go and read dad's letters, the Bible and then find out what they think about you. Don't just read them for information, but for how they express their love for you and receive it."

Jessica came up with every excuse of why she couldn't do it, then she remembered her morning's procrastination. She got up, blew her nose, went to her room and started reading some well-needed affirmation.

Chapter 24. Painful Victory

"I feel like that I'm drifting through life and that no one would really care if I just disappeared. I'm more comfortable with the shadows people cast than being with them," complained Frank.

Phillip sat in the counseling session listening to Frank spilling his guts and watching the reactions from the group. He was very attentive because he'd had the best sleep since being shot.

Looking around the circle, Frank sat at the edge of his seat while petting his imaginary cat, Kevin had his arm around Frank consoling him, Mary rocked in her seat with her knees up to her chin, and TJ had been quiet.

Everyone knew that TJ was there, but he wasn't parading himself.

Phillip figured that Ethan had finally corrected him, or he was biding his time.

Ethan sat in the circle also, inattentive and scribbling in his notepad about something else.

Phillip was sure that the 'something else' was something about him because Ethan hadn't looked him in the eye nor acknowledged his presence. He figured that it was his imagination getting the best of him, until Ethan started the group session by recognizing each person by name, except for him.

He racked his mind, trying to think of anything that he'd done to upset Ethan recently. He'd done everything that Dr. Pitney had requested of him: he kept his journal, and he'd mingled with the other patients.

He did, however, get a brief chance to see Ethan's notepad and saw a drawing of King Tut.

Shrugging it off, he saw that Mr. Abiel behind Ethan and praying for him.

This was the first time that he'd seen him since yesterday, he tried to reconcile on how he could 'stay low and heal' like Ethan wanted him to do and also work within Mr. Abiel's rebuke about 'still being called by God' and 'stop feeling sorry for himself.'

After last night's storm, Phillip felt that his spiritual drought was over. He had a great time with Jesus this morning during his prayers and felt like that he'd been purged.

However, he couldn't relate with his devotional from this morning. It was on I Corinthians 5, about the man sleeping with his father's wife.

Phillip had a difficult time thinking about how incest was going to help him get through his current situation.

He couldn't put any more attention to it as Frank began again, "I wish things could be different. I wish I were worth the time and effort of my wife. I wish she didn't leave me."

With each phrase, Frank was broken more, to the point that he began crying.

Kevin consoled, "Frank, I know what it's like when things get bad," as he gave an overly firm pat on Frank's back.

Kevin continued, "When my son died, I thought of when he would be coming back. He's going to come back more beautiful than any other butterfly. I need to be sure that I'm ready for when he comes."

Phillip's good mood turned dismal, as TJ perked up from Kevin's last statement. TJ raised his eyebrows and smirked at him with a devilish grin. His heart sank as Frank lost control of the conversation, and TJ straightened up, leaning slightly forward towards him and said, "Pastor P.A. are you going to tackle this one or should I?"

Phillip tried to think about Kevin's last statement, but admittedly, he wasn't paying enough attention and couldn't form a reply. He was thinking of the joy he had from being released from his trials last night, how his leg didn't ache that much and how good that he'd slept.

Considering his inaction during the last therapy session and the rebuke that he received afterward, he looked over Ethan's shoulder for help and wisdom from Mr. Abiel, but all he saw was compassion and encouragement, but no hint of what to do.

Still finding that the connection between his brain and tongue was tied into the 'Gordian Knot,' Phillip didn't want to admit that he wasn't paying attention nor give an off the cuff answer. Knowing that he had to present a reply, he cleared his throat and was about to speak to the group for the first time.

Before he could answer, TJ turned to Kevin and said, "Man, the rules to this life are pretty simple. Marriage is antiquated. It's a 'take before taken' type of world. You're what you make of yourself. Life does not owe anything to anyone. Life is all about experiences. Oh, and your son, he isn't coming back. Ever!"

Kevin squalled, "TJ, you mock everyone. Why are you here? Please tell us how you're a self-made man and how taking before being taken has helped you."

As Kevin interrogated, TJ sat there smugly, enjoying the chaos that he'd accomplished.

Kevin became flustered all the more and began yelling, "What have you made of yourself? Because, the way I see it, you're just like the rest of us except you are the worst because you hide and prey on those who have given up the fight. You act as if you are a tough guy, but you're hiding behind a facade just like the rest of us. What do you look like when you look in the mirror without the mask?"

TJ answered in a mockingly singsong manner, "If I were a butterfly, With wings so bright. I would have gone, To the clouds in the sky. Asked them to rain, on the little flowers, To have a very pretty sight, For all day and night."[14]

Putting his arms up in exasperation, Kevin plugged his ears while he said, "Stop it. Not again! I hate that song! Go back into the Hell hole you crawled out from."

TJ jumped up into the middle of the circle and took a bow as if he was entertaining the group.

Not getting the reaction that he wanted, he sauntered over to Mary and sang, "Mary Mary quite contrary, How does your

[14] If I were a Butterfly – Nursery Rhyme

garden grow? With silver bells and cockle shells And pretty maids all in a row."[15]

At the end of the song, TJ looked Mary over inappropriately, causing her to shift in her seat. She adjusted her legs she had under her chin to the point where one could only see her eyes.

TJ raised his eyebrows with a lowbrow statement, "So, how does your garden grow?"

Phillip felt compelled to do something, but he was still paralyzed by her previous actions. He formed a response, but when he caught her eyes, she winked.

Taken aback, his mind went blank as he looked at the clock and began to count the second hand on the clock again.

Ethan finally stepped in and disciplined, "TJ, you need to stop and sit down."

TJ squared off Ethan and continued in singsong, "I do not like thee, Doctor Fell, The reason why - I cannot tell; But this I know, and know full well, I do not like thee, Doctor Fell. [16]"

Then TJ danced around the outside of the circle like a jester, patting each person on the head saying "Duck" each time.

Ethan summoned, "TJ, please sit down."

Surprised with Ethan's patience with TJ's belligerence, Phillip pondered why he didn't have the same patience with him. Not wanting Satan to get a foothold and steal his joy that had started the night before, he quickly dismissed it.

Phillip came out of his reverie when he noticed TJ was quiet, and the group was looking above his head. Knowing that he was the next person in Tennessee Jack's little game and that he hadn't done anything, he twisted around and saw TJ's face in front of his as he loudly said, "BOOO!"

Frank jumped up and down, clapping his hands like he was in kindergarten as TJ exuberantly declared, "I have one for you Pastor P.A.. 'Humpty Dumpty sat on a wall, Humpty Dumpty had a

---

[15] Mary Mary Quite Contrary – Nursery Rhyme – Public Domain.

[16] I do not like thee, Doctor Fell – Nursery Rhyme – Public Domain

great fall; All the king's horses and all the king's men Couldn't put Humpty together again.'[17]"

TJ let out a horse laugh and bellowed, "Get it gimp! You're all alone, and God has abandoned you."

TJ held his finger up to his lip as if he was in deep thought and then overly exaggeratedly said like he was teaching a small child, "Because, he doesn't exist. He is a nursery rhyme you tell yourself to feel better. That's why God was not there for you, nor Mary, nor Kevin, nor Frank, nor Ethan. He's only a platitude that you comfort yourself with."

Struggling with his reply, Phillip didn't feel like he could convey the truth without sounding like the kid on the playground who couldn't come up with anything except "Oh yeah!"

Therefore, he sat there taking his lumps, sure that he looked like a failure to Mr. Abiel.

Wanting to stop the silliness, Ethan suggested, "OK, TJ enough."

TJ responded like a kid talking back to his mother, "Big man, I'm just having fun."

Kevin answered, "TJ, that was a secret. Now everyone's going to know that Ethan is the big man."

Ethan gently smiled at Kevin and replied, "It's all right Kevin, I knew."

Phillip then recalled Kevin saying something about "the big man' losing something and being mad about it. He still was puzzled as to what Ethan was angry about losing. But then he gained a glimpse of his notepad again, and saw what he'd thought was a drawing of David with his slingshot with Goliath in front of him.

Not understanding Ethan's reasoning to draw that scene, he looked at TJ and knew that he'd met his Goliath, one who cursed God while others were paralyzed by their fear. Phillip quietly prayed for strength like David had to confront TJ.

Ethan looked at his watch and said, "TJ, we're waiting."

Looking around the group, TJ said as he took a bow and sat down, "OK, the show is over. Thank you very much."

[17] Humpty Dumpty – Nursery Rhyme – Public Domain

The group relaxed, relieved and glad that Ethan had finally reigned in TJ.

Kevin leaned over to Frank and said, "Are you OK, Frank?"

Coming back to his senses, Frank took a breath and started stroking his imaginary cat again, and said, "Yeah, I'm back. I hate when TJ does that."

In the corner of his eye, Phillip observed that Ethan had reached for his phone and speculated, "What can you lose on a phone?"

Deciding to not unravel the knot in his thought process, he removed it by cutting it into two.

Finding his voice, Phillip got Frank's attention and said, "Frank, pardon me, but I want to respond to TJ. I want to thank him because he's correct. I am broken. I've lost something precious, just like everyone here has."

TJ loudly spoke, "Ladies and gentlemen, he speaks."

Phillip continued, "I've despaired over what has happened to me long enough. I know what it is that I've lost. This 'lost something' is the same thing that each person in this group has lost. Truthfully, it's what the whole world has lost."

Regarding the small group, he saw that he had their attention, including Ethan.

Phillip continued, "We've been in the dark, and our eyes aren't attuned to see it anymore."

Kevin anxiously answered, "What is it?"

TJ mimicked, "What is it?"

The interest of the group emboldened him as he prayed that his words would convey God's truth. Drawing on his years of public speaking, he continued, "What is it we're looking for? What is the one thing that has gone beyond our grasp? We've tried to find this lost thing through knowledge and understanding. We try to fill its void with our independence, conscience or self-injury."

Phillip glanced at Mr. Abiel, who was grinning ear to ear.

He resumed, "However, what we have lost is the hope of heaven, the hope of eternal life, the hope that this world, as good as it seems and as horrible as it becomes, isn't the final destination that God had in plan for any of us but the precursor of what is yet to come, which is perfect."

TJ tried to speak over Phillip, but unrelenting Phillip continued, "We all have desires here on this earth that are fulfilled: when we're hungry, we eat; when we're thirsty, we drink; when we're cold, we can build a fire, but when we have a desire, a demand if you will, for something that is greater than we are and this world cannot supply it, then we must acknowledge that we all have the desire for our lives to continue on. A hope for someplace greater where we can have a life of peace with no strife, a life to be with our loved ones for eternity, a life where we commit no wrong against each other.

We look at the world and can't be satisfied with it, because the probable explanation is that the life we so desperately want was provided once, and we failed, leaving us with a world that has justice that needs to be paid for by everyone of us. We are the ones who've messed up this perfect life by our wrongdoing. However, this life is still available, the price of justice was dearly paid, but it cannot be found here, and that desire should bring us to the hope that this world is not our final destination and that heaven is calling."

Finished, he was glad that he remembered C.S. Lewis[18] speaking about the subject of hope.

He felt like that he was about to preach and thought that he should back off, but noticed that everyone had sat at the end of their seat, with the exception of Frank and TJ.

***

Ethan felt a touch on his shoulder while Phillip was speaking, but ignored it.

He didn't know how to explain the way he was feeling.

All of his doubt seemed to attempt to block his ears.

He heard TJ trying to talk over Phillip, as Frank tried to contain him and listen to Phillip speaking calmly.

---

[18] "Mere Christianity," Chapter Hope (pgs 136-137) C.S. Lewis. "If I find in myself a desire which no experience in this world can satisfy, the most probable explanation is that I was made for another world..... Probably earthly pleasures were never meant to satisfy it, but only to arouse it, to suggest the real thing.

Ethan found himself hearing Phillip over TJ's cacophony, like when one is hearing someone whisper and it makes you want to pay attention to them all the more.

Looking at TJ, he felt that he was just enjoying the sound of his own voice regardless if anyone was listening.

He was mostly speaking about the ironies in Phillip's beliefs, like the holes that keep intelligent people away from Christianity.

Ethan reflected on how he normally agreed with what TJ was saying, but now all that he felt was the hollowness of the argument.

He knew that something inside him had changed him since last night. He was aware that he'd had a huge hole in his life. He'd acknowledged that a long time ago, but hadn't found anything else to fill the gap.

Looking down at his doodling, he thought about how he'd lost many things and wrote down, "HOPE?"

Studying the group, he was amazed at how many smiles that he saw while they were listening to Phillip.

He observed that Mary had relaxed and wasn't hiding behind her knees, that Frank was trying to have peace whenever TJ wasn't ranting, that Kevin was approving with everything that Phillip was saying like the choir during a sermon.

Still, TJ screamed out louder and louder to be heard. He spouted about the traditional atheist lines about how God had hardened Pharaoh's heart and how a loving God wouldn't do that.

Looking at his doodling again, he thought about how hollow the argument sounded, because he knew that TJ, just like himself, honestly didn't care about Pharaoh. Thinking about Phillip's book, he remembered how it stated that we give more benefit of the doubt to Pharaoh because we identify with him, but don't give any inkling to God.

Challenged, he struggled with the knowledge that he was going to have to reevaluate his beliefs. That if that 'truth' he believed was a lie, what else could be?

His conscience, or was it God convicting him to want to reason out these thoughts and not quickly dismiss them, wrestled with God as he did try to reason things out.

He gently heard a whisper, "Come, I can take it" as he saw a memory of a painting of Jesus with his hands out with the scars showing.

Hearing the call, he wanted to respond, but his stubbornness brought him back from abandoning his ideals. He fought against the thoughts of aborting his beliefs now, considering how he had fought for them and had paid a dear price for his right to be right.

Rubbing the groove on his ring finger, he remembered how his beliefs had cost him his wife.

He whispered, "Dear Beth, I miss you."

***

Stealing a glance towards Ethan, Phillip saw that his spirit was troubled.

He mentally said a quick prayer for a blessing on Ethan.

Turning his attention back to the group, he continued speaking, "We all want justice to prevail, but only justice for those who have wronged us, and don't think about the justice that would condemn us.

We don't examine ourselves because we know we are as guilty as the people we blame. We lie to ourselves thinking that blaming others frees us from what we have done.

However, there is hope for all of us while we journey towards our destination at the end of life. We could share each other's burden, go to the cross, and accept His forgiveness. Let us hold onto this hope, because if we don't, we isolate ourselves and become hopeless, wallowing in pity, anger and despair.

Still, today's culture preaches that we should live our lives to the fullest because the grave is everyone's final destination. But no matter how much they say it, they know their position cannot be defended with their science or knowledge.

It's a question that cannot be answered without faith, and don't let them fool you, they are putting their faith into something.

They put their faith in their own knowledge, their own sense of right and wrong and they force others to succumb to their biases by calling it the standard. But they don't evaluate the question of what happens after the grave. They live their lives as if it is everything and that there is nothing afterward.

They want peace, but conflict quickly comes when their faith is challenged. They want hope, but they don't have comfort in their own achievements. They want to live forever, but their vices rob them of extending their lives. They're always striving for something more as if they have a void that they are trying to fill?

If these beliefs resound within you, then don't blame anything or anyone else for your despair, because you have robbed yourself of hope and decided your own fate.

However, I personally put my faith in the One, who has conquered sin, death, and the grave. The resurrected One who has seen beyond the afterlife of the grave and has told us that He can give life everlasting.

This is what gives me hope, especially considering what I've personally been through."

Pausing to catch his breath, he heard TJ still pleading his case, "His truth cannot be proven either. Why believe this?"

Glimpsing Mr. Abiel, he saw that he was laying his hands on Ethan's shoulders. He looked around to see if anyone else saw him doing this and saw that they were engrossed in his presentation of the gospel, instead of TJ.

He quickly prayed for Ethan once more and then confidently continued, "I'm sure you have heard from those who don't believe, that what I'm telling you right now is only a myth that fools believe. They will passionately tell you we evolved from an ooze and then from monkeys. That the universe was created with a big bang and that God had nothing to do with it[19].

Then they will tell you that Christianity cannot be proven.

---

19 Georges Lemaître, was a Belgian priest, astronomer and professor of physics at the Université catholique de Louvain who came up with the idea of the Big Bang. http://www.amnh.org/education/resources/rfl/web/essaybooks/cosmic/p_lemaitre.html

Truthfully, there is no way for today's culture to prove their own stance either because what they believe changes based on what they can prove, which also changes based on the bias of the day or what they believe in at the moment.

Their personal knowledge and intellect have become their religion that they place their faith in and the dogma that they preach. However, they cannot give any hope, love nor salvation in their conviction, but can only give belonging if you subscribe to their belief."

TJ screamed, "Religion does the same thing."

Phillip nodded in agreement and countered, "But I'm not talking about religion, but a relationship with Jesus Christ."

TJ bantered, "Oh boy, the poster child of perfection."

Phillip responded, "I tell you the truth that there are other evidence other than the Bible stating that Jesus lived on this earth, that He truly did claim to be the Christ, the Messiah, the Anointed One and the only way to God, so much so that they killed him over this one claim. Moreover, he rose again after three days just as had been prophesied.[20]

Jesus is the one who said that you have to only believe and have a relationship with him to live a full life now and beyond the grave. He also said that the grave isn't the end and that He's the resurrection and the life and whoever believes in Him will live, even after dying.[21]"

Pausing for station identification, he checked each face in the group and was amazed that everyone was still engaged.

He did see that Frank was seeking comfort by stroking his imaginary cat, but that he was interrupted by TJ, who sarcastically started to clap his hands.

This act had finally won him the whole group's attention from Phillip.

---

[20] "Antiquities of the Jews,Book 18, Chapter 3" Testimonium Flavianum, Flavius Josephus
Cornelius Tacitus in his Annals, xv. 44

[21] John 11:25

Recognizing that he finally had obtained the attention of the group, he said, "Well isn't that nice? You know that today's scholars have discredited Josephus and all the other historians.[22] You're just like the other Christians who so desperately want their myth to be true. So much so, they have to lie and say that NASA has proved their myth true by finding the missing day mention in the Bible. [23]

Why don't you admit your myth is only founded on unrealistic hopes and dreams?"

***

Ethan watched the conversation between TJ and Phillip volley back and forth. He knew that he had lost control of the group, but he was happy that he was getting some questions answered that had been nagging him since last night during the storm.

Like why he had only found more emptiness in his pursuit to answers, which only led to more questions.

Observing the group, he saw that they were engrossed in the debate also.

Examining Phillip, he was personally well aware of his razor sharp wit and knowledge during their discussions when he first got here, but wondered how he'd manage arguing with an unconscionable man that had no moral compass.

Considering TJ, he was surprised that Phillip was holding his own and having a credible conversation without losing his tempe. He was so used to him normally being a thug when openly challenged and not getting his way.

He was glad to see that TJ had brought up the NASA story because he had stumped several Christian's false belief by busting their bubble with this urban legend. He loved using this to show that Christians would believe in anything. Then he mused about a Christian sharing the condescending story of Albert Einstein shaming an atheist professor by telling him that he had no brain[24].

---

[22] http://www.truthbeknown.com/pliny.htm

[23] http://www.snopes.com/religion/lostday.asp

Then he got the pleasure to humiliate another Christian again by their ignorance because he was quoting another urban legend like scripture.

However, he admitted to himself that he was completely lost during the discussion about Josephus.

He jotted down that he'd have to check it out himself, because if there were proof that the Bible was true, and everything that he believed could be refuted, he'd have to check it out and come to his own conclusion with logic and knowledge.

He still felt like he was wrestling with God as he tried to reason things out.

Startled, he looked around as he gently heard, "Come, I can take it" again.

Ethan turned his attention back to the group, seeing that all eyes were still on Phillip, he was glad he hadn't missed anything.

Observing TJ, he saw that he was leaned back in his chair with his hands clasped behind his head with a sardonic smile.

***

Phillip waited on Ethan, astonished as to why he hadn't halted TJ and him from dominating this group therapy.

Looking into Ethan's eyes, he saw a desperateness in them and perceived that his hand was clutching his phone like it was a chain he willingly used for his penance.

Mr. Abiel shuffled from Ethan to behind Frank. He didn't put his arms on him, but just let his presence be known.

He nodded at Phillip, giving him permission to continue.

Taking in a heavy breath, he began, "You're correct, some Christians put more attention into these folklores than they ought, but Christians aren't the only ones who defend their beliefs by unrealistic hopes and dreams.

Both sides of the debate do harm when we try to "defend" our beliefs with stories and controversies[25].

---

[24] http://www.snopes.com/religion/einstein.asp

[25] THE TESTIMONIUM FLAVIANUM CONTROVERSY FROM ANTIQUITY TO THE

314

I agree that some of these arguments like the NASA story could easily be debunked with a quick google search or by going to Snopes and exercising common sense.

The defense of Christianity should be defended by truth and not by hollow hopes. However, in the same breath, one shouldn't interpret something false as truth either. For instance, you stated that scholars have disproven Josephus's TESTIMONIUM FLAVIANUM, but the scholarly debate on this writing has upheld that Josephus's writing to be authentic."

Phillip knew that he was talking over most of the groups heads, but recognized that they were quiet and seemed to be mulling over his answer.

He resumed, "Again, both sides, the Christians, and the atheists, are working from faith and are depending on their faith to be proven that they are right. All have faith because everything cannot be understood by knowledge alone.

Initially, everyone has to reason or wrestle with God and come to their own conclusion about Him. Just like one has to form a hypothesis and test it. Fundamentally, this is faith that can lead to an understanding of God as he reveals himself.

But in my experience, non-Christians do not want to debate but want to discredit . . ."

TJ roared and then disrupted with a litany of grievances, "Christians want everyone to come together and reason, but they are so stuck in their own fucking ways that it makes it impossible to have the conversation. You Christian's have saturated this country, choking everyone with your own beliefs and never taking anyone else's belief in consideration."

Phillip gestured to TJ, pantomiming that he conceded the floor to him.

TJ persisted, "You're against a woman's right to choose what they can do with their own body. You're against all things fun: sex, pornography, gambling, drinking and drugs. You argue about the

PRESENT, Alice Whealey, http://www.roger-pearse.com/weblog/wp-content/uploads/2011/08/whealey2000.pdf

validity of proven evolution. You're against people's natural expression of love for one another.

And yes, I'm talking about homosexuality.

Christian's say that they are full of love, but then they act all superior and look down on all the things that society has evolved too. It's natural to be gay, and Jesus himself had nothing to say about it. It isn't hurting anyone, and if it does, it's because they're holding onto Christian guilt-ridden diatribes."

Hyperventilating but not wanting to lose the floor, TJ continued screaming, "Anyone who believes in this Christianity myth is a fool to put all of their faith in a make believe person who is going to save everyone. There are people in foreign countries who've never heard about Jesus. How could a loving God send these people to Hell?"

Phillip sat there as TJ paused for dramatic effect. He gazed at Ethan, who was as wide-eyed as the rest of the group.

TJ began pacing around the group as if he was preaching, "You Christians don't even agree amongst yourselves. Some Christians say that it isn't the word of God unless it is the "King Jimmy" Bible. You dispute amongst yourself on if parts of your Bible are literal or allegory. You'll abuse each other and then expect the other to respond in mercy. Your membership includes the Westboro hate group and the abortion clinic bombers. And please, don't get me started on the Crusades.

Then there's the ruckus that's constantly being made about the separation of church and state. You Christians have had your way for so long that you believe that you're entitled to have sole rights to privileges and dictate to everyone else what is good and evil.

Christians frequently claim that they're being attacked, but I personally think that it's a leveling out of the playing field. You're just hurt because your 'persecution' is nothing more than all of you being treated just like everyone else, with no special treatment."

To emphasize his point, he pointed at Phillip and said, "I think that it's hilarious that you've spent your whole life in dedication to this God, and he's let you down."

Phillip sat there, taking everything that TJ dished out. Meeting Ethan's gaze, he noticed that he was wincing. He figured it was from hearing his own thoughts out loud.

He watched as Ethan tried to gain control of TJ, but TJ was collarless.

Feeling a hand on his shoulder, he was encouraged to find that Mr. Abiel was standing behind him and praying for him.

Trying to relax his nerves, he listened to tidbits of Mr. Abiel's prayer, but one word stood out from his prayer: purge. That word triggered his memory about his Bible study that he had this morning on the man sleeping with his father's wife.

He recalled the verse that seemed out of place: "For what have I to do with judging outsiders? Is it not those inside the church who you are to judge? God judges those outside. Purge the evil person from among you.[26]

He closed his eyes and drew strength on the part that God is the one who judges those outside.

He thought about the image that Christianity has in the culture, like how Christian's talk more about what they're against compared to the love that God has for sinners.

Rolling all of the thoughts around in his head, he had an epiphany wash over him. That when one is talking more about what they're against, instead of what Christ is for is in the spirit of the antichrist. That any thought that doesn't align with Christ is opposed to Him and therefore is blasphemy. That God is the One who judges. That the Holy Spirit brings the conviction upon someone's spirit and convicts all, those inside and outside the church.

He thought about how some Christians think and act more on what they perceive Christ is against, contrasted to how Christ did think and act himself.

---

[26] *The Holy Bible: English Standard Version.* 2001 (1 Co 5:12–13). Wheaton: Standard Bible Society.

The story of the adulterous woman to be stoned and Jesus' reply to their accusations quickened to his mind, "He without sin, cast the first stone."

Wiping the tear that trailed down his face, he understood that Jesus was the only one that was there that was without sin and could have judged her. But that he offered her grace and told her to go and sin no more.

He dropped his stone and repented of his involvement with this practice of holding the world up to Christian standards.

The revelation that God wanted to bring his kingdom down through his followers who practiced His love, mercy, and grace, renewed and restored him.

Thinking more on this, he was overjoyed because he didn't have to change anyone, but only had to be an ambassador for Christ, telling how good God had been for him.

Phillip turned his attention to TJ, who was showing signs that he was petering out, but relentlessly yelling, I'm not done yet, Christians are fascist, and everyone has to stand up against them."

Phillip watched the group, curious as to why no one paid attention to Mr. Abiel walking around.

Losing his voice, TJ continued ranting, "I'm tired of hearing how Christians claim that they've been discriminated against, persecuted and targeted because they're no longer the dominant belief in today's culture.

The screaming is the loudest especially around Christmas, which is just a good time to get together with friends and family. You Christians must have forgotten that it was a pagan holiday long before the Catholic Church had adopted and had proselytized it.

There's also all the craziness that happens during Halloween as you Christians try to proselytize it also with your Harvest Festivals."

Tired of TJ's litany of accusations, Phillip asked, "Like I asked beforehand, do you want to debate and reason or do you want to discredit? If what we are debating is Christianity, then everything that you've said is true. Christian's are imperfect. We forget that our sin is no greater or less than anyone else's. Some of us speak more against issues than we do exulting Jesus. Some live in their self-righteousness and forget that they are all equal in their need of a Savior. But let's get back to the subject I was talking about: Jesus Christ."

TJ blurted, "Now, you be quiet. Who told you to talk now?"

Phillip felt Mr. Abiel's hands raise off his shoulder as he raised himself onto his cane, answering back, "No, you've had the floor for long enough, and YOU be quiet. Just because you bark the loudest doesn't make you right. You can attack Christianity and me, but when you state your dogma as truth, I will not condone it with my silence.

Every man has a right to form his own opinion and values, so I want there to be a counter to your argument, or are you so insecure in your beliefs that you cannot accept criticism or a counterargument?

You see, my beliefs have been challenged during this recent ordeal, and I've found that they still sustain me. I've rediscovered that everything still comes by faith and that God is strong enough defend Himself when I've questioned Him.

Are you afraid that your argument won't stand a differing opinion?"

TJ shot back, "How bout I just beat the living sh…"

***

Wanting to hear some of the rebuttals that Phillip seemed prepared to give, Ethan was saddened that the conversation had degenerated.

He interrupted TJ by saying, "TJ, sit down. You're not helping your argument by being obnoxious."

TJ glared at Phillip, finally sat down and relented, "Ok, fine, but he cannot hide behind faith as a valid answer anymore," as he withdrew within himself.

Ethan asked the group on if they'd like the discussion to continue, and was overjoyed that they all nodded yes, except Frank, who raised his hand.

Ignoring Frank's hand, Ethan thought about TJ's suggestion and offered to Phillip, "OK, you can present your side, but you can't use the word faith."

Ethan was surprised that Phillip quickly nodded his head in agreement as he said, "That's all right by me. I'm certain that I've established that both Christians and non-Christians beliefs are established in faith."

Ethan spun to TJ to get the debate going again but was interrupted by Frank asking, "Are we done with the therapy session, because if not I've got more that I'd like to say."

Not wanting the discussion between Phillip and TJ to be interrupted, Ethan desired to answer no, but he also had to agree with Frank that the session had been hijacked a while ago.

His duty to the group was before his personal wishes but figuring that he had the group's permission already he supposed that he could let the debate continue.

Sucking his teeth as he thought, he looked down at his notes and saw that he planned on to be talking about step 8 from his book, "Accept things as they are, not as you wish them to be."

Downcast, he accepted that he had to give Frank the floor and contemplated about how Frank was sabotaging his own recovery.

Looking at Frank and wishing that TJ would interrupt, Ethan relented and gave Frank the floor.

Frank asked, "Phillip and TJ, this question is for both of you. In your opinion, why did my wife leave me?"

Ethan watched as Frank bowed his head.

Everyone in the group turned to Phillip, awaiting his answer.

***

Lifting his head and shifting his eyes out the window, TJ responded, "Co'mon Frank, I don't know why she left you. It could be because she found someone better or that she just got tired of you. Anyways, marriage is such a relic that I don't think that it matters anymore. It is like I said earlier, this world is all about the take before it is taken from you and that it does not owe anything to you.

Or, it could be because you let her beat you and you didn't let her know her place. It could have been that she liked a certain side of you, but you were too busy battling yourself and could not love her like a real man because you're a sniveling whiner."

Turning his attention to Phillip, TJ nipped, "I'm already in his head, and we've had this argument too many times. Pastor P.A., he's yours."

TJ withdrew, and Frank's lip quivered as he withdrew also.

Putting his arm around Frank, Kevin asked him, "Frank, you OK? Are you still with us?

Frank weakly replied, "Yes."

Phillip asked, "Frank, was there any adultery or abuse?"

Frank responded, "No, none that I think that I may have been responsible for. She just said that she was done acting like she was happy and that she had fallen out of love with me."

Nodding his head slowly, Phillip said, "OK, well I'm sorry about that. Do you still love her?"

With tears in his eyes, Frank answered, "Yes, I didn't know how much that I loved her until she was gone."

Phillip asked, "How long ago?"

Frank answered, "About three months ago."

Phillip permitted a moment to reflect on all of the reasons of why he was in the ward. He thought about how his marriage was in limbo, how he was no closer to any answers about who Tracy was and how he'd become a target amongst TJ and Ethan.

Aware of all of this, he was somehow able to empathize with Frank as tears came to his eyes because he felt the same hurt as Frank did.

Considering Frank's coping mechanism, he felt burdened as he considered that the only difference between him and Frank was that he opened himself up to Jesus as best as he could, and Frank chose to open himself up to his personal demons.

Wiping his eyes, he said the quick prayer that he'd prayed so often while being here, that God would help him to be real in his faith and to provide him strength and courage.

He answered, "Frank, I'm in the same boat that you are. You know how TJ throws all of my pain up in my face. Well, one of the pains that I struggle with is that ... well ... as far as I know ..."

Lost for words, he paused because this was the first time that he'd accepted that his marriage had had problems for a long time.

Relaxing, he wiped the tears from his eyes and confessed, "As far as I know, my wife has left me because of many misunderstandings and assumptions that she has made. The unknown is the hardest part for me, but I still pray that God will fix things while I wait on Him. The waiting is the hardest part for me, but I have to have ..."

He caught himself because he was going to say faith and continued, "I've to trust that God is also working in Jessica. That He has a plan, and it will be fulfilled."

Together Frank and TJ both gave an exhausted, heavy sigh, which Phillip interpreted as, "Get on with it! " so he answered, "Listen, I offer no apologies that I'm a Christian and that I'm going to explain everything from this perspective. "

Frank replied, "That's OK, it's why I asked you."

Phillip queried, "Are you a Christian?"

Frank answered, "No, I've never thought about it."

Phillip asked, "You've heard that God hates divorce, but do you know why?"

Frank jested, "Well, I thought that it was because He just wanted us to be miserable."

Phillip smirked at Frank's answer as Kevin and Mary chuckled. In the corner of his eye, he saw that Ethan was unconsciously rubbing the groove where his ring used to be, he noted it and decided to be engaged in this conversation instead of the puzzle of Ethan's phone and missing ring.

Once the chuckles subsided, Phillip said, "Yes, marriages do have those moments, but it's because some people have a 50-50 marriage or they only meet the other person halfway. Alternatively, some people approach marriage from only what they can get out of it and then fight to ensure that the other spouse is treating them equally and fair, or as TJ has said, 'Be on the take'"

Frank said, "My ex-wife and I were the 50-50 couple. Our marriage didn't work because it was like a competition on who had done the most or who was better at doing their part. We were constantly trying to prove to the other they were not carrying their own weight."

Phillip answered, "Yeah, it can become that way. We play the blame game, judging what we're not receiving instead of seeing how we're just as unfaithful in what we're not giving either. Because, our desires and expectations are denied, we inflict rejection by not meeting the other's needs. We justify our actions and feel that we have to protect our rights and neglect our responsibility to our spouse because we feel we have been mistreated."

Frank straightened up and answered, "That's what she said. She said that I didn't care about her and that I only cared about work. She said that I took all the fun out of things and that because I didn't love her, she didn't love me. She didn't understand that I did everything because I loved her."

Phillip nodded his head and said, "That must be hard. The truth is that marriage is set up to be 100% to 100%. It's a covenant, not a contract

In a contract, you have an end date and set definitions of expectations for each person to uphold their end of the bargain. The problem with this is a lot of these expectations may be unspoken, or they may be unreasonable, so inevitably we fail."

Frank answered, "But she didn't do what I wanted either. She'd sit home all day just watching TV or talking to her friends. I'd come home, and she'd tell me what all of her friend's husbands were doing for their wives. It was not fair. I had a hard enough time competing with the voices in my head, let alone being compared to others."

TJ rose up and answered, "Man, it's like I said earlier. Life isn't fair."

Phillip said, "TJ, you've had your time to speak, now it's me and Frank's time to talk."

Phillip eyed Frank and said, "While it's true that life isn't fair, the truth is that we don't want fairness. Not really, what we really want is our own way."

Leaning forward towards Frank, Phillip continued, "That's why God hates divorce. It's the ultimate breakdown of society. One only has to do a quick web search to see how divorced families affects society.

Another reason God hates divorce is that God chose marriage as a representation of His love for the church. God designed marriage as a covenant between man and woman to give life and to protect and cherish that life. Just like He brings life when a church acts like a church should, not only looking inward but outward as well. He loves us so very much, just like you love your wife."

Phillip could see that Frank was getting tired of the Sunday school lesson, as he increased the power and speed of the strokes on his imaginary cat.

During the pregnant pause, Frank scowled and said, "So, what! I wasn't the one who left her, she left me. Why did she leave?"

Phillip bit his bottom lip and knew that TJ was going to interrupt again or that Ethan was going to cut him off if he didn't wrap things up soon.

Mr. Abiel sat next to Frank and put his arm around him. While comforting him, he nodded his head at Phillip encouraging him to continue.

Phillip continued, "Frank, you said that you wanted to know the Christian perspective, and you've agreed with everything that I've said thus far, so please just let me finish. "

Frank relented and answered, " All right!"

Phillip recollected his thoughts and continued, "For Christians, marriage is a covenant. In a covenant, one gives up their rights and assumes responsibility for the other party.

Therefore, God gave us examples of Him being a husband, because He isn't going to expect something of us that He doesn't expect of Himself.

Here are some examples. He loves. He leads. He protects. He nurtures. He understands. He initiates. He communicates. He sacrifices. He praises. He forgives. He endures. He provides. He doesn't forsake. He wipes away tears. He dwells with us. He values. He submits. He believes. He redeems. He waits. He denied himself. He gives of himself continually. He rejoices. He sympathizes. He took on our debt. He suffered. He died. He lives. He saves."

Frank interrupted, "OK, but what about me?"

In spite of Frank's interruptions, Phillip continued, "He was rejected. He was neglected. He took sole responsibility and payment for our disobedience. He was cheated. He was tortured. He was shamed. He was beaten. He was lied about. He was disowned. He was forgotten. He was punished, He was beaten. He was ..."

Frank petulantly asked, "Yeah, but what about me?"

Folding his hands together, Phillip looked into Frank's eyes and leaned back.

Letting the silence roll, Phillip thought about how this question summed up the world's main problem with Jesus.

Examining the room, he answered, "I'm not finished, but I'll cut to the chase. I believe that Jesus was perfect in every way and didn't sin. Nevertheless, Jesus took us as an imperfect bride, raised us up, and redeemed us so the relationship can work. He constantly gives of Himself, enters into us and helps us to be holy. He chooses to offer grace through our imperfections and ..."

Screaming, Frank gained the attention of the whole room. He wailed, "OK, OK, I nitpicked. I wanted her to be perfect, just like the world says she should have been. I never told her thank you when she finally did something right, I just looked for the next thing that needed improvement.

The reason that she left me was because of me. It was the world that lied to me, not God. I drove her away.

I admit I did it. I did it. I did it."

Phillip remembered Frank showing off his scars and screaming the same thing earlier, however, this time, the confession was in repentance not in condemnation.

He hobbled over on his cane, sat next to Frank, and let him sob on his shoulder. He patted him on the back and answered, "Confession is good, but it doesn't end there."

***

Wide-eyed, Ethan was surprised at Frank's confession and felt that Frank was the closest to a breakthrough than he'd ever been.

He knew that Frank had to get to the point where he didn't blame anyone else for his failure in his marriage and that he had to get to the point where he had to open himself to the truth that he is fallible.

Phillip making grace the main conversation point didn't surprise him but weighed on him as much as it had on Frank.

Looking at his notepad, he regarded the checkmarks beside each virtue that Jesus fulfilled and that he had neglected during his marriage with Beth. Guilty, he retrieved his phone and read her last text: **Can't wait 2 C U at home!**

He whispered, "I'm so sorry Beth."

Looking at the time on his phone, he had to close things up.

***

Looking into Frank's eyes, he saw that he was cornered by what he had invited into his soul.

TJ broke the silence and sneered, "So, that's your great salvation story. This is what people go to see you for. You're wasting your time because he is mine."

Not wanting to lose Frank when he was this close, Phillip pleaded, "Frank, don't let your demons win."

TJ leveled his stern look at Phillip and said, "You can't have what you don't possess."

Phillip's strength welled up within him as he grabbed Frank's shoulders, saying, "Admitting what you did wrong isn't the end, it's the beginning. Admitting that we have sinned doesn't save us, but believing that Jesus can save you will."

Amused, TJ mocked, "So, only believing that Jesus can save you will save you. Is that it?"

Phillip was taken aback by the recollection of Tracy asking him the same thing.

Losing confidence that only believing in Jesus was enough, he challenged his own belief system as he raced through several scenarios: One can only believe in Jesus and still be obese, one can only believe in Jesus and lie, cheat, steal, and be homosexual. His mind quickened to the verse in James that said that the demons believe Jesus is the Son of God and shudder.

"So, what makes a Christian different from the demons?" invaded his mind.

He knew that an answer had to be found for himself before continuing on. He was familiar with Jesus saying to believe in Him and be saved, but he discerned that being challenged twice from two different sources about this subject wasn't a coincidence. With all the culminating events that had happened to him since being shot, he now knew was for him to grasp the answer to this question

Racking his mind, "What else is there? Well, God wants you to change. We submit to his change."

He thought about his epiphany from last night during the storm then the truth came with its fullness and glory.

Phillip regained the attention of the group and answered, "No believing isn't everything. Christians have to believe, repent and accept Jesus as our Lord and Savior."

That complete thought resonated in his heart because it wasn't just the hollowness of just believing, but knowing that the Holy Spirit works Himself within us during our repentance and the daily reconciliation of Jesus as Lord of our life.

TJ taunted, "OK, so you're saying that belief and by the things people do is what saves them."

Frustrated that he was speaking to TJ instead of Frank, Phillip answered, "No, salvation isn't by what anyone does. We're powerless because of our disobedience. We can only repent and accept Jesus as Lord and Savior, and depend upon His work on the cross and His resurrection.

Because of God's love for us, He sent His only Son to die for the payment of our sin and disobedience. His death was the payment in full for His bride, which is the church, and all are welcome, but in this love story, we're the ones who have committed adultery in our relationship with Him.

Some twist His love into abuse as they claim irreconcilable differences with God, instead of receiving the grace and mercy that he truly gives. Still God chooses to redeem us from what we've chosen to enslave us.

However, we still have to repent and accept Him as our Lord and Savior. As a member of His chosen bride, the Church, we have to submit. We have to respond to Him in love and understand that God is protecting us.

God's love for us is a gift. It isn't something that we deserve or anything that we've paid the price for, but a gift that He paid for dearly and continues to pay for in His patience, which means our salvation.

This has been God's plan from the beginning, which is that His people would be reconciled to Him and that He'd crush Satan under His feet."

TJ blurted, So, this is your great salvation story, God crushing the scary evil snake under His feet. "

Phillip answered, "No, it's deeper than this," as he surprised himself and seized Frank's head in his hands and said, "Frank, do you want to remove the separation between you and God?"

Eye's flaming red, TJ's bellowed, "Unhand me, now!"

Ignoring TJ, Phillip spoke to Frank hiding in the corner of his soul, "Frank, pay attention to me now. Do you want to be free?"

TJ shouted, "Frank, I'm the one who got you through all your struggles. Don't you remember all the pain that you were in when I found you? Remember how I made you strong. Where was God then?"

Phillip prayed, "Jesus, You said that You came to free those in bondage. In Your name, I pray for Frank that You give him the strength and courage to see You for who You really are."

TJ argued, "You don't have to listen to these lies."

Frank said, "Pastor, I want to believe but ..."

TJ spoke over Frank, "Listen, you mother fucking bastard. Your Jesus is a bastard. He made up his immaculate conception. . . "

Phillip said, "TJ, in the name of Jesus Christ I ..."

TJ said, "That's it. I'm going to fuck you up, you motherfucker."

As TJ rose up, Phillip released his hands.

Drawing back, TJ punched Phillip in his chest knocking the wind out of Him.

With a flurry of fists, TJ was on top of Phillip, drawing blood with every connection.

Kevin shirked back.

Mary jumped on TJ's back, screaming, "Stop it!"

Dumbfounded and paralyzed, Ethan sat there with his mouth agape.

Strangling Phillip, TJ thundered, "Just say one more word! I dare you!"

Phillip managed to say, "Frank, claim Jesus."

TJ's grip increased as his eyes glistened redder, pronouncing, "You're mine now, time to finish what the bitch couldn't!"

Seeing that TJ was coming closer like he was going to bite his neck, Phillip rose his hands in front of him in defense as TJ started to bite his hands.

Still strangling Phillip, TJ thrust his knee into his wounded thigh.

Phillip stared at the intensity of TJ's reddened stare, as he fought blacking out.

Mr. Abiel clutched TJ and flung him aside.

After rolling into the chairs, TJ spat, "You have no authority over me."

Mr. Abiel just smiled at the absurdity of that statement.

After retching, Phillip continued urging, "Frank, claim the name of Jesus!"

As TJ tried to get to his feet again, Kevin and Ethan had finally come to Phillip's aid and held TJ down.

Phillip crawled over to Frank and brought himself to his knees as he winced in pain from his thigh and torso that was burning, and laid his hands on Frank and prayed the name of Jesus over and over.

TJ screamed, "Stop it!"

Phillip sustained, "Jesus, Jesus, Jesus, Jesus, Jesus ...."

TJ struggled against Kevin and Ethan, as Mr. Abiel placed his hands over Phillip's.

TJ writhed like a snake caught.

The ordeal continued for several moments, until Frank attempted, "Je...."

TJ screamed, "NOOOOOOOOOOOOOOOO! You're mine!"

Phillip claimed, "TJ, in the name of Jesus Christ, be silent."

Frank stammered, "J – J – J- Je - J – Je – "

Shocked, Ethan looked to Kevin and queried, "What's going on?"

Dodging a headbutt from TJ, Kevin answered, "Seriously! What do you think is going on?"

Ethan requested, "Well, I just want to hear it."

Kevin answered, "You know how TJ's been mad before?"

Struggling with pinning TJ's arm down, Ethan replied, "Yeah, I remember that it was a bad day for everyone."

Kevin gave a grin and answered, "I'd say that we should hold on because things have just gotten interesting and more worse than that day."

He was surprised that a man with two people on him was able to fight back so easily.

TJ roared, "Dr. Bigman, you've failed your wife, and that's why you're alone."

Stunned, Ethan recoiled from the verbal punch more than any physical one he'd received.

The moment of distraction allowed TJ to get his arm free as he began to wail on Kevin's kidney until he released him.

Kevin doubled over, leaving only Ethan to hold Frank down.

Ethan's emptiness grew from what TJ had said. Remembering his authority as the leader, he attempted to shout, "Stop," but he couldn't find his voice and was sure that a verbal warning wouldn't stop TJ.

Knocked down, Phillip got back on his knees and petitioned, "Frank, say Jesus' name. Say you want to be free."

TJ shoved Ethan aside and got his legs under himself. Towering over Phillip, he drew back his fist to pummel him.

Phillip winced in the preparation of the blow but opened his eyes to see that Frank had regained control of himself and raised his eyes upward and finally said, "Jesus, I have wanted to believe in You. I've blamed You for long enough. I'm the one who pushed You and my wife away."

Frank's face contorted, as TJ fought back control. TJ pointed at Phillip and said, "But look at him, is this how you want to be?"

Tasting blood in his mouth, Phillip looked past TJ to Frank and said, "I'm not asking you to look at me, but I'm asking you to look at what God's done for you right here and now. God will not condemn or torment you. Jesus' truth will never leave you to fend for yourself while you are kicked and beaten."

Seeing the rage building in TJ's eyes, Phillip drew up his courage and put his finger on Frank's chest and said, "Jesus wants the best for you while TJ controls you with his standard. Ask yourself, has TJ saved you or enslaved you? Only Jesus can save you."

Tired of the foolishness, TJ ran into Phillip with all of his rage as he roared, "Everything that he's saying is a lie of Satan. Everyone, open up your eyes and see that you're your own God. You're able to determine good and evil for yourself without some do-gooder dictating to you their dogma."

Trying to get his footing again, Phillip felt like he had lost his leg. Struggling up, TJ pushed him back down.

Mary screamed, "Leave him alone."

TJ smirked and shot back, "No, that's what he wants you to do little lady."

Taking advantage of the interference, Phillip scooted to the wall and struggled to sit up.

He saw TJ saunter over to Mary, not wanting Frank to be distracted he called out, "The problem with your theory is that if each of us is like a God, and each of us is determining our own standard of what good and evil is, then we get to determine who makes it and who doesn't. We would get to decide whom we look up to and whom we look down on. We could excuse ourselves from justice and freedom because these are absolutes for everyone else and not relative to us."

TJ turned his attention back to Phillip ambled over to him and started to lift his leg over his wounded thigh, saying, "Yep, just like the religious do."

Sitting resolute, Phillip continued, "Yep, just like the religious do. The thing is that we're all equally sinners in need of a Savior. God's perfection is something that we can never attain by ourselves. The moment that I look at myself and try to compare my goodness to Him, I've broken his first commandment."

TJ began to drop his leg down onto Phillip's thigh, but Mr. Abiel grabbed him as Frank shouted, "I claim Your name Jesus, please save me!"

TJ tried to regain control, but Frank's confession had broken his control over him.

Purified from TJ, Frank went limp and laid on the floor motionless.

Ethan examined Frank and breathed a sigh of relief that he was still breathing.

Mr. Abiel took Frank into his arms and calmed him saying, "Everything's OK now. You're safe because the demons are gone. Peace. Peace."

Silence filled the vacuum, as the whole group sat quietly, digesting what just had happened.

After several minutes, Ethan studied the whole group, clutched his chest pocket, and noticed that he had lost his phone.

He realized that Frank held it in his hand, offering it in shame.

Retrieving his phone, he scrutinized its destruction.

Detached from the world, he stood, grabbed his pen and paper from his chair and disgustedly marched to his office.

Mr. Abiel followed Ethan, only to have the door to be slammed in his face. Not missing a beat, Mr. Abiel began to constantly knock on his door.

Phillip ventured as to what Ethan had lost on his phone. He knew that it was something that he clutched as security or as a weight.

Kevin helped Frank to his feet and took him to his room.

Frank cried, "I didn't mean too."

Kevin consoled, "It wasn't your fault. The one at fault is gone."

Mary looked at Phillip and said, "So, what do we do now?"

Assuming that his tongue exaggerated his injuries, Phillip licked his lips and still tasted blood. He scooted over to his chair, grabbed his cane, got up, and hobbled past Mary to his room wincing in pain at every step.

The victory had been painful, but worth it.

Chapter 25.   We are all Broken

Trying not to hyperventilate, Phillip paced around while murmuring to himself, "That wasn't anything that I did, but You Jesus."

Putting all of his weight on his cane, he divided his attention on making sense of what just happened and how his cane was a part of him now.

Taking deep breaths, he said again, "That wasn't anything that I did, but You Jesus."

Standing still, he forced himself to quiet his mind.

Several seconds later, he decided that he really wanted to talk to Ethan or Mr. Abiel, but looking toward Ethan's office, he'd saw that Ethan was still locked in with Mr. Abiel knocking on the door.

He began swinging his arms around while taking several deep breaths.

Not having any counsel, he asked God, "OK, what's next?"

Hearing the door creak, he saw Mary walk into the pavilion and meander to a seat close to him.

Unnerved that his alone time was interrupted, he shuffled around the pavilion with his cane some more, but he figured she had every right to be out here as he did. However, all she did was stare at him. He was sure it was so she could wait for him to perform another miracle. Feeling guilty that he should give her the benefit of the doubt, he could only think about her first impression in his lap and enjoying his plight.

Tired of being the show, he headed back in.

Mary appealed, "Please don't go, I was hoping that I could talk to you."

Not wanting to be alone with her, Phillip answered, "Maybe some other time Mary. I have had a full day, and I'm tired."

He heard her voice tremble as she choked out, "Oh. OK."

She turned her face away from him, hiked her legs up to her chin and started to rock back and forth.

Clearing the door, he heard echoes in his mind the question he asked God, "OK, what's next?"

Knowing that he had rejected an opportunity to speak Jesus into her life, he justified himself with "All my problems right now are with women, and I don't need another."

Echoes continued piercing his solace, "I'm sure you'll be such a big help for everyone."

Shuffling faster, he tried to outrun his concern. Still he had to walk past Mr. Abiel to get to his room, except this time he didn't want to talk to him like he did before.

Eyes forward, he prayed that he'd not notice him.

His heart sank as Mr. Abiel questioned, "Where are you going? Do you think that you're finished now and that God is done with you? You're still that self-righteous person who followed me from the hospital who hasn't learned your new purpose."

Not wanting to deal with the conviction, Phillip stopped and pinched the bridge of his nose. He tried to rekindle his patience, but spun around and snapped, "If you have such a burden for Mary, then you go talk to her. I'm tired, and I think I have done enough. Goodness, I have spent most of my life in service to God. Can't you see that my life is screwed up and that I'm here for healing also."

Still knocking on Ethan's office door, Mr. Abiel calmly regarded Phillip and answered, "Is being shot going to be used as an excuse for you to get out of the ministry? I've heard you say that you still want to be useful to God, but what you really mean is that you want to be used as you see fit. You want to pick and choose the activities that make you feel good or lifts you up. Well, God saved you for a purpose, and you better be looking for His glory."

Phillip retorted, "I know that, but she …

Mr. Abiel answered, "She's a child of God just like you are and has sinned just like you have."

Phillip defended, "You do know what Mary is and what she's done to me, right?"

Mr. Abiel asked, "Ask yourself?"

Phillip replied, "You're impossible!"

Mr. Abiel smiled and said, "I specialize in the impossible."

Exasperated, he stomped away from Mr. Abiel muttering, "Why can't you understand that I'm hurt and tired. Haven't you ever been hurt and tired?"

Halfway through his room's hall, someone walked by, met his eyes and quickly walked away.

He cocked his head in wonderment on what spooked that person, then he thought of the sight of him being in a mental ward, muttering to himself while breathing deeply.

A small grin crossed his face and grew until it became a full smile. Laughing doubled him over until crying overwhelmed him as his adrenaline-rush flowed out of him.

He realized this was the first time he thought he deserved to be here.

He just wanted to be alone and allowed to rest, not always having someone expecting something from him.

Walking into his room, he closed his door and laid down.

Rubbing the soreness from his leg, he thought through his day so far and how much had changed. At rest, he tried his best to pray through the pain in his leg, but it wouldn't subside.

Then he heard a scratch at the door. He moaned and wished that Lilly would go away.

He attempted to ignore her persistent scratching, hoping that the world would leave him alone.

She began whining, and he muttered to himself, "Demanding little beast," as he slowly raised himself from the bed and shuffled to the dog food and filled the bowl.

Once hearing the dog food fill the bowl, Lilly scratched at the door with all of her vigor.

Limping his way to the door, he let Lilly in as she sprinted across the linoleum with her nails clicking at each step. She hit the brakes and then ran into the wall and started to eat before she had stopped.

Feeling used, Phillip thought about how Lilly didn't even acknowledge his presence. She just sped past him in expectation of what he could give to her.

Wanting to put the day's events behind him, he laid on his bed and tried to forcefully elucidate about Tracy and Jessica. Each time he tried to think about them, Mary impeded his concentration on his own problems. He tried to compel his thoughts past Mary, but the burden for Mary grew heavier in his mind.

Wanting to divert his attention from Mary, he sat up and tried to seek solace in reading his Bible. He began reading John 4

> "... and Jesus, tired as he was
> from the journey, sat down by the
> well. It was about noon."[27]

Knowing the story, he closed the Bible, looked up to heaven and said aloud, "Seriously God, you too?"

He laid down and closed his eyes, hoping that rest would save him from any further conviction.

Slowly lulling into his nap, he was awakened by Lilly jumping onto the foot of the bed.

She gradually skulked her way up to his hands, putting her head under them, wanting to be petted.

He crossed his hands over his chest, as she finally settled down next to his side.

Phillip enjoyed the silence until Lilly started to snore.

Nudging her awake, she rolled over, wanting her belly rubbed.

Understanding that the world was against him from resting, he raised up and looked at Lilly.

He chided, "Oh, I see. It's all about you. You want me to rub your belly after snubbing me for food."

She began to wag her tail.

---

[27] John 4:6 NIV

He scoffed, "No, I'm serious. Do you think that I'm here only for you? That I'm only here for your pleasure. Who is serving who?"

After saying the words, his stomach dropped as he recalled Mr. Abiel's same question.

Further conviction washed over him as he looked at the wall clock and saw that it was exactly noon.

Thoughts of o'er and o'er quickened in his mind, as he thought of relentless waves moving one to where it wanted them.

Admonished, he prayed

> *"Dear God, help me to be obedient to*
> *You in all things and not think that I've*
> *sacrificed enough.*
>
> *You have saved me o'er and o'er: from*
> *my sin, Tracy, and TJ.*
>
> *I know that You've given so much more*
> *than I have and that I've ... that I've ..."*

He wanted to justify himself that he had put others before himself: Ethan, Frank and Kevin, but guilt crept into his thoughts as he meditated on why he shied away from Mary.

He considered his recent record with women. He was shot by a woman, Jessica blew up at him for something that he had no control over and that Mary was the one responsible for Jessica's outburst. He didn't trust women anymore.

Revelation gave way to epiphany as he continued praying,

> *"God, I've been hurt, and I'm not a*
> *strong as I think I am. Please help me to be*
> *healed and restored. Help me to trust again.*
> *Let me know what I am to do."*

Hearing his watch sound off the hour, he saw that it was noon.

He looked at the clock that was passed noon and his watch, recognizing that his watch was slow, he laughed and asked, "Ok, God. I'll read John 4 and see what you want me to do next.

Picking up his Bible again, he continued reading John 4.

He got to the part:

"My food," said Jesus, "is to do the will of him who sent me and to finish his work."[28]

Looking at Lilly, he saw her wagging her tail.

He patted her on the head and said, "Dang you Lilly, you're my best teacher. Between you and Mr. Abiel, I don't stand a chance."

Lifting himself up on his cane and shuffled to the pavilion.

Walking past Mr. Abiel, he saw that he was still knocking at Ethan's door and that he gave a knowing smile that he'd made the right decision.

Phillip asked, "Why don't you knock louder?"

Mr. Abiel shrugged his shoulders and answered, "Why? He hears me, just like you do. He's only ignoring me. Are you?"

Phillip smirked and replied, "You're stubborn and difficult aren't you?"

Mr. Abiel answered, "No, just patient, "as he gave a big toothy smile.

Phillip went back to the pavilion and didn't see Mary.

Feeling relief that he was relieved of his burden, he gave a heavy sigh. But Mary still weighed on his heart.

He double backed towards Mr. Abiel and asked, "Do you know where Mary went?"

Not looking at him, Mr. Abiel replied, "Yeah, she has crawled back into her doubt in humanity," as he pointed to a corner in the main room.

Phillip saw Mary sitting with her back to the wall, ensuring that she could see anyone who approached her.

With his hat in his hand, he met her eyes.

She shifted her gaze out the window, acting coy and in control of the situation.

Sitting in the seat next to her, Phillip said "I'm sorry about earlier. I'm available to talk right now."

She turned towards him, and he immediately noticed that the vibrancy in her eyes was gone, as she venomously spat, "Well,

[28] John 4:34

isn't that convenient for you that you're available to talk right now. I thought that you were different, but you're just like the rest of them."

Catching the tone in her voice, he recognized that she was behaving just like the strong woman who straddled him, not as the meek Mary with her knees up to her chin.

Giving a harrumph, she crossed her arms and looked out the window.

Fighting himself on staying here with her in this mood, Phillip answered, "I don't know about the rest of them, but I came back here, so I could try to understand."

Not turning her head, she ridiculed, "There's no way that you can understand what I've endured. You've spent most of your life in a perfect bubble compared to mine. Damn, being shot would be a utopia compared to what I've survived."

Taking her anger in stride, he knew that her perception was her reality and that there was no reason for him to argue the point on whose life was the worse. Sin had ruined his life inasmuch as hers.

Wanting to draw her out and find out why God had him here in the first place, he asked, "What have you endured?"

He watched her focusing outside more intently, as her jaw tightened and her grip on her crossed arms strengthened as she answered, "Like you care."

He wanted to stand and leave, but stayed settled in his chair and answered, "Well, I'm still here if you need to talk."

He wanted to argue with her, telling her that she hadn't made his life easy either and that it was her fault that his marriage was in shambles.

Dwelling on it more, he recognized that Mary was just the catalyst, lighting the fuse to the bomb that was his marriage with Jessica.

His patterned thinking of justifying Jessica's actions by stating, "Well, that's just how she is," didn't comfort him. It only brought more conviction upon him, piercing through his criticism and preventing him from making Jessica the scapegoat of their marriage.

His neglect through the years had caught up with him, his acting like he was self-sufficient and that he didn't need her revealed his culpability, and his choosing other things above her showed that he didn't desire nor really show love towards her.

Turning his gaze to the oak tree that Mary was looking at, he murmured, "My toleration of Jessica was the catalyst. Me forsaking her destroyed her radiance that she covers up with anger because of my passivity. She cares for me, and I just throw it all away. I need to be more intentional about my love for her."

In his peripheral, he detected Mary shifting her gaze back and forth as if she was struggling not to be vulnerable with him.

He joined her in looking out the window, glad that he had figured out a huge puzzle piece that had landed him here. He wished that he could figure out Tracy.

Looking askew, he kept silent as Mary began tangling herself up into a ball.

Sensing her uneasiness, he knew that it would be a little bit more time till she opened up to him again.

She loudly sighed and looked to see if he'd respond.

He stretched out his legs, relaxing with his arms behind his head.

After several minutes of this, she finally conceded, "There was a time that I thought that I knew what love was, but those people turned around and bitch slapped me."

He saw her shift her eyes over to see his reaction, as he just sat there stonefaced.

She continued, "I felt that if I could only measure up to what people thought, then they'd love me. I thought that if I gave them what they wanted, then everything would be good. Still, it was never enough. I tried to meet their expectations, and they would change the rules to be self-serving. They didn't care about me."

Detecting that she had loosened the tension in her arms and had brought her knees to her chest, he turned towards her, giving her his undivided attention.

Still looking outside, she pursed her lips and continued, "Everyone has let me down, and that's why I'm here right now.

My dad abandoned my mom when I was born, and my mom abandoned me to her sister when she could not take care of me. My uncle sexually abused me and my aunt didn't care when I told her. She just let it happen and sacrificed me to him. I can still smell the sweat and his hairy hands over my mouth as he whispered in my ear, 'There's no need to scream, but sit back and enjoy this.'"

He shook upon hearing her say this as he recalled the same words when he first met her

As each piece became available, Phillip began placing the puzzle of her life together.

She stopped to allow him to respond, but he kept quiet and permitted her to speak.

Trembling, she stared out at the oak.

He figured that she was trying to stuff the memories back in its cage. Seeing her ears burning, he startled when she spun on him. He saw that she was fighting the rage from consuming her again.

Phillip recognized the look instantly as the time when she straddled him. Taking a deep breath, he thought of the events with TJ this morning and prayed that she wouldn't try to overtake him again.

She leaned forward and searched his eyes.

He presumed that she was looking for sanctuary and peace in his.

Giving a frustrated sigh, she looked back to the oak as she continued, "I always have him in the back of my head with him over me and accusing me. I begged for help, but no one would believe me. I tried to distance myself from him, but I lived in the same house.

When I became a teenager, I ran to the first boy who said that he loved me. It was so easy for me to catch one, I'd just flash my eyes and let him have his way with me. I'd stay with any boy at all hours of the night so I wouldn't have to go home.

I remember the day before I turned 18. My uncle got me alone and then told me that he was sorry, but I knew that he only wanted to keep things a secret. The next day, I ran as far as I could because I had finally become an adult.

I found I could still get what I wanted by flashing my eyes. I know that I'd ruined many men's marriages and single men's dreams as they did everything they could to try to hold me down, but I was finally unleashed and in control. I was bound and determined to not be bound by any man. I'd live with anyone who would put me up, but I ran as soon as they tried to get close to my heart. Though it all came crashing down when I … when I …"

Mary stopped abruptly and stared off into space.

Phillip replied, "You don't have to go on, I think I understand."

Hearing him, she came back to reality and began to scoff as she said, "No, I'll continue."

Taking a deep breath and fanning herself with both of her hands, she wiped the tears as she laughed and joked, "I feel like a prostitute in church on a Sunday."

He noticed her demeanor change, as she struggled to continue through sobs and snot, "But it all came crashing down when I became pregnant, and I didn't know who the father was. I was determined to keep the child, but I …"

She searched the ceiling for the right words to say. Satisfied that she had found them, she counted each point off on her fingers as she resumed," I had nowhere to go, I became homeless, I wasn't able to eat, no man wanted to be tied to a pregnant woman, and I lost the baby."

Turning her attention to Phillip, her lip quivered as she said, "Can you fucking believe this?"

Realizing that she had cursed in front of him, she shirked as she said, "I'm sorry. I didn't mean to cuss in front of you. I am so sorry."

Phillip answered, "It's all right, please go ahead and tell me the rest of the story."

He saw that she was surprised that she hadn't lost his attention. He contemplated on her amazement and thought about how some Christian's would've reprimanded her and would've sacrificed the rapport just for their own virtues.

She resumed, "Can you believe this? I lost my baby because I couldn't get anything to eat. But it was really because I'd thought that I'd based my life on independence, but I really placed it on dependence on men. Lying to myself had enslaved me to them, and when I had no goods to bring to the table, they left, and I starved, and my baby died. I was trash that was thrown away."

She cupped her head in her hands and shook as she cried.

Wanting to console her, he stopped because he was afraid that she'd misconstrue his comfort. He wished that he had the right words to say, but knew listening to her was the best thing he could do.

So, he sat with his hands in his lap and silently listening.

Mary continued, "After my baby passed away; I tried to live my life like I did before because it was all I knew.

However, my attitude was more resolute because I knew that everyone I tried to trust had abandoned me. Moreover, I didn't want to have to be in the same situation again.

Now when I hook up, I try to make them mine. But I quickly realized that I was a damaged plaything. I'm just a toy that men discard after playing with it or when a new toy becomes available.

When I recognized that no one really wanted me, I tried to manipulate them and get them to not leave me. I would plead with them 'not to go,' 'That I could do better', but they didn't want my better. They just wanted me out of the way.

I thought of suicide and suffered through a night of binge drinking and cutting. I gave up on the world and felt like giving up on myself. I needed someone to talk with. I needed some help. So, I checked myself in here that morning.

I talked to Mr. Pitney about how I didn't have insurance and how I couldn't pay. He told me not to worry about it and that he would take care of it.

I remember one night when he called me into his office and then closed the door behind me. I knew how the game was played, and I was ready for him to take his payment. After he had closed the blinds, I braced myself for his touch. But I saw his shadow overtake me as he walked to his chair, turned his phone towards me, and asked me what I thought a text message meant.

I took the phone and read: Beth Pitney: **Can't wait 2 C U at home!**

I didn't know what mind game he was playing. I assumed that he was struggling with going home to his wife or him having his way with me.

I figured that if he were going to collect his payment, I would do it on my terms. So, I stood up and put his phone back in his shirt pocket, slid my hand down his shirt and got to his belt buckle. Once there he seemed to come to his senses and jumped up and said, "I think there is a misunderstanding.

Surprised, I said, "Fine, then what do you want me to do."

He said, "Please leave."

That text message is what Dr. Pitney is all torn up about. You can see him clutch his phone every once in a while, and that is the reason why. He changed even more after you arrived.

Other than that incident, Dr. Pitney has been completely professional. He has never approached me on payment, and he has helped me a little. He said that I've got Histrionic personality disorder. I still don't know what that means, but he says that I've got it.

The thing is Mr. Pitney does all right, but I need a change of perspective. He sings the same song and dance as the rest of the world, but just in a different key.

A few weeks later, you arrived, and I recognized you the moment you walked in because of all the newscast and pictures. I knew that you were married, but I needed to know that you were different. I saw that you had something inside that was special. Something that helped you to stand strong in the face of hard times.

Jesus Christ, you were shot, and you're still standing!

I knew you were a pastor and that you knew about love. Desperate, I had to get your attention because I felt that you'd help me find the answers. I knew that you could really help me, but you've only proved that you're just like everyone else who has forsaken me."

Phillip decided to let it slide that she'd conveniently left out her seductive nature as being the cause of his neglect even after her admission that she'd ruined many men's marriages and single men's dreams.

Tucking her knees to her chin as she had done several times, she finished, "That's why I know that you can't help me. It's because you cannot truly understand my pain. You cannot know what it's like not to have hope, but just having feelings of worthlessness and desertion."

Wiping the tears from his eyes, Phillip was sure that Mary was through with her story and not sure how to start his.

Taking Mary's hands in his, he began to pray:

"Jesus, please be with Mary. Let her know the joy that she is in your eyes. Please give me the words to say that would encourage her and lead her to You. Amen!"

Still holding her hands in his, he said, "Mary, if there is no hope for you then there is none for me either. It's not about what we've done wrong, but about what Jesus has done right that saves us.

Our main sin in life is that we're all still eating of the fruit of knowledge of good and evil. We appoint ourselves the ruler of good and evil, determining who is better than we are and who is worse, deciding who measures up to our standard or whose standard we cannot reach.

The problem arises after you've set your standard, then Mr. Pitney sets his and then everyone else in the world comes up with their own benchmark of what good and evil is.

You can almost hear the Devil still promising that we will be like God."

Mary interrupted, "Yeah, I remember that you were saying something about this during this morning's group therapy meeting, but so what if everyone has their own guidelines."

Phillip continued, "Well, life is messy. Some people's lives are messier than others because of our war of ideals. We make ourselves a god and pass judgment on who is worth our time, or who is beneath us so we can abuse them. Or we do everything within our abilities to help others to be better according to our standard, but can't agree on what is truly better for others. But we can't just survive the mess of ideology and morals because we can't agree on what is good and evil, nor can we just throw our hands in the air, give up and look down on other's hard luck.

I believe that there is a standard, and that is that God is holy, perfect and authoritative of what is good and what is evil."

Seeing Mary nod her head, Phillip was sure that she was not agreeing with him, but tracking with his line of thought.

He continued, "Since God is our standard and His standard is perfection, He is who we should measure ourselves up to. Not one of us is righteous enough to come close to God, which makes all of us equal. None of us is greater or lesser than each other. We all fail. Doesn't that give you hope? "

Phillip saw that Mary was trying to understand, but he knew that she would have to think everything through more. He wasn't surprised when he heard her reply, "No?"

He proceeded, "It gives me hope because God is the only one who is able to judge me. I don't have to worry about everyone else who tries to hold me to their standard. It's only Him that I've got to abide with. This is the freedom that Jesus brings, I don't have to worry about those who try to compare themselves to me because I'm going to point them to Jesus. I don't have to worry about those that I don't measure up to because I don't measure up to Jesus either. But He is more gracious than they are."

Mary asked, "So, you're saying that everyone is bad, and that makes all of us equal."

Phillip answered, "Yes!"

Mary inquired, "And that gives you hope?"

Phillip answered, "No, not that by itself. I've attained hope because of the salvation that God gives through Jesus. Knowing that He's my savior from the judgment of my sin is what gives me hope.

Jesus came down from heaven and became one of us. Not as a conqueror demanding our submission, but as a servant who lived this life without committing any sin. Faultless, He took on the punishment of our sin. He became cursed and rejected by dying on our cross as an atoning sacrifice."

Mary tilted her head and asked, "Atoning sacrifice?"

Phillip was glad that she was asking him to define his churchy words as he answered, "Well, you see, justice demands payment for our sin, which is death. Atonement is Jesus substituting himself in our place. It is Him taking on the penalty of our sin, shame and death."

Mary said, "Yeah, but I don't see how ..."

Phillip interrupted, "You told me your story. Will you let me tell you mine?"

Mary conceded.

Phillip started, "First off, you're right. It's my fault that I left you alone in the courtyard earlier to deal with your own struggles. I've also been frustrated in dealing with my own problems and have avoided you because ... well ... uh ..."

Gesturing towards her, he said, "It's like you said, 'You were desperate to get my attention,' and your methods didn't agree with me."

He waited to see if he was delicate enough in his admonition. After seeing the slightest nod of agreement from her, he continued, "If you don't mind, may I tell you about real love. May I tell you my testimony of how I found Christ to be necessary in my life?"

Mary quietly answered, "OK, but I don't expect there to be many parallels between yours and my life because you've had and easy life and have always known Jesus."

Phillip thought, "I wish," along with praying for God to give him courage, strength, wisdom and that his words would be fruitful.

Releasing her hands, he cleared his throat and positioned himself at the edge of his chair, and commenced, "Mary. Mary, you think that I've had such an easy life because you see my relationship with Jesus now. Honestly, my life right now has struggles, but I have Jesus helping me through it. The truth is every Christian has a back-story. You know, the B.C. (Before Christ) part: the hard time when one opposes God as much as they defend their own sin. I call mine the 'Before God got a hold of me' story."

Phillip saw Mary settle in to hear his story and suddenly felt apprehensive in bearing his soul to her. His life had been threatened, his marriage had disintegrated, and now he was having nightmares and seeing things in the shadows.

He also thought of how much his life had changed since the rally at the arena and wondered if he should incorporate the new events into his testimony. He decided not to because he hadn't fully processed the events in his life himself. He could add these things later when he had come to terms with it all.

Breathing in deep, he quietly prayed and then started: "As you probably know, I'm an evangelist preaching Jesus' message of love across America, but that hasn't always been the purpose of my life.

I had the idealistic American childhood: the loving family, my own room, dog, etc. However, there was a part of me that I thought was completely different from anyone else. It bound me to my loneliness for the same reason you stated earlier: I didn't think anyone would understand.

You see, my parents would go on dates and leave me at my aunt's house overnight. For whatever reason, I slept in the same bed as my female cousins and learned about sex at an early age. We continued having sex until my parents moved to another state when I was 6 years old.

I didn't know then that my life long struggle had begun. You see, I was a kid who had found a new toy, but the truth is that my whole life I've struggled with perverted thoughts. I still deal with the temptation daily.

After getting away from it all with only a damaged mind, it was a blessing to have a somewhat normal childhood, although I daily fought seeing girls as sexual objects. Having an outgoing personality, I struggled in relating with girls because there was always an inward battle, so I avoided them because I was humiliated by my sinful nature. I slowly built a wall; protecting them from the beast I caged up.

Moving away also brought another blessing, my parents began to go to church, and they were baptized. Seeing a change in them, I wanted to have the same thing. So, I accepted Jesus as my savior and got baptized at age 8.

Whenever the doors were open, we were there enjoying the fellowship with our extended family at our church. Everything got better in my life."

Mary interrupted, "That's what I'm talking about, your life got better, and mine got worse. I wish I had the same thing."

After hearing her confession of wanting the same thing, he felt like he could stop and walk Mary through the Roman road and the sinner's prayer. He desperately wanted to quit being vulnerable with Mary, but there was a prompting that overwhelmed him to continue

Seeing that she wasn't gathered up into a ball any longer, he found in her a kindred spirit. He felt like he was sharing Mary's burden with her as he told his testimony.

Seeing her attentiveness, Phillip proceeded, "Well, just because I believed in Jesus didn't mean that my life wasn't without its challenges.

My family moved back close to my cousins again when I was in sixth grade. I didn't tell anyone about what had happened with them. I buried my past and shame and learned how to act like everything was all right.

My cousin's had grown up and because of their boyfriends they didn't have anything to do with me, but they had a younger sister who was three years younger than me. I became the cancer, spreading the disease to her as we started to have sex with each other.

I knew better, but I fell into the sin that was waiting for me. It was my fault that I spread the generational curse by having sex with her.

All throughout middle and high school, we had sex, even though I played the game of Christianity.

I lived the poster child life of a Christian: I had the lead parts and solos in the church play, I quoted scripture, won sword drills, played in the church softball league, went on mission trips every year.

Living this Dr. Jekyll and Mr. Christian[29] life, I was constantly tormented by the shameful thought loop that persisted until I was in college. I knew what I did was wrong, but I did it anyways. I felt guilty about it and then say that I'd not do it again, only to repeat the cycle again.

I now believe it was a generational sin, which my wife and I were dead set on breaking with our children. "

Phillip could tell that he'd lost Mary around 'sword drills,' so he said, "Don't get caught up in not knowing about the sword drills, the thing was I was leading a double life. People loved to be around me because of my outgoing personality, but I was torn. Everything that I did was to hide my distress and scandal. My life was all about fooling everyone, maybe even God. The truth was I was only fooling myself.

While calling myself a Christian, I was still having sex with my cousin. I did start to date other girls, but I didn't know how to function around them. Wanting to protect them and myself, I didn't show any affection so they wouldn't' find out my trespass.

Not doing anything with them, I had every appearance of purity, but I didn't understand how to treat them. Every relationship I had was self-destructive because I couldn't let my guard down and let the monster be released.

My bondage was in containing the beast that always wanted to claw its way through. I was very messed up because when I was

[29] Love WhiteHeart, "Don't Wait for the Movie," Sparrow Records, 1986

not having impure thoughts, I was beating myself up, trying to keep all the rules that were set out in the Bible while forgetting them when with my cousin.

Some adults and friends were interested in my well-being and tried to speak Jesus into my life. But ironically, I was screaming out for someone to love me, but I kept everyone at arm's length so they couldn't see my cracked façade. I couldn't let them know that I was the walking wounded. I couldn't let anyone know what was going on with me because I thought that Christianity was that one had to maintain the image of perfection."

Mary took Phillip's pause and asked, "I've never heard this about you. I mean, you're Mr. Christian, and you've felt that way?"

Pausing a little longer, he thought on how unbelievers throw around the word hypocrite so easily. However, believers understand that everyone has their story and moments of when the flesh overrides the Holy Spirit, and they sin.

Phillip answered, "I think that's the lie the world tells people, which is that Christianity is impossible. However, it is like that knowledge of good and evil I was talking about earlier, we're all equal because we are all sinners and in need of God's salvation. This is the thing; every Christian is working out their salvation. We're not perfect, but just at different levels in our walk, but ultimately we're sinners who continually receive God's grace, mercy, and salvation."

Mary thought on that a while and Phillip wrestled with the idea of walking Mary through the plan of salvation, but he still felt the urge to continue with his testimony.

He asked her if she had any other questions or if he could continue.

Mary said, "Please continue, I think that I'm beginning to understand.

Phillip nodded and continued, "Then I started college and got away from everything. I buried myself in my studies and worked with the campus ministry. I kept every impulse in check and felt like I had turned the corner. I felt like I had finally won the battle of sex dominating my life.

That was until I was on a college mission trip to Mexico. While there, I hit it off with a beautiful coworker. Going on a date, her and I became caught up in the heat of passion and temptation. I pursued the relationship for the wrong reason, and she happened to ask me if I wanted to take things further in her room. Being weak, I followed her and things got hot and heavy. We were topless and about to go further ..."

Trailing off, Phillip's voice began to break. He knew that he had to finish the story, but he had not thought about how far Jesus had brought him since that night.

Leaning forward and into his story, Mary prodded, "Yeah, and?"

His voice wavered as he resumed, "Jesus called my name. Jesus simply stated, 'Phillip, what are you doing? Don't you know that I love you more than this?"

**

Mary's eyes got big as she wrestled with the idea of God talking to someone in today's time.

Thinking about her own life, she thought about when she had been in similar situations and her inner soul was screaming 'No' at her, but she ignored it repeatedly until it was muted.

Hearing Phillip's testimony, she began to feel the familiar inner voice starting to stir in her again as it urged her to listen and to understand.

Phillip continued, "I froze. I'll never forget those words. Being at a crossroads in my life, Jesus didn't cast me aside. With no condemnation, He granted me the permission to know the depths of how much He loved me as He simply called my name."

Watching a tear trail down Phillip's cheek, Mary cherished this moment as she felt the tug of emotion, drawing her closer to the love of Jesus.

She did feel that he did understand, albeit not everything, but he did understand the struggle that she now felt.

Her heart sank as he simply whispered more to himself than her, "He called me by my name."

She desperately wanted the same thing. She wanted God to call her by name also.

Listening hard, almost straining, she heard, ""Mary, you've never been alone." It resonated within her as she almost leaped from her chair.

***

Seeing her excitement, Phillip jumped back in defense of what Mary might do.

As she just bounced in her seat, he wiped the tears from his eyes and continued, "At a defining point in my walk, I had to determine if I was content with just playing Christian or was I going to start having a relationship with Jesus.

I told my date that I had to leave because I was having a God moment.

She covered herself right then, and it showed me what I had been doing my whole life. That I built it on covering up and living in shame. Kicking me out of her room, I wrestled with that thought on my walk back to my own.

I felt like Saul on the Damascus road, God had revealed himself to me, and I had to come to grips with the love He was giving.

Please don't misunderstand me; I knew Christ and believed what He did for me, but I didn't fully understand His mercy, grace and love that He had given. I acknowledged Jesus as teacher but hadn't accepted Him as my Redeemer, not as the lifter of my head. I thought of Him as the rule maker, the one I had to grovel to, the one I went to when I asked for pity. Honestly, I didn't know Him.

Hesitating, Phillip reflected about all the women that he had inappropriate thoughts of and proceeded, "Now here's the part I can empathize with you on, Mary, I knew that God is love, but I didn't know what His love was for me. I learned that I didn't know Him as well as I thought I did. I had based my life on lust and shame, I hid in the open so people would think they knew the real me, I suppressed my identity, and I needed to change. That night was the beginning of the work in progress you see now.

I resolved that I wasn't going to be with another woman until I knew who God was. Knowing that he loved everyone even in their sin, I still had a hard time with the fact that Jesus loved me because of my failure. I struggled with having to prove my worthiness, but Jesus demanded no such thing. I didn't know Jesus as love, I only tolerated Him."

Phillip instantly stopped after saying those words. He quickly remembered another girl from his past who had said a similar thing to him. He recalled her saying, 'I don't want you to love me or tolerate me. I just want you to do me."

The conversion with Tracy, that night at the rally, came to his mind. He remembered her asking, "Do you love her or do you tolerate her?"

Withdrawing into his thoughts, he softly said, "I remember her face, but her name was not Tracy."

Snapping out of his reflection by Mary snapping her fingers in his face and saying "Hello, Earth to Phillip. Who is Tracy," he became annoyed because he'd had another breakthrough in his puzzle with Tracy.

Not wanting to lose his train of thought, he checked his pockets for something to write with but didn't have anything with him.

Abruptly, he asked Mary, "Do you have a pen?"

Giving her pen and paper to him, he wrote: Love … Tolerance … Not Tracy … Why won't you do me?

Ripping the paper from the pad, he rose, gave everything back to Mary and said, "Thank you, Macy."

Jaw agape, he fell back into the chair wide-eyed as he asked for the pen again.

Obliging, she handed him her pen again, and he wrote down: MACY!!!!!

Handing the pen back to Mary, she cried to him, "My name is Mary, not Macy. I don't want to be insulting, and I recognize that you're having a moment right now, but can you finish the story? I feel like I'm having a moment also right now, and I realize that you do understand."

Overjoyed that he'd made a breakthrough about Macy, he really wanted to run to his room and let his thoughts race as he put the pieces together, but he recalled how Mary had reacted to him leaving earlier at the pavilion. At peace that he'd written the triggers down and would be able to come back to them.

Also looking into Mary's eyes, he noticed that his defenses to resist Mary's whiles were gone. He prayed God would guard His heart and help him to get to the crux of his salvation.

Putting the paper in his pocket, he stammered, "Where was I?

Mary answered, "Your last comment was,'...I didn't know what love really was. That I just tolerated ...' and then you spaced out on Macy."

Recollecting his thoughts, he looked Mary in the eye, leaned forward in his chair, and divulged, "I didn't know what love really was. I just tolerated sin in my life because I didn't want to truly change. Before God spoke to me, I was comfortable with the status quo of just believing in God. But afterward, I discerned that I had to change."

Mary replied, "So, believing is not enough?"

In disbelief, Phillip shook his head, remembering the same question from Tracy? Macy? Whoever ... the night he was shot.

Lost in his head again, he recalled Macy asking, "And that is it? I believe, pray for forgiveness and then everything is all right? There is nothing else I have to do?

Reverberating in his soul, the echo of those words struck a truth he knew intellectually but hadn't grasped the depth of the verity: believing isn't enough. The verse, "The demons believe Jesus is the Christ and tremble[30]," came to his mind. He knew the truth of that verse, but it was a hard message for him to receive.

He had placed his whole life and faith on the supposition that Jesus as ones Savior to be enough. He thought, "what else is there? The Christian life requires sacrifice and consistency. It requires us to ..."

Excited, he nodded towards Mary's pen.

[30] James 2:19

356

Handing her pen to him again, she said, "Keep it!"

On the other side of the paper, Phillip scribbled, "Not only believe but also repent and accept Jesus as Lord and Savior." He knew that he'd dealt with repentance earlier with TJ, but now he understood it more as it related to his testimony.

He glanced at Mary and was glad that she was accommodating with him among his revelations. Although, he did perceive hints of impatience as he was sure that she was prepared to deal with herself.

Recollecting himself again, he stated, "Believing in Jesus as the Son of God and as your Savior is the beginning. The rest of the Christian life is the belief that we have to repent. We have to turn away from what is separating us from God. Moreover, we've got to accept Him as our Lord and Savior.

Truthfully, I'm still working out my salvation and learning about that. Nevertheless, here's how I understand repentance; it's about three C's: Confession, Contrition, and Change. And you've got to have all three for true repentance."

Grabbing Mary's hand, he asked, "Have you ever had someone who has wronged you and was told to apologize to you for what they did?"

Mary answered, "Yes."

Phillip continued, "OK, good. The thing is that the apology could be a nice and sweet, "I'm sorry" or like a little brat kid being forced to do something he does not want to do and spits out the words like poison. They both confessed but what is the difference?"

Mary responded, "I guess it is the one who meant it."

Grinning, Phillip acknowledge, "You're right! Truly meaning that your sorry is what contrition means. It literally means that you're ground to pieces. You're so sincere in your confession that you embody it. However, let's say that you've got a friend who confesses to you they're sorry, and they really mean it. They mean it so much that they bring you to tears in their confession."

Mary answered, "That's how I feel right now about starting a relationship with Jesus. After hearing this talk, I know that Jesus can love me."

Amazed at Mary's forthrightness and confession, he continued, "All right, now let's say your friend gives you this confession, but then commits the same wrong again. Then they come back and say they're sorry again and really do mean it, but they continue to go and do it again and again."

Mary declared, "Then it wasn't real."

Phillip pleaded, "But they said that they were sorry and that they really meant it."

Mary answered, "Yeah but they didn't change."

Delighted that she understood, Phillip said, "Exactly, the person would have to show evidence of change. It is not that they just confess their wrong, or that they really mean it, but they have to change. Which I believe is the hardest thing.

So much so, that Martin Luther, one of the church Fathers' said, "When our Lord and Master Jesus Christ said, "Repent" he willed the entire life of believers to be one of repentance[31]."

The Christian life is a life of continual repentance to God. It consists of us renewing of our mind, habits, desires, speech, and attitudes. Evaluating them compared to what God has set as the standard of good and evil.

The good news is that God hasn't abandoned us as we try to accomplish this. He continually gives of himself, as the Holy Spirit to assist us and convict us, to aid us in understanding God as reveals himself to us."

Furrowing her brows, Mary repeated, "So, believe in, accept, repent to, and receive Jesus. Got it."

Believing that she truly did comprehend Jesus' love for her and that the Holy Spirit would reveal the rest, he asked her if she wanted to receive salvation.

Mary eagerly nodded.

He began, "Ok, salvation is a gift paid for by the ultimate price. It's what we've been talking about the whole time.

[31] http://www.reformed.org/documents/95_theses.html

So, what was salvation's price? You see, Jesus left all the comforts and prestige of Heaven and came to Earth fully God and fully man. He stood in the gap of sinners and forgave their sins. He died in our place to pay the ultimate price so that we wouldn't be a slave to sin, but to have Him as our Lord and Savior."

Holding out the pen that she'd given him earlier, he said, "So, we talked about salvation having a price, let's talk about it being a gift. Let's say that this pen represents the salvation that Jesus paid for and that it's wrapped up with your name on it."

Mary nodded.

Phillip gestured the pen towards Mary and said, "When is this gift yours?"

Mary answered, "When you give it to me."

Phillip gestured the pen towards Mary again and said, "I'm giving it to you, but when is it yours?"

Mary took the pen and smiled in understanding, "When I receive it."

Phillip smiled back and said, "You're right when you receive it. Jesus' gift of salvation is available to everyone who believes, who repents of their sin, who accepts Him as Lord and receives His gift of salvation. So, don't lose your pen anymore."

Phillip regarded Mary laughing and then saw her working everything out in her head.

Looking at the pen and then back to Phillip, she finally said, "That's all I have to do?" Her laughter became tears of joy as she said, "Jesus loves me."

Phillip waited till she looked him in the eyes again and invited her to repeat after him.

Repeating after Phillip, she prayed:

> Jesus, I'm a sinner that You died for.
> Please forgive me for all of my sins. I believe
> You're God's only Son. I confess that You're
> my Lord and believe in my heart that God
> raised You from the dead and that You can
> save me. I repent and ask that You help me to
> live for You.

Amen.

Smiling as bright as the sun, she exclaimed, "Whew! That was awesome. I feel like I ... I .... Well, I feel new. So, is this it?"

Ecstatic, he answered, "No, there's so much more. Let's see if I can retrieve a Bible for you so you can learn more?"

Wrapping her arms around herself, she gave herself a hug. Then she jumped up and said, "Yeah, let's do this."

She reached down and lifted Phillip up.

Once standing, the room spun around in circles, and he recoiled as pain surged through his leg as it started to wake up. Grabbing his cane, he bit his lip and winced as the blood started to flow back into his leg.

Mary asked, "Where do I get a Bible?"

Phillip started to hobble towards Mr. Abiel and said, "Let's ask him."

En route, he thought about his reluctance on wanting to speak to Mary, but looking at his notes he took earlier he felt the weight of the veil lifting about Macy and his fault between him and Jessica.

Observing Mary's confidence, he thought, "We are all broken, and only Jesus can make us whole."

Chapter 26. Open Door Policy

Ignoring the insistent knocking on his door, Ethan lied his head down and wept.

He couldn't believe what he had just seen. Questions flooded into his head: Was that an exorcism? Was TJ a demon? Was Frank possessed? Was everyone that he was trying to help possessed? How am I going to explain all the destruction and pain that was used by TJ? How was he going to explain this to his superiors?

Leaning back in his chair, he tried to let the day pass. Out of all the destruction, the one that pained him the most was the loss of the last connection to his wife. He fumbled with his broken phone, but it was beyond his ability to repair it.

Closing his eyes and tired of sharing the silence with the persistent knocking, he put some headphones on and tried to play some music but couldn't because of his phone's destruction. Wanting to be left alone, he brought up his music on his computer, plugged in earphones and reclined in his chair.

Hearing Phillip's voice over the music, he wondered if he was the one who was knocking. Cocking one eye open, he saw that he walked away in a huff.

Watching Phillip walk away, Ethan pitied him because he knew that Phillip would've been better in someone else's care. He was sure that he wasn't being any help to anyone. He thought about how his ideology had failed him.

He endured his failure anew as he whispered, "I'm a fraud."

Taking one headphone off to hear if the knocking was from Phillip, he still heard the faint tapping on the door. He put the headphone back on, so he could drown out the world and lose himself in his misery.

He sulked because with his phone broken, he had nowhere to seek solace or comfort any longer. However, he knew the text by heart because it was a millstone on his conscience. **Can't wait 2 C U at home!**

Still not able to give into his wife of 11 year's last wish, he felt that his failure was complete. He knew that he'd considered deleting Beth's text message before as closure, but now he grieved because it had been forced upon him.

Rubbing the groove in his finger left from his wedding ring, he understood what she wanted and wished that he could erase all the reasons of 'the why' she had sent it.

Abdicating his atheism, he cursed, "God, why did You take her from me?" Scanning his destroyed phone, he cried out, "Why did You take my only connection to her?"

So angry that he couldn't see straight, he gazed into the main room and saw Phillip limping over to Mary.

Glad to have a diversion, he smirked and thought "Good luck with her. Enjoy the show."

He mentally compared how Phillip was still strong in all the challenges and adversities that he had faced, but that he was a shell of his former self.

He knew that Phillip's answer would simply be God, but he believed that explanation was a crutch.

For some reason he keyed in on Phillip's cane, he thought of how he had accused Christians of using God as a crutch, but then wondered if it was a bad thing to have something to lean on. Knowing that Phillip could walk without the cane, but not as well without something to support all of his weight.

Catching himself in the allegorical thinking that he hated Christians using to explain ideas about God, he laughed as he contemplated the irritating poem that all the Christians liked: 'Footprints.'

Unsanctioned, his mind bounded to the visuals of the poem: The path of the footprints, the legacy, the past, the weight each step carried.

Shaking the imagery out of his head, he cursed his willpower and muttered, "Damn 'Footprints.'"

Rubbing the bridge of his nose, he felt a headache coming on as the knocking sounded like jackhammering. Still trying to gain control of himself and not wanting to deal with anyone, he increased his diversion from the world even louder.

Wanting to distract himself further, he picked up Phillip's book that he was reading from the night before. He arbitrarily thumbed through the pages and read:

> ...and I've met many people who were white-knuckling the chair in front of them only because of the conviction of the Holy Spirit leading them to decide to follow Jesus.
>
> These people were in conflict with their will or God's will as they fought God. They aren't alone in the struggle because we see a few accounts of people in contest with God: Jacob and his wrestling match, Jonah running away from Nineveh, Elijah on the mountaintop, Peter denying Jesus, Paul before the Damascus road.
>
> The fight stems from one's earthly nature and their spiritual side. You could be fighting God because you think that God hasn't blessed you the way that you think He should. Or you're running from obeying God and choosing your own prejudices. It could be that you've done awesome work for God once, but then someone had threatened you, and you forget that God is stronger. You could've been ashamed because you had denied Jesus and you do not think He would want you back. You could be self-righteous and persecuting God and have the blinding moment on your journey. You could be so

afraid of what other people are thinking of you.

> I think of it this way: God says "Come let us reason together." [32] Meaning that he wants to have an open dialogue with us, but most of us close the door on the One, who knows His plans and the future.

Tilting his head back, Ethan felt the weight of the day. Exhausted, he wished that he could just somehow come to understand everything, but now wrestled with the thought of God wanting to reason with Him.

"How do I reason with You, God? How do I stop fighting You?", escaped his lips.

Picking the book back up, he continued:

> "We see evidence of God working all throughout the Bible in people beyond what they could have imagined.
>
> He wrestles with Jacob because Jacob went overboard on his desires and God gave him a reminder of that day.
>
> Through the extreme of Jonah being thrown overboard from the ship because of his disobedience and swallowed by a big fish, God cared for Nineveh and led them to repentance.
>
> Elijah looked for God in the extremes, but God spoke in the still small voice.
>
> Jesus came to Peter's level as he restored him ..."

Putting the book down, Ethan massaged his temples as he grumbled, "I can't catch a break."

Getting some aspirin from his desk drawer, he swallowed it down as he wished that the dull thuds of his headache would subside.

---

[32] Isaiah 1:18

He felt like he needed to get away on a cruise so he could deal with the overwhelming stress that he was dealing with. But no matter how far he went, he knew that his wife's memory would still follow him.

He scoffed as he thought that he'd be no different from Jonah.

Looking at his destroyed phone, he cursed, "Why can't I catch a break? It wasn't my fault."

His entire being screamed at him on the contrary. The weight of his wife's last text overshadowed him as he yelled, "I want to deal with this right now and not run away, but I don't know how."

Angry at his predicament, he picked up Phillip's book again, switched to another page, and read:

> ... the struggle everyone has is that we all want to play God. We all want to live forever, but then we walk up to the forbidden tree in the garden instead of the Tree of Life.
>
> We listen to Satan's lie, telling us that we can be God, that we can make the decisions of what is right and what is wrong in our life and try to impose our decisions upon others.
>
> Person A would tell person B to how to get better, when person B believes that nothing is wrong with them based on their own standard of good and evil. Then person B would tell person A that they should mind their own business because their standard is meaningless to them.
>
> The truth is that we shouldn't be looking at our standards or comparing ourselves with others who are just as much as a sinner as we are, but come to the real question: Are you better than God and do you personally meet His standard?"

Dropping the book like it had burnt him, Ethan let out a silent scream of frustration after reading that last sentence, "Are you better than God?"

He had recalled those words before as his eyes shifted back and forth, replaying the arguments he had with his wife. He now knew why Phillip vexed him. It was because he had been fighting Phillip, not Beth, in his marriage.

He now knew why he normally could keep his tongue around most Christians, but why he couldn't deal with Phillip. Now he knew. His wife had been using Phillip's books against him when she discussed Christianity.

Remembering Beth's haunting text, he scowled and declared, "Phillip, it's on. Everything has been your fault."

Ethan was about to call Phillip into his office as he saw him and Mary walking to his door. Before Phillip could knock on it, Ethan opened it and was about to let all of his suffering, pain, hurt and frustration out on Phillip.

But before he could pour out his rage on Phillip, his desk phone rang.

He heard Phillip say, "This will just be a second. Do you have a …," but he held up his finger and answered the call, "This is Ethan Pitney."

The caller asked, "Is this, Dr. Ethan Pitney?"

Ethan shook his head in irritation because he had just announced to the caller that he was Dr. Ethan Pitney. He wondered if anyone listens when making a phone call. He tried to settle down because he knew he was angry with Phillip and not this person.

He curtly replied, "This is Dr. Ethan Pitney. How can I help you?"

***

Listening to Ethan on the phone, all Phillip heard was him saying was, "Uh huh! Oh! I understand. OK!"

Walking into Ethan's office, he was surprised to see two Gideon Bibles sitting on Ethan's desk. Grabbing one of them, he lifted it up and gestured to Ethan on if he could have it.

Deep into his conversation, Ethan fell into his chair and waved him on.

Taking that as a yes, Phillip strolled out with the Bible and looked at Mr. Abiel.

Mr. Abiel smiled as he waited for Phillip to close the door and continued his knocking on Ethan's door.

Phillip studied Mr. Abiel still knocking on the door and said, "I'm sure you can just go in."

Mr. Abiel smiled and responded, "Everyone has to open their own door to me, not someone else opening it up for them."

Shrugging his shoulders, Phillip moved on and handed the Bible to Mary and stated, "This is now your personal Bible."

Mary thumbed through it and asked, "Where should I start? I tried reading this once and didn't get that far."

Phillip answered, "Yeah that happens. I'd suggest reading the "Book of John." It is a good place to start to learn about who Jesus is and His love for you."

He watched Mary thumbing through the Bible until she gave up and gave a frumpy look.

He asked for the Bible back, dog-eared the pages for John and said, "You know, another good place to read is 1 Corinthians. It's a letter written to Christians who weren't acting like Christians should. It also has a chapter on love."

Giddy, Mary asked, "Where's that?"

Phillip earmarked 1 Corinthians also.

Mary retrieved the Bible and said, "Thank you for listening and for telling me about Jesus."

She gave him a huge hug and skipped away to her room.

***

"Ethan Pitney, I'm Detective Parks and I calling to inform you that Champ Davis committed suicide today," said Detective Parks on the phone.

Ethan collapsed into his chair and said, "Uh-huh!"

Detective Parks said, "It was a clean suicide. There was no guns or blood. He just took too many prescription sleeping pills."

Despair gripping his heart, Ethan groaned, "Oh!"

The detective continued, "He also wrote a suicide note beside another envelope which had your name and phone number on it."

In dread, Ethan answered, "I understand."

The detective asked, "Are you at your work? I can bring it to you, or you can pick it up."

Numb, Ethan replied, "Please deliver it here."

As the phone call disconnected, he kept the phone to his ear and asserted that his failure was complete. Reproaching himself, he stated, "I can't help anyone. Not my wife. Not Champ. Not Frank or Mary. Not Phillip. Not even myself."

Still holding the phone up to his ear, he observed Phillip "ministering" to Mary.

Shaking his head in amazement, he thought, "I'll be damned, Phillip did rise to the challenge and has been a big help to everyone." Crushed by melancholy, he thought, "Even more of a help than I have been."

He tried to figure out Phillip's secret as he roleplayed the conversation in his head, but he knew that his answer would've been Jesus. Personally, he didn't know how Jesus could fix his situation. He figured that he could tell Phillip his story and let him tell him how Jesus could fix it, but he couldn't get over realizing that Phillip's words were used against him in past arguments with his wife

Seeing Phillip finishing up with Mary outside his window, he watched as he stopped outside his office.

Putting his phone over the receiver, Ethan yelled, "Whoever is knocking, enter."

Phillip entered with the orderly who held the door open for him this morning.

Still playacting the fake phone call, Ethan said, "Ok, that would be great. I'll be waiting for it."

Phillip grinned and stated, "I figured it out. The block is gone, and I figured everything out about Macy and my wife."

Ethan nodded his head in acknowledgment but held his finger up to Phillip to have him wait. He acted like he couldn't get a word in during his fake phone call but the truth was that he didn't want to give Phillip the benefit of his failure.

Not being in any position to assist Phillip, he gave a thumbs up and then covered the receiver of the phone, as he demanded, "Make it quick."

Phillip said, "That's it. I see that you're busy. I'll tell you later."

Ethan mouthed, "Okay," and swiveled his chair around.

Phillip turned away and saw Mr. Abiel turning a Bible on Ethan's desk to a specific page.

He knew how Mr. Abiel had helped him and figured that Ethan was in safe hands.

Ethan's senses came back to him and noticed that his headache had subsided and that the insistent knocking had finished.

Reasoning out his anger on Beth quoting Phillip, he remembered how when he was angry at Beth that she wasn't the one raising her voice, but he was. How he was the one accusing her as she sat there taking it.

Phillip and Beth's question still bounded around in his mind, "Are you better than God"?

He stated, "I'm not mad at Phillip nor Beth, I'm angry at you God."

Turning his chair back towards the desk, he saw his Bible opened there and read:

> For what shall it profit a man, if he shall
> gain the whole world, and lose his own soul?[33]

Stunned, Ethan moved those words around in his head. He wanted to dismiss them, yet the words weaved off the book and into the fabric of his mind and the events in his life: the night accepting his award, the night when Beth left, the night he made Phillip kowtow and now with Champ committing suicide.

What did it profit him?

---

[33] Mark 8:36 KJV

Wanting to claim goodness, he figured that was all he was capable of. Still, he knew that he couldn't truly say that he had ever been his best.

Gain the world and lose my soul?

Grabbing his broken phone, he clutched it tightly, hoping that he wouldn't lose anything more.

Trying faith in God, he closed his eyes and decided to bestow God a little of his attention as he whispered, "God if You're there. I'm as ready as I'll ever be to talk."

Opening his eyes, he was startled to see an orderly sitting beside him.

Remembering him walking in with Phillip, he asked, "Who are you?"

"I am …" Mr. Abiel snickered and finished, "Let's just leave it at that. You and I've got a lot of talking to do."

Flummoxed, Ethan questionably responded, "OK."

Looking at Ethan's broken phone, Mr. Abiel asked for it, causing Ethan to hold onto it tighter.

Mr. Abiel stated, "You've been tormented by that text for far too long. Everyone can see that you carry it like your cross. Please, let me have it."

Ethan hesitantly handed the phone to the orderly, but he couldn't let his grip loosen from it when the orderly tried to take it.

Mr. Abiel relented, released the phone, and asked, "Please tell me about what is troubling you?"

Ethan thought about how weird the day had been and asked, "Who are you?"

Mr. Abiel answered, "Who do you say that I am?"

Ethan chuckled as he said, "The orderlies rotate through here so much I don't remember them all. Sorry, but you all look the same to me, so quit playing games."

Mr. Abiel replied, "I am not the one playing games. You're the one who is clutching onto a broken phone. Please tell me about what's bothering you?"

Ethan figured what could it hurt, so he asked, "How far down the rabbit's hole do you want to go? Mr. …"

Fishing for the orderly's name, Ethan gave a pregnant pause hoping he'd not get another riddle.

Mr. Abiel smiled and said, "Let see, you've called me 'The Company of Fools' before. I'll go with that."

Ethan remembered saying that during his Q&A at the Pelusa award ceremony.

He scoffed, "No really, who are you?"

Mr. Abiel replied, "I am …. OK. Just call me Abiel. Tell me what was on the phone?"

Clutching the broken pieces, Ethan answered, "It's my problem. Just leave me alone."

Mr. Abiel asked, "Have you ever thought that your problem is that you want everyone's approval?"

Confused by the question, Ethan argued, "How can I want approval? I get approval for whatever I want."

Mr. Abiel answered, "That's the problem. You're getting approval from all the places that don't really mean anything to you. You care about if your book succeeds amongst a world of strangers, but then you put on a good face for friends, all the while you're hurting inside because you're afraid that if you let somebody in, you would be seen for who you really are. Then, you wonder if they're going to truly accept you."

Surprised by the no holds bar approach that this orderly carried himself with, Ethan figured he'd diagnose him with a Messiah complex and that it was the reason why he worked in a hospital because he'd have the grandiose delusion that someone is getting better because of him.

Mr. Abiel smiled and said, "It isn't a complex."

Taken aback, Ethan was surprised that he'd known his thoughts.

Recovering, he shot back, "Well, I acknowledge that everyone can't like everything, so I couldn't just be about people's approval."

In a firm straight tone that wasn't condescending, Mr. Abiel answered, "True, you also want someone to love you unconditionally while you don't reciprocate, but continually place conditions on everything they do. So, how do you expect to get what you want when you don't give anything in return?"

Ethan wanted to deny that he didn't take people for granted, but his memories exposed him. His introspection revealed that he'd taken more from Champ than he ever gave. He thought about how Phillip gave more to others than he ever did. His epitome of disregard was Beth listening to his diatribes about how her beliefs separated them and her only response was her undeservedly loving him."

Pulling out his phone and showing it to Mr. Abiel, Ethan screamed, "I did have everything that I wanted, and she was taken from me. She loved me unconditionally and approved of me."

Mr. Abiel answered, "Yes, she loved you unconditionally, and you squandered it."

Faced with unrelenting truth, Ethan buried his head in his arms and started to weep with his phone sticking out of his hand.

Mr. Abiel gave a little tug on the phone, and Ethan released it.

Bitterly, Ethan cried, "It's the last thing that I have from her. It was my fault that she left."

Mr. Abiel put the broken phone down and asked, "Please tell me what is bothering you? Why are you as broken as this phone.?

Wiping the tears on his sleeve, Ethan said, "Well, Beth began to go to this church that some of her friends invited her to. Not thinking anything of it, I let her go because it gave me time to work on my research and book. I thought that it would be harmless and that she'd find how ridiculous religion was by going there.

The problem was that she changed. We were married, and she made the decision to change everything by herself. She knew that I didn't believe in God and that I believed that religion was a mass delusion that plays on one's desire to explain the unknown.

We began to fight so much so that there were times I had to walk away from her because I couldn't stomach what she was saying. She became one of those people who was all sunshine and rainbows. She made me sick with her sugar coating of every situation and always bringing Jesus into it.

Then there was this one night that she wanted me to go to church with her. I gave her the look that I always did, but she didn't drop it. I asked her why she was still with me? She said it was because she loved me. I asked her to leave me alone about the Christianity. I cursed at her about how she was unfair for changing the rules of our marriage. She said she had changed for the better and asked me to give an example of how being a Christian had made her any worse. I informed her it made her weak and simpleminded.

She stared at me and said, "For the sake of Christ, then, I am content with weaknesses, insults, hardships, persecutions, and calamities. For when I am weak, then I am strong."[34]

I was so angry with her that I took off my wedding band and told her to choose Jesus or me.

She told me that she chose Jesus, and I took the wedding band and threw it at her. She stood there and let it hit her in the chest and told me she loved me, but that Jesus was first in her life. She told me how I was getting more bitter, more resentful and drinking more.

I argued that it was her fault.

She asked me if I would at least drive her to the church meeting because it was going to rain.

I dismissed myself into my study as she informed me that she'd see me when she got home, and she left.

She was gone for two or three hours and then I received that text: **Can't wait 2 C U at home!**

I didn't answer the text at the time because I thought that she was simply checking in and letting me know that she was on her way home. I waited up for her a little bit, but I figured that she was caught up in talking to friends.

So, I went to bed still angry with her."

---

[34] 2 Corithians 12:10 ESV

Ethan stopped as expressions of hate, sorrow, bitterness, rage and sadness crossed his face. Settling himself, he wiped his tears.

Mr. Abiel just sat patiently listening intently.

With nostrils flared, Ethan's voice cracked as he said, "I woke up to a phone call to a police officer who informed me that my wife had had a car wreck. He told me that she'd ran off the road and into a tree and that she had died."

Reliving the moment, Ethan's whole body shook. Finding his voice, he said, "Ever since then I haven't been able to catch a break. It was the first chip in my façade. It's when my whole world collapsed.

I was angry with everyone. I blamed her church, her friends, and her God.

I remember her pastor coming over to me during the funeral and trying to console me.

That day I quit being an atheist. I wanted there to be a God so I could hate Him. I wanted to knock this pastor on his ass. I wanted to take all my frustration with his God out on Him. If His God could let that happen to my beautiful wife, then I couldn't believe in him."

Watching for a reaction for Mr. Abiel, Ethan became uneasy that he was just sitting there passively as the story was told.

Biting his bottom lip, Ethan pursed his lips as he worked out the rage as he blurted, "I never found the ring. I tried to, but I've never found it. I wished that my last words to her were not in anger. I wish that I had gone with her."

Ethan looked into Mr. Abiel's compassionate eyes and then nervously chuckled, as he said, "No, it was my entire fault."

Throwing his hands in the air in exultation, he quickly brought them down because he thought he was being foolish. Still elated, he felt a wave of grief wash out of him as he took a deep breath and exclaimed, "Whew! That was great to say. It was my fault."

Tears flooded his vision as he cried, "She loved me, and I treated her like shit. She was even going to come home to me after

I was such a jackass. Why? She was the only one who really approved of me even through all the hell I put her through. Why?"

After several minutes of Ethan weeping, Mr. Abiel broke his silence and said, "I have a gift for you," as he reached out and took Ethan's hand.

Upon Mr. Abiel's touch, Ethan's vision went dark and then slowly began to come into focus.

He looked around and noticed that he was off to the side of a road. He felt the rain on his face and heard someone calling for help.

Turning in the direction of distress, he saw his wife's car crumbled into a tree. He ran to the car and screamed, "I'm here. I'm here."

He came to the door and tried to open it so he could hold Beth in his arms.

He heard her whispering and saw that she had broken glass all around her, and that blood was coming from her scalp, nose and mouth.

He shook the car's door handle and pulled with all of his might to open the door. Tapping on the car's doorframe, he yelled, "I'm here Beth. I'm right here."

With her not responding, he thought that she was in shock, and that explained why she was so unaware.

He banged on the car door and kicked it. When he started to get angry that she hadn't acknowledged his existence, he understood that he didn't exist at this moment.

Resting his head on the door jam, he listened to her whispering but then recognized that she wasn't whispering but praying. With all of his strength gone, Ethan whimpered, "I'm here."

Beth seemed to look him in the face, but he knew that she saw right through him. He whispered, "I love you."

Ethan surveyed the wreckage and saw the tree limb that killed her. He saw that she was pinned in the car and that her dress was stained with blood.

Watching her pray, he heard his name mentioned. He loved hearing her voice again and wished she had spoken louder, but knew that from her perspective that she didn't have the strength nor the ability.

He saw her get a peaceful look on her face as she breathily said, "Amen!"

He watched her shift her head back and forth as if she was looking for something. Apparently finding what she was looking for, she started to stretch for it.

Writhing in pain, she grabbed a cable in her hand and began to fish her phone by its power cord.

Ethan feverishly pleaded, "Forget about it."

After she finally got the phone in her hand, she rested, looked up to heaven and said, "Thank you, Jesus."

She struggled in opening the texting program. She selected Ethan's contact, and then rested a little more.

Sitting helpless watching the events take place, Ethan could tell that her breathing was getting shallower.

She began to cough as thick blood started to ooze out of her mouth. She prayed, "Jesus, give me strength to do this." She wrote out the text and then sent it.

Ethan watched Beth as she studied his contact picture on her phone. She smiled and then leaned onto her side away from Ethan and dropped the phone.

Ethan howled, "NO!" as he beat on the doorframe.

He stood on the hood of the wreckage and tried to pull the limb out.

Tiring out from his struggle, he gazed up and saw Mr. Abiel.

Mr. Abiel informed, "Beth prayed for you the whole time. She wanted you to know the joy and peace she had at that moment. She prayed that God would reveal himself to you. She prayed that Christians would come into your life and help you."

Ethan jumped off the wreckage and walked towards him, "How do you know that?"

Mr. Abiel replied, "Because, I was there."

Ethan screamed, "Why didn't you do anything?"

Mr. Abiel said, "Like what?"

Ethan yelled, "Like what? Like, save her."

Mr. Abiel chuckled, "I did."

Ethan gave a confused look.

Mr. Abiel continued, "Now it's your turn. She desperately wanted you to be saved."

Ethan wanted to argue, but he knew Mr. Abiel was telling the truth. The words started to lose their sting and started to sink in. Now it was his turn. The thing she wanted most for him was for him to be saved.

Mr. Abiel continued, "You assumed the text she sent to you was her notifying you that she was on her way home. But now you know that it means she wants you to find your way home to her."

Ethan fell to his knees, buried his head in his hand, and cried, "It's not fair."

Mr. Abiel asked, "What isn't fair?

Ethan looked up in disbelief, "That she died."

Mr. Abiel answered, "Why is that not fair? Everyone dies."

Ethan said, "She deserved so much better."

Mr. Abiel asked, "Better like this earth with all of its destruction or Heaven? Or better like you? Or better with you condemning her and forsaking her?"

Ethan quipped, "I'm not going to argue about this world being the half empty cup or the full cup."

Mr. Abiel answered, "Three people happened upon a table with a half-filled cup of water on it in the desert. One person says the cup is half full, another says it is half-empty. The third person looked at the other two and said, 'I'll debate later' as he took the cup and drank the water down. He looked at the other two and said, "It was exactly what I needed.""

Ethan asked, "What does that mean?" as he looked around and noticed that Mr. Abiel had disappeared.

Alone, he sat by the wreckage.

Defeated, he buried his head in his hands again.

He heard his phone's text chime and knew that it was the text from Beth.

He grabbed his phone and then noticed it was broken, and he was sitting in his office.

Finally getting his bearings, he heard someone was knocking on the door.

Finding his voice, he answered, "Come in."

Chap opened the door and stuck his head in.

Relieved, Ethan was so glad to see him as he waved him in.

Chap took a seat and said, "You've been on my heart all day. Are you all right? I've been praying for you."

Ethan said, "It has been a life-changing day."

Chap just stared at Ethan's face as Ethan told him the events of the day and about his conviction about the text. Ethan explained everything to him. When reciting the text "**Can't wait 2 C U at home!** " he felt a shiver down his neck to his toes as he remembered his dream.

He pleaded to Chap, "Tell me about Heaven. Tell me about where Beth is.

Chap smiled and said, "Heaven is a glorious place and our hope as Christians."

Then noticing that Ethan was receptive to Jesus, Chap got excited and said, "You believe in heaven? Oh please let me tell you about Jesus' love for you."

Ethan bowed his head and answered, "Please do. I can't guarantee that I can give an answer now, but I'm more receptive."

***

Walking away from Ethan's office, Mr. Abiel and was glad to see Ethan's heart was finally opened and receptive to salvation.

He cheerfully strolled to the front door of the facility and let Jessica and Claire in.

Surprised that the door opened as she was about to knock, Jessica walked in with Claire following her.

Mr. Abiel said, "You're right on time. Follow me."

Part 8.

The Call for Grace

Chapter 27.   Mercy is something to give

Leaning on his cane, Phillip wobbly walked down the hall. He praised God that he wasn't feeling any pain in his thigh and that God had made Himself evident throughout the day. Feeling the warmth of the sunlight on his face, he reflected on how his hope had never been higher while in the ward and was glad that he'd found joy again.

Arriving at his room, he was confused to find the door closed. Walking through the door, he lost his footing by a liquid covering the floor. Lying on the ground, he felt like cursing as his thigh reminded him that he wasn't completely healed. Biting his tongue, he let all his breath out so he could relax.

Breathing in, he smelled the pungent smell of dog pee as he recognized he was laying in it.

He looked to the corner of the room and saw Lilly cowering and averting her eyes as she tried to make herself as small as possible. The tip of her tail wagged gently, as she awaited the boom to come. She quickly glanced towards him and shied away while licking her nose nervously.

He found that he could only laugh at the absurdity of the situation. God had saved him from an assassination attempt, but he had been wallowing in his pity and pain, crying himself to sleep and fearing what was to come. Then, as joy heralded before him, he met his first challenge.

Letting out a hearty laugh, he determined not to let anything ruin this day as he called Lilly over to him.

Perking her ears up, she looked Phillip's way with her tail between her legs.

As he called her over again, she slowly sulked towards him, mistaking his laughter with anger. Getting a foots length from him, she stopped and looked at the floor.

Phillip reached for her, wincing the whole time from the fall and brought Lilly towards him and rubbed her head.

Lilly jumped on Phillip and began licking him.

Seeing the door opening, he yelled, "Stop, there was an accident in here ..."

The door continued to open as Jessica stuck her head in and said, "Guess who?"

Taking a deep whiff of urine, she stepped back into the hallway and gagged.

Catching her breath, she thought about how she wanted events to play out. Then she looked at Phillip sitting in pee, petting on the dog that did it. Not wanting to be deterred, she put on her best face, powered through the stench, walked back into the room and planted both of her feet in the pool as she joined Phillip.

Claire tried to walked in, only to have to catch her breath in the hallway also. Looking in the door, she watched as her mother and dad just stared at each other. Then she saw her dad's cuts and bruises. Before she could comment on them, she was distracted by seeing a real live dog in her dad's lap.

Relieved that the dog was real and not a figment of her dad's imagination, she grinned ear to ear and let it become a full laugh. She was so overjoyed by the revelation that she just considered the dog pee as more evidence to her existence.

Examining Phillip, Jessica remembered that she heard him laughing earlier. Seeing that he had the pee all over him and loving on the dog, she tried to joke, "Well, witnessing you like this causes me to conclude that you're in the right place."

Becoming aware of her tone, she tried to catch the last words out her mouth, but she cursed herself that the first words she said to her husband were barbed.

Mr. Abiel walked in, saw the puddle at the door and said, "I see that nature has taken its course. I'll be back, and I'll clean this up."

Once he left the room, silence rushed into the vacuum that had been between Phillip and Jessica for the last few days.

Feeling an anger swell in him, Phillip thought about how he hadn't felt angry with Jessica the whole time that he'd been in the hospital, but as she stood before him, his anger overwhelmed him. As he continued to just stare at Jessica, the day's events and his memory of his fault in their marriage rushed so quickly in his mind that he couldn't translate them into words.

Claire sat in a corner and called the dog to herself.

Lilly bounded to her, jumping into her lap and licking her face.

Standing up, Phillip looked at Lilly and then at Jessica and stated, "Her name is Lilly, and she loves me."

Lilly jumped out of Claire's lap, danced around her and rolled onto her belly. Thoroughly enjoying Claire's attention.

Agitated and euphoric, Phillip only stared at Jessica bewildered. He wanted to recount his love for her, but her abandoning him had finally seized him as he averted his gaze.

Settling himself, he stated, "I wrote you."

Feeling the awkwardness and really wanting to show Phillip that she'd changed, Jessica responded, "Can we stop right now and will you allow me a do over?"

Full of his self-justification, Phillip was about to reply when Mr. Abiel strolled in with a mop.

He said, "Sometimes others make a mess, and we fall down in it and get all dirty."

Finishing up mopping the puddle, he continued, "Jesus cleans it up and then you just have to pick yourselves up, forgive each other and then move on so you can heal."

Calling to Lilly, Mr. Abiel ordered, "Come on girl, let's go outside to finish the business."

Lilly ran to him, and they left.

Phillip accepted Mr. Abiel's sideways wisdom. Ready to listen, he bit his lip and softened his demeanor.

Taking a deep breath, Jessica started, "Throughout this ordeal, God has worked on me. He has shown me where I've failed and how I can be better. He has shown me that I haven't completely depended upon Him and that I've put too many expectations on you.

He's also revealed to me that I've put others before you and that I haven't loved you like I should. I put Scott, the girls, even myself before you. I had a picture perfect idea of the world and you getting shot was not part of the plan."

Knowing that she was doing the best that she could at giving an apology, Phillip smirked as he replied, "I didn't plan on getting shot either."

Catching the cue that she'd messed up again, Jessica declared, "Phillip, this is hard for me. Yet, I'm trying. I know that I haven't handled anything right and that I don't deserve it but will you please forgive me."

Stunned, Phillip sat in silence because he'd never heard nor seen his wife broken or ever ask for forgiveness. His balance of the fault in their marriage took him off his high horse as he was humbled that Jessica was the better person, by being the first person to start the healing process.

Stumbling through his words, Phillip answered, "I've never stopped loving you, and yes I forgive you. Still, I can't … No. Not just me. We can't continue living like this. You're not the only one to blame for the state our marriage is in. I've forsaken you for way too long, and it's my entire fault that I've neglected to tell you how much that I love you.

I'm also just as guilty for putting things before you. I've put my career and the kids before you also. And I'm sure that my passive-aggressive behavior has made things impossible for us to be together as I sabotage things when you don't do things my way.

I'm also guilty for not protecting you from the wolves in the world. I …"

Jessica let the tears flow as she interrupted, "I have thought about this time and played it around in my head. I wanted to jump into your arms and hug and kiss you all over. But, honestly, I didn't expect you to be filthy. So, I guess this is the beginning of our picture imperfect world."

Advancing over to him, she passionately kissed him on his mouth.

Surprised that Jessica had come to where he was and kissed him, especially in his filth, Phillip finally started to believe that she had transformed.

Amazed at what God could do in a few days in both of their lives, he raised his hands and praised God.

Disturbing their reconnection, Claire exclaimed, "Get a room, guys!"

Phillip felt his heart drop as he waited for Jessica's temper to flare. He prepared himself to be the referee between them, but was surprised when Jessica replied with a smile, "We already have one, and you can leave anytime."

Phillip pulled away laughing, "OK, I'm convinced. I believe that God has performed a miracle. I have prayed for this moment, but I so need to get clean."

Cradling his wife in his arms, he kissed her and then went to the shower.

Closing the door behind him, he hobbled into the shower and let the water cascade over him as he thought of the broken puzzle that his life had become, and how God had gathered and arranged all the pieces together perfectly without him even knowing or assisting.

With tears mixing in with the shower, he was glad that he and his marriage had survived.

***

Ethan sat with his head bowed, but Chap's was prayer was lost to him because he was fixated on the awkwardness of someone holding his hands but was relieved when he finally heard Chap say "Amen."

Lifting his head, he understood intellectually what Chap was talking to him about accepting Christ with open arms, still a part of him wanted to stop and process everything that had happened throughout the day. He was no longer skeptical, he just felt like he wasn't faithful to himself if he did not stop and analyze God. He'd dismissed the existence of God all throughout his life, that Him revealing Himself to him now was overwhelming because his mind hadn't caught up to what his soul believed.

Thinking through the day's events with the exorcism of TJ, the healing of Frank, Phillip speaking with Mary, and his discussion with Mr. Abiel. He was sure that he didn't have any further excuses, but he wanted to ensure that he was doing this for the right reason, and not because he felt like Phillip was a hero, and that he was a chump.

Silence prompted him out of his contemplation, as he became aware of Chap waiting for a response to his delivery of the plan of salvation.

Ethan itched the back of his neck, then slapped his leg and mentioned, "Chap, would you like to meet Pastor Phillip Ashby for yourself?"

Taken aback, Chap stammered out, "OK? I'd be honored."

Relieved to have a way out, Ethan led Chap down the hallway towards Phillip's room.

En route Chap asked, "Ethan, I was expecting a clearer response from you. I'm surprised that after your revelations from today and your confession about Beth's death and her dying words that you wouldn't t want to hide behind your intellect. Faith is more than ..."

Cutting him off, Ethan said, "It's OK, Chap. I've got to think about it. I wouldn't want to just jump in and later feel like I was just caught up in the moment."

Chap said, "Ethan jump in, the water is fine."

Not liking the hard sale, Ethan said, "I need time. Please don't pressure me. Trust me, God is at the forefront of my thoughts now."

Disappointed, Chap backed off and stated, "The Lord's patience is salvation."

Knowing that he meant well and that he was doing his job, Ethan endeavored to not get angry. He was just lost in all of the jargon and catch phrases that Christians used. He remembered when Beth would speak Christianese to him.

The still fresh wound from his new found knowledge of Beth's desire for him, convicted him of being the jerk that he was when she was alive and ashamed that he was now seriously thinking about making a life decision for God after her death.

Not wanting to deal with the tug-of-war in his mind, Ethan hoped walking would help him get past his sentimentality, yet each futile step revealed his hollowness as he subconsciously desired to accept Jesus so he could be with Beth again. The battle raged within him because Beth wanted him to know Jesus and he wanted to know Jesus to get Beth back.

Each step furthered his self-defenses that had led him away from knowing God, then he recalled Beth telling him something about a 'shield of faith.'

His introspection led him to envisage faith being a shield and how his new found faith and every step he now took should be a step of faith. Then he speculated as to what he used as a shield beforehand if it wasn't faith. He concluded that his self-righteousness and pride was what he had used as protection against God.

Understanding washed over him on how a Christian could be vulnerable to God as he trusted, faithed, and believed in Him for protection and identity and that he was shielding himself wrongly behind his id, ego, and superego.

Running his hands through his hair, he was amazed at how easily that revelation came to him. He thought about how it was freeing to depend on someone greater than oneself, to believe and have hope than it was before today.

Stopping in his tracks, he was astonished that he'd thought of God as a someone vice a something.

Chap asked, "Is everything all right?"

Shaking his head, Ethan stammered, "Yes, just had a ... ah ... what do you Christians call it when you get a moment of clarity and understanding about God? "

Smiling, Chap answered, "An epiphany."

Ethan nodded his head in agreement.

Chap asked, "Do you need to talk it out?"

Not answering the question, Ethan began walking again as Chap followed side by side.

***

Arriving at Phillip's room, they were surprised to see Jessica and Claire.

Ethan made an introduction between all parties and asked, "Where's Phillip?"

Snickering, Claire and Jessica answered, "He had to get cleaned up."

Jessica asked, "When can Phillip be released?"

Faced with the idea of Phillip leaving, Ethan's cheerful disposition subsided because he now treasured having him here so he could pick his brain about his new found interest in the Christian faith.

Because Phillip had checked himself in and wasn't a danger to himself or others, Ethan knew that he had no reason to keep Phillip here.

Guilt about his past behavior caused him to recognize that he'd ruined a great opportunity and knew that he'd have to ask for forgiveness.

Trying to manipulate things for his advantage, Ethan turned to Claire and said, "Claire, you said a few days ago that you thought your dad would benefit from being here. Do you think that he's had enough time to work things out."

Claire answered, "Well, I finally met Lilly and discovered that she's real, I see my dad with unexplained bruises and cuts. His home life will be so much better, so I'm satisfied that Daddy does not belong here any longer."

Jessica chimed in, "Where did the injuries come from?"

Grimacing, Ethan found that the one person he thought would be in his corner had changed sides and also brought him back to his responsibilities.

Trying his best to answer the question on Phillip's injuries, he answered, "You see, well, uh. There was a scuffle today during group therapy."

Together, Jessica, Claire and Chap exclaimed, "What!?"

Holding his hands up, Ethan continued, "Believe it or not, it was a God thing and … and … I was going to call you but … but … but … You see, God also has been … "

Relieved, Ethan saw the bathroom door open as Phillip exited while drying his hair with a large towel.

Not noticing that there were new visitors, Phillip interrupted, "Jessica, did I tell you about Ethan. I think he has more problems than I do. He keeps clutching his phone every time that …"

Hearing Jessica and Claire clearing their throats, he removed his towel and noticed that they weren't alone.

Looking around the room, Phillip knew everyone but the visitor that seemed to be with Ethan

The stranger looked at Ethan, began to chuckle as he said to Ethan, "It seems that your secret was never that secret."

Ethan introduced Chap, and then zeroed in on Phillip and said, "Well, you don't have to worry about that phone thing. I don't need it any longer. The question is, are you all right?"

Seeing Jessica's beautiful smile, Phillip felt that things were resolved between them and that they were healthy enough to work towards reconciliation. He answered, "Things are great. My wife is smiling. I also don't have that hole in my memory about Macy any longer."

Claire corrected, "You mean Tracy."

Speaking over Claire's correction, Chap tattled, "Ethan is acting like he has it all figured out, but he doesn't feel like that he deserves God's forgiveness, healing, and grace."

Ethan replied, "It's not only that. I just don't think that I'd be fair to myself in making a rash decision."

Understanding Chap's direction, Phillip asserted, "Ethan, your spirit has been leaning towards this decision all along. If you're waiting until you deserve salvation, you'll never receive it. The truth is that none of us are worthy of God's forgiveness, healing, and grace, which is why Jesus redeems us. We have to get the right perspective on ourselves through Jesus' eyes before we start evaluating our worth to any others or ourselves. Redemption means that Jesus deems us worthy again."

Challenged by Phillip's words, Ethan fought the desire to argue with him intellectually, but he couldn't disagree that Phillip defined how he felt. He never felt worthy. He had failed so many time and had let so many down, starting with himself.

Shame whispered in his ear about his drinking, his marriage, his practice, his relationship with Champ, his marriage with Beth and all those in the ward that he'd failed.

Phillip continued, "That's why Jesus is the lifter of our heads. We are bound to fail, but He makes us worthy again."

Fighting the urge to intellectually shoot holes in Phillip's statement, Ethan decided to seek comfort in it. He became overwhelmed by something that within him flowed and from his chest, through his veins and shook his being when he let the truth wash over him.

Ethan meditated on that word: truth. Then on the word faith.

Phillip added, "Ethan, don't make the decision to follow Jesus based on circumstances alone. Take time with Him in prayer and study as He reveals Himself."

Amazed, Ethan looked up suddenly at Phillip once he said the word 'reveals' and knew Jesus had revealed himself already.

He softly answered, "You're right, Jesus has certainly revealed Himself to me."

Praying silently that God would continue to work within Ethan, Chap smiled after seeing that he was accepting Phillip's words and not wanting to argue.

Charmed by being in Phillip's presence, Chap said, "Amen!" as he took Phillip's hands and shook them as he said, "By the way, I'm so glad to meet you. I'm so glad that you survived."

Phillip fought back his reverie as Chaps said 'survived', but thought of Macy anyways.

he considered the miracle of Jessica and Claire smiling together and not arguing, and recognized that Ethan was taking God's truth in without hate or anger. He understood that Jesus had been at work without him. He had to assume that Jesus had been working on Macy as well.

Taking Chap's hand, Phillip answered," I am too."

Ethan recalled that Phillip had stopped by his office wanting to talk about something. He asked, "You said that you'd figured something out. What was it?"

Hearing another voice come from the door, everyone startled when it sneered, "Isn't this sweet that everyone has gotten together to sing Kum-bah Yah. Are ya going to start holding hands? I want to know the answer also Phillip, what was it you figured out?"

Turning to the door, everyone and was surprised to see Tracy standing in the doorway.

She wasn't the bedraggled woman that she was at the rally, but more refreshed. She wore clothing that was more feminine also: high heels, black sheath dress, fitted leather jacket and a shoulder holder for her gun. Her hair was a messy pixie with strawberry blonde highlights. Her makeup was something that you'd see in a magazine: red lipstick, dark eyeshadow and liquid eyeliner.

Not everything about her was different though, she still had a gun leveled at Phillip.

Chapter 28.   For Grace to Trust Him More!

Lifting his head from a quick prayer, Mr. Abiel watched Lilly sniffing around the trees.

He said to himself, "Well, everyone who has a part to play is almost here."

He watched as Lilly became interested in a squirrel in the trees.

Calling for her, she turned and ran towards him, as a police car pulled up into the parking lot.

He scratched behind her ears as she sighed. Then she perked up from seeing the squirrel again.

Praying that things could be different, he let out an anguished sigh as he watched Lilly change directions towards the police officer who just stepped out of his car.

***

Seeing the gun, Jessica recoiled and felt all her shame come back onto her like a wet blanket. She wanted to shout her displeasure at Tracy and find out why she had done what she had done, but in her concern for herself, she stood speechless.

Paralyzed, she also fought the urge to run, mainly because she didn't want to leave Phillip alone with this woman again like she had last time. So, she just prayed that God would intercede and protect her family.

Claire was intrigued as to how Tracy had gotten out of prison, found a gun, and found her dad again.

Feeling his body pumped full of adrenaline, Chap hoped to follow the lead of the one who took charge. However, he'd never thought of an occurrence like this ever happening, so he neither took the initiative and did what he'd always had done in situations like this; he stood still and waited for someone else to restore normalcy.

Ethan stood forward and asked, "How'd did you get a …"

In a quick movement, Macy bashed the gun grip into Ethan's face and then smoothly trained back at Phillip.

Surprised, Ethan cradled his face as the blood seeped through his fingers. He was sure that she'd broken his nose and split his lip.

Chap raised his hands and sought comfort in asking God for help while Ethan found it odd to now be calling on the name of Jesus.

Upon seeing Macy pointing a gun at him again, Phillip wondered as to what she was waiting for? Unfortunately, his mind disassociated from the actual current event and into a reverie. He recollected the day she had originally shot him. His thoughts weren't about 'being shot' like it was something that had passively happened, but a crisper and clear memory as the day she had shot him. The gun was his only crisp memory, though, his mind's eye blurred everything else that had happened that day, but his hearing was clear.

In the vision, Scott sang *Jesus, Jesus, how I trust Him!* as his family added their voices, *How I've proved Him o'er and o'er* and then the auditorium supplemented their voices to the song into a glorious crescendo, *Jesus, Jesus, precious Jesus!* Leaving him to sing in the present *Oh, for grace to trust Him more!*

He mused on how he'd heard that song several times during his rally and how it was all orchestrated with the music, lights, and passion, but how he'd never contemplated how God had orchestrated His crusade among man. How everyone has their part to play and how God had staged everything thus far. How we're to be His light, His music and His passion. How He continuously moves and swells in everyone's life and we don't even recognize that He's the One, who is affecting events and using us to His glory. How He'll call us to stand for what is holy and to worship him as Lord through all things. How He'll command us to use His authority to further His kingdom on the earth.

Phillip panned around to see the whole audience in praise with arms lifted high in worship to God as their Savior. Panning back across he saw his room, with Jessica, Claire, Ethan and Chap waiting for someone to lead them.

He began to laugh as he looked down the barrel of the gun again. Then into Macy's merciless eyes. He mused about how the Devil's agenda to steal, kill and destroy was behind everything that he'd been through. He thought about how Macy's mission to kill him, the destruction of his marriage and how TJ stole everyone's joy.

Correlating all the events, he kept laughing. Having confidence in God to reveal Himself, he lifted his hands in worship to God and began to sing.

Tis So Sweet to Trust in Jesus.
How I proved Him o'er and o'er.

Not making any sense of any plan, everyone in the room furrowed their eyebrows and looked at each other in bewilderment.

Through his busted swollen lip, Ethan asked Chap, "Is this a Christian thing?"

Chap replied, "No, I was going to ask you if this was a crazy thing."

Macy shifted her eyes to Ethan and mocked, "I don't think that you really believe that I'm serious. I will kill you."

Ethan kept wondering as to why she kept singling him out, but decided that he didn't really want to know that badly, so he kept his mouth shut.

Phillip kept singing, *O for grace to trust Him more.*

Everyone in the room jumped as Macy ran up to Phillip, pushing her gun under his nose and hissed, "Did you hear me?"

Feeling the cold metal under his nose, he evenly answered, "Macy, my life must mean something to you if you think you have to kill me to remove any obstacles or wounds in your life. You need to go to Jesus and find your peace. I forgive you, and I'm not responsible any longer. To save my life I have to lose it."

Macy's eyes widened when she heard her name from Phillip's lips. She backed up in bewilderment.

Phillip saw the chance to rush her, but then Claire asked, "Who's Macy?"

Seeing Macy come out of her astonishment, Phillip cursed the timing, as she trained her gun back onto him but this time her eyes were more wild than before. He noticed that she'd lost her focus.

Jessica pleaded, "Forgive her? Honey, she has a gun."

Still writhing in his pain, Ethan thought, "Forgive her? Forget about forgiving her. Get the gun, beat the shit out of her and then forgive her." Suddenly feeling uneasy, Ethan puzzled as to why thinking this way had never affected him like this before.

Chap wished he were somewhere else and continued to do the only thing he could do at this moment. He kept praying.

Ethan's heart sank when Phillip addressed him while pointing at Macy, saying, "Ethan, this is what I wanted to talk to you about in your office. When I was talking to Mary earlier, God revealed to me that Tracy is truly Macy. I've got to admit that you were right, I had to shift my focus off myself and be about God's work to have Macy revealed to me. I bet you knew that all along. I have to admit; you're smarter than I thought."

Giving a bloody halfway smile, Ethan wasn't sure if he should take credit for Phillip's gratitude yet, considering that Macy had everyone at gun point and he had a broken nose. Wiping his face with his shirt, he thought about thumbing 911 on his cell but quickly remembered that it was broken.

Still not wanting to draw any attention, Ethan cautiously asked Phillip, "Now that you've had the breakthrough, what can you tell us about Macy? "

Phillip gave a look to Macy and asked if he could retrieve the paper he wrote his notes.

She nodded her head in approval.

Taking out the notepad paper where he wrote the triggers, he disclosed, "You see, I was talking to Mary about my past and how I came to know Jesus."

Jessica said, "Who's Mary?"

Ethan answered, "She's a patient here."

Macy buffaloed Ethan in the back of his head with her gun again as she yelled, "You are not in charge here. Do you understand?"

Everyone found themselves, holding their breath as Ethan cradled himself on the ground.

Seeing that she had the gun trained on Ethan, Phillip answered his wife to bring the attention back to himself, "She's the one that you saw straddle me that day you visited."

In disbelief, Macy sardonically chastised Phillip, "You say 'no' to me and fool around here?" as she shifted the gun back on to Phillip.

Trying his best to not lapse into his memory loop while looking down the barrel of the gun, he said, "Please let me finish."

He gave a brief description of what he told Mary about his "God getting a hold of him" testimony to the group.

When Phillip had finished, Ethan moaned in pain as Macy said to him, "After I am done killing Phillip, you are next. So, shut up, unless you'd like to be first in line."

Finally, getting his bearings back, Ethan leaned his back to the wall and stared holes at her. In pain, he licked his lips and thought about Phillip saying that he'd forgiven her. He thought about how he didn't want to forgive her, but how he wanted to make her pay.

Gesturing to Macy, Phillip continued, "... after the Mexico trip, I came back home and tried to explain Jesus to my brother."

Ethan interjected, "Your twin brother," as he put his hands up to protect himself.

Nodding in agreement, Phillip continued, "Yeah, my twin brother. Being identical twins, we weren't much alike, other than having the same face. Anyways, I wanted to talk to him about my trip to Mexico and how Jesus had changed everything in my life."

* * *

Angry that Ethan had spoken again, she wanted to pull the trigger and be done with this sheep, but shock overcome her after hearing that Phillip's brother had been his twin brothers.

Fighting to stay aware in the present, she was distracted by flashes in her memory, recalling that she knew the data, but deemed it impertinent to her mission.

However, while hearing that Phillip had a twin brother, pathways in her synapses reconnected and layers of consciousness revealed that her memories were whitewashed with a painting underneath.

Looking at Phillip, she allowed her vision to blur to the point of where she saw two of him. The name Andrew came to her mind, as she gasped and brought her vision back into focus.

Her pupils started to constrict, and her blood pressure began to elevate as she had flashbacks of training with Andrew.

Agitated, she shook her head and tried to stay in the now.

Renewing her grip on the gun and reality, she aimed to get things back on track as she asked, "So, what happened in Mexico?"

***

Studying Macy, Phillip could tell something was off. He noticed that she became unsteady like she was the night she'd shot him.

Looking into her eyes, he spotted the reddening of the whites and felt like he was going to hyperventilate. Trying to draw longer breaths, he proceeded with his testimony of when he heard Jesus talk to him and the vow that he made with God.

Acrimonious, Macy scoffed, "Seriously? Jesus talked to you?"

Finding it hard to ignore her, Phillip gestured to Macy and pressed on, "You see, the night Macy shot me wasn't the first night that I'd met her. While I was telling Andrew about my testimony and Jesus, she walked in. Being my brother's girlfriend, she had free reign in his apartment. Long story short, my brother had to go to work, and Macy and I struck up a conversation while left alone in the apartment."

Not knowing what else to do, Phillip kept talking as he silently prayed for an opportunity to strike.

He continued, "Talking well into the night, she told me how her and my brother had been together for a while and how she was glad to finally have met me. But the conversation changed when she commented on how uncanny it was that she saw my brother in me and how she appreciated that I talked about God's love freely. She mentioned how she felt like she was tolerated by my brother."

***

Ethan bowed his head in guilt as he recalled Beth talking about God's love freely to him also and how he only tolerated her instead of appreciating her.

He remembered hoping her Christianity was a phase that she was going through.

Then he thought about his new-found faith and wondered if it was a phase.

Seeing the gun and thinking of the events of the day, he didn't think so.

Wiping the blood from his nose on to his lab coat, he smiled as he found it comforting that he could now pray that he'd see tomorrow.

***

Averting his gaze from the gun, Phillip looked deeper into Macy's reddened eyes. He tried not to recoil when he recognized the red eyes elsewhere from dreams, corners that he turned, and when TJ was completely out of control.

Seeing that she still wasn't stable, he nervously swallowed as he worked through the timing and the distance between him and her.

The silence must have been too long because it brought her back to her task.

Figuring that his calculations weren't in his favor, he asked her if she wanted him to continue with his story.

***

Macy's memory shifted like static on a TV as she looked at Phillip but only saw Andrew.

She wanted to drop her guard; however, she had to keep the mission in the forefront. After all, that was why they'd broke her out of prison and sent her back out to finish what she'd started.

She'd been happy to stay in jail, relieved of her duty. But they weren't done with her yet.

Warned by the silence, she cursed her negligence.

Zoning back in, she heard Phillip's question and generically nodded in agreement.

* * *

Phillip realized that Macy was lowering her guard throughout his story. He knew that she was willing to kill for her cause, but he couldn't think of what to do to keep everyone alive.

Taking a deep breath, Phillip continued, "In Andrew's apartment, the conversation lulled, and Macy excused herself and went to the bathroom.

Alone with my thoughts for the first time that night, I prayed that God would help my testimony and the sharing of what Jesus had done would take root into her and Andrew's lives. I think that was also when I decided to change my major at school and learn more about God.

While setting my future aspirations, I turned and was astonished to see Macy stark naked. She sat in my lap and put my arms around her as she caressed my face and kissed me."

Judgingly, everyone shifted their collective accusatory gaze to Macy.

Brazen, she cast her devil-may-care stare at them and then to her gun as each accuser's boldness dwindled.

* * *

Waging a war within her mind, Macy struggled to keep Phillip and Andrew from continuously merging from one person and then back to an individual. Filled with nervous energy by having her story confirmed for her, she did her best to keep still as the battle played out in her mind.

The whitewash that her supervisor created began to flake. She saw the image that they portrayed her as, compared to the different story that Phillip was telling.

She silently argued, "I wasn't the instigator. He was," but the image underneath her façade aligned with Phillip's story.

Doubt surfaced, as she thought, "Phillip's not the villain. I am."

Latching onto her introspection, she couldn't fight the discharge of pain like an ice pick jabbing her brain which erased all traces of any memory that had surfaced.

Familiar with the pain, she tried to stable herself from the confusion. She tried to keep her mind on the task and not to be distracted by Phillip and Andrew's faces alternating repeatedly.

The pain dissipated as she concentrated on the mission.

***

Examining Macy's vacant dead stare, Phillip was surprised that she hadn't flinched or reacted to any of his stories.

Thinking about her current stoic behavior, he contrasted it to her carefree spirit he knew when she was younger. He wondered about what she had been through to get to this point.

A chill disturbed his recollection as he noticed that the only visible change in her was the reddening of her eyes.

Hoping that his storytelling was buying all of them time, he continued, "I stood up and tried to get away from her. I remember her saying, 'Why won't you do me? Your brother will never have to know.'

Almost out of her arms reach, she grabbed a bit of my shirt sleeve and it ripped off. Getting out of the apartment as fast as I could, I got into my car and drove without a destination. I wanted to get away."

***

Dripping with contempt, Macy whispered to herself, "Get away!"

That phrase triggered another memory.

Fighting the hammering in her head, she screamed, "Get away. Get away? Get away!"

She ignored the reaction of the sheep in the room as she pressed through the pain. She recalled a time when Andrew wanted to get away from the training that the both of them were a part of. She remembered that he said that they both were being brainwashed into automatons. She remembered defending the training, because they were both considered to be dead anyways, so it didn't matter what happened to them. She remembered telling him that they had a purpose and that the mission was what was important.

Intense, excruciating throbbing coursed through her, making her want to rededicate herself anew to the mission so the pain would stop.

Staring at Phillip, she licked her lips as he and Andrew kept changing in her mind and she became lost as to who the true target is.

She repeated to herself quietly, "The mission is what matters."

***

Hearing her mutter to herself, Phillip was glad that she'd broken character a bit.

He thought about how he'd really didn't understand her purpose. At the arena, she seemed to be downtrodden and unsure of her goal. Now she was dressed to the nines but still seemed unsure.

He thought that if she'd wanted him to be dead, she wouldn't have been toying with him and allowing him time to talk to others in the room. So, there must have been something that she related to in his sermon that night.

He racked his brain for a clue, but the gun barrel pointed at him didn't help. He remembered one of her questions at the rally, "I believe, pray for forgiveness, and then everything is all right? There is nothing else I have to do?"

Now he understood that he'd known the answer all along but hadn't emphasized it in his own life. That belief in God made everyone no different than the demons, and that repentance played a crucial part in a Christian's spirit, but that was typically overlooked because it isn't popular.

Hoping that he'd delicately strike a nerve, he ended his story, "After a few miles, I was so proud of myself on how I was faithful to God.

Honestly, that was all I thought about during that situation. I thought about how good I was and how God should have been proud of me. I was so satisfied that I'd endured the first test that Satan had thrown at me and that I passed."

He tried to figure out how he could weave repentance into his story, but he felt that his part in the charade was done.

Standing quiet, he awaited whatever action took place tonight as he thought of the song, *How I've proved him o'er and o'er*.

***

Between the throbbing in his head, Ethan ridiculed himself as he thought about Phillip's story, "I'm a failure. Could I say that I'm glad I'm running? I'm a drunk. Champ's killed himself. I'm just pitiful."

Noticing that there was a pregnant pause, he became aware that he wasn't paying attention to Phillip's story, except on how he could correlate it to his own story.

Seeking comfort, Ethan instinctively grabbed his phone out of habit and Macy trained the gun on him.

Phillip exclaimed, "Whoa! Whoa! I'm the one you're mad at, not him!"

Terrified, Ethan slowly raised his hands into the air, hoping to satisfy her suspicion.

He saw her purse her lips and then turn the gun and her attention back to Phillip.

Relieved, he was amazed as to how Phillip sacrificed himself for him. Phillip's valor only solidified his depth of cowardice. Also, the symbolism wasn't lost on him either as he recalled his wife telling him about Jesus' sacrifice for mankind while we were still sinners.

Getting tired of being beaten and others sacrificing for him, he let out a sigh. He stated, "OK, I'd call that a breakthrough. Considering that you ..."

Macy interrupted, "This isn't a therapy session, and he hasn't told the whole story." As she pulled a second gun out from under her jacket.

Peeing himself, Ethan screwed up his courage as his training kicked in as he said, "OK, tell us your story, but not with a gun pointed at all of us."

With the gun still aimed at Phillip and him, Macy gave a harrumph and said to Ethan, "Say, please."

Feeling his heart beating out of his chest, he muttered, "Please."

Holstering the second gun that was pointed at Ethan, she teased, "So, the sheep can be trained. It's like I said, this isn't a therapy session, and you're not in control. Phillip wasn't there when everything got worse."

Pushing his luck, Ethan asked, "How did it get worse?"

Pointing to Phillip, Macy absentmindedly continued, "He's actually clueless about how deep this all goes. He's completely unaware of all the people who are connected. He thinks he knows what happened to his brother, but he doesn't really know the truth."

***

Mr. Abiel waited patiently at the door as Lilly finally finished doing her business and for the police officer to make his way up the sidewalk.

Seeing Lilly bound to the new person once she noticed him, he smirked when she rolled over to get her belly rubbed.

Mr. Abiel joked, "She thinks that everyone is here to see her."

The officer gingerly stepped over her, but almost tripped as Lilly ran ahead to only roll over in his path again.

Mr. Abiel watched as the officer bent his knees in a way to pet her but not get any of her hair on his uniform, but only to be surprised when she bounded up and licked his face.

Wiping his mouth, the officer stood and wiped away the fur from his uniform. Satisfied that he was presentable, he walked up to Mr. Abiel and said, "I'm Officer John Parks, and I called earlier to Mr. Pitney about stopping by to drop something off for him."

Mr. Abiel smiled and said, "Follow me."

Officer Park's responded, "Do you mind if I leave this with you? I trust that you can get this to him."

Mr. Abiel said, "No, I think that considering the day he's been currently having, he'd want you to deliver this to him as quickly as possible. Follow me."

Officer Park's sighed aloud and said, "OK."

Mr. Abiel opened the door as Lilly went running in before them.

***

Once inside, Lilly sniffed the hallway and was excited to have a new scent. Remembering all the new people in the last room she was in, she raced there.

***

Never having been a gunpoint, Ethan felt that he was handling things well. Although, considering how rotten his day had been, he thought about how the day wasn't over yet.

Trying to keep Macy talking, Ethan asked, "So, how deep does all this go? Who's all connected?"

Ignoring Ethan's question, Macy began to laugh as she told Phillip, "All the truth you know is a lie."

Phillip asked, "What do you mean? My brother is dead. That's the truth."

Ethan was surprised to see Phillip's countenance crack, as he got angry from Macy's laughter. He was sure that she enjoyed being in control, not because she had the gun, but because she thought that he needed something from her.

Phillip's face became red as he shouted, "How dare you mock Andrew's death. He died in the line of duty as a hero."

Annoyed, Phillip trailed off as Macy continued laughing hysterically said with a swagger, "He's the red demon eye's that you've seen."

***

"How do you know about the red eyes?" Phillip asked absentmindedly. Then understanding what she implied, he summoned all his strength and yelled, "You're a liar."

While screaming, he saw Lilly turn the corner to the room and jump up onto Macy's leg.

Startled by the movement, he saw Macy train her gun onto the disturbance.

Glad to have the distraction, Phillip prayed silently, "Jesus, I trust You." as he threw the towel he had from showering earlier at Macy, he charged her as best as he could.

***

Seeing Phillip making his move towards Macy, Jessica joined the cacophony as she screamed, "Noooo!"

During that split second, she jumped towards them, concluding that Macy had taken so much from her, and she wasn't going to let her take more.

***

Thinking about Beth, Ethan anticipated Jessica's actions towards Macy as he instinctively put himself between them.

Surprised by his actions, he quickly rationalized that he'd lost his wife because of his inaction and he was bound to stop Phillip from losing his.

***

Terrified, Claire watched Macy get smacked in the head with the towel in her face. As the towel fell from her face, she yelled as Macy lifted the gun towards her dad.

She cringed as her dad lost his footing because of his hip and fell, thus putting his entire frame on top of Macy and Lilly.

She watched as Lilly became aware of her dad's charging and tried to get away but was too late and became tangled in the confusion.

She saw Ethan block her mom from getting into the action, as her mom tried to push her way through him, but only able to grasp enough of Macy's sleeve to get an exact aim and to push Ethan into Macy.

Phillip, Lilly, Ethan and Macy struggled on the floor with Lilly still trying to get away, Ethan with look of confusion as to his part to play, and her dad using all of his might as he attempted to wrestle the gun away from Macy while saying, "Let it go!"

***

With a hint of realization that she may be overcome, Macy's eyes became wilder than ever as she lost the battle on differentiating between Phillip and Andrew's' faces. Their face's blurred together like the colors of a spinning top and then slowly rested on Andrew.

Immediately, she realized that Phillip wasn't her target, but Andrew was the target.

"But they sent me in here for you, not Andrew," said Macy as she tried to figure out what her mission truly was. She knew that it was Andrew at the rally until something triggered in her to target Phillip.

Disgusted, she convulsed as she said, "I've been a pawn."

***

Seeing the confusion on Macy's face, Phillip pushed her gun arm downward but was aware that she still had her finger on the trigger.

***

Ethan was glad that he'd moved Jessica away from the tangled mess but was distressed that he had joined it. Trying to get away, he flailed and elbowed everyone behind him.

***

Chap finally had the presence of mind to leave the room and get an orderly or security to help.

Once clearing the door, he began yelling, "Gun! Gun! Someone, get help."

Then he heard two shots fired.

***

The sound exploded in the small room.
Lilly yelped.
Phillip's body went limp.
Ethan rolled over and doubled over.

Macy laid on top of all, breathing shallowly.

Dark red bled out, spreading around the triad on the floor.

After all the action, silence reclaimed its embrace.

Glad to be freed from the entanglement finally, Ethan stood up by Jessica.

Motionless, Jessica thought that she'd lost Phillip for real this time.

Filled with horror that her dad may have actually died this time, Claire sprang to her feet to find if what she feared was true.

The gun laid on the ground smoking.

* * *

Thinking that he heard something, Officer Parks asked Mr. Abiel if he'd heard it also.

Mr. Abiel stood quietly, agreed that he heard the same thing, and said, "I think that it's coming from Mr. Ashby's room."

Seeing a man run down the halls screaming, "Gun! Gun! Someone, get help!," Officer Park's unholstered his gun, released the safety, and called into his shoulder mike, "Dispatch, I'm downtown with a possible disturbance at ..."

Before finishing his call, he heard the two shots fired and notified. "I'm responding. Send help. "

Turning his microphone down, he looked at Mr. Abiel and ordered, "Call 911 and bring in the cavalry. Then, start getting people out of here."

Still holding the letter to Ethan, he handed to Mr. Abiel and demanded, "Please get this to where it goes."

Mr. Abiel smiled and said, "Trust me, help is on the way," as he slowly walked to Ethan's office.

Officer Park's watched Mr. Abiel's slow gait and sarcastically exclaimed to himself, "Don't get in a hurry. I'm enough to take care of this," as he made his way to the screaming man.

Trying to calm the man down, Officer Park's asked, "Sir, are you all right?"

Chap said to the officer, "Thank God you're here. You've got to get in there. She's got a gun."

Officer Park's asked, "How many people are in there?"

Disoriented, Chap replied, "Umm ... she's got a gun. You've got to go."

Officer Park's put his hands on Chap's shoulders and reiterated, "How many people are in there?"

Coming to his senses, Chap answered, "One woman with a gun, Phillip Ashby, his wife and daughter and Ethan Pitney. There is a total of five people in there."

Creasing his forehead, Officer Park's confirmed "Pastor Phillip Ashby?"

Chap answered, "Yes, that Phillip Ashby."

Officer Park's asked if the woman with gun matched Tracy's description.

Chap nervously shook his head in agreement.

Officer Park's thought about her docile behavior when he had interrogated her, and then how she went crazy when the so-called lawyer said something to make her try to kill herself. Putting the pieces together, he figured that her being transferred to the FBI being bunk.

Shaking his head to get back into the moment, he jeered to himself, "Tracy, we're going to have to stop meeting this way."

He told the screaming man to get outside and to help get others out also.

Leaning against the wall, he prayed, "Jesus, please protect me," as he positioned himself against the wall to Phillip's room and snuck a peak.

He saw two bodies on the ground with blood oozing beneath them with a gun laid to the side and a man with two women in shock. He heard a soft whimper and saw movement underneath the bodies.

Taking a breath, he walked in and cleared his corners. Confident that there was no current danger, he trained his gun onto the pile on the floor.

***

Pushing Macy off him, Phillip rolled over to his wife and daughter.

Straining to stand up, Lilly collapsed and wailed. She scooted herself to her bed in the corner on the linoleum, trailing a pool of blood behind her.

Seeing her struggle, Phillip moved over to her, grabbed a sheet off his bed, and applied direct pressure to the wound.

Lilly yelped and relaxed when she figured out Phillip was trying to help her.

Claire approached and began to pet Lilly.

Focusing on Claire, Lilly licked her hand, laid her head down on Claire's lap, closed her eyes and let out her last breath.

Phillip's lip quivered as he removed his hands from the blood-soaked sheet.

Longing to take away his pain, Claire watched her daddy mourn and wished that he didn't have to deal with any more.

After a few moments, Phillip stood up and walked away from the best friend and teacher that he had during this whole trial.

***

Sitting on the bed, Ethan thought about how he didn't think he could handle anything else this day.

Seeing the cop in the room begin to disarm Macy of her weapons, he just couldn't deny that God had orchestrated events. He was entirely sure that he didn't need any more convincing, and that his faith was sure, and his doubts in God had subsided.

He looked up and said aloud, "God, I believe."

Then he thought of Beth pleading with him to accept Jesus and her text before she died, and added, "Beth, I can't wait to see you when I get home. I love you."

He lifted his arm to wipe his eyes and was surprised to feel his arm begin to burn. Taking his arm out of his doctor's jacket, he winced from the pain.

Once his arm was out of the sleeve, he saw blood dripping from his fingertips.

Getting lightheaded, he exclaimed, "I've been shot."

The cop came over to him, cleaned off the blood and found the source.

Ethan saw a smile on the cops faces as he said, "Sir, you've only been grazed. You'll make it."

***

Officer Parks left the doctor and leaned over the other body in the room. He recognized that she was the escaped convict. He saw that she had blood coming from her lower stomach, so he checked her pulse and breathing.

Noticing that they were shallow but still there, he reached for his mike to call it in but heard the sirens outside.

Pastor Ashby stood over Macy and prayed, "Please Lord, forgive her."

After saying the words, Phillip felt a relief and that weight lifted. He knew that he needed to forgive Macy, but saying it was another thing.

Shocked, Jessica replied, "You really are going to forgive her? How can you?"

Looking at his wife, Phillip answered, "Jesus forgave us even when we rebelled in our sin and shame. He forgave us while he was dying on the cross. I have to do this out of obedience. I have to forgive in faith. I have to forgive as he forgave me. Also, forgiveness is more for me than it is for her."

Jessica argued, "Well, I don't think that I can forgive her because of the pain that she has caused."

Putting his arm around his wife, he comforted, "I know that it's hard to forgive. I would say that it's one of the most difficult things to do as a Christian. Nevertheless, let's get straight what forgiveness is. It's a release. It's a choice to let go of the debt I feel she owes to me.

It's not reconciliation, that's a long and arduous task, and I accept I may never have this with Macy because it's dependent upon both of us.

Nor is it me excusing Macy of all the consequences of her actions, but it's me releasing the pain and suffering that she has caused.

I choose not to hold it against her."

Biting her upper lip, Jessica agreed, "If you say so. I guess that makes sense. Then I forgive her too."

Several paramedics and cops rushed in. The cops promptly removed Macy from the room.

* * *

Outside with the media in front of the ward, Officer Park's answered all the questions about Macy as Claire responded to questions about her dad.

Ethan saw Phillip give him a hand wave of acknowledgment, as he stood waiting for the cops to get their statements from him. Shifting his stance back and forth, he fumbled with the unopened letter from Champ and Beth's Bible to him.

Finally getting away from the questioning, Phillip asked, "So, what do you have there?"

Ethan put the letter in his pocket and changed the subject, asking, "So, now that you know who Macy is, what are you going to do regarding this information?"

Smiling, Phillip said, "Nope, you go first. My weight is gone, but it looks like you've changed what your burden is."

Ethan produced the letter and handed it to Phillip, as he added, "It's from Champ Davis. He was a patient of mine who just killed himself, and it's all my fault. "

Phillip held the letter, and said, "I'm so sorry. You know on second thought, I'll go first," as he reached into his pocket and retrieved the note that he wrote during his discussion with Mary. Flipping the paper over he read, "Not only believe, but also repent and accept Jesus as Lord and Savior."

Phillip pursed his lips, looked at Ethan and with his voice breaking he claimed, "Ethan, I've used you as a target of my frustration as I was lost in my pain and brokenness. Will you please forgive me?"

Ethan held up his uninjured hand and said, "Sir, there is no apology needed. Being there in people's pain and brokenness is in my job description. Anyways, I was going to ask you for forgiveness for the exact same thing. I'll forgive you if you forgive me."

Phillip and Ethan laughed together in commiseration.

Phillip flicked his note with Champ's letter, and responded, "Deal. Well during that talk with Mary, I relearned repentance. You see, I teach that one only has to believe in Jesus to be saved. I now know that is so hollow. That belief in Jesus is only one part of the solution and that the other part is repentance.

I do believe that Jesus is God. I also believe that He has been with me through this whole ordeal since being shot. However, I have to repent because I'm an example that believing is not enough. I've need to repent because I've made Jesus so cheap. I was so full of my belief in Jesus that I never went back to Macy later and repented for what I did wrong. Everything wasn't all of her fault.

I know that by staying alone with her at my brother's apartment was sending the wrong signals to her. I should've left after my brother did. I should've ..."

Ethan put his arms on Phillip's shoulder, and interjected, "You could've never anticipated what she was going to do."

Wanting to plead his case, Phillip began, "Yes, but ..."

Ethan answered, "Yes, but, what? You aren't responsible for someone who transferred all of their pain, suffering, and self-destruction upon you."

Phillip held up Champ's letter and asked, "Just like this letter?"

Ethan shot back, "Yes, but ..."

Phillip answered, "Yes, but, what? How is this any ... "

A gust of wind interrupted their conversation as it tore the letter from Phillip's hand and down through the street.

They both tried to give chase, but the obstacles of the police, new reporters and paramedics wouldn't all them too caught up to it.

Downtrodden, Ethan sat on the curb and thumbed through Beth's Bible as Phillip apologized profusely.

Ethan thought about Phillip's confession about repentance and felt a chill in his body, as he knew Phillip had revealed to him what his problem was. That he would put people in a position to fail him and then blame them for proving him right. That he'd put himself in the lofty position of helping people in his practice to not play the victim as he relished the victim role in his own life. That he acted superior and looked down on those who didn't share his opinion.

Phillip sat next to him still groveling.

Ethan patted Phillip back and said, "Phillip, I shouldn't have made you responsible for the letter. It's my fault."

Phillip was taken aback and sensed a genuine change in Ethan's attitude and answered, "Well, I'm still sorry."

Ethan waved him on and stated, "You know, throughout this day, I've come to believe in Jesus, and I understand the whole repenting thing. Is that all there is? Just believing and repenting."

Phillip smiled and answered, "No, the Christian life is a life of continual believing, repentance, and discipleship."

Ethan said, "Ok, I'm ready. After everything today, I want to start following Jesus."

Phillip said, "I believe you. Praise Jesus."

They both looked up and saw Chap and Jessica standing in front of them.

Jessica asked, "Mr. Pitney, do you mind if I could spend time with my husband."

Phillip answered, "Well, Ethan here has just accepted Jesus."

Jessica smiled graciously at Ethan and then longingly looked at Phillip.

Chap stepped in and asked, "Pastor Ashby, I can handle the rest and let you spend time with your wife."

Phillip regarded his wife and was filled with love for her that he'd not felt in a long time as he answered Chap, "You're right, it's not me who is doing the work anyways. It's the Spirit. Carry on Chap."

Ethan and Chap walked away as Phillip looked into his wife's eyes. Seeing her love for him in them, he cupped her face in his hands and passionately kissed her.

Glad that she didn't pull away from him, but was leaning into him, they kissed more.

Even through the chaos of blinking red and blue lights, they both felt complete in each other's embrace.

Needing to breathe, Phillip leaned back and lost himself in his wife's eyes.

Breaking the silence, Jessica asked, "Is this all done?"

Phillip answered, "I don't know." Pausing, he smirked, "Maybe that's a good place to be. We're in a place where we can only ask for the grace to trust in Jesus now."

Watching her husband's smirk turn to laughter, she asked, "What is it?"

Phillip replied, "Nothing."

Giving a familiar stern look, Jessica said, "Co'mon, we share everything equally now. No more Macys and Scotts."

Phillip answered, "It's nothing really. I'm just thinking about a dream I had. That's all."

Jessica waited and answered, "OK? And?"

Enjoying the blue sky, he said, "I think I'm both the wounded and attacking sheep. I just need to ensure that I'm listening to the Shepherd, so I don't eat other sheep or get eaten myself."

Giving a quizzical look, Jessica nodded and grunted, "Huh?"

"Or it could be that you're the sheep that needs protection from the other sheep chewing on you," Phillip continued.

Jessica gasped and declared, "Phillip Ashby, what are you talking about?"

Phillip answered, "It's like I said. It's nothing but a fever dream that I had about sheep attacking each other after being shot. Let me think it through some more and I'll get back with you."

Jessica asked, "How does that work with once saved always saved theology?"

Phillip answered, "I'll get back with you on that too."

Seeing Phillip smiling at her, she asked, "What?"

Phillip answered, "I'm ready to go home."

Taking each other's hands, they went home complete.

Epilogue

Sitting in the dressing room with his eyes closed, Phillip thought about the last time he was at the Bridgestone Arena. Breathing in and then out, his concentration was broken by a knock on the door.

He looked in the mirror and saw that he was unkempt. Figuring that it was Jessica at the door, he tucked in his shirt and combed his figures through his hair.

Grabbing his cane, he walked to the door and opened it. Where he was met by Ethan. Inviting him in he watched as he shifted back in forth like a little kid with a secret.

He stood there quietly and played the waiting game.

Ethan finally lost the waiting game and said, "Guess who's a national bookseller all by himself."

Phillip was waiting for Ethan to gloat, so he answered, "Let's see ... I've been a national bookseller. So has J.K. Rowling, Stephen King, Ayn Rand, ..."

Shaking his head, Ethan interjected, "OK, let me rephrase. Guess who's a national bookseller all by himself .... today."

Phillip answered, "I think it is a book named <u>Can't Catch a Break</u>."

Ethan smirked and corrected, "OK, smart alec. Its name is <u>Finally, Catching a Break</u> and something tells me that you knew that already."

Phillip gave Ethan a hug and then patted him on his back and agreed, "Yep, I did, and I am so proud of you."

Blushing, Ethan received the congratulations and asked, "So, how are you recovering?"

"As best as I can," answered Phillip as he lifted his cane and continued, "I wish I could get rid of this, but I think that it is a part of me now."

"At least you're still alive," scolded Ethan.

Phillip replied, "Yeah. I know. Changing subjects, in your book, you stated that you met Jesus and that he helped you in reconciling your doubt in Him and the pain from your departed wife. "

Ethan feigned surprise and answered, "Wow, you've read my book."

Shrugging Phillip answered, "Of course, I did."

Furrowing his brow, Ethan cautiously replied, "Yeah, he was there the whole time you were there, and then he left after you had. You didn't know who He really was."

Phillip probed his memory and coming up with nothing, he answered, "No, who?"

Shocked, Ethan said, "You're serious. You don't know." He covered his mouth and said, "Oh my!"

Another knock was on the door, and Phillip stood to get it, but Ethan stopped him and said, "I got to get going. I just stopped by to tell you what you already knew."

Opening the door, Ethan let Jessica in and gave her a hug as he said, "Well good seeing you again."

Jessica answered, "I agree. I'm glad that it is due to better circumstances."

Ethan looked at Phillip and began to laugh in disbelief, as he excused himself, "Well, I was leaving."

As the door closed, Jessica asked, "What was so funny?"

Phillip answered, "Honestly, I don't know. "

Noticing that Phillip wasn't still completely dressed, she grabbed the tie and began to put it over his neck.

She smiled when she saw that Phillip had bent his neck down to help her. She said, "Well, it's a packed house again. I guess people want to hear about your experiences since you were here last."

Finishing the double Winsor, she gathered his coat and helped him into it. Once she caught his eye, she smiled.

Phillip reached up and stole a kiss from her. She giggled as she said, "now is not the time, mister."

Phillip answered, "Anytime is time for a kiss with my love."

Blushing, she stood back and gave him a visual once over to award her approval.

Phillip gave his best pose as she gave him a kiss.

She put her arms on his shoulders as she said, "you're good. You meet my approval."

Then her voice broke as she said, "You be careful out there. OK?"

Phillip nodded and said, "I'll try my best, but I got to go where Jesus leads."

She bit her lip and then turned to leave. Opening the door, she turned and said, "I'll go wherever you go."

As the door closed, Phillip took a deep breath and praised Jesus for the healing in his marriage.

Closing his eyes, he calmed himself as the butterflies wreaked havoc with his stomach.

He muttered to himself, "You'd think I'd be used to it."

Bowing his head, he prayed, "Heavenly Father, You've gotten me through so much. I pray that You …"

Another knock at the door made him pray all the more quickly, "Jesus, please show up and do Your work. Amen!"

Exasperated, he grabbed his cane and answered the door to see Mr. Abiel.

Double backing, he just stood there surprised to see his friend.

Shifting the weight of the basket he was holding, Mr. Abiel asked, "Are you going to let me in?"

Phillip shook his head and moved aside, answering, "Certainly, please come in."

Phillip watched in disbelief as Mr. Abiel strolled in.

Mr. Abiel looked around the room and gave a low whistle as he sat the basket on the table. Turning back to Phillip he said, "Well, I see that you're back to what is familiar."

Gathering his senses, Phillip asked, "Where have you been? I went back to the asylum to thank you, and no one knew where you went."

Mr. Abiel smiled, ignored the questions and gestured to Phillip's cane and asked, "How is your leg?"

Still at the door, Phillip closed it and hobbled back to the chair and answered, "It is doing well. Honestly, it seems to be the only reminder I have."

Mr. Abiel nodded and stared at Phillip.

Phillip continued, "My marriage has been the best that it had ever been." He paused to let Mr. Abiel interject anything but was unnerved by his silence.

Phillip resumed, "The problem was that we became too familiar with each other. I just … well … I just … I was just married."

Phillip heard Mr. Abiel give him an hmm. He remembered his first encounter with Mr. Abiel and how he was quiet then, but he really loved his wisdom and wished that he could have that again.

Mr. Abiel said, "Phillip, you know how I was always there with you?"

Phillip answered, "Yes."

Mr. Abiel opened the basket and took some bread and a wine bottle out as he continued, "Know that I'll always be with you."

Phillip cocked his head and cautiously answered, "OK?"

Mr. Abiel resumed, "Never become too familiar with me that you assume that you know me completely."

Phillip wrinkled his forehead and answered, "I'd love to get to know you better."

Mr. Abiel took the break as he said, "Good. Do you mind if we break bread together?"

Phillip smiled and replied, "By all means."

Mr. Abiel tore the bread, then poured out the wine and blessed them both.

Bowing his head in prayer, Phillip listened to Mr. Abiel's blessing as the veil of familiarity fell away from him as he opened his eyes to only see the broken bread and poured the wine.

Chilled by the presence of God, he ate and drank to the glory of God.

Phillip nodded and said, "I'll go wherever you go."

The ~~End~~ Evangelist.

Word from the author:

I hope that you have enjoyed this book and if you'd like for more, I need your help.

You may ask how I can help. It is simple.

1. Please leave a review on Amazon/Goodreads/etc., even if it is just giving stars.
   a. This will help in increasing visibility and ranking of this book compared to others and hopefully will get the attention of a publisher someday.
2. Tell your friends.
   a. This is crucial, please leave a post on your social media/blog. I am an indie author with no marketing budget nor skills. Please share this book with others.
3. I know you're always supposed to have three points. (At least, my pastor does on Sundays), so, here is my third point. Contact me. This has been a labor of love and I'm available on Twitter @TheEvangelistWK and facebook at https://www.facebook.com/TheEvangelistWillKing

Again, thanks for allowing me to share "The Evangelist" with you.

www.ingramcontent.com/pod-product-compliance
Lightning Source LLC
Chambersburg PA
CBHW061509020726
47502CB00006B/2000